FAST SHIPS, BLACK SAILS

FAST SHIPS, BLACK SAILS

EDITED BY Ann & Jeff VanderMeer

Night Shade Books
San Francisco

First Edition

ISBN 978-1-59780-094-5
Printed in Canada

Night Shade Books
Please visit us on the web at
http://www.nightshadebooks.com

Dedicated to Matt Staggs, pirate extraordinaire

CONTENTS

INTRODUCTION:

A Fascination With Pirates

by Ann & Jeff VanderMeer

At least part of the current fascination with pirates, including our own, has to be about freedom, frontiers, a yearning for adventure and a desire to explore exotic locales. In this anthology of original stories from some of the best writers in the world, you will find all of that and more. From Caribbean intrigue to pirate cooks, from unlikely romance to blood-thirsty attacks, *Fast Ships, Black Sails* has something for everyone. Bestselling author Naomi Novik's "Araminta, or, The Wreck of the Amphidrake," for example, is one part riveting battle, one part mystery, and all parts exciting. Garth Nix, whose work has thrilled millions of readers, contributes a sly and wickedly bold novella with "Beyond the Sea Gate of the Scholar-Pirates of Sarsköe," which features two of the most likeable rogues to ever have their exploits set down on paper. Steve Aylett's side-splitting "Voyage of the Iguana," on the other hand, will make you see life at sea in a completely new and hilarious way. Just to name a few of the many stories here that will delight and entertain you.

In compiling this anthology, we came across several interesting resources, including the comprehensive keeptothecode.com fan site, talklikeapirate.com, and Gail Selinger's wonderful *The Idiot's Guide to Pirates*. We asked Selinger what qualifications someone would have to have to become a pirate. Her answer? "They'd have to have a deep need to be the master of their own fate. Accept death could come at any moment… A total disregard for laws. To go 'on the account' (a voyage) a pirate had to own a firearm and at least one shot of lead and blackpowder. Be a sailor or learn quickly."

But some of what she had to say surprised us, much as many of the stories in *Fast Ships, Black Sails* surprised us. Selinger goes on to add, "I'd say *must love liquor*, but the great pirate Bartholomew "Black Bart" Roberts didn't drink alcohol!" Yes, you can't be drunk all the time. Perhaps even more shocking, "X" did not, in fact, mark the spot: "We have to thank the authors of the 19th and 20th Century for that myth. A pirate crew would never give their captain their individual portion of the treasure to bury—they'd keep it for themselves. They'd kill any captain that tried to take all the treasure for himself. Think about it logically for a moment.

1

They may have been cutthroats and thieves, but why would they make it easy for someone else to find hard fought for treasure?"

One thing about pirates, though, that Selinger thinks is true: people love an anti-hero, "villains with that heart of gold." Within these pages you'll find villains, all right, black-hearted and gold-hearted both. You'll find captains in love with mermaids. You'll find double-dealing, double-crossing, and double-identities. Whether you like your pirates serious or humorous, in the past, the present, or in the future, we hope you enjoy reading *Fast Ships, Black Sails* as much as we enjoyed putting it together.

BOOJUM

by Elizabeth Bear & Sarah Monette

The ship had no name of her own, so her human crew called her the *Lavinia Whateley*. As far as anyone could tell, she didn't mind. At least, her long grasping vanes curled—affectionately?—when the chief engineers patted her bulkheads and called her "Vinnie," and she ceremoniously tracked the footsteps of each crew member with her internal bioluminescence, giving them light to walk and work and live by.

The *Lavinia Whateley* was a Boojum, a deep-space swimmer, but her kind had evolved in the high tempestuous envelopes of gas giants, and their offspring still spent their infancies there, in cloud-nurseries over eternal storms. And so she was streamlined, something like a vast spiny lionfish to the earth-adapted eye. Her sides were lined with gasbags filled with hydrogen; her vanes and wings furled tight. Her color was a blue-green so dark it seemed a glossy black unless the light struck it; her hide was impregnated with symbiotic algae.

Where there was light, she could make oxygen. Where there was oxygen, she could make water.

She was an ecosystem unto herself, as the captain was a law unto herself. And down in the bowels of the engineering section, Black Alice Bradley, who was only human and no kind of law at all, loved her.

Black Alice had taken the oath back in '32, after the Venusian Riots. She hadn't hidden her reasons, and the captain had looked at her with cold, dark, amused eyes and said, "So long as you carry your weight, cherie, I don't care. Betray me, though, and you will be going back to Venus the cold way." But it was probably that—and the fact that Black Alice couldn't hit the broad side of a space freighter with a ray gun—that had gotten her assigned to Engineering, where ethics were less of a problem. It wasn't, after all, as if she was going anywhere.

Black Alice was on duty when the *Lavinia Whateley* spotted prey; she felt the shiver of anticipation that ran through the decks of the ship. It was an odd sensation, a tic Vinnie only exhibited in pursuit. And then they were underway, zooming down the slope of the gravity well toward Sol, and the screens all around Engineering—which Captain Song kept dark, most of the time, on the theory that swabs and deckhands and coal-shovelers didn't need to know where they were, or what

3

they were doing—flickered bright and live.

Everybody looked up, and Demijack shouted, "There! There!" He was right: the blot that might only have been a smudge of oil on the screen moved as Vinnie banked, revealing itself to be a freighter, big and ungainly and hopelessly outclassed. Easy prey. Easy pickings.

We could use some of them, thought Black Alice. Contrary to the e-ballads and comm stories, a pirate's life was not all imported delicacies and fawning slaves. Especially not when three-quarters of any and all profits went directly back to the *Lavinia Whateley*, to keep her healthy and happy. Nobody ever argued. There were stories about the *Marie Curie*, too.

The captain's voice over fiber optic cable—strung beside the *Lavinia Whateley*'s nerve bundles—was as clear and free of static as if she stood at Black Alice's elbow. "Battle stations," Captain Song said, and the crew leapt to obey. It had been two Solar since Captain Song keelhauled James Brady, but nobody who'd been with the ship then was ever likely to forget his ruptured eyes and frozen scream.

Black Alice manned her station, and stared at the screen. She saw the freighter's name—the *Josephine Baker*—gold on black across the stern, the Venusian flag for its port of registry wired stiff from a mast on its hull. It was a steelship, not a Boojum, and they had every advantage. For a moment she thought the freighter would run.

And then it turned, and brought its guns to bear.

No sense of movement, of acceleration, of disorientation. No pop, no whump of displaced air. The view on the screens just flickered to a different one, as Vinnie skipped—apported—to a new position just aft and above the *Josephine Baker*, crushing the flag mast with her hull.

Black Alice felt that, a grinding shiver. And had just time to grab her console before the *Lavinia Whateley* grappled the freighter, long vanes not curling in affection now.

Out of the corner of her eye, she saw Dogcollar, the closest thing the *Lavinia Whateley* had to a chaplain, cross himself, and she heard him mutter, like he always did, *Ave, Grandaevissimi, morituri vos salutant*. It was the best he'd be able to do until it was all over, and even then he wouldn't have the chance to do much. Captain Song didn't mind other people worrying about souls, so long as they didn't do it on her time.

The captain's voice was calling orders, assigning people to boarding parties port and starboard. Down in Engineering, all they had to do was monitor the *Lavinia Whateley*'s hull and prepare to repel boarders, assuming the freighter's crew had the gumption to send any. Vinnie would take care of the rest—until the time came to persuade her not to eat her prey before they'd gotten all the valuables off it. That was a ticklish job, only entrusted to the chief engineers, but Black Alice watched and listened, and although she didn't expect she'd ever get the chance, she thought she could do it herself.

It was a small ambition, and one she never talked about. But it would be a hell of a thing, wouldn't it? To be somebody a Boojum would listen to?

She gave her attention to the dull screens in her sectors, and tried not to crane her neck to catch a glimpse of the ones with the actual fighting on them. Dogcollar was making the rounds with sidearms from the weapons locker, just in case. Once the *Josephine Baker* was subdued, it was the junior engineers and others who would board her to take inventory.

Sometimes there were crew members left in hiding on captured ships. Sometimes, unwary pirates got shot.

There was no way to judge the progress of the battle from Engineering. Wasabi put a stopwatch up on one of the secondary screens, as usual, and everybody glanced at it periodically. Fifteen minutes ongoing meant the boarding parties hadn't hit any nasty surprises. Black Alice had met a man once who'd been on the *Margaret Mead* when she grappled a freighter that turned out to be carrying a division's-worth of Marines out to the Jovian moons. Thirty minutes ongoing was normal. Forty-five minutes. Upward of an hour ongoing, and people started double-checking their weapons. The longest battle Black Alice had ever personally been part of was six hours, forty-three minutes, and fifty-two seconds. That had been the last time the *Lavinia Whateley* worked with a partner, and the double-cross by the *Henry Ford* was the only reason any of Vinnie's crew needed. Captain Song still had Captain Edwards' head in a jar on the bridge, and Vinnie had an ugly ring of scars where the *Henry Ford* had bitten her.

This time, the clock stopped at fifty minutes, thirteen seconds. The *Josephine Baker* surrendered.

Dogcollar slapped Black Alice's arm. "With me," he said, and she didn't argue. He had only six weeks seniority over her, but he was as tough as he was devout, and not stupid either. She checked the Velcro on her holster and followed him up the ladder, reaching through the rungs once to scratch Vinnie's bulkhead as she passed. The ship paid her no notice. She wasn't the captain, and she wasn't one of the four chief engineers.

Quartermaster mostly respected crew's own partner choices, and as Black Alice and Dogcollar suited up—it wouldn't be the first time, if the *Josephine Baker*'s crew decided to blow her open to space rather than be taken captive—he came by and issued them both tag guns and x-ray pads, taking a retina scan in return. All sorts of valuable things got hidden inside of bulkheads, and once Vinnie was done with the steelship there wouldn't be much chance of coming back to look for what they'd missed.

Wet pirates used to scuttle their captures. The Boojums were more efficient.

Black Alice clipped everything to her belt and checked Dogcollar's seals.

And then they were swinging down lines from the *Lavinia Whateley*'s belly to the chewed-open airlock. A lot of crew didn't like to look at the ship's face, but Black Alice loved it. All those teeth, the diamond edges worn to a glitter, and a few of the ship's dozens of bright sapphire eyes blinking back at her.

She waved, unselfconsciously, and flattered herself that the ripple of closing eyes was Vinnie winking in return.

She followed Dogcollar inside the prize.

They unsealed when they had checked atmosphere—no sense in wasting your own air when you might need it later—and the first thing she noticed was the smell.

The *Lavinia Whateley* had her own smell, ozone and nutmeg, and other ships never smelled as good, but this was… this was…

"What did they kill and why didn't they space it?" Dogcollar wheezed, and Black Alice swallowed hard against her gag reflex and said, "One will get you twenty we're the lucky bastards that find it."

"No takers," Dogcollar said.

They worked together to crank open the hatches they came to. Twice they found crew members, messily dead. Once they found crew members alive.

"Gillies," said Black Alice.

"Still don't explain the smell," said Dogcollar and, to the gillies: "Look, you can join our crew, or our ship can eat you. Makes no never mind to us."

The gillies blinked their big wet eyes and made fingersigns at each other, and then nodded. Hard.

Dogcollar slapped a tag on the bulkhead. "Someone will come get you. You go wandering, we'll assume you changed your mind."

The gillies shook their heads, hard, and folded down onto the deck to wait.

Dogcollar tagged searched holds—green for clean, purple for goods, red for anything Vinnie might like to eat that couldn't be fenced for a profit—and Black Alice mapped. The corridors in the steelship were winding, twisty, hard to track. She was glad she chalked the walls, because she didn't think her map was quite right, somehow, but she couldn't figure out where she'd gone wrong. Still, they had a beacon, and Vinnie could always chew them out if she had to.

Black Alice loved her ship.

She was thinking about that, how, okay, it wasn't so bad, the pirate game, and it sure beat working in the sunstone mines on Venus, when she found a locked cargo hold. "Hey, Dogcollar," she said to her comm, and while he was turning to cover her, she pulled her sidearm and blastered the lock.

The door peeled back, and Black Alice found herself staring at rank upon rank of silver cylinders, each less than a meter tall and perhaps half a meter wide, smooth and featureless except for what looked like an assortment of sockets and plugs on the surface of each. The smell was strongest here.

"Shit," she said.

Dogcollar, more practical, slapped the first safety orange tag of the expedition beside the door and said only, "Captain'll want to see this."

"Yeah," said Black Alice, cold chills chasing themselves up and down her spine. "C'mon, let's move."

But of course it turned out that she and Dogcollar were on the retrieval detail, too, and the captain wasn't leaving the canisters for Vinnie.

Which, okay, fair. Black Alice didn't want the *Lavinia Whateley* eating those things, either, but why did they have to bring them *back*?

She said as much to Dogcollar, under her breath, and had a horrifying thought: "She knows what they are, right?"

"She's the captain," said Dogcollar.

"Yeah, but—I ain't arguing, man, but if she doesn't know…" She lowered her voice even farther, so she could barely hear herself: "What if somebody *opens* one?"

Dogcollar gave her a pained look. "Nobody's going to go opening anything. But if you're really worried, go talk to the captain about it."

He was calling her bluff. Black Alice called his right back. "Come with me?"

He was stuck. He stared at her, and then he grunted and pulled his gloves off, the left and then the right. "Fuck," he said. "I guess we oughta."

For the crew members who had been in the boarding action, the party had already started. Dogcollar and Black Alice finally tracked the captain down in the rec room, where her marines were slurping stolen wine from broken-necked bottles. As much of it splashed on the gravity plates epoxied to the *Lavinia Whateley*'s flattest interior surface as went into the marines, but Black Alice imagined there was plenty more where that came from. And the faster the crew went through it, the less long they'd be drunk.

The captain herself was naked in a great extruded tub, up to her collarbones in steaming water dyed pink and heavily scented by the bath bombs sizzling here and there. Black Alice stared; she hadn't seen a tub bath in seven years. She still dreamed of them sometimes.

"Captain," she said, because Dogcollar wasn't going to say anything. "We think you should know we found some dangerous cargo on the prize."

Captain Song raised one eyebrow. "And you imagine I don't know already, cherie?"

Oh shit. But Black Alice stood her ground. "We thought we should be *sure*."

The captain raised one long leg out of the water to shove a pair of necking pirates off the rim of her tub. They rolled onto the floor, grappling and clawing, both fighting to be on top. But they didn't break the kiss. "You wish to be sure," said the captain. Her dark eyes had never left Black Alice's sweating face. "Very well. Tell me. And then you will know that I know, and you can be *sure*."

Dogcollar made a grumbling noise deep in his throat, easily interpreted: *I told you so.*

Just as she had when she took Captain Song's oath and slit her thumb with a razorblade and dripped her blood on the *Lavinia Whateley*'s decking so the ship might know her, Black Alice—metaphorically speaking—took a breath and jumped. "They're brains," she said. "Human brains. Stolen. Black-market. The Fungi—"

"Mi-Go," Dogcollar hissed, and the captain grinned at him, showing extraordinarily white strong teeth. He ducked, submissively, but didn't step back, for which Black Alice felt a completely ridiculous gratitude.

"Mi-Go," Black Alice said. Mi-Go, Fungi, what did it matter? They came from the outer rim of the Solar System, the black cold hurtling rocks of the Öpik-Oort Cloud. Like the Boojums, they could swim between the stars. "They collect them. There's a black market. Nobody knows what they use them for. It's illegal, of course. But they're… alive in there. They go mad, supposedly."

And that was it. That was all Black Alice could manage. She stopped, and had to remind herself to shut her mouth.

"So I've heard," the captain said, dabbling at the steaming water. She stretched luxuriously in her tub. Someone thrust a glass of white wine at her, condensation dewing the outside. The captain did not drink from shattered plastic bottles. "The Mi-Go will pay for this cargo, won't they? They mine rare minerals all over the system. They're said to be very wealthy."

"Yes, Captain," Dogcollar said, when it became obvious that Black Alice couldn't.

"Good," the captain said. Under Black Alice's feet, the decking shuddered, a grinding sound as Vinnie began to dine. Her rows of teeth would make short work of the *Josephine Baker*'s steel hide. Black Alice could see two of the gillies—the same two? she never could tell them apart unless they had scars—flinch and tug at their chains. "Then they might as well pay us as someone else, wouldn't you say?"

Black Alice knew she should stop thinking about the canisters. Captain's word was law. But she couldn't help it, like scratching at a scab. They were down there, in the third subhold, the one even sniffers couldn't find, cold and sweating and with that stench that was like a living thing.

And she kept wondering. Were they empty? Or were there brains in there, people's brains, going mad?

The idea was driving her crazy, and finally, her fourth off-shift after the capture of the *Josephine Baker*, she had to go look.

"This is stupid, Black Alice," she muttered to herself as she climbed down the companion way, the beads in her hair clicking against her earrings. "Stupid, stupid, stupid." Vinnie bioluminesced, a traveling spotlight, placidly unconcerned whether Black Alice was being an idiot or not.

Half-Hand Sally had pulled duty in the main hold. She nodded at Black Alice and Black Alice nodded back. Black Alice ran errands a lot, for Engineering and sometimes for other departments, because she didn't smoke hash and she didn't cheat at cards. She was reliable.

Down through the subholds, and she really didn't want to be doing this, but she was here and the smell of the third subhold was already making her sick, and maybe if she just knew one way or the other, she'd be able to quit thinking about it.

She opened the third subhold, and the stench rushed out.

The canisters were just metal, sealed, seemingly airtight. There shouldn't be any way for the aroma of the contents to escape. But it permeated the air nonetheless, bad enough that Black Alice wished she had brought a rebreather.

No, that would have been suspicious. So it was really best for everyone concerned that she hadn't, but oh, gods and little fishes, the stench. Even breathing through her mouth was no help; she could taste it, like oil from a fryer, saturating the air, oozing up her sinuses, coating the interior spaces of her body.

As silently as possible, she stepped across the threshold and into the space beyond. The *Lavinia Whateley* obligingly lit the space as she entered, dazzling her at first as the overhead lights—not just bioluminescent, here, but LEDs chosen to approximate natural daylight, for when they shipped plants and animals—reflected off rank upon rank of canisters. When Black Alice went among them, they did not reach her waist.

She was just going to walk through, she told herself. Hesitantly, she touched the closest cylinder. The air in this hold was so dry there was no condensation—the whole ship ran to lip-cracking, nosebleed dryness in the long weeks between prizes—but the cylinder was cold. It felt somehow grimy to the touch, gritty and oily like machine grease. She pulled her hand back.

It wouldn't do to open the closest one to the door—and she realized with that thought that she was planning on opening one. There must be a way to do it, a concealed catch or a code pad. She was an engineer, after all.

She stopped three ranks in, lightheaded with the smell, to examine the problem.

It was remarkably simple, once you looked for it. There were three depressions on either side of the rim, a little smaller than human fingertips but spaced appropriately. She laid the pads of her fingers over them and pressed hard, making the flesh deform into the catches.

The lid sprang up with a pressurized hiss. Black Alice was grateful that even open, it couldn't smell much worse. She leaned forward to peer within. There was a clear membrane over the surface, and gelatin or thick fluid underneath. Vinnie's lights illuminated it well.

It was not empty. And as the light struck the grayish surface of the lump of tissue floating within, Black Alice would have sworn she saw the pathetic unbodied thing flinch.

She scrambled to close the canister again, nearly pinching her fingertips when it clanked shut. "Sorry," she whispered, although dear sweet Jesus, surely the thing couldn't hear her. "Sorry, sorry." And then she turned and ran, catching her hip a bruising blow against the doorway, slapping the controls to make it fucking *close* already. And then she staggered sideways, lurching to her knees, and vomited until blackness was spinning in front of her eyes and she couldn't smell or taste anything but bile.

Vinnie would absorb the former contents of Black Alice's stomach, just as she absorbed, filtered, recycled, and excreted all her crew's wastes. Shaking, Black Alice braced herself back upright and began the long climb out of the holds.

In the first subhold, she had to stop, her shoulder against the smooth, velvet slickness of Vinnie's skin, her mouth hanging open while her lungs worked. And she knew Vinnie wasn't going to hear her, because she wasn't the captain or a chief engineer or anyone important, but she had to try anyway, croaking, "Vinnie, water, please."

And no one could have been more surprised than Black Alice Bradley when Vinnie extruded a basin and a thin cool trickle of water began to flow into it.

Well, now she knew. And there was still nothing she could do about it. She wasn't the captain, and if she said anything more than she already had, people were going to start looking at her funny. Mutiny kind of funny. And what Black Alice did *not* need was any more of Captain Song's attention and especially not for rumors like that. She kept her head down and did her job and didn't discuss her nightmares with anyone.

And she had nightmares, all right. Hot and cold running, enough, she fancied, that she could have filled up the captain's huge tub with them.

She could live with that. But over the next double dozen of shifts, she became aware of something else wrong, and this was worse, because it was something wrong with the *Lavinia Whateley*.

The first sign was the chief engineers frowning and going into huddles at odd moments. And then Black Alice began to feel it herself, the way Vinnie was... she didn't have a word for it because she'd never felt anything like it before. She would have said *balky*, but that couldn't be right. It couldn't. But she was more and more sure that Vinnie was less responsive somehow, that when she obeyed the captain's orders, it was with a delay. If she were human, Vinnie would have been dragging her feet.

You couldn't keelhaul a ship for not obeying fast enough.

And then, because she was paying attention so hard she was making her own head hurt, Black Alice noticed something else. Captain Song had them cruising the gas giants' orbits—Jupiter, Saturn, Neptune—not going in as far as the asteroid belt, not going out as far as Uranus. Nobody Black Alice talked to knew why, exactly, but she and Dogcollar figured it was because the captain wanted to talk to the Mi-Go without actually getting near the nasty cold rock of their planet. And what Black Alice noticed was that Vinnie was less balky, less *unhappy*, when she was headed out, and more and more resistant the closer they got to the asteroid belt.

Vinnie, she remembered, had been born over Uranus.

"Do you want to go home, Vinnie?" Black Alice asked her one late-night shift when there was nobody around to care that she was talking to the ship. "Is that what's wrong?"

She put her hand flat on the wall, and although she was probably imagining it, she thought she felt a shiver ripple across Vinnie's vast side.

Black Alice knew how little she knew, and didn't even contemplate sharing her theory with the chief engineers. They probably knew exactly what was wrong and exactly what to do to keep the *Lavinia Whateley* from going core meltdown like the *Marie Curie* had. That was a whispered story, not the sort of thing anybody talked about except in their hammocks after lights out.

The *Marie Curie* had eaten her own crew.

So when Wasabi said, four shifts later, "Black Alice, I've got a job for you," Black Alice said, "Yessir," and hoped it would be something that would help the *Lavinia*

Whateley be happy again.

It was a suit job, he said, replace and repair. Black Alice was going because she was reliable and smart and stayed quiet, and it was time she took on more responsibilities. The way he said it made her first fret because that meant the captain might be reminded of her existence, and then fret because she realized the captain already had been.

But she took the equipment he issued, and she listened to the instructions and read schematics and committed them both to memory and her implants. It was a ticklish job, a neural override repair. She'd done some fiber optic bundle splicing, but this was going to be a doozy. And she was going to have to do it in stiff, pressurized gloves.

Her heart hammered as she sealed her helmet, and not because she was worried about the EVA. This was a chance. An opportunity. A step closer to chief engineer.

Maybe she had impressed the captain with her discretion, after all.

She cycled the airlock, snapped her safety harness, and stepped out onto the *Lavinia Whateley*'s hide.

That deep blue-green, like azurite, like the teeming seas of Venus under their swampy eternal clouds, was invisible. They were too far from Sol—it was a yellow stylus-dot, and you had to know where to look for it. Vinnie's hide was just black under Black Alice's suit floods. As the airlock cycled shut, though, the Boojum's own bioluminescence shimmered up her vanes and along the ridges of her sides—crimson and electric green and acid blue. Vinnie must have noticed Black Alice picking her way carefully up her spine with barbed boots. They wouldn't *hurt* Vinnie—nothing short of a space rock could manage that—but they certainly stuck in there good.

The thing Black Alice was supposed to repair was at the principal nexus of Vinnie's central nervous system. The ship didn't have anything like what a human or a gilly would consider a brain; there were nodules spread all through her vast body. Too slow, otherwise. And Black Alice had heard Boojums weren't supposed to be all that smart—trainable, sure, maybe like an Earth monkey.

Which is what made it creepy as hell that, as she picked her way up Vinnie's flank—though *up* was a courtesy, under these circumstances—talking to her all the way, she would have sworn Vinnie was talking back. Not just tracking her with the lights, as she would always do, but bending some of her barbels and vanes around as if craning her neck to get a look at Black Alice.

Black Alice carefully circumnavigated an eye—she didn't think her boots would hurt it, but it seemed discourteous to stomp across somebody's field of vision—and wondered, only half-idly, if she had been sent out on this task not because she was being considered for promotion, but because she was expendable.

She was just rolling her eyes and dismissing that as borrowing trouble when she came over a bump on Vinnie's back, spotted her goal—and all the ship's lights went out.

She tongued on the comm. "Wasabi?"

"I got you, Blackie. You just keep doing what you're doing."

"Yessir."

But it seemed like her feet stayed stuck in Vinnie's hide a little longer than was good. At least fifteen seconds before she managed a couple of deep breaths—too deep for her limited oxygen supply, so she went briefly dizzy—and continued up Vinnie's side.

Black Alice had no idea what inflammation looked like in a Boojum, but she would guess this was it. All around the interface she was meant to repair, Vinnie's flesh looked scraped and puffy. Black Alice walked tenderly, wincing, muttering apologies under her breath. And with every step, the tendrils coiled a little closer.

Black Alice crouched beside the box, and began examining connections. The console was about three meters by four, half a meter tall, and fixed firmly to Vinnie's hide. It looked like the thing was still functional, but something—a bit of space debris, maybe—had dented it pretty good.

Cautiously, Black Alice dropped a hand on it. She found the access panel, and flipped it open: more red lights than green. A tongue-click, and she began withdrawing her tethered tools from their holding pouches and arranging them so that they would float conveniently around.

She didn't hear a thing, of course, but the hide under her boots vibrated suddenly, sharply. She jerked her head around, just in time to see one of Vinnie's feelers slap her own side, five or ten meters away. And then the whole Boojum shuddered, contracting, curved into a hard crescent of pain the same way she had when the *Henry Ford* had taken that chunk out of her hide. And the lights in the access panel lit up all at once—red, red, yellow, red.

Black Alice tongued off the *send* function on her headset microphone, so Wasabi wouldn't hear her. She touched the bruised hull, and she touched the dented edge of the console. "Vinnie," she said, "does this *hurt?*"

Not that Vinnie could answer her. But it was obvious. She was in pain. And maybe that dent didn't have anything to do with space debris. Maybe—Black Alice straightened, looked around, and couldn't convince herself that it was an accident that this box was planted right where Vinnie couldn't... quite... reach it.

"So what does it *do?*" she muttered. "Why am I out here repairing something that fucking hurts?" She crouched down again and took another long look at the interface.

As an engineer, Black Alice was mostly self-taught; her implants were second-hand, black market, scavenged, the wet work done by a gilly on Providence Station. She'd learned the technical vocabulary from Gogglehead Kim before he bought it in a stupid little fight with a ship named the *V. I. Ulyanov*, but what she relied on were her instincts, the things she knew without being able to say. So she *looked* at that box wired into Vinnie's spine and all its red and yellow lights, and then she tongued the comm back on and said, "Wasabi, this thing don't look so good."

"Whaddya mean, don't look so good?" Wasabi sounded distracted, and that was just fine.

Black Alice made a noise, the auditory equivalent of a shrug. "I think the node's inflamed. Can we pull it and lock it in somewhere else?"

"No!" said Wasabi.

"It's looking pretty ugly out here."

"Look, Blackie, unless you want us to all go sailing out into the Big Empty, we are *not* pulling that governor. Just fix the fucking thing, would you?"

"Yessir," said Black Alice, thinking hard. The first thing was that Wasabi knew what was going on—knew what the box did and knew that the *Lavinia Whateley* didn't like it. That wasn't comforting. The second thing was that whatever was going on, it involved the Big Empty, the cold vastness between the stars. So it wasn't that Vinnie wanted to go home. She wanted to go *out*.

It made sense, from what Black Alice knew about Boojums. Their infants lived in the tumult of the gas giants' atmosphere, but as they aged, they pushed higher and higher, until they reached the edge of the envelope. And then—following instinct or maybe the calls of their fellows, nobody knew for sure—they learned to skip, throwing themselves out into the vacuum like Earth birds leaving the nest. And what if, for a Boojum, the solar system was just another nest?

Black Alice knew the *Lavinia Whateley* was old, for a Boojum. Captain Song was not her first captain, although you never mentioned Captain Smith if you knew what was good for you. So if there *was* another stage to her life cycle, she might be ready for it. And her crew wasn't letting her go.

Jesus and the cold fishy gods, Black Alice thought. Is this why the *Marie Curie* ate her crew? Because they wouldn't let her go?

She fumbled for her tools, tugging the cords to float them closer, and wound up walloping herself in the bicep with a splicer. And as she was wrestling with it, her headset spoke again. "Blackie, can you hurry it up out there? Captain says we're going to have company."

Company? She never got to say it. Because when she looked up, she saw the shapes, faintly limned in starlight, and a chill as cold as a suit leak crept up her neck.

There were dozens of them. Hundreds. They made her skin crawl and her nerves judder the way gillies and Boojums never had. They were man-sized, roughly, but they looked like the pseudoroaches of Venus, the ones Black Alice still had nightmares about, with too many legs, and horrible stiff wings. They had ovate, corrugated heads, but no faces, and where their mouths ought to be sprouting writhing tentacles

And some of them carried silver shining cylinders, like the canisters in Vinnie's subhold.

Black Alice wasn't certain if they saw her, crouched on the Boojum's hide with only a thin laminate between her and the breathsucker, but she was certain of something else. If they did, they did not care.

They disappeared below the curve of the ship, toward the airlock Black Alice had exited before clawing her way along the ship's side. They could be a trade delegation, come to bargain for the salvaged cargo.

Black Alice didn't think even the Mi-Go came in the battalions to talk trade.

She meant to wait until the last of them had passed, but they just kept coming. Wasabi wasn't answering her hails; she was on her own and unarmed. She fumbled with her tools, stowing things in any handy pocket whether it was where the tool went or not. She couldn't see much; everything was misty. It took her several seconds to realize that her visor was fogged because she was crying.

Patch cables. Where were the fucking patch cables? She found a two-meter length of fiber optic with the right plugs on the end. One end went into the monitor panel. The other snapped into her suit comm.

"Vinnie?" she whispered, when she thought she had a connection. "Vinnie, can you hear me?"

The bioluminescence under Black Alice's boots pulsed once.

Gods and little fishes, she thought. And then she drew out her laser cutting torch, and started slicing open the case on the console that Wasabi had called the *governor*. Wasabi was probably dead by now, or dying. Wasabi, and Dogcollar, and… well, not dead. If they were lucky, they were dead.

Because the opposite of lucky was those canisters the Mi-Go were carrying.

She hoped Dogcollar was lucky.

"You wanna go *out*, right?" she whispered to the *Lavinia Whateley*. "Out into the Big Empty."

She'd never been sure how much Vinnie understood of what people said, but the light pulsed again.

"And this thing won't let you." It wasn't a question. She had it open now, and she could see that was what it did. Ugly fucking thing. Vinnie shivered underneath her, and there was a sudden pulse of noise in her helmet speakers: screaming. People screaming.

"I know," Black Alice said. "They'll come get me in a minute, I guess." She swallowed hard against the sudden lurch of her stomach. "I'm gonna get this thing off you, though. And when they go, you can go, okay? And I'm sorry. I didn't know we were keeping you from…" She had to quit talking, or she really was going to puke. Grimly, she fumbled for the tools she needed to disentangle the abomination from Vinnie's nervous system.

Another pulse of sound, a voice, not a person: flat and buzzing and horrible. "We do not bargain with thieves." And the scream that time—she'd never heard Captain Song scream before. Black Alice flinched and started counting to slow her breathing. Puking in a suit was the number one badness, but hyperventilating in a suit was a really close second.

Her heads-up display was low-res, and slightly miscalibrated, so that everything had a faint shadow-double. But the thing that flashed up against her own view of her hands was unmistakable: a question mark.

<?>

"Vinnie?"

Another pulse of screaming, and the question mark again.

<?>

"Holy shit, Vinnie!… Never mind, never mind. They, um, they collect people's brains. In canisters. Like the canisters in the third subhold."

The bioluminescence pulsed once. Black Alice kept working.

Her heads-up pinged again: <ALICE> A pause. <?>

"Um, yeah. I figure that's what they'll do with me, too. It looked like they had plenty of canisters to go around."

Vinnie pulsed, and there was a longer pause while Black Alice doggedly severed connections and loosened bolts.

<WANT> said the *Lavinia Whateley*. <?>

"Want? Do I *want*…?" Her laughter sounded bad. "Um, no. No, I don't want to be a brain in a jar. But I'm not seeing a lot of choices here. Even if I went cometary, they could catch me. And it kind of sounds like they're mad enough to do it, too."

She'd cleared out all the moorings around the edge of the governor; the case lifted off with a shove and went sailing into the dark. Black Alice winced. But then the processor under the cover drifted away from Vinnie's hide, and there was just the monofilament tethers and the fat cluster of fiber optic and superconductors to go.

<HELP>

"I'm doing my best here, Vinnie," Black Alice said through her teeth.

That got her a fast double-pulse, and the *Lavinia Whateley* said, <HELP> And then, <ALICE>

"You want to help *me*?" Black Alice squeaked.

A strong pulse, and the heads-up said, <HELP ALICE>

"That's really sweet of you, but I'm honestly not sure there's anything you can do. I mean, it doesn't look like the Mi-Go are mad at *you*, and I really want to keep it that way."

<EAT ALICE> said the *Lavinia Whateley*.

Black Alice came within a millimeter of taking her own fingers off with the cutting laser. "Um, Vinnie, that's um… well, I guess it's better than being a brain in a jar." Or suffocating to death in her suit if she went cometary and the Mi-Go *didn't* come after her.

The double-pulse again, but Black Alice didn't see what she could have missed. As communications went, *EAT ALICE* was pretty fucking unambiguous.

<HELP ALICE> the *Lavinia Whateley* insisted. Black Alice leaned in close, unsplicing the last of the governor's circuits from the Boojum's nervous system. <SAVE ALICE>

"By eating me? Look, I know what happens to things you eat, and it's not…" She bit her tongue. Because she *did* know what happened to things the *Lavinia Whateley* ate. Absorbed. Filtered. Recycled. "Vinnie… are you saying you can save me from the Mi-Go?"

A pulse of agreement.

"By eating me?" Black Alice pursued, needing to be sure she understood.

Another pulse of agreement.

Black Alice thought about the *Lavinia Whateley*'s teeth. "How much *me* are we talking about here?"

<ALICE> said the *Lavinia Whateley*, and then the last fiber optic cable parted, and Black Alice, her hands shaking, detached her patch cable and flung the whole mess of it as hard as she could straight up. Maybe it would find a planet with atmosphere and be some little alien kid's shooting star.

And now she had to decide what to do.

She figured she had two choices, really. One, walk back down the *Lavinia Whateley* and find out if the Mi-Go believed in surrender. Two, walk around the *Lavinia Whateley* and into her toothy mouth.

Black Alice didn't think the Mi-Go believed in surrender.

She tilted her head back for one last clear look at the shining black infinity of space. Really, there wasn't any choice at all. Because even if she'd misunderstood what Vinnie seemed to be trying to tell her, the worst she'd end up was dead, and that was light-years better than what the Mi-Go had on offer.

Black Alice Bradley loved her ship.

She turned to her left and started walking, and the *Lavinia Whateley*'s bioluminescence followed her courteously all the way, vanes swaying out of her path. Black Alice skirted each of Vinnie's eyes as she came to them, and each of them blinked at her. And then she reached Vinnie's mouth and that magnificent panoply of teeth.

"Make it quick, Vinnie, okay?" said Black Alice, and walked into her leviathan's maw.

Picking her way delicately between razor-sharp teeth, Black Alice had plenty of time to consider the ridiculousness of worrying about a hole in her suit. Vinnie's mouth was more like a crystal cave, once you were inside it; there was no tongue, no palate. Just polished, macerating stones. Which did not close on Black Alice, to her surprise. If anything, she got the feeling the Vinnie was holding her… breath. Or what passed for it.

The Boojum was lit inside, as well—or was making herself lit, for Black Alice's benefit. And as Black Alice clambered inward, the teeth got smaller, and fewer, and the tunnel narrowed. Her throat, Alice thought. I'm inside her.

And the walls closed down, and she was swallowed.

Like a pill, enclosed in the tight sarcophagus of her space suit, she felt rippling pressure as peristalsis pushed her along. And then greater pressure, suffocating, savage. One sharp pain. The pop of her ribs as her lungs crushed.

Screaming inside a space suit was contraindicated, too. And with collapsed lungs, she couldn't even do it properly.

alice.

She floated. In warm darkness. A womb, a bath. She was comfortable. An itchy soreness between her shoulderblades felt like a very mild radiation burn.

alice.

A voice she thought she should know. She tried to speak; her mouth gnashed, her teeth ground.

alice. talk here.

She tried again. Not with her mouth, this time.

Talk… here?

The buoyant warmth flickered past her. She was… drifting. No, swimming. She could feel currents on her skin. Her vision was confused. She blinked and blinked, and things were shattered.

There was nothing to see anyway, but stars.

alice talk here.

Where am I?

eat alice.

Vinnie. Vinnie's voice, but not in the flatness of the heads-up display anymore. Vinnie's voice alive with emotion and nuance and the vastness of her self.

You ate me, she said, and understood abruptly that the numbness she felt was not shock. It was the boundaries of her body erased and redrawn.

!

Agreement. Relief.

I'm… in you, Vinnie?

=/=

Not a "no." More like, this thing is not the same, does not compare, to this other thing. Black Alice felt the warmth of space so near a generous star slipping by her. She felt the swift currents of its gravity, and the gravity of its satellites, and bent them, and tasted them, and surfed them faster and faster away.

I am *you.*

!

Ecstatic comprehension, which Black Alice echoed with passionate relief. Not dead. Not dead after all. Just, transformed. Accepted. Embraced by her ship, whom she embraced in return.

Vinnie. Where are we going?

out, Vinnie answered. And in her, Black Alice read the whole great naked wonder of space, approaching faster and faster as Vinnie accelerated, reaching for the first great skip that would hurl them into the interstellar darkness of the Big Empty. They were going somewhere.

Out, Black Alice agreed and told herself not to grieve. Not to go mad. This sure beat swampy Hell out of being a brain in a jar.

And it occurred to her, as Vinnie jumped, the brainless bodies of her crew already digesting inside her, that it wouldn't be long before the loss of the *Lavinia Whateley* was a tale told to frighten spacers, too.

CASTOR ON
TROUBLED WATERS

By Rhys Hughes

He's almost fifty years of age, Castor Jenkins is, which for a stereotypical Welshman must be reckoned venerable, if not ancient. Not that he takes kindly to being considered a stereotype. He likes to point out that real Welshmen *don't* live exclusively on a diet of beer and chips, nor do they avoid exercise, work and responsibility every waking minute of the day: the fact he does those things is a mark of his uniqueness and it's just a coincidence that the cliché and his individualism are the same.

But in fact there's some dispute about his true age, and it's possible he might be twice as old as he says, for something incredible happened one day that confused the issue. He was sitting in his favourite pub with his best friends, Paddy Deluxe and Frothing Harris, getting ready to play cards and win heavily, as always, when a disagreement about the integrity of past games threatened to spoil the evening. Paddy started it with a complaint about the physical condition of Castor's cards. His argument ran as follows:

"The state of your deck is abysmal, truly it is, and you might as well be playing with marked cards, for all the different beer stains on the backs, not to mention chip fat drippings, surely form patterns recognisable to you but not to us, and so allow you to know what's coming next."

"In other words, to cheat," added Frothing Harris.

Castor Jenkins announced that he resented the accusation, but his friends continued to grumble and the fuss gained momentum and became an unbreakable refusal to play even a single round unless they used the brand new pack, fresh and unopened, that Paddy had thoughtfully brought with him. And there was talk of reimbursement for previous losses, and hints of compensation on top of that, and finally Castor was forced to back down and agree that the beer and chip stains *might* be considered to be arranged in a suspicious manner.

They played with the new pack and Castor lost every game and he soon found himself owing a sum in the region of £100 to both of them. Unable to settle up on the spot, he offered to go out and find a cash machine and return with the money as quickly as possible. His friends nodded.

"That's a reasonable suggestion," they said.

"I'll be back in ten minutes," Castor declared.

He stood and walked out and they watched him with triumph in their eyes, but it was the sort of triumph that a fish feels when it bites a worm on a hook, and so their eyes glittered sickly, waiting to see what trick was in store, for they couldn't imagine Castor would do exactly what he promised without some effort at regaining the upper hand. Ten minutes passed but he didn't appear. An attempt to contact him on his mobile phone proved futile. Paddy rubbed his nose and Harris scratched his chin, but not in that order.

An hour later Castor returned and he was breathing hard and he staggered around the room before returning to his place at the table and sitting down, still panting and mumbling to himself in a language that was either Spanish or Arabic, Paddy and Harris couldn't agree on that, before shuddering and licking his lips and tugging at his earlobes. They gazed at him in silence and he slowly regained his composure and addressed them directly. He said:

"You won't believe what has just happened to me!"

"Tell us," they replied.

"Very well," he said slowly, "but I need a drink to settle my nerves first. You don't mind if I take a sip of your beer? That's better. And yours as well? Sure, a massive gulp isn't the same as a sip, but listen carefully: I was kidnapped! I know it sounds ridiculous but it's true nonetheless. Shortly after I left you, while walking along the esplanade, I noticed a strange vessel anchored offshore, an old-fashioned galleon. Then a boat was lowered from it and began rowing closer and I soon realised there was something unusual about it."

"How unusual?" asked Paddy.

Castor lowered his voice to a whisper. "It was crewed by men dressed like pirates, with black breeches and billowing white shirts, spotted scarves tied around their heads, eye-patches and bristling beards, and many waved cutlasses in the air or carried knives between their teeth, and I imagined that a film was being made, even though I couldn't see a director or any cameras. I wanted to stay and watch, but my first duty was to get your money and so I hurried onwards."

"Very considerate of you," observed Harris.

Castor nodded. "I reached the cash machine, inserted my card, punched in my number and withdrew the crisp notes, but as soon as the money was in my hand I felt myself being lifted up and carried away. A mob of howling ruffians filled the street. They took the cash machine as well, blowing it out of the wall with gunpowder. That explosion disordered my senses, I can tell you! I was so stunned I never properly realised what was going on until it was too late. Everywhere there was chaos, broken bottles on the road, the overpowering smell of rum. When the clouds of smoke cleared I saw that they had bundled me aboard the boat.

"It was at this point I understood that these men were not actors but real pirates. As the history books tell us, pirates don't just attack other ships, they also raid coastal towns, looting and sacking. Porthcawl is a coastal town and ripe for such unwanted attentions. These pirates had obviously decided to make a rapid strike, grabbing what they could and departing before the police arrived. I imagine they were disappointed with their haul, just one cash machine and a single captive, namely myself."

"Not much of a profit there," agreed Paddy and Harris.

"True," sighed Castor, "but perhaps they needed the practise. Anyway I was taken to the galleon and locked inside a narrow cell where I lay in mouldy darkness, my mind filled with thoughts of what pirates traditionally do to prisoners, but after calming down I stopped believing I was destined to walk the plank. If they wanted me dead they would have saved a lot of effort by cutting my throat at the cash machine. So it grew increasingly likely they intended to sell me into slavery. I felt terrible, knowing that you were sitting here waiting for your money, but I had no way of getting a message to you.

"The days passed slowly, and I was sick during a horrid storm, and they gave me nothing to eat and drink but bread and water. When I asked for proper nourishment they laughed in a piratical fashion and treated all my other requests with similar contempt. I began to rot in that prison, but one morning a man more distinguished than the others opened the door and let me out. He was Captain Ribs, he announced, the leader of the pirates, and he had a proposal for me. He led me to his cabin and asked me to sit down and offered the chips and beer I craved. When I was full, he scrutinised me closely and said:

"We're a man short and to run the ship with maximum efficiency I need to find a replacement. You're the only candidate for the position and so I want to offer you the job. If you don't want it and would prefer the life of a slave in the hellish butter mines of Kowpoo, I'll understand."

"I need to think about it. What exactly is the job?"

"Lookout. Our last lookout fell to his death last night, just like his predecessor, and the lookout before him, not to mention the lookout before *him*, and so on. Without a lookout we don't know where we're going and won't recognise it when we get there, so it's a very important post carrying a great deal of responsibility."

"I was about to declare that I wanted nothing to do with responsibility of any kind but then it occurred to me that as a member of the ship's crew I stood a better chance of escaping and paying you the money I owed than if I ended up working in the butter mines of Kowpoo. So I accepted. Captain Ribs was delighted and explained my new duties. I had to climb the tallest mast to the crow's nest and call down whenever I saw anything noteworthy. He gave me a comprehensive list of things considered 'noteworthy' and it consisted of the following: land, storms, whirlpools, treasure ships, rival pirates, reefs, cannibals, whales, giant squid, mermaids, lifeboats, seductive cloud formations, alterations in the shape, colour or tensile strength of the horizon line.

"My job began immediately and I climbed the rigging with a queasy stomach. Higher and higher went I, my fingers rubbed raw on the rough cords, my feet slipping, the sweat pouring off my brow in droplets as thick and yellow as chip oil, but determined to reach the top without admitting defeat. I got there safely, in case you're wondering. The crow's nest was hardly bigger or more secure than a large wok with slippery sides and the precariousness of my position generated little or no contentment in my heart. I wondered how long it would be before I too fell to my doom. Fortunately the sea was calm at this particular time and I was able to discharge my duties to a satisfactory degree. Whenever I spied an object on the surface of the ocean I checked the list to see if it merited a shout. 'Large floating log' did not, but 'Large floating log with a man sitting on it' did. And so it went."

Paddy interrupted the story by asking, "How did you sleep?"

"Badly is the honest answer," sighed Castor, "but I was able to curl myself into a ball tight enough to fit the crow's nest. It was cold at night, even in the tropics, maybe because I was so high up. Don't ask how food and drink was delivered to me: if you do that, I'll also have to explain how I relieved myself! While my fellow pirates far below gorged themselves on watermelon and toast spread with butter from Kowpoo, and drank rum and lime juice, I went largely without, but there were occasions when I was allowed to descend. Each time we docked at a port, I had permission to go ashore with the rest of the crew."

"How many ports did you visit?" wondered Harris.

"Too many to remember! We sailed around the world several times and stopped off in Bombay, Rangoon, Surabaya, Shanghai, Osaka, Lima, Montevideo, Luanda and the strange seaside towns that dot the coasts of Lowest Bo, Zing and the Mediocre Utopia, among others. Once we even docked at Tenby in Wales and I saw a chance to jump ship and make my way back to Porthcawl on a bus, with a change at Swansea, but Captain Ribs detained me and so the opportunity was lost. He had something important to say and I had no choice but to let him say it.

"'Look here, Master Jenkins,' he began, 'of all the lookouts I've ever employed you are the best by far. You always shout out at the earliest moment, you never make mistakes and you haven't yet fallen to your death. You are so perfect I wish I could keep you forever! Promise me that if you ever marry and have a son, you'll name him after yourself and bring him up to be exactly like you in every way. That's how highly I regard you. I hope your friends appreciate you?'

"'That they do,' I assured him.

"And so I remained in the service of Captain Ribs and my work got harder rather than easier. He was driven by some unspecified urge, a quest he was unable to articulate even to himself, and I could never work out if his ultimate goal was a distant country, a horde of treasure, international notoriety or some way of forgetting his past. Whatever it was that motivated him also drew us along, in his spiritual wake, as it were, until we became like sacrificial victims who desire our own demise. I recall with a shiver certain adventures in abandoned temples on overgrown islands, engagements with intelligent apes armed with blowpipes, races against ghost ships.

"We committed our fair share of atrocities. We were pirates, never forget that, and I feel terrible shame at some of the things we did. We pillaged the coastal settlements of a dozen nations. Once we discovered the factory where calendars are made, there's only one in the whole world, and sabotaged the delicate machinery by throwing a spanner into the works, a spatula actually. Another time we sailed the wrong way up a river during a charity raft race, scattering the entrants like the smug middle-class skittles they were. It was a violent career and I risked a horrid injury every single working day.

"On one occasion we sailed up a narrow channel between two obstacles that struck terror into my heart. The first was a vast iceberg, the second was a smoking volcano newly arisen from the sea. The waters of the channel churned awfully and our vessel swayed from side to side, almost capsizing, and I felt like the weight at the end of a metronome pendulum. As we passed the crater of the volcano, the top of the mast and the crow's nest dipped into the sulphurous flames. Contact lasted only an instant but it was long enough for my clothes to burst into fire. Fortunately the mast then dipped the other way and quenched me on the surface of the iceberg with a gigantic hiss. Such extreme occurrences were quite commonplace!

"This life might have gone on forever, or at least until Captain Ribs led us to out deaths, but one cloudy morning I had an encounter that changed everything. The clouds were thick but very low, practically resting on the surface of the sea, but the top of my mast protruded above them. I was able to look out across a vast fluffy expanse and the effect was very soothing. To my astonishment I noticed a man standing on the clouds far away, but this was just an optical illusion. As he approached it became obvious he was a lookout like me, balanced in a crow's nest at the top of a tall mast. We waved to each other. The situation was very dreamy: we seemed to float like angels, the ships below us completely forgotten, and the serenity of the scene distracted us from performing our duties. Suddenly I realised we were on a collision course!

"It was too late to shout down a warning. The snapping of wood and popping of nails was background music to my prolonged descent into the ocean. I was flung out of my nest far into the mass of clouds and through them into the cold salty water. I thrashed and gasped, my senses reeling, my eyes stinging, and by sheer luck my flailing hands grasped a barrel that had floated free from one of the holds. I hauled myself up, sat astride it and found myself blinking into the face of a beautiful woman. We were the only survivors and she permitted me to share her barrel in return for keeping her company. I entertained her as best as I could by telling her strange but true tales until we were cast ashore on a desert island."

"What tales did you choose?" asked Paddy Deluxe.

Castor Jenkins sniffed. "I can't rightly recall. I think that my encounter with the King of the bicycle-centaurs was one. I mended his puncture in return for my life, as it happened. Anyway, we lived on the desert island, the woman and I, in a sort of paradisal harmony, eating fruit, walking on the beach at night and laughing at the stars. For some reason she found the constellations funny, especially Gemini and Cassiopeia, who knows why? Her name was Charlotte Gallon and she was the captain of the other ship, also a pirate vessel. We became intimate and our first child was born less than a year after our shipwreck. I kept my promise to Captain Ribs and named the boy Castor.

"Sometimes the tide brought useful objects to us. Flotsam and jetsam included tennis rackets, old shoes, waterlogged books, rusty batteries, broken stools and a fondue set. Only one empty bottle was ever washed up on our sands, oddly enough, and only one pencil. I tore one of the blank pages out of one of the books, dried it in the sun and composed a message on it. This was our only chance at contacting the outside world but instead of writing HELP and appealing for rescue I decided to contact my best friends, Paddy Deluxe and Frothing Harris, because I respected them so much, and I did this even though Charlotte told me it was a waste. I hurled the bottle into the sea and watched it bob along."

"What did you write?" cried Frothing Harris.

"I merely repeated what Captain Ribs had said to me. I told my two friends how highly I valued them, went into detail about what superb fellows they were, and urged them to name their own sons after themselves, if they ever had any, and to bring them up to be *exactly* like their fathers. That message seemed more important to me than any request to be picked up by a passing ship and delivered safely back into the comforting lap of civilisation."

"We never received the bottle," said Paddy Deluxe.

"Yes you did," stated Castor.

"I assure you we didn't. No message at all!"

Castor pursed his lips. "The ocean is wide and one might think that messages in bottles just drift around forever, but in fact there's an organised system at work to ensure they reach the persons they are intended for. A secret place exists where every bottle with a message is kept until it can be delivered properly. I learned this from a fellow who interviewed me after I escaped the island, calls himself the Postmodern Mariner, an investigative journalist who specialises in the mysteries and dramas of the sea. Anyway, to return to the point, my two best friends *did* receive my message, and they acted upon it too, which is how we are able to have this conversation right now.

"Confused, are you? Let me explain that I dwelled with Charlotte and my son on that island for years and years. An oil tanker eventually picked us up. I worked our passage back to the mainland but I never returned to Wales. I married Charlotte and we lived in relative happiness, with only one argument, until I was accidentally killed by a thrown saucepan, which is how that argument ended. After my funeral, my son went on a touching quest. I had already told him everything and he planned to seek out my two dear friends and settle my debts with them. He searched the pubs of Porthcawl for a long time.

"Finally he entered the pub where that card game had taken place all those decades previously. And here I am! Yes, I'm not the first Castor Jenkins but the second, his son, grown to the precise age my father was when he left to use the cash machine. Remember that I was brought up to exactly resemble him in every way!"

"You *are* him!" blurted Paddy.

"You left one hour ago, not fifty years," added Harris.

Castor sadly shook his head. "I have some sad news. Paddy Deluxe and Frothing Harris are dead and buried. They were your fathers and they raised you in the way my message urged them to do, with the same names and identical thought processes. That's the reason for your identity confusion. It was my father who left this pub to obtain money for your fathers, but it is the son who returns to pay the sons. The time difference also explains why you'll find no evidence of a pirate raid when you walk home tonight: that incident happened a generation ago and the damage has long since been repaired. Now to more pressing matters! How much was owed in total?"

"One hundred pounds," answered Paddy and Harris together.

"Would you like that sum in today's money?"

"Of course!" came the roar.

Castor reached into his pocket and withdrew a single coin, a tarnished penny, which he slapped down on the table. "There you go. That penny was in my father's possession during the original card game. Because of inflation over half a century it is worth £100 *in today's money.*"

Paddy Deluxe and Frothing Harris were speechless.

"I'm glad everything is settled," said Castor. "By the way, the machinery in the calendar factory was never fixed and the wrong year has been printed on every calendar ever since. Curious, don't you think? Don't trust dates from now on, whatever you do. I'm off to the bar for a drink. Then we can toast our ancestors. Come now, my friends, restrain yourselves! Are we not gentlemen? Fighting over a penny is most undignified!"

I BEGYN AS I MEAN TO GO ON

By Kage Baker

They'd been five days adrift when they saw the sail on the horizon.

"Oughtn't we to try and signal?" said young John, and rose in the canoe and was going to pluck off his red neckerchief and wave it, only he overbalanced and nearly capsized them again. Dooley cursed him, and Jessup took their one oar and hit him with it.

"Sit down, you mooncalf!"

It wasn't an especially seaworthy canoe. They had made it themselves out of a fallen tree trunk, slipping out at night to work on it, with the idea that they might escape from Barbados and live as free men on some other island. The first time it had rolled over in the water, they'd lost all the victuals and drink they'd brought with them. The second time, they'd lost the other oar. So they were in a bad way now, and not disposed to be charitable.

John looked around at Jessup, rubbing the back of his head. "But it's a ship," he said. "How else will they see us?"

"They're too far away to see the likes of us," said Jessup. His voice was husky from thirst. "They'll sail this way, or they won't. It's all down to luck."

"We might pray to the Almighty," said John.

"I'm done praying to the Almighty!" Dooley sat bolt upright and glared at them both. "Forty years I've prayed to Jesus! 'Sweet Jesus, don't let me be caught! Sweet Jesus, don't let me be transported! Sweet Jesus, let that fucking overseer drop dead where he's standing!' When has He ever answered me, I'd like to know?"

He had the red light in his eyes again, and John swallowed hard, but Jessup (perhaps because he had firm hold of the oar) said: "Belay that, you stupid bastard. Blaspheming don't help at all."

"Oh no?" screamed Dooley. He threw back his head. "You hear me, up there? You can kiss my red arse! Baisy-me-cu, Sir Almighty God, mercy beaucoup! I'm praying to the Devil from this day forward, You hear me? I be Satan's very own! Huzzay, Satan! *Praise* Satan!"

Such was the force with which he threw himself about in this rant, that he lurched clean over the side and went in with scarcely a splash, and vanished. A moment later he came up again, a little way away on the other side of the canoe,

27

spluttering and blowing. One big fin cut smooth through the limpid blue sea, and Dooley went down again with a shriek cut off in the middle. The rest was bubbles and bloody water.

The other two sat very still, as you might guess.

It was a long while before Jessup felt safe enough to start paddling again, but he did, ever so cautious, while John bailed with his cupped hands. In a couple more hours the sail tacked and made toward them, and John was quite careful to thank the Almighty.

Their rescuer was a brigantine with her aft decks cut down flush to the waist, long and low, and she had a dirty ragged look to her. She flew no colors. A few men leaned at the rail, watching incuriously as the canoe came alongside.

"What ship's this?" called Jessup.

"The *Martin Luther*," was the reply.

"Where d'you hail from?"

"From the sea."

"Ah, Christ," said Jessup quietly, and John looked at him, wondering what he meant. Jessup shrugged. "Well, needs must," he said, and reached up for the line when it was thrown down to him.

The canoe rolled over one last time as he scrambled from it, as though out of spite, but John vaulted up and caught the rail. There he hung, draped down the tumblehome, until a couple of laughing men took his hands and hauled him aboard.

When John had his feet under him on deck he looked around, hoping to see a water butt. He'd never been on any ship except the one that had transported him to Barbados. The fact that the *Martin Luther* bristled with mismatched cannon, and that her rigging was in trim despite her dirtiness, told him nothing. A man came up on deck, and from the fanciness of his coat relative to the other men's John assumed he was someone in authority.

"What're these?" said the man.

"Shipwrecked mariners, Captain," said one of the crew. The captain glanced over the rail at the canoe, which was already bobbing away in the wake. He laughed and spat.

"Mariners! In a piece of shite like that? Not likely; they're redleg bond slaves. Escaped. Ain't you?" He turned and looked hard at John and Jessup.

"Please, sir, we are," said Jessup.

The captain walked round Jessup and John, looking them over as though they were horses he had a mind to buy. "Been out long?"

"Two years, sir," said Jessup.

"And lived this long. Had the fever?"

"Yes, sir," they said together, and John added, "Please, may we have some water?"

The captain grinned. He held out his hand; one of the crew went and fetched a mug of water, and gave it to him. He held the mug up before John.

"The water's for the crew. We're on the account; no purchase, no pay. You'll sign articles and serve before the mast, and take your share, or you'll go back in the sea. Which is it to be?"

John didn't know what he meant, but Jessup said, "We'll serve, sir," and John nodded, thinking only of the water. So the captain laughed and gave him the mug, and he drank deep, and everyone became friendly after that.

There were articles to sign, which were read aloud to them. Jessup made his mark. John signed his name, which drew a whistle of admiration from the ship's clerk. They were taken below and it was filthy there, but very free and easy; they were given clothing to replace the bleached and salt-caked rags they wore, and given sea-chests and hammocks of their own, which John thought was most generous. Later he found out they'd belonged to men who'd died of the fever, but it made no odds.

He felt some qualms at the prospect of being a pirate, wondering what his mother would have said. But if John was clumsy at first learning the ropes, and sick scared the first time he had to go aloft, why, it was better than cutting cane in the stinking heat of the fields, with the flies biting him, and the salt sweat running into his eyes. He liked the blue water. He liked the rum and tobacco and the sea air. He liked the freedom.

Though he learned, pretty quick, that freedom and dead men's gear were all there was in abundance on the *Martin Luther*.

"It's Captain Stalwin's luck," said Perkin, in a low voice. He spat wide, and some of it hissed and sputtered on the hood of the lamp. "No purchase, no pay indeed. We been out these two years, and all we took in that time is one cargo of sugar, and some slaves once, but they was mostly dead, and one ship with chinaware."

"There was that one with the chest of plate," Cullman reminded him.

"One chest of plate," Perkin admitted, "as didn't amount to much when it was divided up in shares, and mine was gone before the week was out once we went ashore in Port Royal."

"There was the *Brandywine*," said Cooper. There were growls and mutters.

"What was on the *Brandywine?*" asked John.

"She had a hold full of dried pease," said Perkin.

"Time was when you'd been grateful for a handful of dried pease, George Perkin," said Cooper. "And there was two sheep on board her, you're forgetting."

"Well, what I say is, if his luck doesn't change soon, Captain Stalwin's looking at being deposed," said Perkin.

Captain Stalwin knew the peril in which his office stood, and stalked the deck with keen hunger, and scanned the horizon with a sunken eye. He could never keep to one course for long; for if they made south a week steady without sighting any vessel, there was sure to be complaint from the crew, and so to oblige them he'd give new orders and away they'd go to the west.

It was nothing like the iron discipline on the ship that had brought John out to

Barbados, where a man must leap to obey the officers and keep his opinions to himself. It beat anything John had ever seen for pointlessness. And yet it pleased him, to see plain hands like himself having a say in their own affairs.

On the day they sighted the ship, Captain Stalwin saw it before the lookouts. John, who was idling at the rail, heard the glass being snapped shut a second before the cries sounded: "Sail ho! Two points off larboard bow!"

Now, they were lying off the False Cape, hoping some cargoes out of the Lake of Maracaibo or Rio de la Hacha might come within easy reach, to either side. And there, creeping into sight off Bahia Honda, was a galleon, as it might be a merchant, and she was flying Spanish colors. Captain Stalwin waited, and watched, though the crew were roaring in impatience to take her; and when he saw she wasn't part of any fleet, he grinned and gave chase. A blood-red flag was brought out and run up, streaming out in the breeze.

The galleon, when she sighted them, was beating hard to windward; but she spread her sails and fled north, and aboard the *Martin Luther* men elbowed one another in glee.

"I reckon she's out of Rio de la Hacha," said Cooper, with a cackling laugh.

"Is that good?" said John.

"There's pearl fisheries there!"

"Might be she's only full of salt," said Perkin, and everyone told him to hold his sorry tongue.

John was kept busy the next hour, running eager up the shrouds as though they were a flight of easy stairs now, letting out all the canvas the *Martin Luther* carried. She bowed and flew, with the white water hissing along her hull, and the white wake foaming behind.

Happy men primed her guns. Cutlasses and boarding axes were handed round. Some men ran to the galley and blacked their faces with soot and grease, to look the more fearsome. The galleon ran, but she was broad and ponderous, like a hen fluttering her wings as she went, and the *Martin Luther* closed on her, and closed on her, like a hawk stooping.

Soon the galleon was near enough to see the painted figure on her stern castle. It was the Virgin Mary in red and blue and gold, her eyes wide and staring, her one hand raised to bless, her other hand cradling a wee Christ who stared and blessed too. It gave John a qualm, at first; but then he recollected the things the Papists were said to do to captive English, which put a different color on the matter. He wondered, too, whether the haloes on the figures were only gold paint or set with disks of real gold.

In ten more minutes they were near enough to chance a shot, and Captain Stalwin ordered the bow guns loaded. Beason, the gunner, got the two shots off: larboard and starboard barked out smart and the one ball went high and fell short, in a spurt of white foam, while the other hit the galleon at the waterline, close in to her keel, and stuck there like a boss on a shield.

"Again!" cried Captain Stalwin, and Cooper and Jessup loaded and primed. Beason adjusted the range with a handspike. They could hear the crack-crack-crack of musket shots from the galleon now—she had no stern guns, evidently—but the musket-balls fell short, and long before the gap had closed Beason had the range right. Fire kissed powder and the larboard shot struck something, to judge from the shatter and shudder that echoed over the water. The starboard shot did worse, to judge from the screams.

When the smoke cleared they saw that the galleon's rudder was broke, in big splinters, though not shot away clean. Her tillerman was desperately trying to bring her about to broadside, with the little she was answering. Cooper and Jessup worked like madmen and Beason fired again, just the larboard gun this time, but that was enough; over the grinding of the rudder's hinge they heard the shot strike, and the fragments showering into the water. The galleon was wallowing when they saw her again, in the red sunlight through the smoke.

But not helpless: she had made it around far enough for her larboard guns to begin firing with some hope of hurt, and what was more her musketmen were now within range. As the *Martin Luther* rose on the swell, a flight of musket-balls peppered the men on her forward deck. John started as Cullman dropped beside him howling. To this moment he'd been smiling like a fool at a play, cheering each shot; now he woke sober and dropped flat on the deck, as an eight-pound ball whistled above his head and punched through the forecourse before sailing on out to drop in the sea.

"Keep her astern!" yelled Captain Stalwin, but the tillerman was already sending the *Martin Luther* slinking around under the galleon's stern again. Close to now they could see what they hadn't noticed before, that two of her stern cabin windows had been beaten into one jagged-edged hole by one of their shots. John thought they could look straight into her when they rose on the next swell, which they did. What came popping up to the window then but a Spaniard with a pistol? He was white and bloody as a ghost, with staring blank eyes. He aimed the pistol full into Captain Stalwin's face, and fired.

There was a click, but neither flash nor ball. The next moment the *Martin Luther* had dropped away and past, grinding into the other vessel, and her crew were yelling and swarming up the side. John looked curiously at Captain Stalwin, who had sagged against the foremast and was trembling. Then the jolt of the swell striking the two hulls together threw John to his knees. He remembered where he was and thought of the gold haloes on the images. Scrambling up he grabbed a cutlass and pulled himself aboard the galleon.

Then he was too scared to think about gold or anything else but fighting off the Spanish who came at him. John was a big fellow, with fists like round shot, and thick arms. He'd been transported for killing a man in a tavern fight, without meaning to; only the man had been snarling drunk and come at him with a blade. John had been fearful of his life and just whaled away at the bugger until he'd stopped moving. So you may guess that John, now armed and even more fearful, cut down the Spanish before him like summer corn.

He stumbled over bodies. A musket-ball creased his scalp and tore his hat away, and he scarcely noticed. His ears were ringing, all sound seemed muffled, and his right arm ached something fierce from beating, and beating, and beating down with the cutlass.

He reached the far rail at last, gasping, and turned to put it at his back—and saw, to his surprise, that there were no Spanish left standing.

There was fighting going on belowdecks. He went to the companionway and peered down cautiously. Blades ringing, kicking, scuffling—a shrieked curse and a shot, and then Beason was coming up the companionway toward him, laughing, wiping his blade.

"We got 'em all," he said.

Captain Stalwin came aboard with the *Martin Luther*'s clerk to take inventory of the galleon's cargo. It was rice and logwood and salt, and some crates of chinaware in a blue pattern of little heathen men and temples. Profitable enough, if you were of a mind to play the merchant and unload the stuff in certain quiet coves, waiting for the smugglers to turn up and have a good haggle.

Nothing a man could weight down a purse with, though, or spend in an hour on rum and sweet companionship; no good chinking coin. A certain sour reek of disappointment began to hang over the deck, above the smells of black powder and death. There were murmurings from the crew, as they set about pitching the dead and wounded overboard. Captain Stalwin emerged from the galleon's hold with a disbelieving look.

"We'll search again," he said. "Tear out the bulkheads. There'll be pearls here, or gold bars, or silver, only it's hidden. It must be! My luck's changed. I felt it spin round like a compass-needle, when that son of a whore's pistol misfired. Ned Stalwin's luck's blowing out of a different quarter now, and our fortune's on this damned ship!"

"It is, señor," said a voice from somewhere down near his feet. "But not in the way you imagine."

John looked down with the rest of them, to see one of the Spanish propping himself on his elbow, smiling a little as he peered up at Captain Stalwin. He had taken a stab in the gut, and was cut above his right eye, so that he smiled through a mask of blood, and his teeth were pink with it. He spat blood now, but politely, away from Captain Stalwin's boots.

"I swear upon the Cross that I will make you a wealthy man. All I ask is a drink of water, and the grace of leisure to expire *before* you consign my body to the sea."

Captain Stalwin fingered his beard, uncertainty in his eyes. Beason prodded the dying man with his boot, in case he should be hiding a dagger. "Liar," he said.

"Señor, I am about to go before God. Would I lie and damn my mortal soul? What I said, I said in truth," said the man. He reached into his shirt and dragged forth something that winked green and golden in the pitiless sunlight. He kissed it and then held it out to Captain Stalwin, snapping the chain on which it had been worn. The chain was soft gold, with the links curiously worked, and it trailed after his gift, which was a crucifix.

Beason whistled. He glanced over his shoulder at the others on deck. John leaned close to see. He took the cross to be made of green glass at first, a faceted rod and the two arms held together with gold work, and the little crucified Christ and the INRI sign in gold. Captain Stalwin seized it, his hand shaking.

"Emeralds," he said.

"Very pretty," said Beason. "But it won't come to much when it's divided up into shares, will it? Have you got any more?"

The man smiled again, and blood ran from the corner of his mouth. "I will tell you where to find them. Water first."

So the captain yelled for water. A cask was brought up and broached, with a drink dippered out for the dying man. He lay his head back and sighed, and asked for a chart. More yelling, then, and hasty searching in the galleon's great cabin before a chart was found and brought up to them, with Captain Stalwin sweating all the while lest the bastard should die first.

When the chart was held before his eyes, the man peered at it a long moment. He looked about helplessly, as though searching for a pen; then giggled, and dabbed his finger in his own blood, and daubed a spot south of Tobago.

"There," he said. "San Cucao. Two hills rising out of the sea. You will find there the mine from which these emeralds came, señor. Very rich mine. Emeralds green as the jungle."

Captain Stalwin licked his lips. "And is it garrisoned?"

The Spaniard smiled again. "Only with the dead. The island was my brother's, and mine; he died six weeks ago, and I was his heir. Now you are mine. All the island holds, I bequeath to you freely, God be my witness."

"Lying bugger," said Beason.

Captain Stalwin drew breath, and looked around. He gave sharp order that the men should get busy moving the galleon's cargo into the *Martin Luther*. John rose and labored with the rest of them, up and down, back and forth, hauling the kegs of salt and the sacks of rice, hefting the logwood. As he went to and fro he would glance over, now and then, at where Captain Stalwin crouched on the deck and conversed with the Spaniard. He only caught a few phrases of their speech together; but every other man of the crew was doing the same as John.

In the days afterward they talked it over amongst themselves, in the night watches or belowdecks, and put together enough scraps of what each man had heard to flesh out the Spaniard's story, which was:

That he and his brother were somebodies in Cartagena, rich in land and Indian slaves, but poor otherwise in their generation. That some ten years since his brother, Don Emidio, having had occasion to travel, was shipwrecked on this little island of San Cucao. It had a spring of fresh water, and enough of the wreck landed for this Don Emidio to live on some few preserved stores while he built himself a raft. When he wasn't working on the raft he would explore the island; and there he found emeralds sticking out of a bluff where the earth had fallen away.

He carried some with him when he put off from the island. When he got home, he took his brother into his confidence. They resolved to go back to the island and mine the emeralds.

Being Spaniards as they were, they did it in proper Spanish fashion, with servants to wait on them and a friar to say the Mass for them, and Indian slaves to labor for them. The overseers cracked their whips, the Indians set to work with picks and mattocks, and soon the brothers had a prince's ransom in fine emeralds, with plenty more still winking out of the earth.

But then, the Indians had all taken sick with the Black Pox. The brothers were supping on board their ship when they heard the news, shouted from the shore. They resolved to flee, leaving the workers there, taking only those servants on board when the news came. They'd a coffer full of emeralds to console them. Only their friar objected; he took a boat and rowed himself ashore, that he might tend the dying and harvest their souls for God.

The brothers agreed to wait seven years before returning to the island, by which time the contagion might reasonably be supposed to have blown away. This was, the Spaniard had said, the seventh year, and the wealth from the emeralds they had carried away with them was now long gone. His brother being dead, he had planned to find a patron to fund his journey back.

Well, as the only patron he found rode a pale horse, he bought him another journey entirely. With the story told, the Spaniard murmured an Act of Contrition and died grinning. Captain Stalwin relieved him of his rings and a fine pearl that had dangled from his ear, and ordered him pitched into the sea.

"They say Drake brought back such emeralds," said Perkin, as he gazed up at the stars. "Like big sticks of sugar candy, and green as... as the green in a church window."

"I seen some like that, once," said Collyer. "I was with Mansvelt when he took the *Santa Cruz*. There was a statue of one of their saints, all painted like, and stuck all over with precious stones. The emeralds was the biggest. I remember, there was one big as a medlar."

"Liar," said Beason. "And that Spaniard was a liar, too. We're sailing straight for some Spanish garrison with big guns, you mark me."

Jessup only shook his head, but John said: "Why would the fellow lie, with him dying?"

"Because we sliced his liver," said Beason. "Wouldn't you be spiteful, if it was you?"

"I'd fret more about the Black Pox," said Cooper. "Belike he was hoping we'd catch it. It's fearful way to die."

"I had the smallpox," said John. "Is it like that?"

"The same, only worse. Your skin turns black and bursts."

"No fear," said Collyer. "There's a keg of vinegar below, and a chest of sweet herbs, taken off that galleon; lavender-flowers and such, that the dons use to perfume their beards. We mix them up with the vinegar and make us pomanders to smell, and we'll keep hale and sound on that island."

"Captain's on deck," muttered Perkin. They fell silent, as Captain Stalwin came up the companionway. He looked at the stars, and drew a deep breath. Then he went to the rail and watched south a while. The green phosphorescence foamed and boiled in the bow-wake, and reflected in his glittering eyes.

San Cucao was just as the Spaniard had said it was, two hills in the sea, poking up steep. It was cliffs most of the way around, with only one bit of shingle beach for a landing. They were able to moor the *Martin Luther* quite close, and from her deck could see the signs that men had been there once; a bit of an overgrown trail leading into the interior, and some stone huts or walls.

Captain Stalwin gave orders that arms should be served out, so the crew grabbed up cutlasses and muskets readily enough. Collyer ran below and fetched up the preventative he'd mixed from the vinegar, and made each man take a strip of sail-cloth and dip it in the reeking stuff. They tied them round their wrists, or stuck them under their hats, muttering about the smell.

All this while there wasn't a sound from the island, baking in the bright sun of noonday; not the cry of a bird, not the call of a monkey, not the drone of a single cicada in its long grass. Its green trees drooped as though asleep.

Silent too the *Martin Luther*'s crew went ashore, with Captain Stalwin leading them, and only a couple of men left on board. No breath of wind, either; John was soaked with sweat by the time they had walked up the beach, and come to the verge where the jungle began, a sort of overgrown meadow. He looked around him uneasily, thinking that all the quiet reminded him of a churchyard. Then he caught sight of a stone cross.

"It *is* a churchyard," he blurted out.

"What?" Captain Stalwin turned. John pointed at the cross. They all stood staring, and now they saw that the humps and hummocks in the vines and long grass were gravestones, grown over here and there, and knew the roofless ruin at the far end must be a chapel.

Jessup reached out and pulled the creepers back from the stone cross. It had a long inscription on it. Jessup, who knew some Spanish, read out: "'Sacred to the memory of Alessandro, born a pagan, in his extremity embraced Christ. A better Christian than his masters.'"

"Here's another one," said Cooper, clearing another stone. This was a cross surmounted by a skull, cut rudely. Jessup leaned down and read:

"'Diego, who became a faithful Christian. Suffered the torments of Hell on this earth, now in glorious repose in Paradise. When all are judged, his cruel masters will beg for a drop of water from his hand, in the flames where they burn.'"

They moved slowly across the meadow, reading carefully, and every few paces uncovered another gravestone. John noticed that they got bigger, the farther down the row they went, and more crudely cut. Jessup read them out, one after another:

"'Baltasar, obedient Christian, betrayed and left to die by Christians who do not deserve the name. Departed this vale of sorrow aged no more than 11 years. Angels carried him up. Devils will drag his masters down.'

"'Juan, humblest of Christians, endured the scourge and lash without complaint, and who for his obedience was left for dead in his hour of affliction. God sees! All the horrors of the Pit will be inflicted on the brothers Claveria.'

"'Narciso, exchanged the sweat and toil of this world for the heavenly kingdom after taking the Blessed Sacrament. He suffered greatly before he died. I had nothing left with which to comfort him. They are damned, both of them, for false and heartless vipers.'

"'Francisco lies here. God be thanked he went quickly and could not see at the end. His soul is with God. Whose ways cannot be comprehended.'

"'Timoteo, Christian. Why was this permitted, O Lord?'"

As they went to look at the last stone, a great rough slab on which the writing was chiseled careless, John put his foot down and felt nothing there to support him. He yelled as he toppled over, dropping his cutlass. Jessup and Beason caught him, and set him on his feet again, pulling him clear of the open grave: for that was what it was, screened over with gourd vines.

Perkin meanwhile had stepped carefully across and pulled the creepers back from the headstone.

"What's this one say?"

Jessup turned and peered at it. "'Brother Casildo Fernandez Molina. Traveler, have the kindness to cover my bones with earth, as you would hope your bones will rest. I bear witness to the perfidy of Don Emidio Claveria Martinez and Don Benecio Claveria Martinez. They are traitors to God. They will suffer and die cruelly, as they left us to die. I bear witness. I am God's hand in—'"

The letters, big angry block capitals, ran right off the edge of the stone.

"But the grave's empty," said Perkin, looking in.

There was an uneasy silence while they all considered that.

"Maybe he got rescued before he died," said John. Captain Stalwin shrugged.

"Dead or alive, he's no enemy of ours. Didn't we do for one of 'em? It's a judgment of God, ain't it?" He raised his voice. "Don Benecio, he *es muerto!* Savvy?"

Nobody answered him.

"We cut his liver open!" shouted Collyer.

"Threw his body in the sea without one prayer!" shouted Cooper.

"Bugger this," said Beason, and stepped warily past the grave to the ruins beyond. "Look! This was his chapel."

It had been a building of unmortared stone, thatched with palm leaves, but they had fallen in years since and were scattered everywhere. A rough-hewn wooden cross had fallen too, and lay worm-riddled at the far end. Maybe the place had served as Brother Casildo's workshop too; broken iron tools lay rusting where they had been dropped, and fragments of cut stone.

When they had poked about long enough to learn there was nothing useful for them there, they came out, and Captain Stalwin spotted the track that led away from the beach into the jungle. It was swift vanishing in green, but it was there.

"I'd reckon the mines'd be this way," he said. "Perkin, go before. Cut the creepers back as we go."

"And be mindful of that friar," said Cooper, looking uneasily over his shoulder.

So they followed the track, and the sun beat down, and the sound of the sea grew fainter. John was looking all around as he walked, with his cutlass held up before him, and sniffing now and then at his little strip of sailcloth. His mother had told him once that if you got the smallpox and didn't die of it, you need never fear it again; but that had been in Hackney. Out here, the old rules never seemed to apply.

It was all silent now on the path, but for the ring and hiss of Perkin's cutlass slicing through the overgrowth. The noise had taken on a comfortable sort of rhythm like music, so they were taken by surprise rather when Perkin suddenly yelled and toppled backward into Jessup.

"What is it?"

"Is it a snake?"

"Back! Back!" said Perkin, who had gone white. "Trap!"

They all staggered back a few paces, and spread out on the path to get a look at what they had narrowly missed walking into. There were creepers dragged craftily across the path. When they'd been green and fresh with the broad leaves spread out they might indeed have concealed what lay below; but they were long dead and withered, and showed clear that someone had dug a little pit in the midst of the track.

"That ain't enough to hurt anybody," said Cooper in scorn, but Perkin pointed a shaking finger at the beam that was laid to one side, with one end projecting out across the pit. He'd come close to putting his foot down on the end of the beam. If he had, his foot had pushed the end of the beam down into the pit, levering up the beam's other end. And the beam's other end—

They followed it with their eyes, silent to a man. The long beam was arranged over a fulcrum of cut stone. If its seesaw had gone up, it had smacked away a bit of wood above it... which was supporting another bit of wood... which was supporting another... and so on, up the steep hillside to the great pile of stones carefully arranged to thunder down on the path if they were dislodged.

"Jesus Bleeding Christ," said Cooper.

"He was a good stonecutter, that friar," said Jessup, with a sick kind of laugh.

"But he didn't catch *us*. Didn't I tell you my luck had changed?" said Captain Stalwin. "Two shares to you, Perkin, for sharp eyes. We'll go on, and every man minds his God-damned feet, and watch close lest there's anything else."

John thought about the friar, left all alone here after the last of the Indians died, and how he must have wandered around in the jungle getting crazier and crazier, setting traps for the two brothers, babbling Latin-talk, nothing left for him but the thirst for vengeance. Was he watching them even now? He'd be emaciated, his priestly robe in rags. Maybe he was lying in wait just around the next bend in the trail, eager to garrote somebody with his rosary beads...

"There's broken tools up here," said Perkin. "And the track's getting wider."

"Are we getting near the mine?" said Captain Stalwin.

"Maybe," said Perkin. He hacked away a few palm-fronds and stared hard through the gloom. "There's something like a shaft. Phew!" He shook his head. "Something stinks."

He hurriedly took his strip of sailcloth and tied it across his face, maskwise, and the others all did likewise except for John, whose strip wasn't long enough. He pressed it to his nose, praying the smell was only a dead pig somewhere. They proceeded with care and in a moment came out in the clearing where the mine-shaft was.

There were no footprints visible; the open sand had long ago been smoothed flat by wind and rain. There were a couple of broken barrels and some baskets, falling to pieces, that the Indians had used to carry dirt. And something in the mouth of the shaft…

Captain Stalwin paced forward warily, his cutlass up, looking from side to side. He got as far as the mouth of the shaft, and no rosary beads came snaking out of anywhere to strangle him. He looked down at what was in the mouth of the shaft—it was a basket, John could see that now—and began to laugh.

"Now, by God!" he cried. "Has my luck changed, or hasn't it?" He bent to the basket and dipped up a big rock that had emeralds sprouting from it like fingers from a hand. The rest of them rushed forward at that, and saw the basket full of rough emeralds, poking out where the sides of the basket had rotted away. Nor was it the only basket; there were others lined up beside it, going back into the shaft, brimful of rough green gems under a thin layer of dead leaves and dust.

John's eyes went wide. He grabbed with all the rest, stuffing emeralds in his pocket, shoving others aside who got in his way. Jessup tried to pick up a basket and it came apart, spilling emeralds across the floor, and Perkin dropped to his knees and snatched them where they scattered. "Look!" he said, pointing down the shaft.

There, just beyond some piled debris, lay another basket. It seemed this was where the choicest stones had been sorted; they were a richer green, they were bigger, and something about the way the dim light glinted on them promised clarity and perfection beyond anything John had yet seen.

Perkin scrambled forward on hands and knees. Cooper vaulted over him so as to get to them first, and in his haste tumbled against the debris that was piled in the way. His knee struck one end of a beam, concealed there. The beam swiveled. Its other end struck smartly on one of the timber baulks that held up the roof of the mine, and knocked it out of true. There was a creak, and dirt and stones fell from above as the baulk tottered—

What happened next John didn't see, for he was running for daylight as hard as he could. He made it, and so did Captain Stalwin, and so did Jessup. Here came Beason and Collyer, sprinting just ahead of the roiling cloud of dirt that belched from the mine shaft, and the muffled roar as the roof fell in.

John was just thinking that Perkin wouldn't get his two shares after all when he and Cooper came staggering from the mouth of the shaft, choking and cough-ing, brown all over as though they'd rolled in mud. When they had been properly laughed at, there was a general idea of gutting Cooper, for being so stupid as to spring another trap and lose them the best of the emeralds. Captain Stalwin, though, lifted his cutlass between Cooper and the rest.

"Belay that. We've filled our pockets, ain't we? And not a man lost when that roof fell in. It's my luck, plain as plain!" He pointed with the tip of the blade at the emeralds lying all about, that they'd dropped in their flight. "Now pick them up, and it's back to the ship with us. We'll come back tomorrow with a shovel or two and see if we can't dig out some more."

John obeyed like the rest, crouching over to collect the scattered emeralds. He was just reflecting on what a pleasant thing it was to be a pirate, picking jewels as though they were strawberries in a meadow, when he saw a bonny green gem lying amidst what he took to be little dry sticks. He reached for the emerald and that was when he saw the arm-bones. He looked along them to the blind, gaping skull beyond.

"Here's a dead man!" he cried.

Captain Stalwin and the others came to see. "Why, it's the priest," said Captain Stalwin, pointing at the shreds of brown robe. "Look here, here's his beads. Ha! He died before he could go lie down in his grave. Well, there's an end to the mystery."

"No," said Jessup, almost whispering. "Who shot him?"

They all fell silent then, staring at the skull, which did indeed have a round hole in it. Beason reached with the tip of his cutlass and tilted it, and a musket-ball rolled out of one of the eye sockets.

"And another thing," Jessup went on, keeping his voice low. "He's rotted away long since. What is it that stinks so now?"

Now, for all the sweat and heat of the day, John felt cold. Beason wetted a finger and held it up, and turned to look at the bit of jungle from which the wind was blowing.

"Don't smell like carrion by itself, though," he murmured.

"Carrion or cabbage, I've no wish to meet it any closer," said Captain Stalwin. "We'll just creep off the way we came, shall we? Quick march, boys, and quiet. My luck will get us back safe."

So saying, he turned; and the shot rang out and dropped him in his tracks, with a little explosion of blood at his buttonhole like a red rose worn there.

John just had a glimpse of someone ducking down, before he threw himself flat. More shots came, as it seemed from some three or four snipers, and all of them in the jungle through which they had just come. Beason yelled some orders, and John dodged through the jungle back of the friar's bones and fell flat behind a log, where Beason had already taken shelter. Jessup and Perkin were behind a log a few feet away, and Collyer came running, clutching his arm where a musket-ball had stuck. They didn't see Cooper again.

Beason already had his musket loaded by the time John rolled over. He laid the barrel of it against the log and fired across the clearing. John loaded his own musket and did the same, as did Collyer and Perkin, and for some few minutes it was hot work there. Musket-balls tore through the green leaves all around them.

"That fucking Spaniard *was* a liar," said Beason, as he reloaded. "Didn't I say it? Who'd listen to me, eh?"

Jessup crawled over and jerked his thumb at the trees behind them. "We retreat through that, we can get to the other side of the island! Make our way around to the anchorage again!"

Beason aimed, fired, and then looked where Jessup was pointing. "Ay," he said. So they retreated, firing as they went. In a moment they came out of the jungle on the other side and there was the blue sea, all right, but before them was a sheer drop down a cliff. Beason looked to and fro distractedly, as a shot or two came zipping out of the jungle behind them; then John spotted a little track that ran across the cliff's edge.

"Where's that go?" he cried.

"But that was where—" said Beason, before a musket-ball cracked into a boulder and sent rock shards flying in every direction. He ducked and they ran, with Collyer cursing because one of the shards had hit his thigh, along the little track. It did get them out of the line of fire from the jungle pretty quick, putting the shoulder of the hill between them, but it rose, too. In another moment they were climbing, all exposed, where the trail switchbacked up the flank of the hill and vanished over a ridge.

By great good fortune their pursuers did not follow to pick them off like flies on a wall. Over the top of the ridge they hurtled, all together, and down through a little maze of bushes and then—

John halted, and the others ran into him as into a wall.

They had emerged into a clearing, and here was the source of the smell. Three or four huts stood around a central fire-pit. The stink was compounded of smoke, and the camp's latrine, which was brimful noisome, and a mountain of clam and mussel shells and fish bones; all that, and the crucified man that dried in the sun at the cliff's edge.

Even so, the place had a peaceful air. The sea-wind blew through the dead man's hair, and the sea broke softly on the rocks below, and a little stream bubbled down to one side… and there was a rhythmic *thump-thump-thump* that suggested someone in no particular hurry. An Indian woman sat at the door of one of the huts, pounding roots in a mortar.

John and the rest stood petrified, for it was surely only a matter of seconds before she looked up and saw them. Now, she raised her head…

And did not see them. She had no eyes. She had barely any face.

"Jesus," said Jessup faintly. "The Black Pox."

John groped for his bit of vinegar-soaked rag, and plastered it over his nose and mouth. Another woman came out of one of the huts. Maybe she'd been beautiful once, with her hair black as a raven's wing and lustrous; but she groped her way by touch along the side of the hut to the stream, for where her eyes had been were two pink masses of scars. As she bent—quite close to them—to fill her gourd with water, John saw that her nose and lips had been eaten off by the pox too, as though she'd been in a fire.

John looked away, and as quickly looked for somewhere else to look; but he'd seen enough of the poor crucified bugger to tell that he'd been a black-bearded fellow, and that they'd stripped him down to a loin-rag before they'd stuck him up there. A gull had been busy pecking at the face…

He ain't been up there any seven years, John realized. The friar had been dry bones long since picked clean, but this was fresher meat.

"They can't see us," said Beason, no louder than a breath. "We can walk through. Come on. Quick and quiet."

They stepped forward, walking soft as they could, and must pass one by one under the cross, stepping gingerly around the bits and odds that lay there. John spotted a glint of gold and green; Beason noticed it too, and dove on it quicker than John could. He held it up on its bit of broken chain to stare. It was a crucifix, as might be twin to the one they'd taken off the Spaniard on the galleon.

"Now I'll tell you what," Beason whispered, "This will be that bastard's own brother, and they did come back, but they was caught—"

A dog leaped up from where it had been sleeping, and barked furiously at them. The woman pounding roots took no notice, seemingly deaf as well as blind, but the woman with the water-gourd turned inquiringly, and two other women came to the doormouths. They too were blind, were horribly disfigured. They caught up sticks and came forward tentatively, waving them, groping with their free hands outstretched. The dog growled and leaped, running from the women to the *Martin Luther*'s men and back, trying to guide them. It ought to have been funny but it wasn't; John's hair was fair standing up, and he was more afraid of the blind women than of anything he'd seen since he'd been transported.

"Oh Christ," said Beason, and shot the dog. "Run for it."

John ran, out in front of the others. He bounded like a goat along the track, that continued on the other side of the village, in its narrow way between the clifftops and the hillside. He could hear the panting breaths of the others as they followed him, knocking pebbles that clattered down the cliff to the shingle-beaches below. Soon he could hear shots as well, though they came from ahead and not behind. Then there was the echoing roar of one of the *Martin Luther*'s guns.

"Those sons of bitches!" yelled Beason, panting. "Move, you great ox!"

He pushed past John. They rounded the side of the hill where it came down and found themselves looking into the anchorage from the other side. There was the back of the ruined chapel; there was their longboat, halfway to the *Martin Luther* and full of armed men. There was only Cullman and Jobson on deck to fight them off, and Cullman's left arm had been no use since taking the galleon. They were crouched behind the great gun in the waist, trying to get off another shot at the longboat without catching any musket-balls.

Beason ran close enough for range, reloading as he went. As one fellow went up on one knee in the bow to aim at Jobson, Beason dropped him with the sweetest shot John had ever seen. John attempted to load on the run but made a mess of it, spilling black powder everywhere. By this time Jessup and Perkin had reached them, with Collyer limping close behind. They took positions behind the grave-stones and commenced firing at the longboat's crew, only praying that Cullman and Jobson had the sense not to sink the longboat with an eight-pound ball.

It was over in a minute more, for the men in the longboat had to cover two targets at once, and couldn't do it. When the shooting stopped, there was no more damage to the *Martin Luther*'s crew than Collyer's right ear, which was mainly clipped away by a ball from the longboat. He crouched, bleeding like a stuck pig and swearing most vile, as John peered out from behind Brother Casildo's gravestone.

"There's nobody moving on the longboat," he said.

"What about that bugger hanging over the gunwale?"

"I see three shot-holes in him," John replied. He got up cautiously and walked out on the beach. One by one the others rose and followed him. Cullman and Jobson hallooed from the ship, waving their hats.

"How do we get the boat back?" said Perkin.

"Anyone know how to swim?"

"Me," said John, and regretted it at once, thinking of Dooley's sorry end.

"Out you go, then," said Beason.

So John prayed as though it was a Sunday, and for all he knew it might have been, as he stripped off his coat and hat, and kicked off his shoes. The water was bright and clear as he waded out, nothing like sorry old Hackney Brook, and a beautiful blue except for the crimson place where the dead man hanging over the gunwale had bled into the water. And the Lord must have listened to John's prayers and nodded approvingly, for John made the side of the boat in safety, pocked up in splinters and musket-balls as it was, though he had to haul the dead man out as he scrambled in.

Now he saw that there were two other dead men floating a little ways off, face down. Three more were lying in the bottom of the boat, all shot to pieces except for one pockfaced lout who was lolling back with open eyes and bared teeth and a knife clenched in his fist—

With a scream the fellow sat up, and John screamed too and caught him by the wrist, and they struggled together a long moment, with the thwart cutting into John's shins something cruel. Shots rang out from the beach, but hummed past like bees; at last John broke the bugger's arm. He got the knife away from him and ran it into him twice, just where he supposed the heart might be, and the man gasped once and died. John pitched him out of the boat and sat there shivering, for all the heat of the sun.

When he'd done puking over the side, he rowed back to shore.

John did wonder what had become of Captain Stalwin's luck, that was supposed to have changed. They all puzzled over it, after they'd elected Beason captain and were sailing away from there; and Perkin's idea made the most sense, which was that the luck under consideration was *their* luck, which was to say the whole crew's. Changing for the better, therefore, had included getting rid of a sorry bastard like Stalwin.

The other tale was what had really happened on the island, and they worked out several different stories for that, sitting under the stars as they drank their rum. Captain Beason's story seemed the likeliest, viz.: that the overseers had been left on the island with the Indians, but, being hardier, had survived the disease; and that they'd taken the Indian women, foul-faced or no, and murdered Brother Casildo. So they lived until the brothers Claveria Martinez came back, in seven years' time.

The brothers must have come ashore armed, not expecting anyone to have survived. One of the brothers must have been taken alive, with all he brought ashore, including fresh arms and ammunition. The other must have gotten away, back to Cartagena, and in course of time took passage on the galleon that ran afoul of the *Martin Luther*.

The *Martin Luther*'s crew debated what they ought to do next. There was some talk of going to Port Royal, but that was a chancy business; if the wind of diplomacy was blowing the wrong way, a poor hard-working captain might find a lot of Royal Marines demanding to see his privateer's commission, and confiscating his spoils, and indeed he might just be hanged to soothe Spanish feelings.

So in the end they went to Tortuga, where there were always folk willing to do business. The galleon's cargo was disposed of, a buyer found for the emeralds, and every last penny of the profits counted out and divided up in fair shares amongst the crew. John and Jessup walked away from the *Martin Luther* rich men, at least as far as John was concerned. His pockets were like to burst for the weight of his money.

"What'll you do with your share?" he asked Jessup, as they walked along. There were yellow lights beckoning through the trees, and a smell of good food and drink, and music. Jessup shook his head.

"Get myself a new name, and put this business as far behind me as ever I can," he said. "Go somewhere no one knows my face. Set up in business, live quiet and die rich in my bed. You'll do the same, boy, if you've any wit."

"I reckon I will, ay," said John.

They parted. John considered Jessup's advice, and knew it was good advice, and heard the voice of his mother in his ear telling him it was good advice too. He fully intended to follow it; but the yellow lights beckoned so, and he could hear women laughing, and he thought he'd just go celebrate his good fortune first.

He met a pretty French whore, who showed him where the best turtle stew was to be had, and where the best rum was served. They had a pleasant evening indeed, or at least what John could remember of it afterward, and she showed him a great many other things too.

Next morning the sun was too bright, and John wandered queasy and penniless along the waterfront, squinting at all the sleek rakish craft moored there. He was hoping to find some of the *Martin Luther*'s crew, as might be willing to oblige an old shipmate with a loan. He didn't; but before long he came to a ship taking on kegs of powder, and some men were talking there, with a look about them of cutlasses, and smoke, and easy money.

John listened to them chatting a while before dropping a friendly remark or two. By and by he joined the conversation, and pretty soon one of them asked him if he cared to go on the account.

John, ever so grateful, said he'd like that very much indeed.

They sailed next day, and had taken a galleon full of wine and silk before the week was out.

AVAST, ABAFT!

By Howard Waldrop

"The *Pinafore*'s gaining on us, Your Majesty!" yelled the bosun.

The Pirate King swung his spyglass aft.

"Put out more sail!" he hollered. "And wet 'em down."

The ship's deck was blurred as the crew brought out canvas, lashed ropes to buckets, threw them alongsides, and hauled up seawater. Others climbed in the rigs, unfurled sails, pulled up the bucket-lines, and poured them over the filled sails.

The deck was slippery as owl snot in a matter of moments.

"Bosun. See to the cargo," said the Pirate King.

The cargo was five daughters of another general. They'd seen them on the shore having a picnic when they had stolen the ship out of Penzance. They'd put a crew out in a boat, run ashore, and grabbed them. They'd do very well for ransom, on this, the crew's first return to sea and piracy.

The pirate crew had all been Lords of the Realm who had gone bad years ago, and made a life of brigandage, but they hadn't been very good at it, being too sentimental. There'd been another in a long series of disappointments; they'd all reformed and taken their former places in society.

That hadn't worked out either. A few weeks ago they'd had a reunion, decided to steal a ship, and take up their former ways.

"We've done well on our first day back at the job," said the Pirate King. "Well away from land; hold full of ransom. If it weren't for that damn Rackstraw and the *Pinafore*; he's closing on a course that'll suck our wind as he closes." He put down his spyglass as the ship, with more wet sail out, left the jagged dot of the *Pinafore* further back on the horizon.

The crew, its present work done, had gathered around the Pirate King.

"What we've never heard, Your Majesty," said the bosun, "is how you yourself first became a pirate."

"Really?" asked the Pirate King. "I'm sure my story's much the same as yours. Next but one youngest son, not a chance for the peerage, waning family fortunes since the Enclosures and Industrialization—" somewhere aboard a mouth organ began a sprightly tune, and the Pirate King began to bob up and down.

"When I was a lad, and hardly knew a thing—

"My old pater pledged me to the service of the King.

"I powd—"

"Majesty!" yelled the bosun, the only man-jack aboard not in the circle around the Pirate King, who was looking through his spyglass. "The *Pinafore* gains again!"

"Look lively, lads! Pray for more wind. Singing continues at eight bells, attack and repel boarders notwithstanding."

After they'd wet sails and put out all canvas, the crew of the *Pinafore* had gathered around Captain Rackstraw as he told the tale of how he had first come to the Navy. A concertina played belowdecks, and Captain Rackstraw bobbed lightly. He was describing his twelve-year-old self.

"I powder-monkeyed up and I powder-monkeyed down

"And never again saw London t—"

"Captain, Captain!" yelled the first mate. "We again gain on the pirate tub!"

"Land Ho!" yelled the lookout from the crow's nest. "The pirates make for it. Two points off the starboard bow."

The concertina stopped, and the circled crew let out a sigh of disappointment.

"Sorry, lads," said Ralph Rackstraw. "When I was one of you, I know how much we all enjoyed a good sing-round. We'll have a real rip-snorter as soon as we free some captives and hang a few pirates."

"Smoke!" yelled the lookout. "Smoke from the island."

Rackstraw watched through his spyglass. The island was barely a dot, but fronds of smoke curled up from it. Then more, lighter smoke came from the left end of the place.

"Answering smoke!" shouted down the lookout. "Same four big puffs and a small one."

"That's no volcanic vent," said the Pirate King. "There are people there, and they've seen us." He turned back, looked toward the gaining *Pinafore*. "We can put the island alongships, protect our side, slug it out with the Navy ship, though we're outgunned," he said.

"Bring me the charts!" he yelled to the first mate. "We sure don't want to put in at a British provisioning station. I don't remember there being land for six hundred leagues."

"It's unknown to me, and not on the maps," said the bosun to Captain Rackstraw. "We're off the main lanes, and the Canaries and Azores are far south and behind; the Bermoothes a thousand nautical miles WSW."

The crew, including Dick Deadeye (who for some reason the rest of the crew loathed), had gathered round, hoping for some chanty or other, despite the Captain's earlier words. When none was forthcoming, they dispiritedly went back to their duties.

"Ready the cannons!" said Ralph Rackstraw. "He'll put one side to shore, and run his heaviest guns out seaward, in shoaling water, so we can't cross the T on 'em. Helmsman, keep on him like he were a fox trying to go to earth, and we the lean hound."

"Aye Aye!"

The smoke continued from the two ends of the island as it grew larger.

"They're certainly talking to each other," said the bosun to the Pirate King.

"That they are, and such a small island, too. Typical high mountain in the middle. Charts show no bottom here, so it must be like one of the Pacific ones, rising straight up from the seafloor for miles. Very atypical for the Atlantic. Rest of the island probably like a ring around the mountain." He took his spyglass away from his eye. "I think I saw a waterfall off the far side, and it's inhabited, so there's fresh water. If we settle the *Pinafore*, we can at least fill our water barrels and be ready for a long run somewheres."

The ship closed with the island. "Start soundings! Helm! Make for the indentation on the port side of the island. A bay or cove mayhaps. Look lively, make ready the cannons, O my Lords of the Realm."

"Yo!" yelled Captain Rackstraw aboard the *Pinafore*. "Make ready for battle. Break out the munitions. Riflemen, up the yards!"

Sailors ran like ants and scrambled up the ratlines. Powder monkeys disappeared belowdecks and returned with long cylinders and passed them up to the men in the rigs.

Dick Deadeye admired their precision as he lashed a wooden trough to the foretopmast. These new munitions could scuttle any pirate tub. He nodded skyward, thanking whoever it was was responsible for science and such…

The stolen ship had long since disappeared around the headland. The island loomed larger, such as those he'd heard in tales from old Cook's sailors. Smoke, and the answering smoke rose up.

As the Pirate King's ship rounded on the port beam, the lookout yelled down: "There's females on the rocks."

With a squeak like a vole a half-naked girl slid off a boulder in the middle of the estuary. She slapped the water with her long green tail. Instantly, squeaks like bedsprings echoed off the island, and with a flurry of spray, like sunning turtles wakened by an otter, dozens and dozens of fish-tailed girls left their rocks and went into the lagoon. They abandoned whatever they had been doing, leaving fruit, mandolins, and half-eaten oysters atop the boulders. In an eyeflash, it was as if they had never been there.

Above on the mountain, more and more smoke rose.

"They's gone now!" came the lookout's cry.

"They's gone now?" yelled up the Pirate King. "My God, man, you went to Eaton! Speak the Queen's English!"

"Your pardon, Sir," shouted down the lookout. "Brevity being the soul of wit, I thought the signal more important than the noise. The females—strange indeed, Sir—who formerly lay about the rocks in the estuary seem to have departed."

"See your brevity is occasionally nuanced with conjunctions and gerunds," said his commander.

"Aye aye, Sir!" yelled the lookout. "And a pleasant day to you, too, Sir!"

As the *Pinafore* rounded the curve in the island, the lookout yelled there were women swimming about.

"Women?" yelled Rackstraw. "Well, we'll have to be very careful they're not in the line of fire when we close battle."

Women? the crew was thinking. The only thing they liked better than singing was the possibility of unaccompanied females on remote islands.

Here and there a long-haired head bobbed up in the water, then disappeared to reappear hundreds of yards away.

"Damn but they can swim!" said Rackstraw to the first mate.

There happened to be another pirate ship far around the island at the back edge of the lagoon, where a creek entered the river just before it dumped into the bay. The ship stood at anchor, creaking on its chain from the river current. It was washday and the yards hung with breeks, blouses, vests, and head-scarves.

"Damn but I'm tired," said the bosun to the first mate. "Tireder than the time in the shoals off Africa where we crawled on our hook for three days after a week of no wind."

"Why are you telling *me* this?" asked the first mate. "I was there!"

"Just passing the time while we await the Captain's pleasure, which seems to be waiting," said the bosun.

"Something disturbs the fish-girls!" yelled down the lookout. "To seaward."

The Captain, in his fine courtier's outfit from two centuries before, ran out of his cabin. He had been there, putting the finishing touches on his manuscript "The Great Cocodrillo of Time," which he would post to the Secretary of the Royal Society as soon as he reached a civilized port. He hoped it would be published in the Proceedings. He had been a Fellow since before he took up his life of crime. He waved his great hook in the air. "Strike the wash! Weigh anchor! Ready the guns!"

The ship was a blur from the deck upwards. Bright clothes rained down as if from a piñata. Cannonballs rolled across the deck, men jumping and dodging.

"Move out where we have a clear field of fire!" yelled the Captain. "It may be the Boy, though he usually doesn't scare the fishy-folk." He looked up toward the forested mountain. "The Indians are certainly agitated," he said. Then he preened his mustaches with his glinting hook. "Perhaps for a change this will be an interesting day, methinks."

"Aye, sir," said the first mate.

As they rounded the point in the *Pinafore*, Dick Deadeye froze stock-still. It was as if he were living a dream; he was translated to a higher state of consciousness that included a perceptual breakthrough and had a paradigm shift. It was like having déjà vu two times in a row.

For he suddenly recognized this island, as if he had been there before or had been born there but had not seen it for a long time. He knew the bay, the rocks with the musical instruments and bitten-into fruit, the long curve of the lagoon, the woods on the mountain, the rising smoke.

It was as if he had heard of it long ago in a lullaby.

And then it came to him, and he went running to the ship's tailor, whose battle-station was in the repel-boarders-starboard gang.

"Pockets!" yelled Dick Deadeye. "Pockets! Run off scads of pockets. They're mad for pockets!"

"What? What?" asked the tailor's mate. "What kinds of pockets? What material are the clothes? You don't just run off pockets. You put them in."

Dick Deadeye strained his brain. "Furs, I think. Skins! They have no pockets of their own."

"Who we talking about?" asked the ship's tailor, himself, putting his cutlass point-first into the *Pinafore*'s deck.

"Boys!" said Dick Deadeye. "Boys bereft of parent or guardian; boys who suffered early perambulatory mishaps," he said. "I heard tell."

"Find these boys; we'll measure them, their clothes, and then see about pockets," said the ship's tailor.

"I'll pay well for pockets," said Dick Deadeye. "We'll put them as trade goods on shore, see what they take, run off more."

"Dammit man," said the tailor's mate. "You have to put pockets *in*; what you want's bags, wallets, budgets."

"They *can't* be wanting those. I'm *sure* it's pockets they crave," said Dick Deadeye.

"See us later," said the tailor. "We've got some pirate hash to settle."

Dick Deadeye climbed back up to his battle-station in the foretopmast. Cowardly men, afraid to run off a few dozen pockets. The whole crew hated him. That was probably because they didn't like *their* day in the barrel.

"They're flying the Roger," yelled down the lookout to the Captain. The man swung his spyglass to seaward. "Chased by a British man-o'war."

"Prepare to sink 'em both," said the hook-handed Captain. He watched the pirate tub heave into view. "He dares to fly a Roger with a crown above it in my presence. The second because I sink all men-o'war on sight, as you know."

"Aye aye Cap'n!" the crew yelled.

"Roll out Large Willy!" he yelled. The crew groaned but hopped to. It was stowed amidships, pointing forward, and took up all the room. There were two removable sections in the port and starboard gun rails to which it could be trundled. When it was run out, the breech reached halfway to the other railing and the ship listed to the mouth-side. It was the largest gun afloat. "Put him to port!" the Captain yelled, pointing with his hook.

They groaned again, but with levers and movable gears, swung him around.

"And for the first volley," said the Captain, "give 'em a whiff o' the grape!"

They groaned louder. Why have the largest gun on any ocean if you had to come in so close as to use it for a giant blunderbuss? Why not sink the bastards with solid shot a mile off? Nevertheless they started bringing up boxes of broken horseshoes and busted anchor chains they'd bought at their last port, and shoveling them down Large Willy's barrel…

Before they came within sight of the river, the Pirate King said, "Drop anchor here! We make a stand to port. Run all the guns out that way. Take the two-pounders up into the rigging. Make 'em pay. Bosun—take the hostages to shore and guard 'em."

Horns blatted and whistles blew. Feet pounded. The port rail bristled with cannon and firearms.

"Just as I figured," said Rackstraw. "They're putting the island to their starboard. Very well, prepare the first volley."

Dick Deadeye, in the rigging, put his charge in the wooden trough. Good thing Buttercup had gotten them these. Anyone could have Congreve rockets as H.M.S. issue. These were the new Hale spin-stabilized kind, with angled vents for the exhaust gasses, so there was no need of the unwieldy sticks. Dick shrugged on his leather coat and face-mask with the big mica eyepieces and awaited the command from Captain Rackstraw. Five more charges waited on the arm beside him.

"On my command, volley fire," said Rackstraw. He watched through his spyglass. "Fire!"

The air became a massed streaking of fires that converged on the pirate tub. Followed by five more volleys in rapid succession.

"Damn!" said the Pirate King. "Who the hell uses rockets except to signal anymore?" He ducked as a low one, the size of a man, crossed above the deck. "We're not some heathens to be scared by noise and smoke!"

"Pardon, Your Majesty," said the first mate. "But our sails, rigging, yards and masts are afire."

"Put out the fargin' fires!" he yelled. "Prepare to show 'em what-for."

Then there was a terrific explosion that took away all the masts and sails and everyone on the deck of the Pirate King's ship.

"What in hell happened?" asked Rackstraw. "The whole damn thing blew up. Did they set off their own magazine?"

"Uh-oh," said the first mate. "Look sir, beyond."

Rackstraw saw through the ghost forest of broken spars and burning canvas of the stolen ship a larger ship looming behind it, a huge cannon to port. That ship, too, flew the Roger. It was coming to get them."

On the mountainside, the smoke signals grew more frantic.

It had been a beautiful day, with only broken cloud and a bright sun, the kind made for wash-day, sunning mer-folk and Indian dances.

"Weather abaft!" shouted down the lookout to the hook-handed Captain. The crew was waiting for Large Willy to cool before throwing in more powder-bags.

"Weather?" yelled up the Captain. "We've not seen weather in five months. Are you drunk up there, Cecco?"

"I'm not drunk nor fooling," yelled the Italian. "And when I say weather, I mean weather!"

The Captain was conflicted.

"Ahoy!" he screamed. "Simultaneously batten down the deck and prepare to fire!"

The crew looked at him.

"You heard the Captain!" yelled the first mate, perplexed as the crew. "It's the caress of the hook to anyone doesn't follow orders!"

They all tried to do three things at once. It's a wonder hands or feet weren't nailed to the deck in haste.

"Weather on us!" yelled the lookout, as all their hats and scarves blew off their heads.

It was dark as midnight under Silver's skillet. They grabbed whatever they could hang on to; rails, rigging, each other. The gale whipped the lagoon to a froth. Wrack and spume obscured the man-o'war—no telling where it was. It was useless even to yell; the words whipped away like paper.

As soon as the lookout warned of a change in the weather, Rackstraw had the ship battened down and the slow-matches taken below, and the men ordered from the riggings. It hit the like hurricane the *Pinafore* had gone through under Corcoran six years ago. The ship seemed to jump its cable length as the storm hit. "Put out a sheet anchor!" Rackstraw yelled to the crew. At least they wouldn't be dashed on the rocks though they might be rounded.

The men tensed at the rails. All the gunports on the gun deck were opened toward where the original pirate ship had been. There was a glow through the rain, orange-yellow, where the burning ship might be.

"When the blow's over," yelled Rackstraw to the bosun, very close by, "prepare to go pick up those hostages on shore."

"If they're not blown away, too. Aye, sir," said the bosun.

Through the roiling wet, as much water as air, a shape formed, came near, from windward. After a second it turned into the second pirate ship, coming broadsides.

Everyone in both ships yelled behind their pistols, rifles, and cannon, ready to fire. It was going to be dreadful.

And then both lookouts screamed at the same instant: "JESUS H. CHRIST!" Everyone turned their heads to seaward.

A huge black galleon of two centuries gone came by, sails furled, moving against the scud and wrack, surrounded by corposantos, trailing a blur of dying sparks.

Everyone on the British man-o'war and the huge pirate ship stood still, trying to avert their eyes (as if they could keep from looking). The ship sailed on, the storm blew off to its stern and faded away to westward. The sun came out and a gull squawked from above.

The sound of tom-toms came on the still-calm air.

"Make about to the river anchorage!" yelled the hook-handed Captain.

"Prepare to pick up hostages," yelled Rackstraw.

The two ships moved apart without so much as a backward glance at each other.

Sunset. The *Pinafore* had picked up the hostages and set course back for Wales.

The hook-handed Captain's ship lay at anchor off the creek and river. Out toward sea, the mermaids were back on their rocks, singing each to each.

"Yo!" yelled Jukes from the lookout. "Four specks and a spark to westward!"

"He's back!" yelled the hook-handed Captain. "This time, he's mine!" He turned to the crew. "Ready Large Willy. He's still primed to fire. Maximum elevation, hit them when they cross."

The crew cranked at the elevating jacks.

The specks grew larger against the darkening east. The spark circled them like an electron in orbit, as described by Rutherford.

"Fire!" yelled the Captain, bringing down his hook, and Large Willy deafened them, and a load of horseshoes and nails flew upward like shot at a grouse.

Far to the east, the *Pinafore* sailed on toward its port. Below, on the decks, Rackstraw and the officers danced with the General's daughters. Lanterns hung in the rigging and on the rails; concertinas vied with fiddles and guitars; a mouth-organ joined in. On deck, all was gaiety and merriment; the men singing along to those sentimental ballads they knew.

Far above in the rigging, Dick Deadeye leaned over the crow's nest side. He looked westward, aft, from whence they had come, and the world of the island was fading, like a half-remembered dream, on the night.

Dick Deadeye was crying.

ELEGY TO GABRIELLE, PATRON SAINT OF HEALERS, WHORES, AND RIGHTEOUS THIEVES

By Kelly Barnhill

C urator's note: *The following pages were found in a cave on an islet eleven miles southwest of Barbados. The narrative is, of course, incomplete, disjointed and unreliable, as is the information contained within its pages. There is no record of Brother Marcel Renau living in the Monastery of the Holy Veil during the years in question. There is a record of the order for the execution of a Gabrielle Belain in St. Pierre in 1678; however, no documentation of the actual execution exists. Some of this narrative is indecipherable. Some is lost forever. Most, if not all, is blatantly untrue, the ravings of a lost sailor gone mad without water. As to the conditions in which these writings were found: this too remains a puzzle. The cave was dry and protected and utterly empty except for three things: a human skeleton, curled in the corner as though sleeping; a two-foot length of human hair, braided tightly with a length of ribbon and a length of rope, laid across the hands of the dead man; and an oiled and locked box made of teak in which these documents were found. Across the lid of the box the following words had been roughly scratched into the wood, as though with a crude knife or a sharp rock: "Bon Soir, Papa."*

I do not know if anyone will ever read these words that I place on this paper. In our order, we have copied, transcribed and preserved words—both God's and Man's—for the last thousand years. Now, as I expire here in this waste of water and wind and endless sky, I write of my own disappearing, and this, my last lettering, will likely fade, drift and vanish into the open mouth of the ravenous sea.

I have always had a lovely hand, which is why I was ever drawn to this vocation. The word of God deserves a deft stroke, a sure line of ink to paper, to mouth, to mind. This is an old skill, of course, made increasingly obsolete by our advances in mechanization. Still, my copies of the Psalms brought men to tears—even il-literate men. They coaxed confessions out of princes and extended the honor of many a wavering maid. I do not write this to boast—what use is boasting to me now? Rather, as my life ebbs and ebbs and ebbs away, I cannot trouble myself with false modesty or concealed pride. I became a monk to lay the work of my hands and the prayers of my heart at the feet of the Savior, and this I have done since I took up the cowl. Except when I have not. And for those, God will forgive me or He will not. It is out of my hands.

I do not write these words to absolve myself, or even to save my beloved Gabrielle. Gabrielle has proven, for once and for all, that she neither seeks nor requires any assistance from me. And why should she? Why should anyone?

Two days before Gabrielle Belain (the pirate, the witch, the revolutionary) was to be executed, a golden bird flew low over the fish market, startling four mules, ten chickens, countless matrons and the Lord High Constable. It flew in a wide spiral higher and higher until it reached the window of the tower where my beloved Gabrielle awaited her fate. People say that she came to the window, that the shadows from the bars cut across her lovely face. People say that she reached out a delicate, slightly freckled hand to the bird's mouth. People say that she began to sing.

I stood in the hallway with the two guards, negotiating the transfer of food, water and absolution across the threshold of the wood and iron door that blocked Gabrielle from the world. I did not see the bird. I did not hear song. But I believe them both to be true. This, of course, is the nature of existence: We believe, and it *is*. Perhaps God will turn His back on me for writing such heresy, but I swear it's the truth. Gabrielle, like her mother before her, was a Saint Among Men, a living manifestation of the power of God. People believed this, and it was true, and no demonstration of the cynical power of bureaucrats and governments and States could unbelieve their believing.

Gabrielle Belain, at the age of ten, walked from the cottage where she lived with her mother, past the Pleasure House to the shore. The moon, a thin slash on a glittering sky, cast a pale light on the foamy sand. She peered out onto the water. The ship, hidden in darkness, was still there, its black sails furled and lashed to the tethered boom, its tarred hull creaking in the waves. She could *feel* it. Actually, there was never a time when she could not feel it. Even when it was as far away as Portugal or Easter Island or the far tip of the continent, she knew where the ship was. And she knew she belonged to it.

Four porpoises bobbed in the waves, waiting for the child to wade in. They made no sound, but watched, their black eyes flashing over the bubbling surf. A mongrel dog, nearly as tall as she, whined piteously, and rubbed its nose to her shoulder.

"You can't come," she said.

The mongrel dog growled in response.

Gabrielle shrugged. "Fine," she said. "Please yourself. I will not wait for you." She waded in, caught hold of a porpoise fin, and swam out into the darkness, the mongrel dog paddling and sputtering behind her.

The sailors on the quiet ship watched the sky, listened to the wind. They waited. They had been waiting for ten years.

By the time Gabrielle was thirteen, she was the ship's navigator. By the time she was fifteen, she was captain, and a scourge to princes and merchants and slave traders. By the time she was eighteen, she was in prison—chained, starved, measured and weighed for hanging.

At night, I see their hands. I do not see their faces. I pray, with my rattling breath, with the slow ooze of my blistered skin, with my vanishing, worthless life, that I may see their faces again before I die. For now, I must content myself with hands. Gabrielle's hands who thwarted governors, generals and even the King himself, and her mother's hands, who healed, who prayed, and God help me, who loved me. Once. But *oh! Once!*

Gabrielle's mother, Marguerite Belain, came from France to Martinique in the cover and care of my order as we sailed across the ocean to establish a new fortress of prayer and learning in the lush, fragrant and sinful islands of the New World. It was not our intention to harbor a fugitive, let alone a female fugitive. We learned of Marguerite's detention through our contacts with the Sisters of the Seventh Sorrow, several of whom waited upon the new and most beloved lover of the young and guileless King. Although the mistress managed to bear children in her previous marriage, with the King she was weak wombed, and her babes flowed, purple and twisted, into her monthly rags with much weeping and sorrow in the royal chambers. Marguerite was summoned to the bed of the mistress, her womb now quickening once again.

"Please," the mistress begged, tears flowing down those alabaster cheeks. "Please," she said, her marble mouth, carved always in an expression of supercilious distain, trembling, cracking, breaking to bits.

Marguerite lay her hands on the belly of the King's beloved. She saw the child, its limbs curled tightly in its liquid world. The womb, she knew, would not hold. She saw, however, that it *could*, that the path to wholeness was clear, and that the child could be born, saved and whole, if certain steps were taken immediately.

But that was not all she saw.

She also saw the child, its grasping hands, its cold, cold eye. She saw the child as it grew in the seat of power and money and military might. She saw the child as it set its teeth upon the quivering world and tore upon its beating heart.

"I cannot save this child," Marguerite said, her leaf-green eyes averted to the ground.

"You can," the mistress said, her granite lips remaking themselves. Cold power trumps grief. "And you will."

But she would not, and was duly imprisoned for the duration of the pregnancy, whereupon she would be guillotined as a murderess if the child did not live, and as a charlatan if the child did.

It did not. But Marguerite was spirited away, disguised and smuggled into our ship of seafaring brethren before the palace ever did turn black with mourning.

It was on the eighteenth day of our voyage that Marguerite gave me leave into her chamber. It was on the eighteenth day of our voyage that a storm swirled from nowhere, sending the wind and sea to hurl themselves against the groaning hull, and striking the starboard deck with lightning.

Was it the lover, people asked, or the lightning that produced such a child when she bore a babe with glittering eyes?

Gabrielle. My child. I am supposed to say the issue of my sin, but I cannot. How can sin produce a child such as this?

On the thirty-first day, a ship with black sails appeared in the distance in the morning. By noon we could see the glint of their curved swords, the ragged snarl of ravenous teeth. By mid-afternoon, the ship had lashed itself to ours and the men climbed aboard. In anticipation of their arrival, we set food and drink on the deck and opened several—although not all—of our money boxes allowing our gold to shine in the sun. We huddled together before the main mast, our fingers following prayer after prayer on our well-worn rosaries. I reached for Marguerite, but she was gone.

A man limped from their ship to ours. A man whose face curled in upon itself, whose lashless eyes peered coldly from a sagging brow, whose mouth set itself in a grim, ragged gash in a pitiless jaw. A mouth like an unhealed wound.

Marguerite approached and stood before him. "You are he," she said.

He stared at her, his cold eyes widening softly with curiosity. "I am," he said. He was proud, of course. Who else would he be? Or, more importantly, who else would he desire to be? He reached for the cowl that hid the top of her head and shadowed her face and pulled it off. Her hair, the color of wheat, spilled out, poured over the rough cloth that hid her body from the world, pooled over her hands, and around her feet. "And you, apparently, are she."

She did not answer, but laid her hands upon his face instead. She looked intently into his face, and he returned her gaze, his hard eyes light with tears. "You're sick," she said. "You have been for… ever so long. And sad as well. I cannot heal the sadness, but I can heal the sickness. He, too, suffers." She pointed to the pockmarked man holding a knife to the throat of our beloved Abbot. "And he, and he." She pointed to other men on the ship. Walking over to the youngest man who leaned greenly against the starboard gunnels, she laid her hand on his shoulder. "You, my love, I cannot save. I am so sorry." Tears slipped down her cream and nutmeg skin. The man—barely a man—a boy, in truth—bowed his head sadly. "But I can make it so it will not hurt." She took his hand, and squeezed it in her own. She brought her pale lips to his smooth brown cheek and kissed him. He nodded and smiled.

Marguerite ordered a bucket to be lowered and filled with seawater. She laid the bucket at the feet of the captain. Dipping her hands in the water, she anointed his head, then his hands and his feet. She laid her ear upon his neck, then his heart, then his belly. Then, scooping seawater into her left hand, she asked the pirate captain to spit into its center. He did, and immediately, the water became light, and the light became feathers, and the feathers became a red bird with a green beak who howled its name to the sky. It flew straight up, circled the main mast and spiraled down, settling himself on the captain's right shoulder.

"Don't lose him," she said to the captain.

In this way she healed those who were sick, and soothed the one who was dying, giving each his own familiar: a one-eared cat, an air-breathing fish, a blue albatross and a silver snake.

When she finished, she turned to the captain. "Now you will return to your ship and we will continue our journey."

The captain nodded and smiled. "Of course, madam. But the child in your womb will return to us. She was conceived on the sea and will return to the sea. When she is old enough we will not come for her. We will not need to. She will find us."

Marguerite blinked, bit her lip so hard she drew blood, and returned to the hold without a word. She did not emerge until we made land.

Our brethren that had preceded us met us on the quay and led us to the temporary shelters that crouched, like lichen, on the rock. That the new church with its accompanying cloister and school were unfinished, we knew. But the extent to the disorder was an unconcealed shock to all of us, especially our poor Brother Abbot, whose face was stricken at the sight of the mossy stones upon the ground.

Brother Builder hung his head for the shame of it. "This is a place of entropy and decay," he muttered to me when the Abbot had gone. "Split wood will not dry, but sprouts mushrooms, though it has heated and cured for days. Cleared land, burned to the ground will sprout within the hour. Keystones crack from the weight of ivy and sweet, heavy blossoms that were not there the night before."

The Abbot contacted the Governor who constricted laborers—freemen, indentured and slaves—to assist with the building, and soon we had not only church and cloister, but library, bindery, stables, root cellars, barrel houses and distilleries.

Desperately, I hoped that Marguerite would be allowed to stay. I hoped that the Abbot would build her a cottage by the sea where she could keep a garden and sew for the Abbey. Of course she could not. The Abbot gave her a temporary shelter to herself, forcing many of the brethren to squeeze together on narrow cots, but no one grumbled. At the end of our first month on the island, she left without saying good-bye. I saw her on the road as the sun was rising, her satchel swung across her back. Her hair was uncovered and fell in a loose plait down her back, curling at the tops of her boots. I saw her and called her name. She turned and waved but said nothing. She did not need to. The sunlight bearing down on her small frame illuminated at last that which I had been blind to. Her belly had begun to swell.

Gabrielle was born in the vegetable garden that separated the Pleasure House from the small cottage where Marguerite lived and worked. Though the prostitutes gave her shelter ostensibly in exchange for her skills as a cook, a gardener and a healer, it soon became clear that her gifts were greater and more numerous than originally thought. As Marguerite's pregnancy progressed, the gardens surrounding the Pleasure House thrived beyond all imaginings. Guavas grew to the size of infants, berries spilled across the lawns, staining the stone walkways and steps a rich, dark red, like blood coursing into a beating heart. Vines, thick and strong as saplings, snaked upwards along the whitewashed plaster, erupting in multi-colored petals that fluttered from the roof like flags.

Marguerite, when the time came, knelt among the casaba melons and lifted her small hands to the bright sky. Immediately, a cloud of butterflies alighted on her fingers, her heaving shoulders, her rivers of gold hair, as the babe kicked, pressed and slipped into the cradle of leaves that cradled her to the welcoming earth.

The girls of the Pleasure House saw this. They told the story to everyone. Everyone believed it.

After Gabrielle was born, Marguerite scooped up the afterbirth and buried it at the foot of the guava tree. The girls of the Pleasure House gathered about her to wash the baby, to wheedle the new mother to bed, but Marguerite would not have it. She brought the baby to the spot where the placenta was buried.

"You see this?" she said to the baby. "You are rooted. Here. And here you will stay. The captain can believe what he will, but you are not a thing of water. You are a child of earth. And of me. And I am here." And with that she went inside and nursed her baby.

For months, the Abbot sent a convoy of monks to the little cottage behind the Pleasure House to argue in favor of a baptism for the babe with the glittering eyes. Though I assume it was well known that the child was the product of the one time (but *oh! Once!*) that Marguerite Belain consented to love me, we had chosen to believe that the child was a miracle, conceived of lightning, of sea, of the healing goodness of her mother. And in that believing, it became true. Gabrielle was not mine.

She would not consent. No water, save from the spring that bubbled a mile inland, would touch her daughter. She would not bathe in the sea. She would not taste or touch water that came from any but her mother's hand.

"She will be rooted," she said. "And she will never float away."

After a time, the girls of the Pleasure House emerged to shoo us off. They had all of them grown in health and beauty since Marguerite's arrival. Their faces freshened, their hair grew bright and strong, and any whiff of the pox or madness or both had dissipated and disappeared. Moreover, their guests, arriving in the throes of hunger and lust, went away sated, soothed and alive. They became better men. They were gentler with their wives, loving with their children. They fixed the roof of the church, rebuilt the washed out roads, took in their neighbors after disasters. They lived long, healthy, happy lives and died rich.

Gabrielle Belain was never baptized, though in my dreams, I held that glittering child in my arms and waded into the sea to my waist. In my dream, I scooped up the sea in my right hand and let it run over the red curls of the child that was mine and not mine. Mostly not mine. In my dream a golden bird circled down from the sky, hovered for a moment before us and kissed her rosebud mouth.

When Gabrielle was six years old, she wandered out of the garden and down the road to the town square. Her red curls shone with ribbon and oil, and her frock was blue and pretty and new. The girls of the Pleasure House, none of whom bore children of their own, doted on the child, spoiling her with dresses and hats and dolls and sweets. Though, in truth, the girl did not spoil, but only grew in sweetness and energy and spark.

On the road, she saw a mongrel dog that had been lamed in a fight. It was enormous, almost the size of pony, with grizzled fur hanging about its wide, snarling mouth. It panted under the star apple tree, whining and showing its teeth. Gabrielle approached the animal, looked up at the branches, heavy with fruit and held out her hand. A star apple, dark and smooth, fell neatly into her little hand, its skin already bursting with sweet juice. She knelt before the dog.

"Eat," she said. The dog ate. Immediately, it stood, completely healed, nuzzled its new mistress, shaking its tail earnestly, and allowed her to climb upon its back. Once in the market square, people stopped and stared at the pretty little girl riding the mongrel dog. They offered her sweets and fruits and bits of fabric that might please a little child. She came to the fishmonger's stall. The fishmonger, an old, sour man, was in the middle of negotiating a price with an older, sourer man, and did not notice Gabrielle. A large marlin, quite dead, leaned over the side of the cart, its angled mouth slightly open as though attempting to breathe. Gabrielle, a tender child, put her hand to her mouth and blew the fish a kiss. The fishmonger, satisfied that he had successfully bilked his customer out of more gold than he had made all the week before, looked down and was amazed to see his fish suddenly flapping and twisting in the rough-hewn cart. The marlin leapt into the air and gave the customer a sure smack against his wrinkled cheek, before hurling itself onto the cobbled path and wriggling its way to the dock. Similarly, the other fish began to wiggle and jump, tumbling and churning against each other in a jumbled mass towards freedom. People gawked and pointed and gathered as the fishmonger vainly tried to gather the fish in his arms, but he had no idea what to do without the aid of his nets, and his nets were being mended by his foul-mouthed wife in their little hovel by the sea.

Gabrielle and her dog, realizing that there was nothing more to see, moved closer to the fine house and tower that served as the Governor's residence and court and prison. To the side of the deeply polished doors, carved with curving branches and flowers and images of France, was the raised dais where men and women and children in chains stood silently, waiting to be priced, purchased and hauled away. The man in the powdered wig who called out the fine qualities of the man in chains on his left did not notice the little girl riding the mongrel dog. But the man in chains did. She looked up at him, her freckled nose wrinkled in concentration, her green eyes squinting in the sun. She smiled at the man in chains and waved at him. He smiled back. He couldn't help it.

The child began to sing, softly at first, and no one noticed. I stood in the receiving room of the Governor's mansion, waiting to receive dictations for letters going to the governors of other Caribbean territories, to the Mayor and High Inquisitor of New Orleans, and to the advisors to the King himself. This was our tribute to the Governor: rum, wine, transcribed books, and my hands. And for these gifts he left us mostly alone to live and work as pleased God.

Through the window I saw the child who came to me nightly in dreams. I heard the song. I sang, too.

The people in the square, distracted by the escaping fish, did not notice the growing cloud of birds that blew in from the sea on one side and the forest on the other. They did not notice how the birds circled over the place where the people stood, waiting to be sold. They did not notice the great cacophony of feather and color and wing as it descended on the dais.

Two big albatrosses upset the moneyboxes of the traders, sending gold spilling onto the dirt. A thousand finches flew in the faces of the guards and officers keeping watch over the square. A dozen parrots landed on the ground next to Gabrielle and sang along with her, though badly and off-key. And hundreds of other birds—and not just birds of the island, but birds of Africa, England and France, spiraled around every man, woman and child, before alighting suddenly skyward, and vanishing in the low clouds. Gabrielle, her song ended, rode slowly away. It was several moments before anyone realized that the dais was now empty, and the slaves waiting for sale were gone. All that was left was an assortment of empty chains lying on the ground.

For weeks after, the Governor, who had invested heavily in the slave-bearing ship, and had lost a considerable sum in the disappearing cargo, sent interrogators, spies and thieves into every home in the town, and while no one knew what had happened or why, everyone commented on the strange, beautiful little girl, riding a mongrel dog.

From his balcony atop the mansion, the Governor could see the road that led away from the town, through the groves of fruit trees, through forest, to the Pleasure House and the little cottage surrounded by outrageously fertile gardens. He could see the golden-haired woman with her redheaded child. His breath was a cold wind, his face a merciless wave. A storm gathered in the town, preparing itself to crush my little Gabrielle.

I went with the Abbot to the cottage behind the Pleasure House, prepared to plead our case. It was not the first time. As the grumblings from the mansion grew louder and more insistent, we wrote letters in secret, sending them to the other islands and to France. Marguerite, dressed in a plain, white linen shift, her golden hair braided and looped around her waist like a belt, laid out plates laden with fruit and bread and fish. Gabrielle sat in the corner on a little sleeping pallet. She was nine now and able to read. She came to the Abbey often to look at bibles and maps and poetry. What she read, she memorized. Once she was heard reciting the entire book of Psalms while perched high in a tree gathering nuts.

"Eat," Marguerite said to us, sitting opposite on the wooden bench and taking out her sewing.

"Later," the Abbot said, waving the plate away impatiently with his left hand.

"Your child is not safe here any more. You know this, my daughter. The Governor has his spies and assassins everywhere. We could hide her in the Abbey, but for how long? It is only at my intercession that he has not come this far down the road, but neither of you are safe within a mile of the town."

"We need nothing from town," Marguerite said, filling our glasses with wine. "Drink," she commanded.

I brought my fist to the table. Gabrielle sat up with a start. "No," I said. "She cannot stay. I will accompany her back to France, and the Sisters of the Seventh Sorrow will protect her and educate her. No one will know whose child she is. No one will know of the Governor's hatred. She will be safe."

Marguerite took my fist and eased it open, laying her palm upon my palm. She looked at the Abbot and then at me.

"She is rooted here. I rooted her myself. She will not go to the sea. There is nothing more to say. Now. Eat."

We ate. And drank. The wine tasted of flowers, of love, of mother's milk, of sweat and flesh and dreaming. The food tasted like thought, like memory, like the pale whisperings of God. I dreamed of Gabrielle, growing, walking upon the water, standing with a sword against the sun. I dreamed of the taste of the mouth of Marguerite.

The Abbot and I woke under a tree next to the stable. There was no need to say anything, so we went in for Matins.

The next day, a ship with black sails appeared a mile out to sea. The girls of the Pleasure House reported that Marguerite went to the shore, screaming at the ship to depart. It did not. She called to the wind, to the ocean, to the birds, but no one assisted. The ship stayed where it was.

Soldiers came for Gabrielle. Marguerite saw them come. She stood on the roof of her house, and raised her hands to the growing clouds. The soldiers looked up and saw that the sky rained flower petals. The petals came down in thick torrents, blinding all who were out doors. With the petals came seeds and saplings, rooting themselves firmly in the overripe earth. The soldiers scattered, wandering blindly into the forest. Most never returned.

The next day, a thicket of trees grew up around the Pleasure House and the little cottage behind, along with a labyrinthine network of footpaths and trails. Few knew their way in or out. Whether the girls of the Pleasure House grumbled about this, no one knew. They appeared to have no trouble negotiating their way through the thicket, and trained a young boy, the son of the oyster diver, to stand at the entrance and guide men in or out. If an agent of the Governor approached, he darted into the trees and disappeared. He was never followed.

The morning of Gabrielle's tenth birthday, a storm raged from west, then from the north, then from the east. It was as though the sea had transformed itself from bringer of life to predator, and it stalked us, preparing to pounce. Everyone on the island prepared themselves for the worst. Anything that could be lashed was lashed. We boarded ourselves in, or ran for high ground. Outside, the wind howled and thrashed itself against our houses and buildings. The sea churned and swelled before rearing up and crashing down upon the island. Most of the buildings remained more or less intact. At the Abbey, the chapel flooded, as did the library, though most of the collection was salvaged. Several animals died when the smaller stable collapsed.

Once the rains subsided, I journeyed through the thick and cloying mud to check on Marguerite. I found her kneeling in the vegetable patch, weeping as though her heart would break. I knelt down next to her, though I don't think she noticed me at first. Her pale hands covered her face, and tears ran down her long fingers like pearls. She turned, looked at me full in the face with an expression of such sadness I found myself weeping though I did not know why.

"The guava tree," she said. "The sea took it away."

I could see that it was true. Instead of the broad smooth trunk and the reaching branches, a hole gaped before us like a wound. Even the roots were gone.

"There is nothing to hold her here," she said. And for the first time since the night in the ship's hold during the storm all those years ago, I reached my arm across her back and coaxed her head to my shoulder. Her hair smelled of cloves and loam and salt. Gabrielle stood on the rocks at the shore, gathering seaweed into a basket to be used for soup. Her mongrel dog stayed close to her heels, as though she might, at any moment, go skipping away. From time to time, she peered out at the water, as though trying to catch a glimpse of something hovering just past the horizon.

Two weeks later, Gabrielle Belain was gone. She slipped out to sea on the back of a porpoise, and she did not return, except at last in chains in the belly of a prison ship.

From the window in the library, I saw the ship with black sails unfurl itself, draw its anchors and sail away. From the forest surrounding the Pleasure House, a sound erupted, echoing across the shore, down the road, and deep into the wild lands of the island's interior. A deep, mournful, sorrowing cry. A dark cloud emerged over the forest and grew quickly across the island, heavy with rain and lightning. It rained for eighteen days. The road washed away, as did the foundations of houses, and gardens and huts that had not been securely fastened to the ground.

The Abbot went alone to the place where Marguerite wept. He brought no one with him, but when he returned, the sun reappeared, and Marguerite returned to her work healing sickness and coaxing abundance from the ground.

Every day, she made boats out of leaf and flower and moss, and every day she set them in the waves, and watched them disappear across the sea.

The captain called Gabrielle to his quarters when the pain in his chest grew to intolerable levels.

"The weight of the world, my girl, rests upon my chest, and even your mother wouldn't be able to fix it this time. That's saying something, isn't it?" He laughed, which became a cough, which became a cry of pain.

Gabrielle said nothing, but took his hand between her own and held it as though praying. There was no use arguing. She could see the life paths in other people, and was able to find detours and short cuts when available to avoid illness or pain or even death. There was no alternate route for her beloved captain. His path would end here. This she could not redirect.

The red bird whined in its cage, flapping its wings so piteously, Gabrielle thought her heart would break.

"I thought that bird would die with me, but he looks like he's in the prime of his life. Don't lose him, girl." He did not explain, and she did not ask.

The captain died, naming Gabrielle his successor, which the crew accepted as both wise and inevitable. As captain, Gabrielle Belain emptied many of the ships heading towards the holdings of the Governor, as well as redirecting ships with human cargo.

The bird remained in his cage for two years next to the portal in the captain's quarters, though it hurt Gabrielle to see it so imprisoned and alone. Finally, after tiring of his constant complaining, she brought the cage of the red bird on deck to give the poor thing a chance to see the sun. The mongrel dog growled warningly, then whined for days, but Gabrielle did not notice. There the bird remained on days when it was fine, for another year, until finally, she whispered to the bird that if he promised to return, she would let him out for an hour at sundown. The bird promised, and obeyed every day for ten days. But on the eleventh day, the red bird did not return to its cage.

The next morning, a mercenary's ship approached from the north, and fired a shot into the starboard hull. It was their first hit since the crew's meeting with Marguerite Belain eighteen years and nine months earlier. The ship listed, fought back, and barely escaped intact. Gabrielle stood on the mast step and peered through her spyglass to Martinique. A storm cloud churned and spread, widening over the thrashing sea.

Down in the ship's hold, Gabrielle rummaged and searched until she found the empty rum barrel where she had placed the boats made of leaf and flower and moss, which she had fished out of the water when no one was looking. She took one, then thought better of it and took ten and threw them into the water. She watched them in the waning light, move swiftly in the calm sea, sailing as one towards Martinique.

Gabrielle Belain (the witch, the pirate, the revolutionary) became the obsession of the Governor, who enlisted the assistance of every military officer loyal to him, every mercenary he could afford, and every captain in possession of a supply of cannons and a crew unconcerned about raising a sword to the child of a Saint Among Men. The third, of course, was more difficult to come by. A soldier will do as he is told, but a seaman is beholden to his conscience and his soul.

For many years, it did not matter. Ships sent out to overtake the ship with black sails, navigated and subsequently commanded by the girl with red hair, flanked as always by a mongrel dog, found themselves floundering and lost. Their compasses would suddenly become inoperable, their maps wiped themselves clean, birds landed in massive clouds and ripped their sails to shreds.

In the beauty and comfort of the Governor's mansion, I took dictation from a man growing sick with rage and frustration. His hair thinned and grew gray and yellow by degrees. His flesh sagged about the neck and jowls, while swelling at the middle. As he recited his dictation, he moved about the room like a dying tiger in a very small cage, his movements quick, erratic and painful.

When Gabrielle was a child and still living on the island, she was an unfortunately located tick to the poor Governor, a maddening bite impossible to scratch. When she boarded the pirate ship and gained the ear of a captain who was both a matchless sailor and ravenous for French gold, she became for the Governor an object of madness. He outlawed the propagation of redheaded children. He made the act of bringing fish back to life a crime punishable by death. He forbade the use of Gabrielle as a given name, and ordered any resident with the name of Gabrielle to change it instantly. He sent spies to infiltrate the wood surrounding the Pleasure House, but the spies were useless. They could have told him, of course, that Marguerite Belain went to the surf every morning to set a small boat upon the waves that sailed straight and true to the far horizon, though it had no sail. They could have told the Governor that every night a blue albatross came to Marguerite's garden and whispered in her ear. They told him no such thing. Marguerite instead led the spies into her home where she fed them and gave them drink. Then, she led them to the Pleasure House. They would appear a few days later, sleeping on the road, or wandering through the market, examining fish.

The Governor, gesticulating wildly, dictated a letter to the King, asking for more ships with which to capture or kill the pirate Gabrielle Belain. He detailed the crimes of the pirate—twenty-five ships relieved of their tax gold, eighteen slave ships either freed or vanished altogether, rum houses raided, sugar fields burned—all these I wrote to his satisfaction, confident that the King would, as usual, do nothing. In the midst of our audience, however, a young man threw open the doors without announcing himself and without apologizing. The Governor, sputtering with rage, threw his fist upon the desk. The young man did not stop.

"The black ship," he said, "has been lamed."

The Governor stood without breathing. "Lamed," he said, "when?"

"Last night. They hailed *The Medallion* who brought the message presently. They have taken refuge on the lee of St. Vincent. The injury to the black ship is grave, and will take several days, I am told, to remedy."

"And the ship who lamed it. Is it sound?"

"They lost a mast to cannon fire, but the ship, crew and instruments are sound. Nothing lost, nothing," the young man paused, "*strange.*"

The Governor walked across the room, threw the doors open with such force that he cracked one down the middle. Whether he noticed or not, he did not acknowledge, nor did he take leave of me. The young man also left without a word. I laid my pages on the table and went to the window, the prayers for the intercession of the Blessed Mother tumbling ceaselessly from my lips. I stood at the window and watched as a dark cloud gathered above us, and rumors of lightning whispered at the sky.

On the first of May, 1678, the ship with black sails was surrounded and beaten, its deck boarded and its crew in irons. Messages were sent to the islands of France, England and Spain that Gabrielle Belain (the pirate, the witch, the revolutionary) had been captured at last, and her death had been duly scheduled. The citizens of Saint-Pierre brought flowers and breads and wine to the edge of the wood surrounding the Pleasure House. They lifted their children onto their shoulders that they might catch a glimpse of the woman who was once the girl who brought the fish to life, and who rode on the back of a porpoise, and who inherited the saintly, healing hands of her mother.

The day before Gabrielle Belain was to be executed, a golden bird visited the window, hovered on the sill, and kissed her mouth through the bars. This the people saw. This the people believed. In that moment, Gabrielle began to sing. She did not stop.

The Governor, as he welcomed representatives from neighboring protectorates and principalities, attempted at the pomp and protocol befitting such a meeting. He heard the song of the girl pirate in the tower. His guests did not. He heard it and it grew louder and louder. He rattled his sword, ran shaking hand through his thinning, yellowed hair. He attempted to smile, but the song grew louder.

The people in the market square heard the song as well. They heard a song of flowers that grew into boats that brought bread to hungry children. They heard a song of a tree that bore fruit to any who was in need, of a cup that quenched the thirst of any who felt the want of water. She sang of a kiss that set the flesh to burn, and the burn to seed, and the seed to growth and abundance. The people heard the song and sorrowed for the redheaded child, barely a woman now, who would die in the morning.

The song kept the Governor awake for the rest of the night. He paced and cursed. He made singing illegal. He made the making of music a crime worthy of death. Were it not for the planned celebrations surrounding the death of the pirate, he would have slit her throat then and there, but dignitaries had arrived for a death march, and a death march they would see.

In the moments before the dawn crept over the edge of the sky, the Governor consented that I would be allowed into Gabrielle's cell to administer absolution. And perhaps baptism as well. She stood at the window where she had stood all night and the previous day, the song still spilling from her lovely mouth, though quietly now, barely a breath upon her tongue. I offered her three sacraments, and three sacraments she denied, though she consented to hold my hand. I thought she did this to comfort herself, a moment of tenderness for a girl about to die. When the soldiers came to bring her to the gallows, she turned to me and embraced me for the first time. She placed her mouth to my ear and whispered, "Don't follow."

So I did not. I allowed the soldiers to take her away. I did not fight and I did not follow. I sat on the floor of the tower and wept.

Gabrielle, still singing, walked without struggle in the company of soldiers, all of whom begged her for forgiveness. All of whom told her stories of how her mother had saved a member of their family, or blessed their gardens with abundance. Whether she listened or not, I do not know. I remained in the tower. All I know are the stories people told.

People say that she walked watching the ground, her mouth still moving in song. People say she stepped up onto the platform as the constable read the charges against her. He had several pages of charges and the people began to shift and fuss in their viewing area. As he read, Gabrielle's song grew louder. No one noticed a boat approaching in the harbor. A boat made of flowers and moss and leaves. A boat with no sail, though it moved swift and sure with a woman standing tall at its center.

Gabrielle's song grew louder, until with a sudden cry, she threw her chained hands into the air and tossed her red hair back. A mass of birds—gulls, martins, doves, owls, bullfinches—appeared as a great cloud overhead and descended over the girl blocking her from view. The Governor ordered his men to shoot, which they did, but the flock numbered in the thousands of thousands and while the square was littered in dead birds, the mass lifted nonetheless, the girl suspended in its center, and moved to the small craft floating in the harbor.

The Governor, his rage clamping hard upon his throat and heart, ordered his ships boarded, ordered his cannons loaded, ordered his archers to shoot at will, but the craft bearing the two women skimmed across the water though no wind blew, and vanished from sight.

This I learned from the people in the square, and this I believe, though the Governor put out a proclamation that the execution was a success, that the pirate Gabrielle Belain was dead, and that anyone who claimed otherwise risked imprisonment. Everyone, of course, claimed otherwise. No one was imprisoned.

That night, I stole gold from the coffers of the Abbey and walked down the road to the harbor. I purchased a small skiff and set sail by midday. My beloved Abbot, I'm certain, knew. The stores where such treasures are kept are always locked, but the Abbot left them unlocked and did not send for me after my crime.

I am, alas, no sailor. My map, one that I copied myself, paled, faded and vanished to a pure white page on my third day at sea. My compass was devoured by a passing fish. I have searched for a boat made of leaf, but found only salt. I have searched for two faces that I have loved. The only things I have loved. Gabrielle. Marguerite. The Abbot. France. Martinique. Perhaps it is all one. One curve of a wanton hip of a guileless god. Or perhaps by believing it is one, it becomes one. Perhaps this is the nature of things.

I have dreamed of their hands. I dream of their hands. I dream of a garden overripe and wild. Of a woman gathering the sea into her hands and letting it fall in many colored petals to a green, green earth. I dream of words on a page transforming to birds, transforming to children, transforming to stars.

SKILLET AND SABER

By Justin Howe

T he week after I first boarded the *Able Fancy* Hogg spoke to me: "Bootstrap tastes best with water, pounded into little strips of shank, and roasted over an open fire."

He might well have been talking to the skillet, though I was in the vinegar-reeking kitchen when he said it, on my way to the fore-closet to get Captain Quilt another measure of rum. I was cold and wet, and the day before someone had stolen my belt. The decision to seek my fortune aboard the *Able Fancy* was now proving to be misguided indeed.

The ship pitched. Everything swayed—even the fire behind the stones. I had to step lively or let my trousers slip down to my ankles and be singed. Hogg had no such trouble, strapped atop his stool in a denim harness, his leg stumps braced against the wall, and his crutches in easy reach.

"Better keep your trousers up," Hogg said. "At least aboard this ship. The Captain gets enough ideas as it is." Hogg laughed and spat. His wide mouth stretched with every spit and I counted all eight of his teeth. Four on either side—his mouth had a monstrous symmetry that the rest of his face only emphasized. His bulging eyes set so far apart as to be almost beside the ears, and wiry hair sprouted from his scalp, nostrils, and down his arms to his very knuckles.

Hogg reached over his head to grab one of the bundles of twigs tied to a post in the wood. "Marjoram—or was." He brandished the bundle under his nose. Little remained of the spice but the black broken twigs, the leaves long since plucked. Hogg undid the knot with a pull.

"Here."

"Good of you, sir," I said as I looped the twine about my waist, unconsciously slipping into the tone of my upbringing when my family had aspirations of making me a valet. The twine pulled tight and was a bit thin, catching more on the bone of my hip. But at least it kept my britches from falling.

"I'll use the rest as a soak," Hogg said, snapping the bundle in half and dropping it into the maw of the pot. The stench of vinegar rose from there—acidic clouds that made the air shimmer with eye-biting clarity. He stirred the mixture until the twigs sagged and bowed.

"What's your name?"

"MacDaniels, sir," I said.

"What did he send you down here for, MacDaniels? More rum? Har—I've drunk rum that would make them blind." He granted me a nod of his chin. "I've had brew that would make a man cut his switchel with cider.

"Aye, Robert?" he asked, addressing the skillet. The instrument showed no peculiarities. Its black cast-iron was pocked in places with rust, and the surface coated by a sweating sheen of melted lard.

"Robert remembers," Hogg went on. "He was there. Dutchmen or not, Robert stuck with me. Traedo almost got us. It got the others, but not us. We lived in the jungle for years eating rats and tree bark—but we made it out."

I made to pass this madman, but he spun on his stool and thrust out the skillet to stop me. Hogg's great rubbery face peered close to mine. His sweat was a sour reek in my nose.

"Would you know what it was like on Traedo?" The iris of Hogg's eye swam within its globe. "What with the Dutchmen pissing down on us ten times a day? Traedo makes Banda look like a sandy cove. Marjoram, nutmeg, and peppercorns—enough to make the mouth water to look at, but no game to hunt, no food to eat, only spices as far as the eye can see. Would you know what that does to a man?"

"Certainly nothing good, sir, I'm sure," I replied, humoring the man until I could leave.

Hogg cough-laughed. His eye bulged even wider until I feared it might burst and splatter me with ooze. My dearest desire was to be free of this man, but the thought of life above deck gave me no solace. Where could I go? Certainly fate had cast me adrift.

The ship pitched again, freeing me to be tossed against the shelf where Hogg kept his dying plants. A great gust of rosemary assaulted my nose as the cabin rattled, clay pots and jars clicking together.

Hogg kept his balance, wedging himself between the shelf and the firebricks. He'd thrust one of his stumps up against the andiron. Its end started to smolder, yet Hogg paid no notice. He was back again on his side of the tiny kitchen, reaching under the shelf for a clay pot. With a hook of the skillet, he lifted the lid to reveal murky seas of submerged fruit and foliage.

"Pickles. Soak them in brine overnight." He let the lid fall with a clank. "But what would you know of such a thing? Har. You look like you have as much flavor as a scum of sea foam."

What came over me then I cannot say. Possibly it was simply hunger—or maybe simple frustration. Without a word, I bent down to lift the lid myself. The brine was cold, the bits of foliage slippery. My fingers closed upon a round fruit and with a toss I had the morsel within my mouth.

I did not know what to expect—certainly nothing as richly textured as this pickle. It shocked my tongue and sent a tingle of garlic and brine throughout my mouth. My lips puckered, but I continued my mastication undaunted by the yellow-eyed stare of the cook. One of Hogg's bushy brows twitched into an inquisitive arch as I swallowed. Quite possibly, he wasn't as mad as he looked.

"It's too bad we have no bay leaves," I said, sucking the last of the flavor from my teeth.

"Take the rum, MacDaniels," Hogg said. "Take it and tell the Captain I need an assistant."

And that's how I began, the assistant to a legless pirate cook.

Hogg taught me to be fierce. I'll give him that. A scavenger by temperament, he could take the greenest side of pork and tease out enough choice meat to serve the crew. I learned to pillage pantries while my crewmates took liberties with women and inflicted barbarities.

And how they ate—every man for himself including the pet monkeys and macaws. Did they care that Hogg and I had figured out exactly sixteen uses for pumpkin rind, or whether a mango pit could serve any purpose once it had been stripped to a hairy husk and stepped on?

Not a bit.

Open mouth, shovel in whatever was set before it, and swallow. One time I even saw a needle and button disappear this way. Hogg and I spent whole watches over the fire tending the sooty pots. He had accumulated a host of odd implements to serve us in our duties: an ancient helmet for stoking the coals, a carpenter's wedge for breaking nuts, rupturing fruit-rinds, and piercing the plating of various fish and reptiles. I ground flour with a rock and wielded a ladle as well as any jack-tar a saber. When I suggested augmenting our collection with possibly a plundered fork or a rolling pin, Hogg swung his head until his jowls shook.

"Robert would never allow it," he whispered with a wink and a nod to the skillet.

"Yes," I said and let the matter lie. Let him keep council with the skillet. Surely it gave better advice than most of our fellow mates. They knew nothing more than drinking songs.

One evening while Hogg napped in his denim swing, I took hold of the skillet—or attempted to, but the instant my fingers circled the handle they were seared quite painfully. I cursed and went to the rain barrel to let my hand soak for a time. The gumbo was scalded, and Hogg blasted me to the quick over it. But by now his tirades barely disturbed my course. I had more pressing worries for I had found out who had stolen my belt: none other than the *Able Fancy*'s Captain, Duvaliar Quilt himself.

A vain man, Captain Quilt kept a Milanese barber to shave his cheeks bare each morning and ensure his brown curls fell in spiraling ringlets to his shoulders. Quilt wore stockings, kept his shoes polished, and looked at me with nothing short of a leer.

The situation was growing desperate. Soon, I was certain, if Quilt failed to seduce me in this fashion, he and a pair of his men would hide in the hold and wait for me to walk by on some errand. I vowed to avoid this ordeal, and in pursuit of this end, I learned from Hogg a tincture of jimson weed, a draught of which made a man see the Devil, while a drop or two kept him slow and sluggish. "Makes you the life of the party," Hogg had said.

I was up to dosing the Captain eight times a day and feared the time when the Devil might arrive in a cloud of brimstone. My hand trembled every night when I brought the Captain his dinner.

"Where have you been, MacDaniels?" Quilt exuded one evening. We were east of Tortuga, coasting in a calm sea.

"Hogg tell you where his treasure's buried yet?" The Captain swayed in his seat at counterpoint to the ship's motion, still wearing the embroidered silks we'd plundered off a Spanish Merchantman the week before. (I'd succeeded in obtaining six strings of red peppers, some salt, and several sacks of corn in the raid.) Quilt had his hat brim turned up so he might whittle at the butt of his pistol with a knife. He put his whittling aside while I arrayed the plate before him. We'd been having shark for two days now, seasoned with pickled jicama.

"Hogg's mad—mad and unlucky. Found him on the beach of some desert isle up to his nostrils in Carib savages—carrying that blasted skillet and talking about being stuck on Tranda—or whatever the Devil's isle's name was."

I nudged aside the mate who lay sleeping at the table, his browned cheek flat in a puddle of wine, and I set down the dish. Quilt jabbed a sliver of fin into his mouth and chewed. "A good cook, though."

"That he is, Captain," I said, refreshing his rum from the open barrel.

"You're a well-mannered man, MacDaniels. Not like the other dogs around here." Quilt gave me a wink and drained his cup while I shuddered.

"Another," he said, wiping his mouth on his silk sleeve. I poured until waved to cease, whereby I retreated. In my haste I came within three strides of the canopied bed and dodged a step to my left, putting myself within a quick sprint to the door.

But I needn't have worried for the Captain stared straight-ahead, moving his lips a bit to make his moustache tremble. For a breath, I thought that my time had come. My Adam's apple plummeted as heavy as a stone. But Quilt remained seated.

"Tell Hogg," the Captain finally said, "I want a feast prepared. I expect to rendezvous with Cutter Takk within a week. The two of us, Takk and I, together, we'll give the sea her share of blood, and we'll profit sweetly by it. Cutter Takk is a great man. He's been shot, sabered, and near blasted half in half by a cannon."

"Look at us," Quilt shouted giving the mate's chair a kick. The fellow slumped to the floor without a pause in his snoring, and I took out my napkin to wipe spilt wine from the table.

"In Port Royale they say Takk can't walk down the street without a host of men dying. What have I got?" The Captain sniveled. His shoulders rolled with agitation, and his head shook until the curls pelted his cheeks.

"The world will learn to fear the name of Quilt." With that the Captain snatched up his pistol. He cackled and waved the gun about the room. I made awkward dance steps, staying as well as I could out of the path of the muzzle. As I fled over the door's threshold, I caught sight of the Captain's handiwork upon the pistol-butt. The sneering face of the Devil glared at me.

A feast—from a ship with a kitchen as large as a closet and more rumtilliumption aboard than hardtack? Our flour had birthed weevils a day out of port. Half our apples had turned to slime, and the ship's cat had slept in the butter. Hogg did not care. He made no reaction to the news of the Captain's plans. He let the cat sleep, shaved the butter, and mashed the weevils into paste.

"Flavor makes the man," he'd say with a tap of the skillet.

We had smooth sailing for the week, nothing but clear skies and gentle breezes to push us on our merry way from morning to night. Or such were the glimpses I had upon those occasions I was above deck emptying the slop bucket. Below deck another order reigned, one of sweat and toil. Hogg and I exchanged more farts than words, communicating in our cooking closet by grunts, tastes, and smells.

Was the broth too weak? A touch more cardamom on the terrapin? Did it matter that a number of peppercorns were in fact mouse droppings? These questions and more kept me occupied all my waking hours until I dreamed of nothing but simmering soups and mashed mofongo.

The day of the full moon, we made anchor in a secluded bay. Captain Quilt busied the men with target practice. Fire danced in his eyes with each flash of the powder. For once his hair was in disarray, projecting at sharp angles from his scalp. By noon he twitched and jumped, reaching for his gun whenever a shadow lingered in his vision a bit crookedly. Truth told, in my distracted state, my administrations of the jimson had been somewhat haphazard for a few mornings now. A little after noon while Hogg and I set up our cooking station upon the beach, Cutter Takk's sloop, *The Deed*, passed the headland and entered the lagoon. Her white sailcloth billowed, and she fired a ten-pounder in salute. Quilt marched into the surf up to his knees and waved while *The Deed* set down her boats. At the head of the front boat a blackened figure waved back with mechanical bends of his arm. A small shape sat beside it, and I took it to be a rucksack of some kind.

The Captain was right—Cutter Takk had been shot and sabered and near blown half in half by a cannon. If not for the expedient alliance of a corset maker, a cooper, and a coat of tar, Takk's innards would have spilled upon the deck. As it was, the man lived inside a contrivance of leather, wood, and whalebone, the assemblage keeping neck straight and back erect. His head resembled a pitted melon, bleached by the sun, and plugged into the muzzle of a blackened cannon. Whenever Takk moved, he creaked.

But strangest of all, Takk's mother traveled with him. What I had first taken to be a rucksack turned out to be a wizened crone no taller than an apple barrel. Mother Takk, the men called her, and as my own mother had sold me into bondage to pay off the family debt, I was ill-disposed to like her. She wore a black gown of homespun cloth with a shawl about her thin shoulders. She was spindly limbed and delicate as a spider, with hair gray as tarnished steel and eyes blue like bits of coral. The mate lifted her in his arms upon the beach as easily as he would a bale of feathers.

"By the Devil himself, Takk," the Captain was saying with a smile when I arrived with the rum barrel.

"Quilt—ye old dog, how the lads been?" Takk's melon formed a grin.

"I'll find out soon enough." The Captain winked at me.

I broke open the rum and left them to their laughter.

By the fire Hogg worked like a beetle, cutting shallow trenches in the sand with his stump-ended legs. Robert dangled from a thong at his side, while Hogg held court to our collection of simmering pots, the steaming kettle, a host of root vegetables buried to bake within the coals, and the butchered body of a lamb set on a spit to roast. I took up a silver platter of cabbage and shredded crabmeat and was about to return to the Captains when I found my way impeded by the miniature frame of Mother Takk. She had silently crept over to the fire on my heels, her pellet-blue eyes regarding me from within their web of wrinkles. Her shriveled nose twitched.

"May I help you, Mum?" I asked, but she paid me no mind. Instead her spindly legs brought her to the side of the fire. Hogg sensed her approach and gave a grunt. Mother Takk looked him up and down before reaching into the left sleeve of her black gown. Her hand hunted within until finally she removed a painted box no rounder than a doubloon. With a flick of the thumb Mother Takk had the box open, and a pinch of snuff administered to both nostrils. She sneezed thrice and went to our prep table where she thrust her finger, the same I might add that had just been up her nose, into the au jus. She brought the oil up to her tongue for a lick. The logs snapped in the heart of the fire. Mother Takk's mouth dipped into an even more sour expression. She tsked and shook her head.

"What kind of witchcraft is this?" Hogg roared. "I'll have no one scoff at my lob-scouse. MacDaniels, get this shrew away from my sight. She's liable to turn the butter sour."

Hogg's great face trembled, and his right hand took hold of the skillet. "I'll have none of this. You hear me."

Mother Takk went on tsking and shaking her head.

I returned the platter to the board and went in haste to stand between the two, the cripple on my left and the crone on my right. The heat off the fire brought sweat to my brow. Hogg's lower lip jutted out in fulminous rage as the sparks danced around us. Mother Takk made keening noises—some semblance of speech peculiar to herself but which was as incomprehensible to me as the language of birds.

A shout came from the beach, Captain Quilt's voice. "Where the Devil are you, MacDaniels? Get over here with the victuals."

I swore and gripped the wallet about Hogg's neck. "Look to the lamb. It's liable to scorch."

"But the witch vexes me," Hogg replied, brandishing the skillet. Its greasy sheen perspired in the firelight. "It's not just me either. Robert says she's nothing but trouble."

"That might be true," I said, glancing towards Mother Takk. She blinked at me, cooed once, and let out another keening torrent of gibberish.

"MacDaniels!" The shout came again—a touch of fire behind it. I took up the platter and went back down the beach to meet Captain Quilt and Cutter Takk.

By now both crews had reached the first stages of general intoxication. They swilled from plundered glasses and chalices. Meerschaums flared and aromatic cigarellos passed from hand to hand, filling the air with a sweet texture. A negro of Takk's crew played a fiddle while a Welshman of our own played the pipe. I laid the salmagundi on the table—a long platform stolen from the customhouse in Almadoro and set in a declivity beneath the trees someway up the dunes from the surf. Church pews had been arranged as chairs about the table and kept company by likewise pilfered sacramental candles. Day was fast descending into night, and the moon broached the horizon white as a skull.

To and fro I went from our fire to the table. With each trip Hogg fumed a bit more. Mother Takk had perched atop the prep table with her legs bent and her knees almost to either side of her chin; a disapproving bird of prey that cackled whenever Hogg set down the saltshaker.

"I did not spend my years on Traedo boiling my boots to have some harridan sit over my shoulder and twitter at me." Hogg swung about on his crutches kicking up sand. He made a great fuss, knocking plates together and slamming down pot lids.

"It'll pass, Hogg," I said, clapping my only friend upon his thick shoulder. "She'll be gone with Takk on the morrow."

I must admit to the sin of pride, which increased with each trip to the table. How I delighted in the expressions whenever I set down a tureen of steamed clams or the corn pottage flavored with fire peppers, sausage, and sea turtle meat. There were tears in the crews' eyes when I brought out the lamb, its carcass birthing the wonderful aroma of mint and rosemary. I was serving out an ample portion to Cutter Takk when he brought his hand up with a creak.

"That is quite all right," he said. I noticed the discarded plates of delicacies before him. He had barely touched any of them. "Yes. All right. I think I've had enough."

Captain Quilt, who up until then had gorged himself upon each dish, looked at Takk from his end of the table, a bit of crabmeat stuck to his chin.

"Everything to your liking, Cutter?"

"Hardly," Cutter Takk replied. "You call this food?" With a series of jerks Takk creaked his hand into a disapproving gesture and pointed at the lamb. "It's not fit to feed a dog."

I nearly struck the man. If I had, it is quite certain I would not be alive to tell this tale.

"Not fit to feed a dog?" Captain Quilt said with incredulity. He held a piece of mutton up to his nose and examined it a moment before dropping it into his mouth. He chewed and swallowed. "You think your cook could do better?" Quilt made a great show of glancing about. "Well bring him out and let's see."

Quiet descended around the table, the two intermingled crews eyed one another with a curious expression. Hands began to hold knives in an altogether different fashion. I retreated a step from the table.

Cutter Takk creaked. "I wager she's been watching your cooks for much of the evening."

I guffawed, and all eyes swung towards me. "She's your cook?" I hooked a thumb over my shoulder and pointed. "She's been watching us all right, twittering like a buzzard."

I had had enough of this man maligning our handiwork. Insult me, fine; threaten to defile my body, sure; but insult Hogg's cooking? That I would not stand.

I laughed again. "She could hardly teach Hogg how to hold a ladle."

Cutter Takk's corset groaned like a great oak badgered by a typhoon. He threw aside his napkin and stood.

"MacDaniels," Captain Quilt piped. "Hold your tongue, man." The Captain was on his feet now, making gestures trying to defuse the situation. His eyes were red rimmed and the ends of his silken sleeves were spotted with grease. "We'll have none of this badinage about the table. It is clear what must be done."

He pointed to Cutter Takk. "Let's make a wager—your cook against mine. Hogg versus Mother Takk."

Cutter Takk jerked his neck about to face Quilt. "Who will be the judge?"

"Why, I, of course." Captain Quilt bowed with a flourish, dipping his cap feather into the rum.

"If I win, I strip your man," Takk said with a nod at me, "and skin him like a goat."

Quilt blanched a moment, looked to me, and shrugged. "Deal. The man has been no use to me at all and the night warrants entertainment."

I hardly had any time to react for just then a great scream rang out of the night, a low mournful howl coming from the edge of the cooking fire.

"Hogg," I cried, and ran.

He lay in the sand when I reached him, moaning and foaming at the mouth. Mother Takk had not moved from her perch but rocked back and forth, crooning to herself.

"Blasted witch, what have ye done to him?" I shouted, and made to throttle her. Hands were upon me in an instant, Captain Quilt and shipmates who had followed me from the table.

"Well, MacDaniels," Quilt said, "looks like you're the cook now. Better start before the fire burns down."

I could say nothing. Rage boiled throughout my body. Two men lifted Hogg from where he lay and carried him to a bench to recline. Robert fell from his hand, and I crouched to retrieve the skillet. As always the black steel burned to the touch, but I grit my teeth and held my grip. Mother Takk unbent herself with a chirp. Her son creaked beside her. The bleached melon rolled a fraction to regard the moon.

"We settle this in two hours," he said, his teeth shining above the black collar.

Quilt nodded. "Aye."

Soon a second bonfire spiraled up into the night, and the crews went back to the table where they resumed their feasting. I stood over Hogg, trying to read some advice from his cataleptic form. His rubbery jowls hung slack, and rivers of perspiration plastered his hair to his forehead. It was as if in an instant the great weight of years had pressed down upon him.

"What did she do to him?" I asked the stars, but they made no reply, indifferent as they were to my plight. I returned to the fire and pondered my fate. Since leaving home I had been the plaything of Fortune. Her fickle nature had tossed me about and whirled me senseless as a beaten egg. But I took heart, knowing though she played rough, never once had she deserted me. I pledged myself to her trust for some time longer and called a halt to my brooding. I gave Robert a spin and caught him by the handle. Mind you the skillet still scorched, but I welcomed the fiery touch. Such was the heat a plate of scalvagee enjoyed in the oven.

A weight in my pocket drew my attention, and I pulled out the bottle of jimson tincture.

"The meal's not done yet," I told the supine shape of Hogg. It would be pie, but a pie unlike any other. Not a sweet thing at all, but one flavored by spices and loaded with enough jimson to bring forth Mephistopheles himself.

The two hours passed in a shower of sparks and cursing. Before long the moon hung as a beaded pearl in a velvet field of black.

Captain Quilt stood as I approached the table with the pie. I'd draped a napkin over it to keep the steam from dissipating into the night. The assembled crews murmured about the table, their intoxication by now shifted into the lowland precincts of cruel inebriation. Mother Takk hovered some way off with a covered platter of her own.

"Thought you had fled," Cutter Takk said. The darkness emitted chortles about me. From either side, Mother Takk and I approached where Quilt sat at the head of the table.

I laid my dish before him and pulled away the napkin. A gout of steam curled off the crust. My pie was a variation on the Nor'easter's dunderfunk moistened by a hint of rum and with a stuffing of diced spinach and squid like I had once seen a Gaetano make years ago. Hogg himself would have been impressed. I cut a great wedge and dropped it upon a plate before the Captain. His whiskers twitched, but before he pounced Mother Takk came forward and pulled the lid from her own platter. There lay in the center of the dish a golden cluster of honeyed dough similar to what the Dutchmen call waffles but baked in the molds of musket bullets and heaped into a mound.

"Well, well," Captain Quilt said with gluttonous admiration. He bit the end of his finger and looked from one dish to the other. "Takk, my man, I'll have to take the evidence under consideration." Quilt took up his fork and dug into the pie. "Remarkable," he said after downing the first slice. "Cut me another, MacDaniels."

"Aye aye, sir."

He swallowed two more after that, rubbed his lips upon his sleeve, and then went to taste Mother Takk's honeyed dough-boys. I had a clear view of the Captain's jaw as he chewed and chewed, my fate hanging in the balance between his taste buds and his dental work. Men leaned close around the table, and even Cutter Takk had creaked his upper half forward to observe the proceedings.

Captain Quilt exhaled a sigh and stretched himself the length of his chair. He rested his hand lightly upon his belly where his silver buttons held tight his jacket. He shook his head and blinked at the candles, his eyes wet and gleaming.

"I can't make up my mind," he said.

Cutter Takk cursed and let one fist drop to the table. "Blast it Quilt! You dare suggest this hobbledehoy can compete with my mother's cooking?"

Mother Takk trilled an arpeggio of indignation.

"Judge for yourself," I replied, for by now I had gone well beyond trepidation to the back end of my fear where some semblance of desperate courage hid. Fortune held my fate (along with a generous helping of jimsonweed), and I cut another wedge off the dunderfunk.

"If the Captain would be so good," I said.

Cutter Takk snorted. "I think I'll stuff your carcass full of straw and hang it from my boat." He grabbed hold the wedge straining his black-tarred corset. Takk folded the slice in half and shovel-fed it down the tunnel of his mouth. He chewed with his mouth open, displaying the mash of spinach and squid to the assembled host. He made a great show of revulsion, swallowing, and frowning.

"Revolting," Cutter Takk declared.

Mother Takk came forward with her plate. With a peck of her finger she brought a ball of candied dough up to her son's lips. Cutter Takk puckered and swallowed the delicate offering. This exchange was repeated until the dish gleamed empty. I moaned with disgust. Cutter Takk strained to his feet. His massive frame towered over me, reeking faintly of tar. His spinach-lined teeth glinted above the rim of his collar.

"Hold him down, while I sharpen my knife," Takk said

It was then that I damned Fortune and dropped my dish. Several pairs of hands took hold of me.

"A toast," Captain Quilt called out from beyond my limited and restrained view. "To the Devil," he said. And a pistol shot rang out in the night.

Whatever Devil the jimson had placed before the Captain's eyes I shall never know. The bullet flew wide and merely kicked up a column of sand. Yet that bullet saved my life, for earlier that day, unacknowledged by any of us, the ship's cat had crept over to the island aboard one of the long boats. Old Jenny had succeeded in scavenging most satisfactorily, and the shot woke her to the height of apoplexy. In an instant the feline leapt upon the table, scattering food and plates about. Quilt flung the smoking pistol after her tail. The Devil's face spun and grinned end over end, striking the candles off the table and right onto Takk's tar-coated corset.

Cutter Takk burst into flames with a sudden rush of balmy air. His conflagration warmed the table and made Captain Quilt's face blossom a fierce, malevolent red.

"I am the Devil," Quilt said, "and I do the Devil's work."

The assembled crews reacted in contrary fashions. Quilt's men struck at Takk's, while Takk's made to save their captain. Since the two acts were in direct opposition, and tar a most suitably flammable substance, it was quite clear that the plight of Cutter Takk was accelerating to a dire end. His mother ran to him, but Takk's flailing knocked the woman to the ground. He shrieked while the clumsy melee of grunts and pistol shots erupted about him. Fists lashed out, knives slashed, and the rum was spilt. I found myself released and forgotten, making great haste to hide myself under the table. Mother Takk cowered beneath there, and I admit to staving the woman's head in twain with a dropped plate.

Above me Captain Quilt was wielding his saber to and fro, striking friend and foe alike. The mate, the barber, both lay on the sand bleeding, their heads split and oozing.

A pair of combatants wheeled across my view—a swart member of Takk's crew and a Bristol man I despised for having once had the audacity to speak against my gull stew. The Bristol man held a lit candle, the swart fellow a pewter spoon, their combat a harried thing of clumsy swats. They crashed into the forest where more lethal weapons like rocks and branches might be found.

"The life of the party," Hogg had said. From my vantage point I had a clear view as Cutter Takk ran towards the surf, his body sheathed in flames like a torch. He tripped over a rum barrel, rolled in the sand, and got to his feet again.

Captain Quilt followed close on his heels, repeating his diabolical mantra: "I am the Devil. I do the Devil's work. I am the Devil. I do the Devil's work."

Half Quilt's left ear was gone, and his clothes showed jagged holes. Cutter Takk fell again—this time at the edge of the surf. He thrashed in the water, smoldering and creaking, as the Captain strode into the waves.

Quilt raised the blade. I shut my eyes and heard a series of pops as the corset's bindings were severed. Takk's screams expired into a series of short gasps. I crawled from my place and ran, bits of mutton and cabbage stuck to my trousers. Cannons sounded. Out on the water, *The Deed* and the *Able Fancy* had joined the fray, their skeleton crews espying the conflict and lending support to their respective sides with grape and powdershot.

The glow of the cook fire drew me like a moth to a flame. In the circle of light, Hogg stood, his body hunched forward to lean upon his crutches.

"Har," he laughed, and his face was pale and grim of cast. "Well done, MacDaniels. Well done, my man!"

Out of the corner of my eye, Captain Quilt emerged into view. His curls hung limpid as seaweed upon his shoulders, his face a mask of wolfish intent.

"I am the Devil," he panted. "I do the Devil's work."

Hogg let out a hoot and swung himself forward, ambulatory as a hermit crab. "The skillet's yours, boy. Take it!" As if by some feat of magnetism, the handle found its way onto the palm of my hand. I spun on my heel and faced the Captain, the dying embers of the fire touching the confrontation with a tint of red.

Quilt swung the saber, and I parried with grease-encrusted, blackened steel. Back and forth, we danced across the sand, skillet to saber. The blade grazed me in spots, but I gave back my own, connecting with an occasional slap of Robert's flat end.

Hogg's voice called out suggestions: "Watch the swing! Duck! Lay him one in the snoot!" and "Har!"

My arm stung up to my elbow, and there seemed to be no end to the Captain's energy.

"The Devil," Quilt said. "The Devil. The Devil."

I ducked a high swing of the saber, but before I could counterattack, I was off balance and lying in the sand.

"Remember boy, the flavor makes the man," Hogg said.

Quilt gave forth an exultant shout of glee. He made to undo his belt. "The Devil's work," he cackled maniacally.

As his britches fell I swung the skillet between his legs. Quilt let out a yelp and fell to his knees. Another clout on the side of his skull, and I rose unimpeded to my feet.

The Deed burned out in the darkness of the lagoon, the *Able Fancy* nowhere in sight. The smell of powder and burnt cassava filled the night. I took up Captain Quilt's saber and thrust it deep into his back.

"I'll have nothing more to fear from you," I said. "Right, Hogg?"

Hogg lay upon the bench, clearly dead.

"Flavor makes the man." I said, and laughed, tucking the skillet into my belt. Hogg's voice still spoke in my ear. He told me of certain marinades favored by the Carib Indians when spicing human flesh. Fortune might have marooned me upon this shoal, but I wouldn't starve—not on this island.

There would be enough here to eat, Hogg told me so.

THE NYMPH'S CHILD
by Carrie Vaughn

G race couldn't see the captain. The Marshal had chained them to opposite sides of the same wall, a partition jutting into the prison cell. She closed her eyes and imagined she could feel him through the foot of stone and mortar that separated them. Weak as a child and tired as death, she hung on the chains, iron manacles digging into her wrists.

"Grace? Are you awake? Can you hear me?" From around the edge of the wall, Alan called in a hissing whisper. She only had to move a few steps to see him. If she could move.

She worked her jaw, stretching her face, still sore from the beating. "Yes."

"You must plead your belly. The Marshal can't hang you. I won't see you hanged—"

"No. I'll die with you, there's nothing else for me."

"God damn you, Grace."

She chuckled painfully. "You as well."

She'd sail off the edge of the world with him. She very nearly had, that time through the Iron Teeth. This was simply another journey, and it would be over soon. Rope around her neck, a moment of fear, then nothing. That was fine. She only wanted to see him one more time.

She heard him take a wet breath; he was bloodied from his own beating. "Mister Lark. You are the finest first mate I have ever known. You have never disobeyed an order from your captain before. So. I order you to live. I order you to live and raise our child. Do you understand me?"

"Don't ask me to do this, Alan. Please don't ask." Her face was so bruised, she couldn't tell if she was crying. Her whole body was numb.

The iron door of the dungeon opened. The Marshal of Hellwarth and a squad of his men entered, fanning out before the captain and first mate of the *Nymph*.

"Captain Alan. Mister Lark. Well met."

The Marshal still didn't know about her. They beat her when they stormed the *Nymph*, but didn't examine her beyond a cursory search for weapons. The Marshal was in a hurry to hang the whole crew before they mounted some spectacular escape. Her hair was cut short, a ragged mat above her ears. Her breasts were bandaged flat. She fooled everyone, because no one believed a woman would sail with pirates.

"I have confessions for you to sign. It will expedite the process."

She spit in his direction, a bloodied gob of mucus. Couldn't tell if she managed to hit anything. "Bastard," someone muttered.

"Do it," Alan said in a low voice. "Tell him."

"No." *Live. That's an order.* But he wasn't the captain anymore if he didn't have a ship.

Chains clinked—Alan straightening. When he spoke, his voice was clear, commanding. God, he was still the captain, damn him.

"My first officer cannot sign your confession, Marshal."

"Why not?"

"I'll tell you alone. Tell your men to leave." The Marshal frowned, and Alan said, "For God's sake, what can I do to you now? I give you my word this is no trick."

The Marshal sent his men away, so the three of them were alone. And Alan told him.

"The name is wrong."

"On the contrary, I have all Gregory Lark's aliases listed—"

"Grace Lark. Her name is Grace Lark."

She closed her eyes. It was all over now. They'd still kill Alan, but she would have to live. And remember.

The Marshal, a stout man, imposing, determined, with slate-gray hair and well-trimmed sideburns, came at her, knife in hand. He tore open her shirt, ripping away buttons. Cutting away the undershirt, he found the bandage. Then he cut through the bandage. She stared at him all the while, but he wouldn't meet her gaze.

Amazed, he backed from her a step or two. He only stared a moment, then looked away. Almost tenderly, he closed the edges of her shirt.

"There's more. She's with child. I must plead her belly for her since she refuses to do so herself."

"Damn." Louder, the Marshal said, "You sent my men away because this is one story you don't wish to spread."

"I see we understand each other, Marshal. Do what you will to me. I'll sign anything. But spare her."

The Marshal of Hellwarth went to the other side of the wall. A key turned in a lock. Pen scratched on paper. Alan signed away his life.

"Thank you, Captain. As for the rest, I will do what I can."

"Thank you," Alan said, sounding relieved.

Grace fought her chains, but only succeeded in cutting her wrists. Fresh blood clotted on dried scabs.

The Marshal called his men. Two went to unchain Alan. When they brought him toward the door, he came into view. He twisted in his captors' grips to look at her.

His face was bloody, his pale hair matted into a cut on his forehead. He could barely keep his feet without the help of the soldiers. She wanted to rush to him.

"Remember your orders," he said, and they dragged him away.

"Mister Lark will be staying with us a little longer," the Marshal said to his lieutenant. Then they left her there, alone.

She called his name. She shouted after him, her voice husky and ragged, because she had forgotten how to scream like a woman.

They hanged the crew in batches. Six times she heard the gallows floor drop and the ropes creak. Captain Alan they hanged alone. The crowd cheered.

Gregory Lark was listed hanged with the rest. The Marshal moved her to a different cell, gave her a change of clothes, and she was Grace again. He held her for two months, until her condition became indisputable. Then, he blindfolded her and packed her into a carriage. For a full day the carriage traveled, with Grace blind to all. At the end of the journey, he set her on the road.

"You have your life and your secret. It is the least I could do for the honor Alan showed. I only ask this: you must never set foot on a ship again. You must promise."

"I promise," she said, her voice flat. The Marshal removed the blindfold and remounted the carriage, which turned and departed in a cloud of dust.

She looked around. A village nestled nearby, a fishing village right on the coast. The sea would always be nearby to haunt her.

Grace the Widow, as she was known in Rowfus, wondered at how a pound of cod could cost more than a pound of beef in a coastal town. But the fish were off this season, apparently. Her tavern, the Nymph's Child, would serve beef stew tomorrow, then. She packed the meat in her basket and returned home.

She took her time, walking along the docks. Rowfus was a poor excuse for a sea port. Most of the big cargo ships sailed on up the coast, where the large cities and roads essential for trade lay. Smaller ships stopped here for repairs and provision. A few others docked to take advantage of low port fees. The Marshallate kept a lighthouse and a small garrison of elder soldiers on the rocky edge of the land, ostensibly to dissuade pirates. A single road traveled up the hill, inland. It was a tired place, with a few rows of plank-board buildings scoured gray by wind and salt, and a few piers painted black with barnacles and slime. Most of the activity came from a thriving colony of fisher folk who didn't care if another ship docked here ever again. Them, and the gulls that wheeled and cried above their boats.

A new ship had arrived, anchored some distance out. She was one of the fast new galleons, with enough cannons to level Rowfus if she chose. Not that anyone outside the town would notice if Rowfus were leveled. The Marshallate garrison didn't seem concerned by the ship's presence. Grace didn't recognize her.

Mainly, Grace was looking for Kate, to make sure the girl wasn't wandering off with stars in her eyes when she should have been minding the tavern. Beautiful Kate, with her blond hair and lithe figure, and a spirit that carried her around town with a tilt to her chin. Proud, some folk said, and if Grace was proud of her daughter's pride, then let her be doubly chastised for it. Kate scared her to death sometimes. Grace would come home one day and find the girl had flown off to an adventure or three. That thought weighed in her belly like iron.

After all, that was what Grace had done, and look where it brought her.

Her tavern, the Nymph's Child, had a painted sign above the door that showed the figurehead of a sailing ship: a woman in a rippling gown, her dark hair streaming along the prow, who held an infant in her arms. An odd notion, some said. Grace told them that if ships were called "she," then why shouldn't they have children?

She came into the tavern through the back. From the kitchen, she heard voices. At first she thought Kate was begging stories from a patron as usual. Then she caught an anxious edge to Kate's voice, and heard that the patron was asking most of the questions—about the Nymph, about Kate's parents. About the story of the treasure.

Quietly, Grace edged into the room along the wall to have a look. She saw a ghost on the verge of harassing her daughter. He was a young sea captain, clean shaven, with a full head of dark hair. His clothing was good quality—wool coat and linen shirt—but weathered, well used. A tricorn hat sat on the table by an untouched glass of brandy.

The stranger looked up, over Kate's shoulder, his attention caught. He smiled in recognition.

"Grace Lark. Well met," said David May.

Sixteen years had treated him well. He'd filled out, grown muscles and a proud figure, weathered hands and a hard expression. He had bright, searching eyes. That much had stayed the same.

Grace wanted to tear him to pieces.

She stepped past Kate, dodged the table and lunged at him. Grabbing his collar, she shoved him out of the chair and slammed him against the wall. By God, the boy was six inches taller than her now. But she was still hard as steel, and still—in their memory at least—his superior officer.

"How dare you—how in bloody hell's dungeon do you dare come in here asking about the treasure?" She wrapped his shirt and coat in her fists and dug them into his neck. "You know it. They all bloody well knew it. There was no treasure!" Her heart raced with the old memories.

"I know," he said, his voice tense but his eyes steady. He didn't struggle at all. "I know it, sir."

"I should kill you. I should kill you for even standing here alive and well, you bastard." But she let go. He stumbled, keeping his balance against the wall, never taking his eyes off her. His hand went to his belt and the sword sheathed there, but she turned her back on him. "Kate, get everyone out. We're closed for the day."

Patrons stared. Grace had broken up a fight or two in her time, but she'd never lost her temper. They seemed happy to leave when Kate asked them to.

Grace turned back to David, who donned a tired smile.

"Lark—your daughter. She looks like him. She looks like Captain Alan. The hair, the eyes—she has this look on her face like—"

Grace rubbed her brow, running her hand across her graying head. "I know. Don't you think I know?"

When everyone had gone and Kate had barred the door, Grace invited David to sit. She went through a list of other tasks she could send Kate on. Then she thought better of it. The girl sat with them, fidgeting, questions obviously boiling on her lips.

"Why are you here?" Grace asked him.

"I need to know how you crossed the Iron Teeth."

She rolled her eyes and laughed. "Is that all? Well, Davy May." She slapped the table in front of him, rattling the glass of brandy. "I need to know how you escaped the Marshal of Hellwarth."

They stared at each other for a long time, silent, waiting to see who would break first and fill the pause. Sixteen years—he wasn't a cabin boy anymore, and she wasn't a pirate. They had to judge each other all over again.

"It's *Captain* May," he said at last.

She raised her brow. "The new ship in the harbor?"

"The *Queen's Heart*," he said.

"Very nice. Especially considering the last time I saw you was in chains in a prison yard. What did you do to be set free? Let the guards have a go at you?"

"The Marshal couldn't hang a twelve-year-old boy any more than he could hang a pregnant woman. He put me on one of his own ships. He… reformed me."

The Marshal of Hellwarth was a strict old man with the sense of honor of a long-lost age. Pirates he caught and hanged. Women and boys—could never be pirates, could they? How strange, what his mercy had saved.

"Mum?" Kate looked very solemn, lips pursed and brow furrowed, when she said, "Gregory Lark—Gregory Lark was my father."

David's eyes went a little wide, and he hid a smile with his hand. Grace—bloody hell, she was going to have to explain it all.

"No, Kate," Grace said, equally solemn. "Gregory Lark was your mother, dressed as a man and fallen in with pirates."

Kate took a long moment to turn this over in her mind. Then, as pieces dropped into place, she stared at Grace with open-mouthed wonder, like she might stare at a giant, or a dragon. Oh, the stars in her eyes had suddenly gotten very big, Grace thought with a sinking heart.

"*You?*" Kate said, her bottled excitement bursting under pressure at last. "You sailed on the *Nymph*? Grace Lark—*Gregory* Lark. You were first mate! First mate of the *Nymph!* You always told me women don't go to sea, the superstitions of sailors won't let women sail, and yet *you*—you never told me!"

"God, Kate. If it ever got out that anyone from the *Nymph* lived, people would beat down our door for word of the treasure. I didn't tell anyone. Especially you. You've watched the boats come and go since you were a baby. I didn't want you getting any more ideas than you already had."

"What really happened? Did you do it?" Kate said, seemingly impervious to words of caution or explanation. She glanced sidelong at David, and her voice fell to a whisper. "Did you kill Captain Alan?"

Grace had heard the stories as well as Kate had—the stories about the *Nymph* were Kate's favorites—and she'd kept her mouth safely shut all this time. The *Nymph* was a pirate ship, but her captain and crew loved adventure more than gold, and that was why they sailed the Strait of the Iron Teeth, a passage of jagged rock and treacherous shallows that were guarded by a dragon to boot, not for the treasure that lay at the other side but to say that they'd done it. In fact, when the crew did find treasure, it tore them apart: the crew accused Captain Alan of hording it; Alan buried it so that none would have it; the first mate, Gregory Lark, killed Alan, and then the crew killed Lark for revenge. There were a dozen versions, with more arising every year. Grace always told herself that Gregory Lark was someone else and people could say anything they liked about him, she didn't care.

The moments passed and Grace remained silent. If she spoke, her voice would crack, and she would be finished. Kate had on a beseeching expression, so eager she nearly trembled. Just like Alan when he'd said, *We can do it, Grace. We can sail the Iron Teeth.*

Kate bit her lip and looked at David, and Grace looked at him as well. She nodded a little. He returned the nod. If he was willing to take on the task of telling Kate, let him have it.

"She didn't kill him," David said to the girl. "Far from it. Captain Alan was your father."

Kate furrowed her brow and her gaze fell. She sat like that for a long time, with David and Grace watching her. Once or twice she acted like she might say one thing, then changed her mind, and finally said, "And he really was hanged at Hellwarth? He's not going to come through the door, a shadow from a story, is he?"

"I watched him die," he said softly. Grace looked away. She hadn't had that privilege—or doom.

Kate twisted her fingers in her lap. "What was he really like? Do the stories tell any truth at all?"

"He was the best and bravest man I ever knew," David said. "When I find myself in a fix, I ask, 'What would Alan have done?' and come out better for considering the answer. I knew who you were as soon as I saw you because you have his face and his sea-gray eyes."

Her eyes were going red, now. Then, she smiled shyly. "Really?"

"On the soul of my ship, I swear it's true."

"Mum—do you miss him?"

"I do. Every day I do." Sometimes she looked out to the ships and swore she saw the *Nymph*, sailed by Captain Alan, come to take her away.

"Mister Lark, sir. Ma'am—" David said, "I truly didn't wish to disrupt your life here. You of all people deserve peace and quiet. But this is a matter of life and death. I must know how you sailed the Iron Teeth."

Grace smiled crookedly. "Don't you know? You were there."

"You locked us all in the hold. That's where Blount got the idea you'd hidden a treasure."

The tale was famous:

The crew set the sails. A strong wind followed, and they moved fast. Alan was at the rudder, and when the crewmen realized where their course was headed—toward the rocky pinnacles reaching up from the ocean like clawed hands—they set up a cry. Was he mad? Did Alan mean to kill them all? *Do you trust me?* he'd said, a wild grin on his face. Most of them did, to the ends of the earth and beyond. But a few, Blount and others, threatened mutiny. That was when Lark appeared with a musket leveled at the lot of them, and four more stacked behind, loaded and ready. He ordered them all below decks and locked the door behind them. There'd be no mutiny on his watch. The crew, David among them, spent the entire journey arguing: did they break free and mutiny, despite Lark and his muskets? Did they trust the captain and wait it out? Every shudder that rocked the hull, every roll they made over every wave, each man held his breath and prayed. The *Nymph* moved fast and sure, and six hours later, Lark opened the hold and the Teeth were behind them. Alan and Lark kept the secret of how they did it, and the stories that spread about a hidden treasure seemed credible.

Only Lark—Grace—still lived and knew the truth.

She said, "We never dropped anchor. We never landed—you could tell that, even locked in the hold."

"That's what we told Blount, but he sold us out anyway, didn't he? He thought the dragon must have dropped a chest of gold on deck mid-flight because of some deal you made with it."

"You see," Grace said, leaning toward Kate. "Alan's reputation was so fantastic, even among his own crew, they had him making deals with dragons."

"Grace, please—"

"Why? Why is this a matter of life and death?"

"The Strait of the Iron Teeth is the shortest distance between Hellwarth and Elles. The Teeth are probably Hellwarth's greatest defense against Elles' warships."

"They can always sail around, if they want war with Hellwarth."

"Yes. But if a messenger sailed the Teeth, word would reach Hellwarth long before an enemy fleet arrived. We could prepare."

Thoughtfully, Grace played with the collar of her shirt. "When Elles sends a fleet to take Hellwarth by surprise, it will be up to you to warn the Marshal. You've become quite the dutiful patriot."

He blushed, looking for a moment like the boy who had stumbled onto the ship, wet behind the ears and eager to please. Alan had kept the boy close, protected him, taught him what he knew, turning it into a game so he would learn better. He'd been almost a son, like the best cabin boys were to the best captains. Alan had seemed to like having an almost-son.

Was that why he had seemed so pleased when she told him she was with child? Why he'd been so desperate that she live? What would he have thought of a daughter?

She continued, "You're here under the Marshal's orders. He told you that Gregory Lark still lived."

"Sailing the Teeth was my idea. When I told him my plan, he said I should come find you."

"Why should I help you? He killed Alan."

"This would save many lives. If I can bring warning in time—"

She raised her hand, stopping him mid-breath. "You've turned into a noble young man, David. Alan would have been proud."

Slouching over the table, David breathed a sigh heavy enough he might have been holding it for sixteen years. "All this time, I've felt like I'm betraying him, serving the Marshal. But—I owe him my life. That means something as well."

"You survived. You stood by Alan as long as you could, and then you survived. That's as he would have wanted it." *Live.* That word, his voice, haunted her nightmares. She wondered what haunted David's.

"Will you help me, sir? Will you tell me the secret?"

She laughed. "Can't you guess? Don't you know what made the *Nymph* different than every other ship? You and the Marshal are the only ones who know Alan's and my secret, and you still don't know?"

"What a riddle. What made the *Nymph* different? She was a ship of legend. Her captain was a pirate, but with a code of honor. He never sought treasure for its own sake—only enough to keep up his ship and pay off his crew. She sailed free, under no nation's flag. She navigated the Teeth, she outran the Marshal until one of her own betrayed her. She was proud, beautiful, an honor to serve like no other ship has been for me since. All that made her different."

It was Kate who said, "She had a woman on board."

The wind cut through the strait like daggers, and the *Nymph* had it behind them. They raced to the Iron Teeth, too fast, too many sails unfurled, and the crew shouting in outrage. Even locked in the hold, the screams echoed topside.

Alan had grinned. "I feel bad, really I do. But it's better this way."

"Aye," Lark had said with a sigh.

Alan kept tight hold of the wheel and steered them true.

The rocks towered, rough and dark, shining with damp. They cast wide swathes of shadows, so that the strait was always in twilight.

Then, the pinnacle of a tower of rock moved. The shadow spread, and two great wings made a canopy over the water. Some of the rock wasn't rock, but scales, which sparkled when the light struck them. A snake-like neck stretched up to a dagger-shaped head, and wide jaws gaped open. The silver teeth inside were like the jagged strait itself. Both would happily swallow anything that crossed their paths. The Iron Teeth and the dragon were the same.

The *Nymph*'s captain and first mate gazed up at those teeth and felt not fear but wonder.

"Are you ready, Grace?" the captain called, and this time the first mate's answer was joyous.

"Aye!"

She yanked her kerchief off her neck and pulled apart the buttons of her shirt.

"You're beautiful!" Alan shouted over the wind.

"You're a maniac!" she shouted back, laughing.

Running away from him, across the deck to the ship's prow, she pulled the bandages off her chest, left them trailing on the wind and tangled in rigging.

The dragon groaned, a guttural sound that made the water tremble and pressed around the ship like a weight. The great, wicked head looked down on the *Nymph*. The wings flapped once, and the ship rocked back. Then the beast jumped to a lower perch, and he was in front of them, staring them down, and they were racing into his jaws.

Standing at the railing, leaning over the water, bare chested, breasts freed, Lark raised her arms to the dragon. Wind and sea spray lashed her.

When the beast sighed, hot breath washed over her. Its wings folded back, and its scaled eyelids drooped.

"A lovely vision," the dragon said in a deep voice that sounded like crunching gravel. "Why don't I see more of you? Why does your kind not sail?"

"I don't know," she'd said, taken aback by the question, because before the monster the usual reasons scattered like dust. "I really don't know."

The dragon let them pass.

He flew overhead, guiding them through the rocks and shoals. All the while Lark spoke to it, told stories and sang songs, though many of the songs he asked for were ancient, and she didn't know them. When they'd cleared the last of the rocks, the dragon bade them farewell and returned to his lonely perch.

When Captain Alan released the crew, the Iron Teeth were behind them, and he and Mister Lark never revealed how they'd done the impossible.

David stared wide-eyed. This amused Grace—the solution was so simple he hadn't seen it.

Grace nodded. "Putting the crew in the hold kept my secret while I talked to the dragon. Think what Blount would have done if he'd known a woman had been giving him orders all that time."

"You talked to the dragon? *Talked* to it?"

"He can be soothed by the sound of a woman's voice, and by the sight of her body. Seems he lost his mate some few hundred years ago and misses feminine company. He only wants a few words, a sweet voice to tell him how brave and strong he is. He's really not a bad fellow, but ships in his territory make him ill-tempered. As for the rocks—if you keep to the right-hand way and have a steady hand at the wheel, you'll pass them by."

"That's all?" David stood. "Grace—Mister Lark, sir. Will you come with me? Will you sail the Teeth one more time?"

She almost said yes before she could think to stop the words. *That* was her life. She'd left it involuntarily. Why not go back? Why not, indeed? Her lean body had grown soft and curved with years and weight. She'd never be able to carry the disguise now. And she had the tavern to run. That life was gone. She'd left it involuntarily, yes. But people always left their lives involuntarily, didn't they?

"I can't. I must return the Marshal's honor in kind. I promised him I'd never set foot on a ship again."

He nodded, not surprised by the answer. "Do you miss the sea?" he said.

"No. Thinking of sailing reminds me too much of Alan."

Kate half-jumped from her chair "I'll go. Take me. I can learn to sail, I already know all the parts of a ship, I watch them come and go every day and I've always wanted to sail. You need a woman to pass through the Iron Teeth. Please take me."

Grace nearly hit her. "Kate, sit down."

She didn't sit. Grace's daughter glared back at her, rebellion in her eyes. Grace had known this day would come, when she would tell her daughter to do something—and Kate would realize Grace had no power over her. Damn Davy May a second time for bringing this on.

"Kate. Sit down," Grace repeated. Kate sat. "Kate—you're all I have left in the world. You're the only reason I left Hellwarth alive."

"If you tell me to stay, I will. But this is my chance. My only chance."

David added his pleading gaze to hers. "The *Queen's Heart* has room for a cabin boy, if you can advise her how to dress like one. I'll guard her with my own life, as well as Captain Alan looked after me. She'll be safe."

Didn't they see how simple the answer was for her? That there could only be one answer for her, and no amount of reasoned argument would change that?

"No," she said. "Not on anyone's life. Not for all the world's wealth. Now, Captain May, this reunion has been pleasant enough, but get out of my tavern."

He didn't move right away, and Kate made a sound that might have been a stifled sob. Grace stood. She couldn't beat David in a fight, not anymore. She could rely on her reputation, though. Her anger. She trusted that the captain of a ship like the *Queen's Heart* wouldn't start a fight here.

Finally, David nodded at her, touching his forehead in a salute as he replaced his hat on his head. Then, he left.

Kate looked like she might scream, as if one of the tantrums of old had returned. Her face flushed, her lips trembled. But she didn't scream, she didn't say anything, not even *I hate you*. She turned and fled to the kitchen.

"Kate!" Grace called after her, wanting to say a hundred things. *Let me explain, let me give you all the reasons you shouldn't go, I want you to have a better life than mine, and a better life isn't at sea*—but it was no good. The girl was off to her bed to have a good cry.

Over the years Grace had listened to a hundred stories that painted her as a villain, the traitorous first mate who shot his captain in the back, who ended the glorious voyages of the famous *Nymph*.

Only now, at this moment, had she ever felt like a villain.

At midnight, the only audible sound was the rush of waves running along the coast. They were regular, constant in form, but in detail they always changed. Some waves struck heavily, some lapped, some were large, some small. One could listen to the waves for a lifetime and never guess their patterns.

"Your eyes are bright as the moon on the waves," Alan told her, when he'd first wooed her.

"You got that line from an untalented minstrel, didn't you?" she'd said, smiling.

"Who am I to say whether he had talent? I passed him by in the marketplace, it was the only line I heard. Perhaps the next was better. But if I'd waited for the next, I'd have been late meeting you."

She'd laughed, because he was so heartfelt, and it probably happened exactly like he said.

What would Alan say if he saw her now? He'd have hated what she'd become: soft, frightened, not a bit of adventure left in her. *I'm only following orders, sir.*

The moon shone on the waves this night. The *Queen's Heart* was still anchored in the harbor.

Though Grace went to bed long after dark, she did not sleep, but listened to the waves instead, so that she also heard the shutters over Kate's window open, heard a rustling and scraping as someone climbed out the window. The girl thought to avoid waking her by not using the door, but Grace knew all the tricks.

Still dressed, Grace rose from her bed and went out to the common room, then through the front door. She caught Kate sneaking around the side of the building. Hands on her hips, frowning, Grace blocked her daughter's path.

Kate wore her cloak and hugged a satchel close to her chest. This wasn't a stroll, this wasn't just wanting a last look at the new galleon. This was fleeing. In her mind's eye, Grace saw a little girl with gold hair, a round face, and wide eyes staring up at her, filled with guilt at some petty crime like breaking a clay jar or tracking mud through the kitchen.

But that wasn't the Kate who stood before her now. Now, a young woman, lips tight with determination, looked her straight in the eye. When had she gotten to be so tall? Why hadn't Grace noticed?

"You can't stop me," Kate said. "I'm going. I'll fight you if I have to, even if you are Gregory Lark."

Grace didn't believe that name really held so much terror. It was a story, a fairy tale.

If she hadn't had Kate, she wouldn't have remembered what Alan looked like at all. And what would Alan have done at this moment? *Let her go, or you'll never have a chance to say goodbye.*

"You'll cut your hair and bandage your breasts," Grace said. "You'll learn to walk and speak like a boy. You can never forget for a moment that you're playing the part of a boy. Do you understand?"

Quickly, bird-like, Kate nodded.

"The men who like boys—David will keep them off you. But you must learn how to look after yourself. Tell David he must teach you how to fight. I trust David, but no one else, and he might not always be there to protect you. Do you understand, Kate?"

"Yes, yes I do—" And suddenly she was crying, without a sound, tears wet on her cheeks. Grace opened her arms and the girl came to her, hugging her with all her strength.

"Come back to me safe, Kate," Grace said, whispering, because her throat had closed and her own tears were falling. She had so much to tell Kate, so much more advice to give, but there wasn't time, because the tide was turning and David was no doubt waiting at the pier. But she had time for one last piece of advice. One last, desperate plea. "And for God's sake, don't fall in love with your captain."

68° 07' 15"N, 31° 36' 44"W

by Conrad Williams

I.

Stars wheeling at his back, Captain Low comes on like bad weather, like something separated from Nature, a different kind of force, one driven by rum and pain and vengeance. Steel in his teeth. Blood on his hand. His own? He's not sure. He doesn't really care. No time to stop and think about injuries, men felled, kills made. Two weeks out of Liverpool on *The Pride o' The Mersey*. The stink of gunpowder raking his nostrils, the sour taste of fear in his throat. Madness rising.

Fetter's in his brain, scouring it out with smoke and shadow like a smithy's iron. Jacob Fetter, the ocean's bowel, the bottom-feeder, the shitehole. One month previous, on a rain-sodden November night, some dark harbour south of a moon they couldn't see, north of wherever, hell most probably, Jake Fetter and his crew slithered in and butchered Captain Low's men. All good men. All hard, mahogany men, weathertan and muscleknot, able to take their grog, maybe they'd have taken a keelhauling with barely a grunt.

Seven and thirty of us… now we are but one.

That harbour ground, that battlefield… ice chased off by hot blood, turned to brown syrup by morning. Barrowloads of sawdust wheeled in. The corpses wheeled out, some of them in pieces. Fetter had stolen every man's tongue, and done for every eye with a wooden fid. He'd whistled a merry tune while he did it. A tune Low didn't know, but that remained in his thoughts like one's first encounter with death.

Low had chased Fetter's shadows from Plymouth to Portugal, from Brest to the Bering Sea. His new crew, a ragbag of scurfy rats handpicked from the dregs of humanity, fallen from a brothel half-cut, eager for work, know his name. Know his past. He has that pull. No strong men left. So he has to invite wraiths on board his ship.

Seven and thirty of us… still we are but one.

The crew talks and he drifts among them, learning, understanding, finding out. First Mate, Mr. Gray, makes his introductions while Low tries—and fails—to avoid the noxious blasts of air that shoot from between his teeth.

"See Mr. Kidney there, Captain, with the ulcerated leg that will not heal? He won't have it taken off. He might be on his way out but he throws himself into every battle, first man up, first man in, a red flag wrapped around those weeping sores. "Shoot me," he cries. "Shoot me and have done." He wants his gold from you for that leg off, see. Amputation means no pay. Anything else, death for example, would be a bonus. This man has a great debt of pain to his past. And mark my words, Captain. He'll never fall. He's weak, but he'll fight till his seams part. That dog's drenched in bad luck. His leg will rot with him still using it before he gives up the ghost.

"Mr. Tamsin next, Sir, at the quarterdeck, folding the colours. Made of tar and wood and salt. Cut him, he'll bleed seawater. Been a brother to these waves since he were a nipper. Survived a fall into shark-infested waters, once. Big one bit him in the chest, ripped his breathers open. He was so close to death he could have touched the ragged hem of Its cloak. Came back though, somehow. Came back and now you know whenever he's near, for there's the sound of the ocean as he pulls in another breath. Some round here won't have it. They steer clear of him. Reckon he's a ghost, or a warning."

"This is all fascinating, Mr. Gray," Low says, closing his eyes. "All fascinating and of great help to a man who likes a bit of character. But, see, and don't take this the wrong way, Mr. Gray, but, see, only man I care about, asleep, awake, only man I *think* about is Jacob Fetter."

And Mr. Gray slinks back, bowing his head, as they all do. He knows how they mutter behind his back; the deep corners of the ship's waist contain a fug of gossip and concern.

He's obsessed, he is. It'll be his undoin'. Fetter's won afore a vengeful blow's been aimed.

He doesn't mind the chatter. No crew of his have ever dreamt of mutiny. As long as they keep the decks swabbed, keep their eyes on the horizon and their hearts cold. Low claps his hands. Heads turn. Tired, soulless eyes, dogs' eyes. Sharks' eyes. Tired pirates. Ruined men.

"Word has it you lot are worthless," Low says. "Word has it your best days were ten years back. A shambling crew, you lot, now. Sleepwalking. Readying for your final bed. Well I'm not having any of that. You come work for me, there must be some steel left in your blood. Youth? Muscle? Means nought to me if there's no fire to fuel it. And I know all about fire. I can see it in you. You might be tired, ready to drop even, but I know rage when I see it. I won't ask you to do anything I'm not ready to take on myself. I'll wash with you, eat with you, fight with you. And when we fight… Oh Lord, men. When we fight, it'll be with the force of the Atlantic at our backs. I promise you ten gold doubloons each and a lifetime of rum, a ship to rival *Queen Anne's Revenge*, if you help me run Jacob Fetter to ground. One last, great task. A defining time. History is upon you men, each and every one of you. What say you to that?"

He turns on his heels as the cheers pile against the sails, yet as swiftly as a mask torn from a face, his smile is gone. His heart has a fathomless chill.

The water, at night. Might be oil. Might be black ice. Might be blood. A gruel of dreams. A froth of souls, of brave men too afeared of showing the truth of their feelings. Men who died hard and did not cry. Did not scream for their mothers. As you will, Jacob Fetter. As you will.

II.
33°09'N, 24°06'W

We hit glass. Sea becalmed. I can see the reflection of the gleam in my eyes when I lean over the side and look into it. I give the order for the powder room to be cleaned and the sails to be taken down for repairs. These men might be damaged, but I'll not need to talk to them again; they don't need me telling them where to put their noses when there's no foam at the bow.

"Those sails down, Cap'n, there's going to be a lot of hot necks in an hour or two."

I stare at the man addressing me. I don't remember where I dragged this one from. Some cobbled street running with wine and blood in Lisbon? A beach filled with nets and bodies on the toe of Italy? His skin is like stewed tea. His voice marks him out from one of the ports of the southwest of England. Plymouth, perhaps. Or Bristol. His eyes will not fasten on me.

"What's your name?"

"Robert, sir. Robert Greenhalgh."

"Mr. Greenhalgh, I'm grateful to you for your concern. At midday, the crew can go below decks for two hours. You, on the other hand, will stay here with me, monitoring the weather and watching for raiders. Do you understand?"

"Clear as this water we're sitting in, *Cap'n*," he said, though again I couldn't shake the feeling that his pronunciation of the word was muddied with sarcasm or disdain.

I was about to take my leave of him when he shifted his stance. He squared up to me. I felt the hairs prickling at my neck; my wrist brushed the handle of my cutlass. He was unarmed. He wore a curious smile, though that might in part be helped by the scar that wormed up from his jaw across his left cheek.

"The men are with you," Mr. Greenhalgh said. "For now. But already there's talk.

"*How's he know, this Captain Low, where Fetter is? How's he know which way to turn?*"

"I'm captain of this ship," I said. "That's all you need, by way of an answer."

Mr. Greenhalgh closed his eyes deferentially. I was unnerved by the sight of open eyes sinking into their position. A tattoo, not uncommon among pirates. I had seen it before. A reassurance, that they might continue to keep watch, even as they slept. Greenhalgh nodded, backed away.

"Mr. Gray!" I shouted. I was angered by the nervousness this man had unearthed in my gut. I did not like him. "Mr. Gray!"

It turned out Greenhalgh was not a direct acquisition of mine. I tried to keep my temper in check as Mr. Gray explained how he had come to be on board at the time of our casting off from Liverpool. None of the men knew him. He'd been asleep in the crew's quarters and gained favour by handing out pieces of dried mango.

"He sailed with Captain Rainer out of Hull a dozen times," said Mr. Gray. "He's brought back heads from the Barbary Coast and some say he has a fortune in Chinese silver. He's an experienced salt. He could be of help to us."

"He's a stowaway," I said. I stared at the horizon, flatter than the underside of the rulers I used on my waggoners. I imagined Jacob Fetter out there, smoothing the water with his hands. "Watch him."

Do I fear Jacob Fetter? I sense him sniffing the waves at some dark prow, all the light from the stars hurtling into his eyes, giving him the vision of angels. And no matter how many miles divide us, he can see me. He can see the loose threads on the scarf at my throat, the beard, the long hair and the tricorn. He can see the tremor in my left hand, where the ligaments and nerves never quite healed after the brawl in Sour Heart's Hollow. He can see the sweat in every pore. He can see the cloud over my eyes. He can see deep into the chambers of my heart where the blood moves cold and sluggish as slob ice in Antarctica. He sees me better than I see myself.

Still waters persist.

The turtles we brought on board have all been devoured. We're having to eat hard tack in the dark of the hold so as not to see the weevils in our food. Mr. Tamsin caught an old porpoise. He argued that it wasn't bad luck because it had risen to the surface to die anyway. He boiled it in the cauldron but it was bad eating. All other attempts at fishing have been in vain.

I cornered Mr. Greenhalgh and asked him if he had any of his mango strips left. "No sir," he said. He offered me a piece of coconut.

"Quite the larder, aren't you, sir?" I said.

I challenged him about his illicit boarding of my ship. He apologised fulsomely and said that it had been an ambition of his to sail with me. "You are gaining a reputation throughout Europe," he said. "A fair man, a good captain. A brother in a fight."

"You served under Captain Rainer?"

"Yes sir. For eight years."

"And did you make good hauls in that time?"

"Yes sir. In 1794 we overwhelmed a crew of seventy-five belonging to *The East Wind*, a schooner from Baltimore returning from the Orient. Spices. Silks. Ivory. Wine and olive oil. There were twenty of us in Captain Rainer's sloop."

"*Red Freedom*, no?"

Greenhalgh smiled. "Yes sir. You know your history."

"I'm impressed," I said. "And flattered. Where is Captain Rainer now?"

Greenhalgh smiled again. I was irked by it. The man was able to convey his emotions without making them explicit in the things he said. He was patronising me. "I can't tell you that, sir. Captain Rainer swore us all to silence."

"Of course," I said. "And anyway, it's Fetter I'm interested in. No clues there, I expect?"

A shake of his head. "The last I heard regarding Captain Fetter, he was alternating between the Mediterranean and the northwest coast of Africa. He works hard, sir."

I nodded. "I work harder."

I was about to take leave of him when he touched me gently on the elbow. I swallowed the urge to lash out at him.

"Pardon my tongue, sir. I don't mean to speak out of turn, nor to sow a seed, but Jacob Fetter captains a warship, the like of which has not been seen since Blackbeard's day. He has a crew of one hundred and fifty. Young, hungry men. Fit men. You might well be obsessed with catching Fetter's tail, but I suspect you occupy merely a tiny portion of his brain." He sucked his teeth. "You're a memory. Not a concern."

His heavy-lidded eyes. Eyes on eyes. Scar or no, the maddening suggestion of a smirk at his lips. I leaned in close. "Be careful, Mr. Greenhalgh. As a stowaway, you've contravened the law. And I might, at any moment, decide to punish you for that."

"I am here to serve you, sir," he said. "If I have spoken out of turn, then I apologise. My words, always, are intended as an aid, nothing more."

I sent him with Mr. Horrocks to the cannon. "Prepare the ship for battle," I told them.

End of the fifth day in sleeping water, Captain Low, alone on the poop deck, watching the stars, remembering a day on a bluff overlooking Port Kincaid. His father teaching him how to find the Pole Star. How to navigate across oceans using only those points of light in the sky. They had built a fire together, Low impressing his father with his knowledge of tinder, of siting. He had knelt close to a knot of dry grass, sheep's wool and down. Breathed gently upon the centre of the heat he had driven into the wood with his whittled stick. The barest tremor from his lips, a ghost's kiss: the smoke thickened, its core a sudden yolk.

He feels that tremor now. Low opens his eyes to the fingers of air touching his face. The stars in the water turn suddenly indistinct, like chalk marks softened by a thumb.

"Mr. Gray!" he calls, pulling off his shirt and unlashing the great halyard of the mainsail. "All hands on deck!"

They left us for dead, and Death had His fill. He took His time and picked the harbour clean. But some of us He missed. The ones you'd have thought were first on His list: the crippled, the diseased, they slipped through His fingers. Fetter had six days on us. Six days before we got the sloop repaired and making a wake. We buried many dead. We swabbed the decks of a lot of blood. We put our brothers in the water. We drank ourselves to oblivion singing their names under a storm.

48°18'N, 29°47'W

The ship plunges on. The wind in our faces. A mist of spray in the air. Getting colder. The sweat of the lads on the ratlines. The occasional hit of tar, of strong wood, of spanked sails beating out our intent across the sea. Dolphins glint like bodkins sewing our route into the water. Hunger has sharpened our minds. No cloud. No land. Five days adrift, as still as corpses, a long time to lose yourself, to let him get away. But I was on to him. I knew we were heading the right way. North. Always north. He had no other direction in him. I saw his face in the powder of the stars and the strange rash of light in the deeps. Even as my hands and feet grew numb, my breath shocked to white, I could sense how he would feel as I crumbled him under my fingers. There was nothing to him. He was akin to these icebergs muscling up against my ship. He had an intimidating air, but he was drifting. And if I chipped away at him, bit by bit, one day he would collapse, reveal his cold, blue heart.

A noise from up in the nest. All eyes turned to the northwest. From the horizon, after a minute or so, a pale red colour bled into the night.

"Mr. Gray! A change of course if you please. Thirty degrees port."

The light was dying by the time we were able to identify it. A ship on fire, its bow blasted into burned, black fingers. It was leaning hard on its starboard side, the keel lifting out of the water and all I could think about was an old, diseased whore I had visited in Rangoon when I was a young man, hauling herself out of a stinking bath. I sent out a party of six to investigate, led by Mr. Gray.

They returned just after the sun slipped the horizon. Mr. Gray was standing at the prow, his hands cupping his mouth. *No survivors. No survivors.* A report of what he had seen. A prediction for all of us on board *The Pride.* I don't know.

All of the heads had been emptied of tongues, their eyes dashed out. I imagined a man in a room unfolding a sopping, crimson handkerchief.

In the dark and the rain. The swell and bottoming out of the ship. The fists of iced wind. Nothing to do but huddle and think. Sup the ladles of rum and gunpowder. You piss where you sit to keep yourself warm. You wonder how life might have gone had you made another turn as a boy on the shadow-line. The fingers of your hands are task-hardened, so calloused you can slice the ball of your thumb with a blade and you will not bleed. No chance of such luck with the heart. Still tender as a lamb's. No great love arcs to strengthen it. No matrimonial blows. A novice in romance. You never married. You never had sons. Well, not that you knew of. Down in the bilges, away from the crew. Through the maggot-infested seams of the ship. Into the stench-black pits of wood and saline. Here you feel it is almost safe to cry.

Morning emerges. An albatross keeping pace off starboard. Stiff breezes from the southeast. Mist. A bone-coloured sun. Clean air. Mr. Tamsin cooks one of the turtles rescued from *The Clarion*. We convene beneath the mainmast. I thank the men for their efforts. For their trust. I tell them the weather will not hold and that conditions will deteriorate. Some of the men are smiling at me as I speak, with genuine affection. I know these lads will follow me to the waterfalls at the edge of the Earth if I were to ask. Some are expressionless, determined. Others cannot meet my gaze, but they nod their heads. They know me. They believe in me. Their belief in me props up the sagging belief I have in myself. Was it ever there? Was it ever there?

The ship turns. The soft shadows realign themselves on deck. A black hand skids elongated over the devil's seam, fingers splayed, unGodly, as if reaching for something it never deserved. A cry. A surge of bodies. Men grappling at the broken remains of Mr. Lerner tied against the bowsprit.

"Cut him down," I call out, needlessly.

He spills to the deck. Somebody says, *Mosey's Law*. Mr. Lerner's eyes are squint-tight shut. The tan in him has turned the grey of whaleskin. His teeth are clenched, protruding from the peelback lips as if making an attempt to escape. Perhaps it is a scream behind them that has created the shape. You might almost lever the ivories open, reach in and pluck it from the tongue. A glassy, fragile thing cast from the branches of the lungs: the outline of terror.

"Turn him over." Your voice, but you'd swear you never opened your mouth. Mr. Greenhalgh scoops his bare foot under the cadaver and flips him on to his guts. You bite down hard on a rebuke at the man's insensitivity, because here's madness. Mr. Lerner's back has been so thrashed by the cat that his spine shows through his swollen, lacerated flesh.

"This was done after he died," Mr. Greenhalgh says, picking at his teeth with a bent nail.

"I'd have thought God the only being who might divine that knowledge, Mr. Greenhalgh. Or are you keeping secrets from us? Do you want to tell us something? Do you want to confess?"

"Dead men don't sing songs," Mr. Greenhalgh said, then turned his back on me, began scooping rope into his thick arms. "We'd have heard him squeal like a harpooned humpback. We'd have been able to do something."

"Then how did he die?"

Mr. Greenhalgh turned around, that maddening ghost of a smile. The slow unblink of his eyes. The pale, staring tattoos. "I'm not the ship's sawbones," he said.

"Mr. Lievesley!" I did not take my eyes off the insubordinate rat.

The ship's doctor assessed the body, and, nervously twiddling with his pince-nez, told me there were flecks of pink, bloody froth around Mr. Lerner's mouth, consistent with death by drowning. "I can't confirm whether it's salt water or drinking water."

"It doesn't matter," I said. I called the men together. I told them that the person responsible for this murder would escape the death sentence if they came forward immediately. Nobody did.

"In that case, my trust has been abused, as has that of the rest of the crew. Mr. Gray, organise a watch. On deck and in the sleeping quarters. When the culprit is unearthed, it will be Davy Jones' Locker for him."

Did my voice break, a little? As I was standing there, my hand shaking like some old man with the palsy, as I voiced my hard threats, was part of me trying to tell me that the murderer would never be exposed? That it was Fetter who had somehow transported his evil, by way of a storm cloud, perhaps, on to *The Pride*, and walked among my men without being detected. Perhaps the crew felt a prickle of cold as he passed, or a jag of pain behind the eyes. Perhaps they found they could not focus on his shadow as he moved. Their gaze slid away, repelled by his monstrousness. I had never set eyes on him. But he filled my mind like some inoperable canker. Sometimes I imagined him beneath the sea; its surface nothing but the vast acres of a billowing black cloak. When the storms began to blow, he would rise and, at some awful moment, he'd swing around and show me how the features sat on his face. And I believed upon seeing him, my eyes would simply turn to dust and trickle from my head.

Two days since we buried Mr. Lerner at sea. The food is all but gone, save a stinking batch of coconut husks already gnawed to the quick. I gave the order to bring down any seabirds, but the skies are emptying, this far north. When the albatross returned, none of the crew were prepared to aim their muskets at it. My own misfired in the cold. I was barely strong enough to lift the weapon in my hand. Another two bodies were found in the evening by Mr. Greenhalgh and Mr. Rees. Rees told me that he had spent the whole day with Greenhalgh, making nets to see if they could catch some fish. Mr. Rees is a good man, too thick for deviousness. I believe him, which lets Greenhalgh off the hook for Mr. Lievesley timed the death at some point that afternoon. The dead men, Mr. Abbott and Mr. Lucy, were naked, their ribs gleaming through the mess of their chests like pieces of ivory buried in rubies. They had frozen to the cannon they had been draped over. Mr. Horrocks had to use an axe to release them.

63°28'N, 29°47'W

While I was discussing weather systems and charts with Mr. Carver, Mr. Gray sidled up to me, in that way he has. He drew me to one side. I covered my mouth and nose, pretending to be disgusted by the grisly show. I smelled Mr. Gray's carious words, regardless.

"Mr. Low. Sir. We've drifted a little. Down to this hard patch of weather I suspect. But we're still on course. Give or take."

I nod. Look at him. "All very good, Mr. Gray. But there's something else stuck in your throat. And it's not ship's biscuit, I'll warrant."

"No sir." He appeared nervous, embarrassed even. "This Fetter, sir. Jacob Fetter. I don't know him. I wondered if you might tell me a little about him."

"No reason why you should know him, Mr. Gray. He's my rogue, not yours."

"With respect, sir, we're on this ship chasing his shadow. All for you. He's as much a part of our nightmares as yours now. We deserve to know the shape of our quarry."

I chewed on this for a while. But I could not disagree with him. "Jacob Fetter was born at sea. His mother was a shark. His father was a raft of dead coral. Some January night, in that unreserved glacial darkness that smothers the Earth perhaps once a year, the coral gave up its unHoly seed and the shark drifted through it. By the time she emerged from the fog, she was dead, and Fetter was fully formed in her belly. His mother, the shark, did not give birth. Fetter devoured her inside out. He has gills, Mr. Gray. He is cartilaginous. His eyes roll back into his head when he takes a bite of his supper. If you get close enough to him, while he sleeps, and look into his black throat, you'll see row upon row of serrated teeth reaching back into his gullet. He cannot eat anything that is dead. At the first hint of night, he must slip into the water. He must constantly be on the move. If he stops, he sinks to the sea bed and dies of suffocation."

"Mr. Low…"

"When he makes love, he rips his women open with a razored penis and slakes his thirst on their blood. When he prays, the moon turns red. If you see his shape in the clouds at midnight, you will go to sleep in fever and wake up blind. His breath is carrion. The wake of *The Iron Mantis* churns so mightily that typhoons emerge from the sea. I have it on good authority that when Fetter relieves himself overboard, the steam of his piss turns into phantoms that can dissolve the skin."

"Mr. Low…" Whispered now.

"I don't know, William," I snapped, and he seemed more shocked by my use of his Christian name than anything previously uttered.

He stepped in closer to me, as if we were spies conspiring on a street corner. "The men, they are with you," he said. "But I don't know how strong your credit with them will prove. They… we are pirates. We live for the chase, for the fight, for the silk and the sovereigns. We want to get drunk, and not on this watered-down piss. We want to fornicate and eat fresh food. We want to sun ourselves in a sandy cove. We're not stupid, Mr. Low. We know this life, it's either feast or it's famine. But our pockets are deep. And there's nothing at the foot of them. And you telling me you don't know this man. You don't know his size or his colour. His creed or his needs. It doesn't put steel in my heart."

"He is where we are going," I said. "The burning ship must convince you of that."

"There are more pressing matters, sir. In my opinion. We have a killer on board. Where are the investigations? Where are the suspects?"

"We are all suspects, Mr. Gray," I said, staring into his sun-blasted face. "At least the body proved to me that at least one of us has some bite, some animal in him."

"Murder?" said Mr. Gray. "You condone it? Among our own?"

"Not at all," I said. "But this is no treasure hunt. This isn't a year of festivities, all mates together drinking and whoring all the ports of the western seas. This is a blood hunt. This is vengeance."

He was about to protest, but this time it was I to duck into his space, to drive the point home. "What would you have me do, William? Spend a day or two rooting out the bad apple? Mete out some justice? And then back on to a cold trail, the men more resentful, more hungry? You say they're with me, for now. Then let me strike while I have a backing. We can dig through the muck after the deed's been done."

"A backing, you say?" Mr. Gray's voice was suddenly tired, breathy. "How many of us will be left once our bow is chopping at Fetter's foam?"

"Three bodies, Mr. Gray. Three murders. There is no guarantee there'll be more killing."

"And, Captain, there is no guarantee there won't be."

He comes for me, but not at night, not when I am alone, struggling to sleep. He comes when I'm in the middle of my toilet, or pinching my nose to drink down the slime of our water in the galley's barrels. He comes when I'm sharing out the hard tack or stepping in to halt a squabble between shipmates. I see his shadow slide across the wall of my quarters like tar drawn into spiderish lengths. His breath is scentless; the cold has burned out all traces of his interior. He touches the skin of my throat and I feel every shred of me become the chill sludge of every dead thing found on the ocean bed. I can't wake up screaming. No such relief. I have to bite on the panic. I have to force the smile. The men see one speck of this madness in me and we are all done for.

We go on. We must go on.

Mr. Gray is up aft with the "bring 'em near." He's convinced land is less than a day away. Clouds on the horizon. I'm too weak to get off my bunk. I can no longer tell which of my hands is the damaged one; both shake like fury. Another body this morning. Mr. Tamsin, frozen so hard to the deck that even Mr. Horrocks' axe would not shift him. Red splinters flew out at every blow. I saw Mr. Kidney drooling.

Mr. Dendy, in the crow's nest, calls out. There is a clamour for the port side. Mr. Gray points a confirmation. A little while later, a white line trembles above the horizon. Land. I'm barely able to hold myself upright, but now I'm cheering with the other lads. Where there's land there's food. Where there's food, there's scavengers. And where there's scavengers, there's Fetter.

It takes an agony of time to reach that solid, icy bluff, and another hour or two to find an access point where we can drop anchor. I order the armoury to be opened. Muskets for everyone. I doubt any will work in this cold, but the men deserve to have their courage bolstered. I feel only the slightest pang of doubt when I realise a gun is being passed to our secret killer. But events have overtaken us. Gun or no, the bodies will pile up.

I choose a landing party. Myself, Mr. Greenhalgh, Mr. Dendy, Mr. Burbidge, Mr. Taylor and Mr. Horrocks. I am tempted to take Mr. Lievesley with us, but again I must think of those left on board. I pull Mr. Gray to one side.

"William, I apologise. I know you would want to come with us, and God be my witness I wish you were at my shoulder, but the truth of the matter is that I need you to be my eyes and ears back on *The Pride*. I trust you with my life. And it vexes me to say that you're the only person I do trust right now."

"Then if that's the case, we ought to turn around and sail back to Liverpool. Forget all this. Forget about Fetter. We are dead men, Captain."

"If I go back without facing him, death would be the least of my worries."

"Sir…"

"My decision is made, Mr. Gray. You have command of *The Pride*. If we are not back within a single arc of the moon, you may cast off."

I do not look back. Mr. Greenhalgh and Mr. Taylor take up the oars and row us into a cathedral of ice. The hollows of the bergs flicker with the palest blues and greens. A pirate's eye is well-trained for prettiness; yet all the treasures he has plundered over a lifetime of robbery and violence cannot prime him for these sights. The bluster and blague of the ship has been shed; we drift in awed silence. I wonder about Fetter, about his eyes trawling these same lofted ceilings and glittering buttresses. I wonder if his soul might have lifted. If he might have felt the cold spike of his own mortality.

Is he running away or drawing me in?

The colours change. Blood frozen into the snow as we clamber on to the ice shelf.

Something has been ripped apart here: blood has hosed in lines over twelve feet away. Surely no man was the author of this atrocity. We fan out.

Mr. Burbidge finds what remains of the corpse a little while later. The dead man's tarred petticoat breeches had been torn open. A blue and white checked shirt was similarly ravaged; a few feet away, a woollen cap and some shoes contained a mush of blood and fat and bone. Mr. Horrocks is copiously sick. I order the men to follow me.

I feel panic that we might have arrived too late. I don't want my confrontation with Fetter to be nothing more than my feet scuffing through his remains. But some glint in the clean knife of the air tells me he lives on. Two hours of tramping through snow, the cold numbing our edges, and we find his ship. We stand in shocked silence. There is a hole in the hull and the mainmast has been downed. The ship leans against the ice shelf as if pausing for breath.

"Careful, lads," I advise. We watch the ship for some time, but there is no movement. A hundred and fifty men. Nobody on board? I can't swallow that, yet I bid my companions follow me and approach that crippled vessel.

Once we find a way on to the listing deck, we quickly search for food. There might be crew below decks, but the smell of fresh meat and bread is too great to resist. The doors are hanging off their hinges, there is blood on the ropes; if any crew are on ship, they are no longer alive.

A wet, growling sound rises into the torn sails.

"Bear," says Mr. Greenhalgh, as if he were casually describing something passing along the harbour in Hull.

I follow his gaze down to the ice. Two large polar bears circling, wagging their heads this way and that whenever they rear up on to their hind legs. Their muzzles are sopping and pink.

We eat quickly, but sensibly. Too much and we'd suffer stomach cramps which would be the death of us out here. We pack as much as we can carry for our mates on *The Pride*. And then, as we prepare to leave, Mr. Burbidge touches me on the arm.

"Begging pardon, Captain. I thought I heard something below."

With the food inside me, I feel my daring return. I bid Mr. Taylor accompany me. He unsheathes his musket. My instinct is to examine the captain's cabin first, to see if any trace of Fetter remains. I want to inhale his stink, top up the hatred, but the cabin is empty of anything to damn the man. It has the air of a room seldom used; perhaps Fetter's disdain for the British Navy runs to a refusal to inhabit the quarters of any officers he has usurped. In that, I feel a grudging admiration.

"Captain Low!"

It is Mr. Horrocks, although I didn't recognise his voice: it is broadsided with shock. We find him leaning over the officer's padlocked water barrel, trying to keep his gorge in check. The cold has prevented the bodies from decay, but the carnage here is worse because it appears stylised, rehearsed, even. It does not possess the randomness, the savage fingerprint of nature. There must be a dozen men entangled. I can't work out where they begin or end.

"Pull yourself together, Mr. Horrocks," I tell him. "What did you expect to find down here? Tea and cake?"

Mr. Greenhalgh on the stairs, calmly picking his teeth. "No polar bear did this," he says. "And those outside have been planted. Bite marks post-mortem. Not the cause of death."

"Mainsail mast was taken down with an axe, sir," calls Mr. Dendy from amidships.

"And that hole was blown from the inside out," Mr. Horrocks observes, rising palely from the belly of the vessel. He wipes his mouth with a handkerchief. "No cannon was fired upon this ship."

"This is a trap," says Mr. Dendy.

"No," I say. "This is a diversion." I gaze at the bodies before me. The ship's hauls are scattered about them, coins, pearls and emeralds densely coated with the eructation of the dead. It was like some ghastly confection, something one might be served in the dining rooms of palaces in Vienna or Versailles.

"I for one," says Mr. Horrocks, "would be happy to be diverted. Can we go back to *The Pride* now?"

"Not yet," I say. And, suspecting that his body will not be here: "We must find Fetter's remains."

I don't know why I passed this profane, unactionable order. I have no more idea of what Fetter looks like than the others. But I reassured them that I will identify his corpse, should the others' doughty redistribution of the bodies unearth him.

We work hard and fast, unknotting limbs, stacking the dead like firewood. We none of us touch the loot; it seems unreal, unimportant, although there is enough wealth here to see the crew of *The Pride*, and their families, into dotage and beyond.

We move through the ship. The gold and the gore is strewn with equal abandon.

By the end of it, Mr. Greenhalgh is whistling a merry little tune.

"Fetter did this," I say. "He did all of it."

"Why?" asks Greenhalgh, his cool little smile suggesting he knows the answer.

"He's afraid," I say. "He's been looking over his shoulder for so long he's got a crick in his neck."

"Afraid of you?" asks Greenhalgh.

"He'd be wise to be," I tell him.

"Our time's almost up," Greenhalgh says. He blinks slowly. Time turns into something ice-coated. The tattoo becomes his gaze becomes the tattoo. I no longer register which is which. Maybe he has eyes in the back of his head. He can watch me at all times.

"I'm sending the crew back to *The Pride*," I say.

"What about you?"

"Us," I correct him.

"Us? I don't follow."

"That's right, Mr. Greenhalgh. I'll be following you. We go on alone. Until Mr. Fetter turns up."

I sense the others staring at us.

Despite the cold, the breath from our throats furring the air, the temperature in that cabin feels tropical.

"Sir?" Mr. Dendyburbidgehorrockstaylor says. I don't know who. I don't care. There is just me and Greenhalgh and his butterfly eyelids.

"Go back to the ship," I say.

The light might have faded. The others might have gone. We might have frozen to death and what I'm looking at is the last thing the back of my eyes ever registered. But then...

"After you, Captain."

"No, Mr. Greenhalgh. I insist." I wave him to the door with my cutlass.

Once upon the ice, he hesitates. He does not look at me when he asks: "Which way, Captain? I see no footprints to tell us Mr. Fetter passed this way."

In his shadow, I stare down at the snow. "Oh, but I do, Mr. Greenhalgh," I said, and prod him.

North.

IRONFACE

A Vignette

by Michael Moorcock

Whoever christened the planet Venice named her well. Her golden surface crossed by a million regular waterways, from space resembled a papal orb. Clouds followed the canals in season and emphasised rather than obscured her geometric character. What could be more natural than to discover on a planet so named the delicate sailing gondolas and elegant barges her inhabitants used for trade and battle? Venice was a rich and lively world. More space travellers deserted to her than to any of her nine or so rivals whose ranks included Ur 17 and the extraordinarily beautiful New Titan, whose colonists risked every danger to enjoy those yearningly lovely landscapes.

Like all inhabited worlds, Venice was forbidden to the great rockets of the IPS. The mercantile vessels of the Terran service were, moreover, constantly challenged by privateers in their subtler, sometimes faster ships using the more erratic solar winds for power. The second intergalactic war had destroyed whole star systems and left by common consent the planetary prizes unspoiled. Surface conflicts were confined to the conventional weapons of each region. On Venice these included battle barges of enormous dimensions, their hulls driven by sails whose canvas covered distances measured in fractions of a mile rather than cubed metres, and speedy little gondolas employing oars as regularly as they used wind. These boats darted along the wide natural waterways like bugs, their oars so many articulated limbs. From space on the great V-screens they appeared as natural creatures endowed with minds and purposes of their own. Ironface the pirate had used those gondolas very successfully in pursuit of his business, taking full advantage of the confusions and disguises offered by war, until the planet was his. For the past half-century, however, he had required little use of them.

There were few land wars on Venice. Canals occupied four-fifths of the planet's surface. All traffic was conducted by water. Explorers had long since discovered that symmetry, formed in the nativity of their geological qualities, was characteristic. Even the howling, fruitful terraces of Arcturus-and-Arcturus owed their existence to this familiar phenomenon.

In his long *Epiconeon* Ironface, whose real name was Cornelius and elsewhere was nicknamed "The Dutchman," wrote:

Catching the solar winds, the vessel brakes and turns
Upon the brane and all the multiverse is hers.
The yearning void calls out, gloriously perverse,
She spurns a dozen planetary advances.
This latticed orb of silver, gold and glowing pearl
Sustains all reverses and her purse remains
Both threatening prize and perilous temptation.
Yet still my patronage and brain are hers
There can be no occasion, no threat or lure
To drive me from my chosen station.

His ship is called *Pain*. He stands on her poopdeck, proud and insouciant, glorying in the beauty he commands. She is the most peerlessly perfect vessel in all spacetime.

Her sails still strain against the pressure of countless billion winking photons; her holds are already crowded with the booty of a dozen beautiful planets. Within her mysterious envelope of atmosphere, created from stolen technologies, her crew crowds her decks to look down on a world they have come to love.

Ironface the pirate is a ruthless poet, a courteous thief, commander of a vessel feared and familiar, envied as much for her ethereal loveliness as the accuracy of her destructive arsenal. Only *Remembered Lombardy* could hope to challenge her in open space. He motions with his hand, giving the order for his men's descent.

With feelings close to pleasure, Venetians, training their glasses upon her as she materialises in their upper atmosphere, recognise her vast, exquisite lines. They know how rigorously her captain honours the conventions. Ironface comes to take his ten-year tribute fair and square, according to the articles signed by all the pirate brotherhood save one, the rogue Cervantes, who roams the barren backlanes of space between the outer stars, his pickings scant and sordid..

Captain Cornelius, the Dutchman, is an enigmatic figure to his men and to his mistresses. His verse is studied so they might know him better but it only adds to his mystery. It reveals little of his character save that he relishes wine and sensuality and favours beauty over friendship. A lonely figure, he stands smoking a pipe stuffed with oily black opium shag, offering his commands with quiet economy. As usual before taking his boat to the surface, he dines only with his bosun Peetr Aviv, a woman almost as distant from the crew as himself, and just as respected. None can say they like captain or bosun, but they obey both with a confidence, offering no other commanders a loyalty so well rewarded. When *Pain* completes her long tour of violent adventure every man, woman or child aboard will be worth a fortune great enough to buy presidents and kings.

Ironface gives the order. The boats break free of their mothership, darting eagerly down, through blazing, sun-tinged clouds, to fill Venice's morning with a grave commanding dignity.

The pirates have come at last. Only a few, watching them from their decks and towpaths, resent Ironface's power. Some nobles even drop to their knees, bowing in respect for the inevitable, as vassals once paid homage to a feudal lord.

By evening Ironface is among them, broadcasting his requirements to all the rival factions on the planet, instructing them, canal by canal, how much they must give and in what form, be it bullion, provisions or people. His price is high, but the price of defiance is higher.

When the barges are filled and brought to the great central basin called The Winters, inventories are carefully tallied and receipts supplied. Then the recruiting begins to replace a skilled complement killed in battle or retired.

Peetr Aviv stands on her elegant prosthetics making notes, quietly relaying orders. Ironface, his features engulfed within the simply engraved mask he adopts in public, sits to one side of the bosun's desk, his glowing, melancholy eyes fixed on the distance, looking towards Saint Marx's islet where once, it is said, he courted a novice and lost her to the only enemy whose superiority he has ever acknowledged and whom he calls God.

At last, after a week, the peaceful tension is dispelled. Their tolls all taken, the pirates prepare to leave, while Saint Marx's bells sound the end of the taxing. In return for this levy Venice will know protection for another decade. Captain Cornelius nods to Peetr Aviv. The ledgers are signed off by pirates and canal captains in a flurry of silken pomp and brilliant armour. The skiffs rise skyward into the broad ribbons of cloud. Those whose eyes strain at their scopes see *Pain* standing for a moment to catch the solar winds, her instruments glowing and winking in the shrouded, perpetual twilight of her decks. Then she's gone, a vast and fleeting glow against the black glare of space. A memory of loss and impossible glory. Once again, briefly, the multiverse has granted Venice an audience with her unsentimental soul.

PIRATE SOLUTIONS

by Katherine Sparrow

Mary Read 1692–1720

You could feel their heat. Not a metaphor, I don't mean that, I mean literally the room grew warmer when they were in it. They were both so powerful. Whenever Anne and Jack (they weren't named that then, but that's who they were) strolled into the room you got contact highs from their lust. People who would never make out would find excuses to go to the bathroom together and come back with monster hickies. Everyone always wanted to sit near them because of their heat, and because they always said the thing you wish you'd said but only thought to say a billion blinks later.

When I first joined the Freebooter tech collective Anne and Jack were happy to have another girl in the group, but otherwise they ignored me. I could stare and stare at them all day long, hiding behind my black-rimmed glasses. But then one day Anne looked at me, and then Jack looked too, and we all just sort of fell toward each other. Like gravity. Like magic. Like there was a God.

You know that feeling you have all the time that if you were just somewhere else things would be better, more perfect, cooler? I never felt that around them, not for a second. They were the exact center of where I wanted to be.

Everything started when we were celebrating one night. It was just the three of us since the other ten had gotten popped at an antiwar direct action. We had just gotten over the flu so we stayed home and programmed like fiends. We worked for like twenty hours straight, and then finally quit and just didn't want to think anymore.

We made a fancy dinner in the crumbly kitchen, and Jack found this ancient bottle of rum in an old wooden box in the back of a closet. We always found crazy stuff in our squat, like control-top pantyhose with mice living inside or huge cracked jars of mentholatum. The rum was a score. It was corked and dusty. The insides looked dark and thick as molasses.

Jack opened it and took a swig without even smelling it. He kissed Anne. Anne kissed me with sugarcoated lips and a toffee-leather-burnt-cream taste. I'm not usually gonzo for liquor, but I wanted more. Jack popped in some beats from an old ska cassette that had a pounding drum-line. We passed the bottle around and around, and a new kind of drunk rose up in me. Like swallowing light bulbs and glowing from the inside. Like being full of helium and wanting to jump all over the place. I bounced up and down a hundred times a minute as the rum snaked down my throat.

"More?"

"Yeah."

By the bottom of the bottle Jack swayed from side to side like he was on a boat, Anne waved her arms around like she was in a knife fight, and I bounced up and down a thousand times a minute.

"There's something in the bottom," Anne said, looking down the bottle like a spyglass. "Something gray. Looks like a bone. Or a piece of wood."

"Drink the worm!" Jack yelled as he began to play air-drums.

Anne tipped the bottle toward the ceiling and drank it all. She stuck out her tongue, black with rum. Nestled in the middle of it lay something shriveled. She bit down on it, then kissed Jack. Jack kissed me and pushed his tongue into my mouth. Shards of dust and death coated my tongue and teeth.

We swallowed. We choked and gasped for air.

I felt the hempen halter tighten around my neck and squeeze the life from me. I felt the fever-death of childbirth. I raged against the shortness of life and damn the church and England! Damn the lords and ladies and everything but brine is swine! I screamed as I died and then rose up from the murky tangle of seaweed and bulb kelp. I breathed in fresh air and stared astonished at Jack and Anne. My Jack. My Anne. We saw who we truly were. The sweetest hope, then laughter and dancing and....

The next morning we downloaded nautical maps, made lists of what we needed to take, and argued over what kind of ship we wanted. When the rest of the collective came home from jail, we told them where we were going, pointing to the little wisp of an island that almost disappeared at high tide and curled around like a question mark in the aqua waters of the Caribbean sea.

"Isla d'Oro."

"It's not marked."

"It's not named."

"Yes, but that's her name," Jack whispered.

"What are a bunch of programmers going to be on an island?"

"You'll see."

We didn't expect the rest of the collective to come, but after we told them our plan, they were all in.

We packed up our servers, boxes, solar panels, and a zillion cables and monitors. We tied them on top of our school bus. We dumpstered hundreds of oak pallets, tore them apart for good wood, and loaded up the back of the bus. We threw away our cell phones, watches, and radios. We drove east and south toward Florida. The bus didn't break down. Cops didn't harass us. We only got lost a couple of times. Fate or her little sister Luck rode with us all the way to Pensacola Bay.

We found our sloop in Brown's Marina—some millionaire had been restoring an old ship before he hanged himself off the boom after losing his fortune. We bought her cheap and renamed her *Rackham's Revenge.* She wasn't much to look at—rotten Jacob's ladder, softened-wood poop, mold all over the lower decks—but the fo'c's'le and abaft masts rose straight and proud. On the crow's nest you could see her lines and wooding were planked true, and she was wide enough to carry our crew and cargo. It took all thirteen of our collective a month of patching wood, weather proofing, and tying knots as big as fists before she was seaworthy. Just before we set sail, Anne and I swung out in harnesses toward the mermaid figurehead on the prow. We pried the old lady off, and nailed on our new ambassador—a fey looking man with golden horns, bare chest, and blue knickers that did little to conceal his small, proud erection. Jack stared at him and blushed, which made the likeness all the more apparent.

We set sail with oakum and tarred hands, and cheered as the wind picked up and blew us southeast. We navigated via sextant and compass, and learned the details of sailing as we went. We earned our sea legs, one mistake at a time. The sun rose, the moon set, and rain fell as waves slapped against our gunwales in choppy water.

Every day was Talk-Like-a-Pirate-Day, at first as a joke, and then because we loved it. Everyone got new pirate names, except Anne, Jack, and I who'd already found ours. On sunny days we talked about our mission all day long as we lay on the deck and embroidered hand-made patches onto our coats. We unfurled rubbery solar panels over the deck as soon as Anne and Malfunction hacked together a satellite feed and got us online. We programmed lazily, exploring our options and data-modeling.

It took us three weeks to get there. Three weeks of water and feeling like all the land in all the world might have disappeared.

"All hands ho and turn her starboard!" Skurve shouted from the crow. We watched our island grow larger as a steady nor' eastern blew us in.

"Lower the iron lady and load up the jolly boat!" Anne yelled.

We left two men on board. The rest of us rowed to Isla d'Oro, which sat like a mirage on the water, just like I'd seen when I drank the rum. My hand trailed through the water as I leaned over the fore-bow. Yellow fish with swirly tails and translucent jellyfish with visible organs swam below. I jumped into the water as soon as we neared shore and swam with dolphin-kicks and butterfly strokes. I flopped onto the sand and stared up at the bluest sky.

The others reached shore. We ran up to the palm trees on the hill. Breathing hard, we sprinted across the flat rocks that led to the hills of the northern point of the island.

"There!" Jack cried, and ran faster.

"There! Beneath the red rock and white stone!" Anne yelled.

We dug with shovels and pickaxes. We sweated and sang and didn't lose hope even when we reached five feet down and there was nothing. Ten feet down and the ground started crumbling inward. Water rose up from below. Then we heard a thunk.

With ropes and pulleys we hauled up a rusted metal trunk. Anne twisted the handle just so, pressed three metal ingots inlaid into the top, and kicked at the lock. It popped open.

Treasure. Beautiful treasure for us and us alone! It had lain here all these centuries, untouched and perfect. I counted the glowing bottles of rum with an anxious lust. The collective looked to us for permission. Anne, Jack, and I nodded our heads. The boys uncorked the first bottle and drank. I watched with envy. When it was my turn, I drank the bone-rum as if it was the only liquid that could quench my thirst.

Jack collected the empty bottles, wrote short messages inside, and chucked them into the sea.

Anne Bonny 1690–1723

History cuts the rope between then and now, telling us it was all so different we couldn't possibly understand. They take away our stories to make us weak and forget that we have always been fighting. With the rum came memory.

Imagine the moment of mutiny, when the captain has just gone apeshit one too many times, and maybe he's about to kill someone you like, maybe a kid he press-ganged, and men spontaneously rise up and take the boat. Of the beautiful things in the world, that's one of them.

We're much luckier than the original pirates. We were able to stock up on vitamin C, potable water, and food supplies. Jack, Mary, and I insisted on it. The others didn't understand, not really, until they drank the rum and remembered the hard times: the scurvy, the rat plagues, and the dying a little every day because there was never enough sleep or water or food.

It is a strange thing to discover one's destiny, or to be press-ganged into it, as the case may be. Our old anarch friends needed us, and so we came to the island.

We're here to find pirate solutions for pirate problems, Jack liked to say, and that was as good a description as any. We tamed the red-hooded crows and used them to watch for incoming boats. We swam down to the trans-Caribbean cable and spliced into it to forge a wicked OC384 connection. We perfected our hardtack. We programmed bits and pieces of software, creating action and reaction as solid as our anchor chain. We cooked whatever we caught—even squid the size of tetra.

There was never enough time in the day to get it all done. I could code for twelve hours and only get a little closer to our goal. Like swimming against the current, our progress, despite our best efforts, was slow.

One day I sat near the fire and played with sand, running it through my fingers. I watched the water. My head was full of code and the fear that I'd never get it all right. A stray comma can ruin everything. Mary sat beside me. Her short hair had grown longer. It made her look girlier, but she still had her edge. She still wore that "I'm shy, but really I'm a predator" look that made me want to devour her. Jack stood talking to the twins—Cannonball and Cutlass—but kept glancing over at us with yearning eyes. I stared back until he blushed and looked away. I know what you're thinking Jack, I thought. He's as easy to read as an open dirty-picture book.

Dred sauntered across the beach and crouched over the treasure chest. His long rope-snake hair trailed down his back. He popped open a bottle of rum. The rest of the collective suddenly showed up. We all pretended not to be lusting after it—not obsessed with who would get the bone. We all lied. Syrop passed around a platter of small, charred fish.

Crunch, crunch, crunch. Waves lapped at the sand, each one a little closer than the last as the tide came in. It reminded me of recursive loops and the way things done repeatedly, a little different each time, change the world.

Red grabbed his guitar and plucked out a tune that thrummed like a discordant mash-up. He chewed the ends of his red beard as he played. I drank rum and passed it on. Madwell got the bone and chewed slowly with a faraway look to him. The rum distorts reality, but the bone twists your soul into a different shape entirely.

We opened up another bottle. Skurve made rolly cigarettes from pipe tobacco, and the air filled with the smell of smoke and salt water. Jack played his bongos and began singing. No words, just ululating sound. Malfunction harmonized and sang about water, ocean, and freedom to do the impossible. It wasn't good music, but it was our music.

Rum like the sea's milk filled my throat. I stood and swayed as the tempo picked up. All the code, all the hacking problems fell away as I slowly spun around the blazing red tongues of fire. I picked up speed and began to dervish like an unstoppable, destructive virus. Others rose and we became the rage of everyone murdered too young to have made a difference. We flung curses and hope up and out into the world. The song grew louder. We jumped into the air like gravity might fail, and then pounded our legs into the sand. Cannonball faced Skurve. Their sunburned faces glowed in the firelight. They matched their movements into large, competitive gestures and then fell onto each other and rolled away from the firelight, making loud, gasping animal noises.

Mary ran at the fire and jumped over it, playing with skin, cloth, and safety. She landed on the other side and flung her over-long sleeves into the flames. When they caught fire she swung them around in circles and turned and ran like a phoenix, shrieking with laughter, into the sea. I followed her, watching as the water extinguished the flames. Mary turned and stared at me with an inner fire. She laughed as I dove into the water and emerged beside her. Jack stumbled in behind us, pausing for a moment as he watched us tear our clothes off. Then the liquid embrace took all of us and rocked waves over our flailing, twisting forms. My lovers whispered to me with every touch that all this folly was my destiny.

I woke up the next morning dry-mouthed and fuzzy on the beach. Others lay naked and scattered like seaweed across the sand. A bird screamed overhead. One of our crows swooped down on ebony wings. "Crawk! Caw!" she yelled.

I shielded my eyes and stared at the horizon. A boat, tacked hard and moving fast, stirred the waters of the world's edge. She was the kind of ship that didn't exist in this day and age, just like our ship. She's coming here. She's coming home, I thought. Things are going to get really interesting, or I'll eat the bottle with the bone.

Jack Rackham, 1691–1720

The ship, like an itch, like a void, rode toward us all morning. Look away! Touch wood and spit! Ask the kraken for a reprieve, but still she grew larger. She sailed three times or more the size of our *Revenge*. Black sails like the fear of night whipped through the air. Golden Chinese characters stood scrawled upon her starboard.

I wanted her. I wanted our crew to stand on her bow and let the wind run ragged. I wanted that ship like I'd never wanted anything in my life.

An arm snaked around my waist and pulled me backwards. Anne whispered in my ear, "It's an old ship. Like ours, Jack. Think for a moment, okay?"

I turned to her and winked gallantly.

"Have you been in the rum already?" Anne asked.

"Maybe."

"Lay off until we meet them, okay?"

I nodded. Her words reeled me in. Pirate thoughts were seductive, and once I started thinking with them, like a song or a rhythm, it was hard to think any other way. "Sure," I said. "Sorry."

Anne punched my arm with force enough to raise a welt. She wandered off toward Mary who stood watching the horizon with a lovely frown.

We waited until we knew she headed straight toward us, and was not perhaps some themed cruise ship or fishermen's boat. We rowed out to *Rackham's Revenge*. If this storm on the water wished for battle, it would be at sea or nowhere else. But perhaps they were friends, not foe.

I buttoned a calico coat over my striped undershirt as I took the helm. I swayed with the sea swells and inhaled the sweaty musk of sea wind.

"Raise the sails, aft and fore!" The words fell like paper from my mouth, like old words written by dead men.

We sailed like an arrow aimed at her portside. Another bout of ship lust rippled through me, but this time I tamped it down like tobacco in the pipe. I mellowed it to a slow burn.

"Tighten the sails!" I ordered.

The distance between us narrowed. A figure rose and stood broad legged on the ship-bow. A billowing red silk coat whipped around him. He pointed at me.

A mighty voice rose from the shrouded ship, using a powerful bullhorn.

"We come to join you," a voice said with a heavy accent, and then repeated the words in Chinese.

"They're here for our treasure!" I yelled. "Or maybe not," another me added. I raised my bottle, but then remembered I had promised not to drink.

Suddenly, the wind fell from our sails and we lay dead in the water.

"No!" I yelled. "Damn the skies!" But it was not the winds of fate who failed me, but our crew who lowered the sails and readied the jolly boat. I glared at the yellow-bellies, but before I could order them back, Anne looked at me with eyes to wither my turnips.

"Relax," she hissed. "Mellow out."

Only when I saw the red captain walk to his small boat did I run to our jolly and let myself be lowered to the water.

Anne, Mary, Dred, and I rowed to them. Bits of white foam hit my face. Their small boat measured twice the length of ours. If I couldn't take their entire ship, perhaps I could steal their jolly?

Stop, I told myself, but the inner pirate looked through my eyes with a stubborn lust.

Our crew threw ropes across the water, and we drew our boats together. The red captain stepped forward and straddled both boats. I stared at her t-shirt, sure I was mistaken, but no! The captain of this magnificent ship was a woman?

I sighed. So what? No big deal, I told myself. She bore a shaved head with a scar that wound around her skull.

"Captain Jack," I muttered and managed a half-bow.

"Captain Ching," she said and nodded her head.

"Captain Shmaptain," Anne said.

"Would you like some tea?" Captain Ching asked in careful English. I was prepared for fisticuffs or swordplay. But tea?

"Uh. Sure."

She took a glass flask from the folds of her coat and passed it to me. It was tar black and smelled like wood chips. As I swung it to my mouth, I heard the clink of something within. Then the liquid touched my lips and a demonic desire flushed through me. The tea was mixed with bone-rum!

"Oh," I said, unmanned by this strange change of circumstance. Anne grabbed the bottle and drank, then passed it to the others.

We sailed back to Isla d'Oro and followed the Chinese women as they ran to where they pried a boulder from a hill and found their own hidden cache of bone-rum.

They told us the story of how their collective, the Wôkòu, had found an old bottle on the beach with a message inside. A message I myself had written. A day later they discovered a bottle of rum in Ching's government apartment. When they drank it they left behind their work of creating autonomous cyberspaces inside the great firewall of China and sailed here, much as we had done. They all wore cropped hair and glasses of a style most geekishly becoming.

We stood around like shy dogfish wanting to play with each other. Then Madwell showed one girl the software he was working on. She pushed him aside, pointed at a line of code, and corrected it.

All awkwardness fell away like foam on the surf. We gathered around monitors and spoke the true language we had in common. It cleaved my heart to the tenderest cut to see such ease and solidarity.

The next day another ship appeared on the horizon. And another. Ships flowed toward us like migrating auks, bringing flocks of geeks from across over the world.

The Marauders, the Corsairs, the Buccaneers, the Infidels, the Pieras Noblas, and dozens more sailed in. Each had received my message. Each found their own cache of bone-rum upon the island, and brought with them necessary skills we needed for our mission.

The Germans were big bratwurst-bellied men who'd welded together shipping crates to make their ship. The French were thin cross-dressers who'd never held down jobs and brought huge rounds of stinky cheeses with them. The Cubans were fierce and rowed in on houseboats. The Indians brought a treasury of spices. All of them understood, without quarrel or bickering, why they were called to Isla d'Oro. The rum was nothing in comparison to the real treasure we would steal.

Every night the captains joined me in gathering up the empty rum bottles, stuffing notes inside, and throwing them out to sea. Our message was simple: Join us.

Ships kept coming. They lay moored and silhouetted against the setting sun. I stared at them as I sat with another man's sad memories lodged within me. There'd been battles fought and lost, sunken boats, and a life much too short and violent. I settled my gaze on the horizon and wondered if this present story would also end with keelhauls and hangings.

Sam Flowers, present day

Falling like flying. Air like freedom. Splash. Hard water turned warm as it wrapped around me. I sank and then surprised myself by thrashing upward, desperate for life. My head broke through into air. I treaded water and watched the thousand-light cruise ship churn away from me. What a shocker—I even suck at suicide.

Ah hell. Oh shit. I should have stayed on that boat. I should have taken pills instead.

I floated in the salty water and stared up at the big fat stars. Why am I here? Why is it all so empty? Bull kelp rose like a submerged sea raft beneath me. It carried me along in a sea current like a magic carpet full of sand flies. The night passed and the sun rose and burned me.

My life played before me like a plotless French movie: no girlfriend, boring office job, stringy hair.

You meant nothing. You were worthless.

Is that you, God? Because you sound kind of mean. You sound just like I expected.

I gulped down salt water and cried. I picked sea leeches off my balls and stared at them. Dolphins came by and poked me with their stubby heads. They made stupid dolphin sounds as they took bull kelp into their mouths and swam.

"I'm not one of those dolphin lovers," I told them.

They swam on with their secret dolphin schemes.

My head turned into a rotten watermelon. My arms swelled like kielbasas. My nipples were ripe cherries. "When do I get to die?"

Aah-awk? said the dolphins.

I drank sea martinis and chatted with all the girls I'd never kissed. They had big breasts like flesh marshmallows. They were covered in glittery fish scales. When did all the girls become mermaids? The mermaids became pirates who rose up around me. They wore sea-gray clothes and grayer skin. They glared at me with watery gray eyes.

"Captain Calico Jack," one said and tipped his barnacled hat toward me. "Awrk?" he added.

"Fuck off," I said.

"Anne Bonny," another said. She spat flotsam at me.

"Mary Read." This one pointed a pistol at me and fired salt water.

"Skurve."

"Madwell."

"Dred."

Thirteen in all, they spoke to me like they were real. I laughed at them and tried to drown.

"Wake him up. He needs to drink water."

"You think he found a bottle?"

"No."

"We should throw him back in the water, maybe."

"Are you talking about me? I feel like shit, Heaven sucks." I spoke through a cottony mouth. Palm trees swayed above me.

"He speaks. Hello."

A woman my age stood over me and nudged me with her knee.

"Ugh. I'm still alive, aren't I?"

"Yep. I'm Anne. She's Mary." Another one stood beside her. They were tanned like popular girls who'd lain out all summer. They had legs and seemed happy. I disliked them.

"I jumped from a cruise ship. Dolphins took me here. I wish they hadn't. Wish I'd drowned."

"Fascinating," Mary said.

"Is he up?" A thin man came up and put his arms around both girls. I hated him instantly.

"Hi, I'm Jack."

"Fascinating," I said, and sat up. A bottle lay near me. I grabbed it and drank.

"That's not—" Jack said.

Rum burned my throat.

I looked at them and saw gray-blue pirates. The image flickered away. "Freebooting lunatics," I muttered, then wondered what freebooting meant.

Anne brought me a water bottle and I drank, but wouldn't let them take the rum. I stumbled to my feet with a bottle in each hand and saw hundreds of computer geeks hunched over computers wrapped up in clear plastic casings. Each geek was either too thin or fat, and had an obvious disregard toward basic hygiene. Cables lay bundled and interconnected across the sand. "Christ. I'm marooned with nerds? Thanks, God." I glared upward.

Mary, Anne, and Jack headed toward empty monitors and keyboards.

"Steady as she goes, mates," a man in a pink shirt yelled.

"Keep true! Tack hard! Apt get install Chaos! Then mutiny! Then freedom! Keep true!"

"Activate the mock-autonomous-network!"

"Activated!"

"Employ the water diversion! Launch vegan!"

People typed furiously. "You all suck brine," I said, angered by how vibrant they all seemed. I raised the bottle. I needed water, but it was the wrong hand and I took another swig of rum.

I swayed and almost fell onto the wooden planks of a ship deck see-sawing back and forth.

What?

I looked around and saw a pirate ship with a billowing Jolly Roger whipping off the ship's mast overhead. Around me a salty crew scrambled to stay upright as the ship tilted toward a huge wave. Six men put all their weight behind a cannon and pushed it to the ship's edge. They kicked wooden wedges behind the wheels, and then ran to the next cannon. A captain held a spyglass and stood with one foot on a wooden box, staring forward. As he lowered it I saw it was Jack.

I ran to him. "I don't understand…"

He snarled and thrust the spyglass into his pocket. He grabbed the helm and spun the wheel hard to the right.

I looked across the water and saw ships flying St. George's Cross.

England? "We're fighting England?"

Jack raised his weathered rifle. He fired toward the ships. He turned and said, "A sea battle is a hard death, child. Make your peace. Ready yourself for the end!"

We swooped down into another stomach-wrenching wave. To our left I spied another ship. She flew a ragged red flag. To our right lay another. Maybe this is death. Maybe this is me dying. I hoped, and then hoped it wasn't.

With the next wave I fell down hard onto the ship's splintery deck.

Except I didn't.

My knees hit hot sand.

"I'm hallucinating," I said. "I'm probably dying." No one even looked up from the computers. I stood and wandered among them as a sound like a thousand crabs scuttling over the sand ebbed and flowed as they typed away.

A woman yelled, "The autonomous network churns trouble up from the deep!"

"Does she slow? Does she bow under the weight?"

"She does, but slowly! We wait! We must wait to slip in the bold and slythy kraken, hold steady!"

"Yar, ye swashbuckling assholes," I said. The rum was making me talk funny. I tried to drink some water, but I got rum again by accident.

Yelling rose all around me and I stood on the pirate ship again. A massive English galleon sailed toward us. We were a rowboat in comparison. We were mosquitoes. Other galleons followed the ships to our left and right as they sped away.

Black cannon nubs pushed out from the lower decks of the English ship. A cannon boom hit the air, followed quickly by two more. Our ship rocked backwards. Clouds of smoke billowed up from below. One man laid limp and screaming on deck with stumps where his legs should be. Another man caught fire and jumped overboard.

Jack scowled and raised his rifle. He shot once more toward the galleon.

Boom. Wood sprayed up from the decks below.

Boom. A cannonball lodged into our mast. A groaning wooden scream filled the air.

Boom. Three more men dead.

Our ship began to sink. Men staggered forward and lit one of our two cannons. A black mass zoomed toward the galleon. A hit! Then another!

Yet still we sank. Still the galleon fired upon us without mercy. I ran to Jack. "What can I do?"

Nothing.

Because I stood on a beach, delusional and disoriented. "I'm dying!" I yelled. I raised the correct bottle this time and drank water.

A man swearing in Italian stormed toward the sea and threw his laptop into it. He yelled and cursed.

"Cloak the feed! Fire at will!" a woman said, her head looking up from her monitor for a moment, before hunching over again.

"She's slowing down! She's crippled!"

"Hold steady! Wait until she's three-quarters gone!"

More rum found its way to my lips. I would have sworn my hand never raised the bottle, even as the rum slid down my throat.

A wave crested the edge of the pirate ship and hit me. It pushed me off the deck and into the ocean. Among the waves were dozens of men yelling and drowning.

Boom! A cannonball punched another hole into our ship.

Boom! Our mast tottered over.

The galleon turned and left us to our watery death. Someone clutched my arm. It was just a kid, barely even a teenager. A wave crashed into us. When I resurfaced he was gone. With the next wave I didn't come up but breathed salt water into my lungs. My chest convulsed, struggling to get air. There was none. I sank down into water that grew darker with every yard. I hit bottom and died. Finally, I thought as the last of me floated away. Finally, it's over.

But no.

I fell forward onto the deck of a different pirate ship. A female captain stood along the ship's edge and watched sinking ships in the distance as we sped off, unseen. Tears ran down her face. We sailed around the edge of an island until we were out of sight, and she strode toward a huge trunk sitting on deck. She knelt and opened it. I walked forward and saw dozens of scrolls piled up inside. The ship circled the island. On the far side of it we turned into an inlet full of pirate ships. We sailed into the bay to the sound of yelling and clapping.

I awoke to water streaming over my face. I opened my mouth and drank. When I'd had enough, I pushed the flask aside. Mary helped me upright. She smiled and I saw her pirate—like a glowing ember—lodged within her. Beside her stood Anne and Jack, tired but unscathed.

Behind them computers lay tangled on the beach. I heard the sound of music and celebration coming from behind the palm trees.

"What happened?" I asked.

"A battle."

"We shut down the internet for a couple of hours via a dummy network. Freaked everyone out," Mary grinned. "Hell of a diversion."

"Before it fell, we hacked into some Cayman accounts, diverted funds, and then destroyed all records and backups. That was the hardest part, but the Moroccans and Chinese cracked it. We stole some islands," Anne said.

"What?"

"Seventy-four uninhabited islands." Jack grinned. "That's what our old friends wanted. That's what we want too. A home. More ships will be coming to join us."

"It will take them a while to figure out what we did. By then, we might even be ready for them," Mary said.

"I saw a sea battle."

Jack nodded. "'Twas fearsome and bloody. Would you like a drink?" He held up an almost empty bottle of rum.

I wasn't thirsty any more, but I took the bottle and drank. A piece of bone slid into my mouth. I hesitated, and then bit into it. Rope squeezed my neck as the landed lords looked on and applauded. I cursed them all with my last breath. Then the noose loosened, and I was reborn.

WE SLEEP ON A THOUSAND WAVES BENEATH THE STARS

By Brendan Connell

I.

W hite, hot sand strewn over with shells and then a great sweep of green; an island rich in vegetation, investigation revealing all sorts of tropical fruits, some of which the crew was familiar with, while others none of them had ever seen before—in the shape of stars, swords and crescents. Large, brightly plumed parrots squawked in the trees and small brown-furred monkeys leapt from branch to branch and chattered while, from the depths of huge ferns, the height of a man, came the pleasant scent of land—welcome indeed to those who had been six continual weeks aboard a ship after being thrown off course by a storm.

It seemed like an ideal place to gather in supplies. There was a fresh-water lagoon in which fish swam and octopuses clung to the rocks. Dozens of giant land tortoises sat on the beach. There were groves of coconut trees.

Some men were sent to gather fresh water, some bread fruit. Six tortoises had been slaughtered for their afternoon meal and men sent into the interior to see what hunting could be done, while La Motte, ship cook, a short, round, balding man with sensual lips and lively eyes, prepared two giant fires, one for his cauldron, the other his weighty cast-iron skillet.

After bleeding the turtles, removing the entrails and assiduously trimming away the fat, he braised their flesh and then set it to simmer with a little claret, bay leaves and various spices.

With sweat pouring down his face he stood, legs somewhat apart, stomach stuck forward, going about his art as if he had been in some famous Paris kitchen cooking for lords and ladies instead of on an island, he knew not where, using his skills to feed thieves and cut-throats.

Late in the afternoon a number of shots could be heard in the distance.

"It sounds like they are having some luck with the game," Lagoverde, first mate, a quinquagenarian, an Italian, a man with a long, thin jaw said.

La Motte: "It would be nice if they were to bring in an eater of ants or a few monkeys, for such a variety of cutlet would augment the meal nicely."

"For me, I am happy as the sun with a plate of simple seafood. And indeed, though I like flesh meat well enough, I am always happiest with haddocks, oyster pies or a plate of sweet periwinkles."

"Then you have chosen the correct career," the cook said, his words peppered with the vaguest hint of hauteur, "for in truth we have eaten little more than bream, cod and flour for the past fortnight."

"A sailor's life."

"One might as well call it the life of a madman. What I would not give to be able to press my lips against a white young lettuce every now and again!"

A figure could be seen making its way along the beach, towards the cook-site. Long strides. The sun to his back. His own shadow preceding him.

"Any luck, captain?"

"Indeed I have," the latter said, opening his sack. "I have captured a crabbe-criarde, which cries like a little cat, a hermit crab hosting a *Calliactis tricolor* and a few interesting echinoderms. The rocky shoals, at the far end of the beach, are rich with a diversity of life."

This individual, who was addressed as captain, and therefore we must assume was in a position adjudicative and determinative over others, merits a description. Extraordinarily tall and thin, his head was crowned by a thick, full-bottomed white wig, somewhat the worse for wear. His face, remarkably pale for someone who had spent a great deal of time sailing in tropical climates, was like the skull of a horse and his lips seemed to sit in a perpetual frown. He wore a collarless grey coat with deep cuffs and a long overcoat, both lined with grey, and black breeches, white stockings and shoes with large brass buckles. His name was Nikola Bruerovich.

The dish was just then beginning to let off a strong and pleasant aroma which stretched itself out on the air, journeyed to lagoon and jungle and tickled the nostrils of the crew and made those fellows agitate their legs in the direction of the little beach camp.

A mass of accent colours, blonde beards and long wispy black moustaches, bright red sashes and brown jack boots; semi-aniline faces embossed with carefree grimaces, some men with willow legs, some with spruce, others with legs of oak, strong, burly knuckled fellows able to stand their ground against hurricanes or men. There was Bull-Milo, a fellow of little intelligence but great strength, Amraphel, who wore a beard long and sharp as a pike, and Martini, a small Italian remarkably skilled with a blade; as well as a great diversity more, from the rough-finished to those with polished foreheads and sharp teeth.

Then, from out of the jungle, came the others, the hunting party, their faces eaten by grins, sabres waving in hands, muskets prodding five small beings. Hollering and laughing, these men walked forward with a group of natives between them—in palmetto skirts, long, oily hair brushed forward, so as to completely obscure their faces.

La Motte opened his eyes wide

The captain frowned.

The men gathered round in interest, laughter and jests.

"Let's bake them like apples!"

"No, we'll have La Motte fricassee them!"

"The girl looks tasty enough to eat raw!"

And then:

"They have something on their bellies it seems," one individual said. "A tattoo or scar."

He pressed his finger to an old man's stomach and then let out a cry, for the thing had opened up, like the mouth of a shark, showed two rows of jagged teeth, bit off the tip of the finger—a splash of orange and then the wounded pirate, frenzied, cutlassed the native and blood excited the desire for more blood, crewmen joining in to slaughter, exterminate those with the long, oily hair—sound of pistols, thrust of blades, till, in just minutes all but one lay wasted bleeding on the sand.

"Stop!" the captain cried. "You men who spend your lives searching for treasure—do you not see that what we have before us is a treasure in itself? I want this interesting specimen kept alive, for I believe it is worthy of study."

A small female sat quivering in the sand, in the midst of the corpses of her people.

II.

One might ask how it was that so many rough men were obedient to this rather decayed-looking gentleman. The answer was quite simple: he was both cruel and generous.

He never took a larger share of loot than his men—having the said loot divided equally amongst all. In the same way, he never ate better food than the rest. Yet he was exacting in his demands for discipline. The slightest breach of conduct would have him blow out the brains of the offender.

It must also be said that he did not lack bravery. For, during assaults, he did his part, coolly and methodically killing men as if he had been gathering specimens from a tide pool. He had never been known to laugh, smile, cry or raise his voice in anger. If he raised his voice at all, it was only to be heard. He seemed a man totally devoid of emotions.

He had been born in the Republic of Ragusa, brought up watching the ships in the harbour, the water splash against the rocky shore. As a young man he had studied at the University of Padua where he distinguished himself by writing a 4,970 Latin verse epic in dactylic hexameter on the lunar eclipse, a work of technical excellence, though dry in the extreme. He fought several duels and dabbled in invention, map-making and botany. Later, he had spent fourteen years sailing the known world, composing a work on tides which, when it was finished, was promptly condemned by the most Holy Roman Church for certain theories it set forth that were at odds with the idea of a single supreme creator and ruler of the universe.

Treated with sudden disdain by the higher ranks of society, met with silence by comrades in science, he swore off the world, procured a ship, gathered together a crew of desperate but for the most part intelligent men, and set out to make his fortune.

III.

Swimming amidst creeping ludwigia and undulated crypt, schools of dazzling fish gazed up at the jolly boat as it coasted from shore to ship and ship to shore, supplying; hold soon stocked with about fifty living land tortoises which could be kept alive and killed as needed, thus offering a steady supply of fresh meat. Also brought aboard were about four hundred coconuts, and numerous other fruits and a good supply of fresh water.

Then a fragrant breeze filled the sails of the *Sparrow*, a miraculous ship, a sloop, an incredibly fast vessel with pontoons of coconut-shell fibre attached to its sides, making it almost impossible for it to sink even during the most raging of storms; and it skimmed over the ocean; behind it, a group of fins following for many a league.

IV.

The captain was working on a tract entitled *A Catalogue of Sea Waters, Their Moods and Concomitants.*

"Come in," he said brusquely, not even lifting his head from the page he was vigorously covering with lines of fine handwriting.

The door opened and Lagoverde entered the small and crowded cabin; on one wall was attached a table of trigonometry next to a huge thermometer. Shelves were stuffed with books and manuscript pages and scientific apparatus were stored on every side, versorium nestling against circumferentor, a nonius in one corner, in another stood a dusty, neglected looking-glass.

"She has been cabined separately as you requested and God willing she will not lead the men to any kind of monstrous temptation."

"Anyone who attempts to violate her will be flogged to pudding."

"I'll let that be understood."

"And how is she behaving?"

"Well, she refuses to so much as touch her hammock, preferring instead to crouch in a corner on a pile of straw like a beast, her tongue hanging out over her stomach. She cries a great deal and spat out the cooked food offered her but became ravenous at the sight of raw tortoise entrails and seemed to relish a few fresh guavas that La Motte put before her."

"Have La Motte shave her head—and tell him to be quick about it, as I want to examine her cranium, which seems surprisingly healthy, this very evening."

V.

Later Captain Bruerovich, as he had said, went to examine the creature. With her head now shaven, her already large eyes appeared even larger. He was surprised by the delicacy of her skin; touched her face and noticed that it excited the action of her larynx; touched her cranium, took note of all the surface peculiarities, letting his long, thin fingers, nimble as wasps, travel from the ethmoid bone to the mandible, and then back to the sphenoid.

Around the lofty heights of his mind thoughts gathered, dispersed, gathered again, like drifting clouds. Infamy slaughtered by fame. The discovery caged, displayed throughout the capitals of Europe, astonishing princes and princes-elect, loosening their purse strings while making the women of court squeal like mice.

The captain spent the following days in assiduous study of the creature. The desk in his cabin was strewn with notes, measurements, diagrams.

"Nature, hereditary, has fitted her with a most unusual structure—and I must ask myself why."

Gauge her jaw, assess her limbs; try and determine, along Anaximanderrian lines, by what transmutation she had come into being; if there was any possibility of a common progenitor.

VI.

"A ship to larboard, Captain."

"What variety of ship?"

"A galleon."

"Nationality?"

"She's flying a Portuguese flag."

The captain finished the sentence he was writing, placed his grey goose-quill pen back in its holder, rose from his seat and made his way on deck.

"What do you think?" he asked Lagoverde.

"It is a large vessel."

"Indeed. And undoubtedly holds booty to match its size."

"But it is clearly a risky enterprise. There must be three men to every one of ours aboard her."

"True enough, but our men are restless. If we pursue the prize, they will fight hard, if we forgo it, they might turn morose."

"Yes, they are thirsty for blood."

"First we must cripple this oversized bastard," the captain said. And then to his chief gunner: "Jacques, cut away its masts."

The *Sparrow* was armed with nine bronze cannons, a few of these ornately decorated with scrolls and escutcheons. The gunners worked off a guidance table that the captain had written up, using chain-shot to take down the rigging of the ship, after which they fired carcasses, incendiary ammunition, in excess of forty rounds per gun until they were no longer safe to load.

It was then that they boarded; faced the odds of over two hundred to their seventy; the deck a veritable hell.

The captain calmly ran his cutlass through one man, exploded his pistol at another.

Fire danced on all sides to a chorus of screams and curses. Heads tumbled from shoulders, and limbs, in bursts of blood, went flying from trunks. Faces distended in horror, some men were thrown overboard to be swallowed by the waves, others butchered on the spot.

A Portuguese grimaced so that his gums could be seen. Bull-Milo, wielding a large axe, lopped off his left arm while, nearby, one of the crew of the *Sparrow* felt a projectile take off one of his ears—a far better fate than that of the first mate of the galleon who, moments later, had a bullet shatter his skull.

Captain Nikola Bruerovich nodded his head in approval, looked to his left, saw: Mademoiselle Savage standing before him, a huge knife in her hand, her arms flecked with blood.

Their eyes met for a moment. Then our hero turned and continued his methodical work of exterminating all resistance aboard the ship; after which, the deck having been made slippery with gore, the hold was inspected: good quantities of minted silver and cochineal, as well as other items of value.

That night, while the men were celebrating their victory and mourning the death of their shipmates—both functions requiring the playing at reverse Diogenes (barrel in stomach rather than stomach in barrel)—the captain stayed sequestered in his cabin. The next day, the crew were cheerful, singing and joking while they went about their tasks, for the voyage was now turning profitable, but the captain seemed downcast, his frown longer than usual, his manners more clipped. His soup that day he barely touched; of claret he took two cups.

VII.

Lagoverde was presented with a sight that surprised him. The looking glass, long neglected, was now hung, its surface polished, prominently on one wall where the table of trigonometry had once been. The captain himself had no time for talk, for he was busy—washing his wig!

The first mate scratched his long chin, made his way to the kitchen.

La Motte sat with a length of light-blue silk on his lap, a needle in hand.

"What are you doing?" the Italian asked.

"Making a set of female garments."

"Eh! And who, pray tell, are they for?"

"Well, the only femme on board obviously. Captain's orders. It seems her grass skirt has gone out of fashion."

Lagoverde went on deck.

"Who would have believed it," he murmured to himself, gazing out at the bloody sun as it descended beneath the waves.

VIII.

As bizarre as their romance might have seemed, it was fitting—for no mortal woman could have ever thawed the rigid ice of Bruerovich's heart—the task being reserved for something else—a specimen; a dark cave full of slime and spiders for the first time flooded with light. And a strange but true fact: the most violent passions are often between beings who share no common language.

The crew did not laugh or joke over the matter. For they knew well enough how lonely the life of a sailor was and there was a certain pathetic element in this high-seas romance which made them silent on the subject; their lips sealed by a mixture of awe and pity—maybe even fear.

And it is often difficult to say why one being is attracted to another and why it is that every man, at some point in his life, will fall in love. There was not a great outward change in the captain's behaviour. He was still as rigid as ever, his lips still as unsmiling, but behind the closed door of his cabin, those slender strips of flesh became tender.

It was during this period that, casting their fishing nets, the pirates pulled up from the sea a strange creature—a serpent with a head that closely resembled that of a human child. La Motte diced it into sections and served it, batter-fried, for lunch.

IX.

The weeks that followed were prosperous, full of butchery, fire and shrieks. The ship flew past cone-shaped islands, glided along the rippling scales of the sea, skimming over white horses and dyeing them red with foaming blood, the crew happily indulging in despicable behaviour. They attacked no less than seven ships—two Dutch, a Spanish, a French, two English and another Portuguese—divesting them of gold and silver, cochineal and indigo.

It seemed that the native girl had brought them good luck.

The captain had taught her to use pistols, had given her a brace of them, and these were stuffed into a sash of bright blue silk, which was wrapped below her mouth, around her thighs. She wore a pair of loose-fitting, brightly coloured trousers; a brocade vest, parrot-green in colour; and a tasselled hat, shaped like the roof of a pavilion.

And she, in these adventures, would always become excited, homicidal—a terror to those poor souls attacked—for to them it seemed truly as if they were being confronted by maniacs and monsters, a band come from hell.

She found a certain ecstasy in extreme violence. During one assault, she jumped on a man, straddled his neck and choked him to death with her thighs. On another occasion she was caught gnawing on a human foot, but this in no way disgusted the captain—possibly he even found it charming, as lovers often do the foibles of their beloved.

And on those days when the fighting was the most ferocious, the native girl's appetite for love was most keen and Bruerovich, trembling, pressed his lips to those hands, beneath the nails of which might have been found deposits of human flesh.

X.

Dark grey. Steady, light precipitation. She leaned against the gunwale, her eyes gazed off, dreamy, letting her body absorb the drizzle, which ran over her face, made her clothes cling tightly to her lithe form.

When it rained she was always like that, lost to the world, absorbed in nature; and the captain kept his distance, being to some degree awed; and later, glancing in her eyes, he thought he could make out faraway vistas, palm fronds, mysterious sun-drenched beaches on which beings swirled together in worship of the waves—an enigma his analytical mind refused to confront; for Mademoiselle Savage was an odd mixture of boldness and shyness, brutal enthusiasm and sadness. She could scratch and bite but also hug tenderly. She carried with her some primordial inscrutability, was a path which led back to those days of formless void; waters under heaven and boiling rock when the world was born.

"What do you make of her?" La Motte one day discreetly asked the first mate.

"She is an animal picked up from the islands."

"Which means?"

"Just that."

XI.

A dead calm. Evening. The captain stood on deck, gazing out at a purplish sunset, Lagoverde by his side.

"I think this will be my last voyage."

"Indeed!"

"Indeed."

"You are retiring then?"

"I have always thought Greece would be a nice place to go… to live peacefully, to study the marine life there while walking over the land once inhabited by Pythagoras and Sophocles.

It was at this point that their discourse was cut short by the approach of Martini.

"Pierre, the powder monkey, is ill," the latter said.

"It is probably simply a bilious complaint caused by some bad piece of fish La Motte served," was Bruerovich's comment.

"That is not the kind of sickness the boy has. He has a fever."

The captain and his first mate went to investigate, saw the boy lying in his hammock, face glistening with sweat. He was wracked with pain and coughed violently.

"How long have you been feeling ill?" the captain asked.

"I haven't been quite myself for the past few days," the patient murmured. "If you have something that would make me feel better…"

Nikola Bruerovich examined his body, saw the rash on his chest.

"It is typhus."

"This is bad," Lagoverde said.

"Yes, it is. I want the entire ship to be cleaned, from top to bottom—throw the bedding overboard, swab the cabins with vinegar. And, by no means, let any man near my cabin."

The next day the boy died and they wrapped his body in sheets and threw it overboard.

"It's never nice to throw a colleague to the fish," sharp-bearded Amraphel said, "but it does mean more grain for the rest of us."

XII.

The captain's orders were followed to the letter and the problem seemed to be under control, as, for three days there was no sign of the pest. But then, on the fourth, Bull-Milo was found unable to rise from his hammock and, eight hours later, died.

That same evening two more members of the crew came down with the sickness. The next day another two. The day after a full seven.

These men, who regularly faced death in the form of battle with smiles on their faces, trembled before this invisible, virulent enemy. Some stained their throats with rum. Others remembered prayers of their childhood. But strong and weak, drunk and sober alike were ravaged.

Men writhed in their hammocks; a few lay on deck, hallow eyes staring up at the blue sky. One, hallucinating, saw the ship enveloped in the flesh of a giant sea snail. Another, singing, said he was having a musical competition with demons.

While some recovered, others did not. Within a week a half-dozen crew members had been cast to the waves.

XIII.

On a certain morning Lagoverde knocked on the door of the captain's cabin.

"Do not come in," was heard from within.

A moment later the captain showed himself.

"She has got the pest," he said.

Lagoverde did not reply. There was nothing he could say and truly this world is as fleeting as a flash of lightning.

She became delirious and Bruerovich found it difficult to keep her in bed.

He tried, in that brief period of time, to squeeze some answers from nature, to unweave its very fibre. He frantically studied his books, consulted his mind, ground together powders; made the girl drink water infused with sulphur, smeared her body with tar diluted with spirits, filled the cabin with vapours and smoke.

Dozing off briefly, he imagined that thousands of hands were crawling towards him, pushing themselves against his lips, demanding their pressure; a frightful obscenity that transferred itself to inanimate objects when he awoke—glasses, table, grey goose-quill pen all begging him for his affection.

XIV.

Her breathing was very weak; her face appeared to be melting like a candle. Stomach exposed, the mouth thereon wore an awful grin. Her large eyes stared at the captain, the pupils endowed with a bronze immobility. Then she turned her head away.

He got up and left the cabin. His heels clicked against the boards; his steps steady. The few on deck went about their business in silence. The gentle splash of water against the hull.

A bubble.

A drop of dew.

He stood on the bridge of the ship and gazed out over the water—an endless meadow, a vast blue-green carpet. The ship floated on the lonely sea, in the distance a mass of dark clouds rested on the horizon and his lips were set firm.

XV.

When he re-entered his cabin, he was surprised to find that she was not beneath her bedding, but rather sat on the floor, completely naked, in an odd position; ankles locked behind neck; body covered by a thin, slimy film.

"You need to get back to bed," Bruerovich said, approaching.

The jaws on her stomach opened; she snapped at him, would not let him near her; and so he stood back, watched as she began to shiver violently, writhe; jaws now protruding from belly, stretching themselves forth; and eyes migrating.

Around her he noticed gobbets of flesh, toes, terminal members of the hand.

"What transformation is this!"

Gasping, she began to flop around the cabin; gills quivering, a deposit of sticky yellowish gelatine left on the floorboards in her wake.

The captain's right hand agitated, as if it had a volition of its own, wished to seek out a quill and take notes, but the convulsive situation before him made him see necessity and so he called in the aid of a few men and, together, they cast a net around her, dragged her on deck, a swirl of tempestuous movement.

"It wants water," Lagoverde said.

Captain Nikola Bruerovich was silent for a moment, and then gave the order, watched as the load was hoisted to the gunwale and, a moment later, with a splash, the object fell into the blue; a glistening flash and she was gone, lost in that expanse which might be called the largest of teardrops.

But there was no time to recite poems, no time to sing deep ballads of passion for freedom or dolorous life.

"Ship to port, Captain. A frigate."

"Flag?"

"English."

"How many are we?"

"Forty-seven."

The captain turned to Lagoverde. "Do you think we can take her?" he asked.

"I do not know, but I would not mind killing a few Englishmen."

"And you shall."

VOYAGE OF THE IGUANA

By Steve Aylett

In the course of researching my unpublished novel *Velvet Dogs* I heard tell of an elderly gentleman who had in his possession a collection of ancient ship's journals—first-hand records of the great days of sail—and resolved to seek him out and ask him if he would lend me some money. The hermit-like figure which greeted me in a Bristol attic some months later was nothing if not eccentric, as he sat in a corner stroking a dry fern.

"This is one of my few remaining pleasures," he explained in a whisper, and embarked upon such a rampant fit of coughing that I feared he would expire then and there; he soon recovered, however, and told me the details of his life until I could barely see. Bringing the conversation around to the subject of finance I established that he had in his possession a full eighty pounds, and offered to invest this sum in porkbelly futures.

One of the items he removed while kneeling to search through an old oak chest was a thick, leather-bound volume such as I had originally heard tell in connection with this slavering gentleman. Taking up and leafing through its autumnal pages, I immediately recognised its likely value. At my questioning its authenticity, however, the ancient man took sudden umbrage, producing an antiquated musket the size of a water buffalo. As I took my leave he was hollering that he was inflatable. Thus I inherited the text which is here entitled *Voyage of the Iguana*.

The log relates the events of a most undisciplined sea voyage. Captained by a Samuel Light Sebastian in 1808 for the East India Company, it was rarely mentioned with anything less than hollering ire and stabbing daggers.

As Captain of the *Iguana*, Sebastian's main occupation seems to be throwing empty bottles at passing Hammerheads, which he constantly asserts are "sneering" at him. His term is characterised by languid indifference and a startling ignorance of seamanship—he was frequently known to give the order "Bows full to stern," a manoeuvre which would entail sawing the ship into two equal halves and folding it into a sandwich.

Especially after reading the account, many questions remain unanswered. What was the ship's course? How could it make half the journey without ballast? What was so horrific about the native ritual performed on August 7th that it caused Sebastian and the First Mate to black out? And most intriguingly, where did Sebastian keep his log?—he seems never to be parted from it. Few clues are yielded by maritime records—Sebastian's name seems largely to have been struck out of history. On returning to England in March 1809 he was frantically demoted to "man without honour, abode, or employment" and it seems to have been a full two weeks before he was once again at sea, as Captain of a 54-gun store-ship which Lord Cochrane commandeered and deliberately blew up to surprise the enemy....

27th May. SSW. Sailed out of Bristol harbour with a fair wind. Introduced myself and First Mate Leggahorn to crew, who responded with mirth. One man stood peeing over rail throughout. Second Mate Forfang interrupted my speech by yelling an obscenity, at which crew erupted into laughter. Morale high.

28th May. SWW. High winds. Leggahorn lost his hat and seven men restrained him from leaping overboard to retrieve it. Remarked to young apprentice Batch that nothing excused such behaviour, at which point all eight men stumbled back and trampled us underfoot.

29th May. SSS. Heavy seas—Mr Byron continually turns his back on wheel and leans laughing at activities of crew as course deviates. Leggahorn and myself forced to separate Forfang and bosun fighting at entrance to saloon—Forfang hammered my head repeatedly against door as big sea came aboard and lifted Leggahorn and bosun on to the fore yard. Everyone swore like the devil. Mr Byron remarks that the incident will provide me with something to tell my grandchildren.

30th May. SSE. Fair sailing again—rain let up, no sea aboard, bosun died down and wind dropped. Forfang lifted me up by the leg and pushed me against the sterncastle, with a mighty yell. All's well.

31st May. SSW. Drenching thunderstorms, big sea aboard, funeral for bosun marred by returns of body. Mizzen-boom sail blown to ribbons. Went to question cook as to hull damage, but he had the gall to say it was not his concern. Spirits raised by Forfang, who is still celebrating yesterday's fair weather. Sent first mate aloft to look for funny clouds.

1st June. SWS. Ship snugged down, lower topsails, fore staysail, reefed fore coarse and spanker. Crew fighting on deck. Leggahorn told us at dinner an amusing story about man who was eaten by a panther. Giving bosun seven lashes for firing musket on deck but wind blew him overboard.

2nd June. NNE. Spoke to Forfang in my cabin about morale, but swinging lantern which struck head upset his mood and he pursued me about the table, until in a position to dash my head upon it, with access of loud laughter. Have determined to indulge in draughts tomorrow. Leggahorn seen hollering obscenities on the topgallant footropes.

3rd June. NNW. Trouble in galley due to lack of food. Stray barrel below burst and flooded passage with rum, at which crew fought to lie down, gurgling and yelling obscenities. Leggahorn and myself strolled deck in coats and seaboots, sat down to play draughts. Pieces vanished instantly on opening case. Struggle getting back to cabin through men in passage.

4th June. NNS. Ventured above with ship's dog, which flew overboard on being released for exercise. John Tunny tells me through blur of waves that it is a bad start to a voyage when one cannot tell where ship ends and sea begins. Agreed with a laugh, at which he took offence and waded away.

5th June. SSN. Shortage of meat and provisions which cannot be explained. Am in process of checking cargo books. New bosun—Piper. Forfang tripped on the cathead and flew into a rage, breaking his own leg.

6th June. SWE. Provisions underloaded. Gathered crew on deck to inform them but could not make myself heard above the thunder and waves. Forfang hurled heavy barrel at my countenance. Harker continually pees over rail.

7th June. WWN? Leggahorn taught crew hornpipe dance on deck—seven overboard. Spoke to Batch in cabin about his duties as apprentice, but he was knocked out by falling ceiling. News of provisions provoked Berringer to wail "That's it lads, we're done for—damned to hell one and all." Could not help but admire his attempts at diplomacy.

8th June. Strolled the deck today, supervised manning of crossjack braces. Parkins and others swore at me through wind and rain. Turtle blown aboard. Hit Leggahorn while laughing on starboard rail. Bad omen.

9th June. Am worried about ship's doctor, who on boarding ship at start of voyage, was suffering from typhoid. Had to retire straightway to rest and nursing by Mate, Leggahorn. Weather still stormy. Batch joined us for dinner—turtle. Flippers had been stolen by certain members of crew, who attached them to their ears and performed demonic ritual. Had those responsible scrub deck, but were washed overboard. Memorial service held, but was washed overboard. All now fastened below save for Harker, who is peeing over rail.

10th June. A glorious morning. Calm sea. Sail repairs going ahead well. Blue skies and fair sailing. Forfang in good spirits, despite broken leg. First mate singing on deck. Ten overboard.

11th June. Fair weather continues. Mr Byron sets his features and lashes himself to the wheel. About midday Forfang punched First Mate Leggahorn, who had been standing in good humour on the poop. Forfang unrepentant. John Tunny tried to heave him overboard, but Forfang knocked him out with lower brace. All's well.

12th June. Had the crew mending sails. Hold taking in water. Took Batch to rail and spoke of the sea. Showed him how to annoy the Hammerheads.

13th June. Spoke to Forfang about his dribbling, at which he took a fragment of plank and attempted to strike me, screaming and foaming as Leggahorn wrestled him out of cabin. Polished my chinaware.

14th June. Bosun devoured by second mate. Laughter.

15th June. Fair weather. Sails and Forfang bellying out. Position uncertain. Crew either working well, sleeping, or drowned. Exception is Harker, who seems never to cease peeing over rail.

16th June. Berringer calculates that following our present course and allowing for cross-currents our position will be "the death" of him. While shaving in clear air on deck, Forfang reminded me about the mizen topgallant bunt lines which were severely damaged in storm, and gaining an unsteady grip upon my leg, tried in fits and starts to pitch me over port rail. Making headway in steady wind. Leggahorn at hold ceiling supervising repairs.

17th June. Position still uncertain. Gathered all my charts and instruments together and bundled down to the cook with them, but he was of no aid whatsoever. Stood on forecastle, watching sunset. Perhaps I am becoming a broken man.

18th June. Leggahorn told amusing joke at dinner—pig and trampoline. Will repeat it to Lord Cochrane. Hurled bottles at Hammerheads and watched them becoming annoyed. Gave rat some bread.

19th June. Spoke to sailmaker at work on the poop, and was hit by flying mackerel. Sailmaker, looking up from his work at that moment, collapsed hollering with laughter. Had finally to be carried below and given a whiff of salts.

20th June. Found tiny terrapin on deck. Laughed and laughed. Have determined to nurse it back to health. New bosun—Landis—drowned in his own snot.

21st June. Assembled crew on deck and told them joke—pig and trampoline. One man shouted an obscenity but the others laughed. Repairs still underway.

22nd June. Albatross for dinner. Bad omen.

23rd June. Forfang forced my head through porthole and wrenched at it from other side, with able help from all hands. Cried out loudly for assistance, and Leggahorn appeared in high spirits, eating grapes one by one and attempting to lighten my mood with quips. Onset of darkness put an end to their exertions. All's well.

24th June. Heard more reports of Harker peeing over rail for long hours. Went up on deck and confronted him. He was peeing over rail. "Listen to me, man, all this peeing over the rail has got to stop," I told him. He merely looked a little pained and hurt—I went away feeling somewhat ashamed. Cast a glance back and found he was peeing over rail. Suppose he has designs on the Captaincy.

25th June. Alarmed by the change in Batch, the apprentice, who has taken to standing unrobed in entrances. Unresponsive to my offer of an orange, or indeed to anything. Confronted Berringer on deck and suggested that we consult the charts together, to which he replied that I should go below and consult "the devil." Forfang turned to me today and yelled piercingly. Appointed new bosun—Parkins—who on hearing news jumped overboard.

26th June. First Mate Leggahorn informs me that crew have taken to eating their trousers. Told him joke about snail and theatre ticket. Laughter.

27th June. Hearing violent shaking of canvas, went forward to see cause. Only Batch prodding it with oar. Crew in low spirits. Attempted jollity by hurling starfish in artful manner, but hit Forfang in face.

28th June. Leggahorn gave swimming lesson off forecastle to Tobias, burly cargo loader, who was taken up by waves and slammed insensible against our bows.

29th June. Went below to visit doctor, who gripped my arm and gasped something about "damnation."

30th June. Ship adrift on still water—no wind at all. New bosun—White. Much perturbation caused by Batch standing at rails and grieving that he saw a rhino in the water, and called for hours that crew go to its aid, but none else aboard saw such a hapless beast. Leggahorn and myself questioned cook as to likelihood, but he seemed unable to answer.

1st July. Watched the sneering Hammerheads. Mr Byron unlashed himself from wheel and fell to deck with groan. Leggahorn and myself sat on the quarterdeck, sketching dogs from memory. Batch stood amidships and upended rum-barrel on head, standing in silence thereof a full hour. John Conk mutters about sausages.

2nd July. Bosun yelled "Green fields—baloo…!" and leapt from the foremast. Memorial service disrupted by Forfang discharging musket at surfacing pilchard.

3rd July. Nobody remembers what we are carrying, and I must confess our destination eludes me. Batch says it may have been coconuts. Harker pees over rail. Leggahorn says if we cannot remember it it cannot be important. John Tunny grasps me by the arm and moves his lips without a sound.

4th July. Had to belay Forfang's order that crew eat their own legs, though crew clearly dismayed at sudden change of plan. Still no wind. Rats uneasy.

5th July. Still no wind. John Conk entertains crew by kicking his own head. Leggahorn makes a cloth effigy of his mother. I stay below, practising mime.

6th July. Investigated hold with lamp. Found dry pickle on shelf. And book filled with pictures of swans. Several upright beams—probably part of ship. Three empty barrels—one so covered in moss that I have installed it in my cabin as a comfortable chair. Leggahorn offered to organise what he termed a "snot party" in the hold, but I did not question him further.

7th July. Wind picked up. Leggahorn knocked unconscious falling from hammock. Hazlitt fired musket at surfacing blowfish—target exploded with great velocity, blinding him in one eye. New bosun—Fennel—constantly rounds on imaginary attackers and screams of a "conspiracy." Crew stare at me through rigging. Rat overboard rescued by Mr Byron.

8th July. Heavy seas. Confronted Berringer on deck and commended him for his skill as a mariner—a remark which provoked him to spit into the wind and yell inaudibly through the crash of the waves, holding up a jellyfish and tearing it in half and jabbing a finger at my chest. Told him to keep up the good work, and went to supervise manning of braces.

9th July. After brief survey it seems nobody remembers name of ship. Searched cabin books unsuccessfully for reference. Batch says it may have been *Coconuts*. Big sea aboard. Nobody on deck save for Harker peeing over rail. Ventured above in coats and seaboots, confronted him at rail. Bellowed over the storm that he should go below. He replied that the men would not approve of his peeing down there. I suggested with a mighty yell that he might cease peeing, but his expression as he turned to me was disconcertingly blank.

10th July. Heavy seas. Lowered Forfang over side to read name of ship. Hauled up claiming to have seen a bison. Three men overboard. Forfang informs us with a gasp of exhaustion that he was never taught to read.

11th July. Damage done to navigational equipment by Leggahorn with sledgehammer during storm. Some charts soaked in cabin spillage, others eaten for dinner by Leggahorn, second mate and myself. Story about broken fruit—how we roared!

12th July. Bosun began rounding on himself and careering across the quarterdeck, punching his own nose. Leggahorn told him to simmer down but he started up again in the afternoon, juddering amidships and pitching over rail. Memorial service disrupted when Forfang hollered from the ranks that the hull was covered in edible crustacea and all hands leapt overboard.

13th July. Fair weather today. Interrupted Berringer as he was hauling on main braces. Halting his oaths in mid-volley he turned to me and spat in recognition. Asked him how long he had been a mariner, to which he replied twenty-five "bloodthirsty" years, and added "in God's name" that he would not be here today were it not for the charity of my "black and empty heart." I thanked him and he struck my countenance, at which crew's spirits were revived and they struck up a shanty, dancing lustily on deck. Twenty overboard.

14th July. Sentenced Batch to fifty lashes for tugging on lantern. Piped all hands amidships to witness punishment, but were washed overboard. Forfang and I caught in the mizen braces, where waves soon rendered us senseless. Leggahorn remained below, smoking my pipe and reading Smollett.

15th July. Hazlitt fired harpoon at surfacing anchovy—complains that loss of eye affects his aim. Became offended at my suggestion that he choose a larger target. I stayed in cabin for the rest of day, trying to remember my name.

16th July. Issued pay today, with lukewarm response from crew—many looked blankly at money without recognition, and some, after brief examination, swallowed it down. Bad omen.

17th July. Having a fair wind, set our foresail and ran aground with a sound which Leggahorn compared to "the shout of a moose"—indeed he blocked the passageway for several moments laughing uproariously as I tried to go above. Found that most of crew on deck were similarly occupied, bent double and hollering with mirth despite damage to vessel. Black outcrop towered over sails and big sea spumed out of the breakers. Harker yelled while peeing over rail that the only individual capable of mending that kind of damage was the god of hellfire. Leggahorn put a comforting hand on my shoulder and was washed overboard. Consulted cook, who held up biscuit and ranted, pointing at it and himself with loud assertions. Taking on water—crew disheartened at having to sleep in rigging.

18th July. Myself, Leggahorn and John Tunny entered cargo hold and rowed across in barrels to inspect hull damage. Leggahorn held lantern under visage and contorted his countenance. Informed him of the graveness of our careers. Laughter.

Outcrop intruded through gash in hull—John Tunny suggested we keep it for ballast. He and Mr Byron created powder keg ignited with muskets, setting sails alight and ship adrift. Bows full to stern. Spider in cabin!

19th July. Navigating shores of this dark isle hindered by list of vessel to starboard. Concerned for crew, who are so long at sea that they seem unaware of land's significance. Hazlitt voiced the uncertain opinion that it was some sort of pudding. Mr Byron states openly that he would like to have the wheel "covered in wool." Weather calm and warm. Gave Leggahorn fifty lashes for molesting figurehead.

20th July. Came upon palmy bay and resolved to go ashore. Commanded Mr Byron to let go the anchor, but he remained unmoved. Took the efforts of eight men to wrestle it from him, provoking his tears. Told him to get a grip on himself. Left him aboard with Harker. Rowing out, saw that ship was called *The Iguana.* Crew disconcerted. On landing, crew ignored my instructions on unloading of provisions and ran hollering into the jungle. I camp alone this night under tree. Used lamp to signal ship that all is well.

21st July. Crew came bellowing out of the jungle covered in mud. Leggahorn reported that he had discovered something of importance, then showed me his belly and ran away. Hazlitt walked laughing down the beach, arms akimbo and a melon balanced on his head. John Conk passed by, kneeing himself in the groin. Forfang beat the life out of me with an oar and told of a crocodile encountered in jungle. Spoke alarmingly of his attempts to "embrace" it, an enterprise thwarted by the depths of an interceding stream. Hazlitt repeatedly fired musket at sand and broke into hysterical laughter. Leggahorn told him to speak his mind, then showed him his belly and ran away. Forfang missing in jungle. Crew buried me and fell into drunken stupor.

22nd July. Crew amused themselves with shooting at coconuts into which were carved my own features. Excused myself and went for a brisk swim.

23rd July. Savages attacked as I attempted to entertain crew with impersonation of hen—took us prisoner and broke our spirit by pouring rum into the sea. Leggahorn screams incessantly. John Conk shakes like a patient of Bedlam. Ordered Berringer to communicate our friendly regards to the savages, at which he grasped the arm of one and began to sob openly. Hazlitt cheerily remarks upon our good fortune at not being washed into sea when we were vomiting earlier.

24th July. Savages tied us down and clubbed what Berringer translated as "the living bloody daylights" out of us with branches. Batch tells us about Moses and then rouses indignation by breaking into laughter. Berringer has identified our location as "the devil's own continent," and indeed there are countless snakes.

25th July. Savages clubbed us again, wearing colourful masks today and pausing only briefly to answer my enquiries. Berringer said that their masks were "Gali-masks" and that they referred to the snakes as "Bo-Mambas," which are apparently capable of "sucking the ruddy life out of the lot of us." Have determined to take on the responsibility of Batch's education—informed me today that he had forgotten the meaning of the word "happiness."

26th July. Savages clubbed us again today. I advised Berringer to comb his beard. His snarled, spitting response was inaudible above the screaming of his crewmates.

27th July. Savages stated today while clubbing us that it was their intention to "bake" us and dine "laughing" upon our scorched frames. Leggahorn stares at me. Morale low.

28th July. Expended arduous thought on how to deal with savages. Leggahorn suggests I promote them to bosun. Conferred with cook, who responded with loud access of sobbing. Savages count our limbs and draw calculations in sand, chattering with easy laughter and rupturing tree-trunks with their bare hands.

29th July. Savages scattered by crocodile which came thrashing out of the jungle and up to Berringer, biting his arm and lying beside us with a leer. Our screams rose immediately in pitch but this seemed only to increase its amusement. For-fang appeared and we begged him to loose our bonds, which he accomplished by firing among us with a musket. John Conk fainted. The rest of us screamed with such abandon that the savages ran to our aid, scattering again under Forfang's fire. Untied, a relieved Leggahorn thanked Forfang with a gasp of exhaustion and knocked him senseless with a rock.

30th July. Surveyed ship with spyglass. Saw Harker, peeing over rail. Signalled with musket that all is well. Mr Byron fired back, wounding Hazlitt and sending crew hollering into jungle. Forfang takes crocodile on lead during exploration. Weary round-robin naming of reptile, during which I vote heartily for Jonathan—crew spat into fire and agreed on "Darly." John Tunny added with a sneer that it was probably just some animal "made of leather." It is good to see them taking an interest.

31st July. Instructed several of crew as to difference between ferns and coconuts, with orders to load the ship with coconuts and freshwater. Myself, Leggahorn and others penetrated deep into the jungle, exploring the area where Forfang "had his frenzy," Hazlitt "carved a chimp" and Leggahorn apparently "talked for hours about steam." Soon, however, we were in unexplored territory and John Conk began whining and repeatedly blowing his nose. Discovered many temples dedicated to the worship of snakes, gazelle and other insects. Our guide, a savage whom Ber-ringer refers to as "Death," told us that many rituals took place here, including one during which a toad was pulverised by a heavy stone mallet, sacrificed to the infernal fury of the god Rakata, and then examined. Crew prayed before a few stone images and left earrings, trousers and such as tribute. Returned to find ship filled with ferns. Shall remain another day.

1st August. Gathered coconuts and spoke of our adventures. Berringer joked that he was a wanted man and showed us a dagger, claiming that it was "the very one." Batch surprised us all by strangling a trout. Forfang tried to ride on Darly's back but kept dismounting in a hurry. Leggahorn and I exchanged jokes about ash—how we roared!

2nd August. Crew gathered coconuts and taught Death a hornpipe dance. Results were so unnerving that everyone begged his assurance that he would not repeat it. Berringer gripped my arm and brandished a fistful of seaweed at me with sundry assertions. Told him to "simmer down." Consulted cook as to sailing conditions, at which he retreated deep into jungle. Dawson entertained us with a song about bats. John Conk kept time by clubbing his own head. Hazlitt began to rant and drowned his accordion. All's well.

3rd August. Gave John Tunny fifty lashes for raping a dove. Leggahorn said he was tired of supervising loading of coconuts and ran around camp showing everyone his belly. Forfang remarked rampantly upon my neglect in failing to converse with crocodile, and stood over me watching my initial efforts. Having knelt and bid the beast Good-day I could not establish as to whether it was well and Forfang kicked me away with a roar. Berringer told us of his time at Clerkenwell. Laughter.

4th August. Leggahorn, Hazlitt and myself went to waterfall in jungle. Hazlitt claimed a carp was smiling at him. Gathered a few coconuts. In our absence Forfang promoted Amberley to bosun and maimed him with a marlin's nose. Funeral service disrupted when Death broke from the ranks and embarked upon a hornpipe dance.

5th August. Fogg approached me with a belt. I departed to a sandbank where crew were burning flags. Hazlitt threw in a crab which exploded with such a deafening report that the savages ran to our aid, careering back into the jungle under a volley of muskets. Crew hollered a shanty, each verse of which ended "Kill the Captain for his trousers." John Conk kept time by stabbing himself repeatedly in the back and Death, though unsure at first, soon picked up a few words. All's well.

6th August. Cook came juddering out of the jungle yelling that every animal in the world was after him—I was just telling him to have a shave when a bleak-featured panther peered through the leaves and proceeded to pounce amid the crew, who awoke and began discharging muskets at each other, tearing their trousers from the mouths of tigers and bellowing obscenities—I know not fully the number of beasts which pursued us from the beach but a dozen cats of the sneering variety swam alongside our landing-boat, from which we hurled coconuts and volleys of inventive abuse. Crew boarded ship and stumbled hollering amid coconuts, punching each other and pitching overboard. Told Harker that all was well and that we were underway. Peeing over rail, he relayed the order to Mr Byron, who unlashed himself from the wheel and collapsed with groan into coconuts. Lion conveyed aboard clasped to anchor—bit Hazlitt on the arm and stumbled amid coconuts as sails bellied out and we moved off, low in water and overrun with deadly jungle cats. Barricaded door of cabin with coconuts and settled down to pipe and Smollett. Crew say goodnight to one-another and fall asleep lashed to rigging.

7th August. We are safely escaped from the island and no man has suffered disease, save for ship's doctor, who as a result of venturing on deck has contracted malaria. Cook still a little feverish this morning but when I sat aside his bunk and enquired as to our coordinates he suddenly revived, strangling empty air and shrieking with laughter. Gave him a coconut and told him to rest. Forfang wrestles lions on deck. John Conk apparently complains that Darly is lashed to rigging too close to him, and asks to be moved. Crew jeer. Leggahorn and myself have lunch with Death, who tries to describe native ritual and resorts to demonstration, causing Leggahorn and I to black out. Leopard in the bulkhead.

8th August. Three lions trapped in saloon—tempted in by barrel of coconut milk. Berringer locked door laughing and swallowed key, halting in mid-holler and gasping for medical assistance. Leggahorn carried doctor on deck and all hands leapt overboard.

9th August. At dinner Leggahorn made as though to expound a theory as to where we are, and breaking into laughter concluded "At sea." Just then Berringer entered and, guessing at what had been discussed, drove Leggahorn's head thirty times against the table, leaving him wild-haired and unresponsive. Saw Darly, whom I still secretly address as Jonathan, dancing today.

10th August. Forfang wrestled two lions and a leopard into landing-boat, setting them adrift. John Tunny remarked indignantly that they weren't even rowing. Told him to simmer down. Crew unlash themselves from rigging and climb down with easy laughter and conversation. I slap Forfang on the back and awake on the wheel box. All's well.

11th August. Heat very strong today. Leggahorn resourceful in organising network of gangplanks over coconuts on deck. Crew burn a few flags. Forfang gave Darly a kick in the belly for snagging his trousers. Darly made gurgling sounds in throat and thrashed his tail, knocking over buckets. He's not all there, if you seek my opinion.

12th August. Hot sun. Sea calm. Batch teaches Death to foam at the mouth. Death quickly becoming one of the crew. I walk on deck, laughing about coconuts. Crew glare at me, unmoved. I remark aloud that we shall not lack for food, and go swiftly below as Berringer stands.

13th August. Hot again—no wind. Ship low in still water. Threw a few coconuts at the Hammerheads. Death joined me at rail demonstrating new skill—commended him and spoke of the sea. Showed him the sneering Hammerheads. Crew hack out strips of canvas and rig up hammocks on deck. Some make a man out of coconut shells, naming it Old Shaky. I go below and look at pictures of greyhounds.

14th August. Still no wind. Crew awoke complaining of bad dreams and visitations from the dead. I went before crew with the conviction that those who are dead remain so. John Tunny belligerently asserted that he possessed the ruddiest bum on the high seas—I retreated with the repeated assurance that I believed him.

15th August. Still no wind. Mr Byron lashed himself to wheel hollering "It's a typhoon lads—biggest I've ever seen," until Forfang knocked him senseless. Went and thanked him on behalf of the men and awoke near the cathead. John Conk struck up a shanty about bloody murder, keeping time by clubbing himself over the head with an oar. Batch confers aloud with his grandfather. I go below and thoughtfully devour coconuts.

16th August. No wind. Spoke to Fogg at rail, commending him for his steady service. He did not regard me but whispered urgently for silence so that he could "hear the actors speaking." I looked out to sea, but could perceive nothing but green fields. Advised him to go below and rest but he pushed me aside yelling that he had paid for this balcony and "on t'balcony I'll stay!"

17th August. Berringer entered cabin with cutlass today and made remarks. Told him I would give them consideration, at which he left hollering with laughter. I consult with my mother and she tells me to "simmer down."

18th August. I stroll on deck, ducking under hammocks. Leggahorn reports a "large, angry face" off the starboard bow and I respond with hilarity. Batch grows a mushroom in his hat. I roll up a chart and, striding, shout through it from the sterncastle that coconuts are the stuff of life. Crew strike up a shanty and dance on deck, pointing in amazement at empty air. I ascend to crow's nest and set light to my trousers, dropping them into sea like burning bird. New bosun—Old Shaky. Forfang and Death ensnare a magistrate. I go below, laughing.

19th August. Leggahorn and I attempt to sit Darly at table but he writhes off and away. Finally achieved by tying him in chair with length of cable about belly. Seated facing away from cabin door, turned to leer at John Conk who entered heartily and fainted. Laughter.

20th August. Carved miniature pelican from coconut today. Spoke to Harker as he was peeing over rail—told me it was "a voyage and a half, this one" and laughed himself scarlet. Leggahorn and I spend the afternoon hallucinating. Sun sets through tattered sails as Berringer shoots a gull. All's well.

21st August. Leggahorn and I hallucinate all morning, and then take Death aside to teach him rules of pontoon. Crew gather round, placing bets, but to everyone's alarm Death wins and begins dancing his joy—eight men fall unconscious and two leap overboard. Four strong men tie him to mast and forbid him to participate in any such game. He seems confused though eager to comply.

22nd August. Watched basking sharks at rail. Remarked to Mr Byron that it were good to spend one's life doing nought but drifting around with one's mouth agape, to which he agreed and added that he would do the same were he in my position. In the afternoon, ship overrun with pirates who fastened crew below at sabre-point and set fire to Old Shaky. Complimented the Captain on his colour-ful garments. Captain said his name was Murder and, inspecting with a frown the deck arrangement of planks and coconuts, asked me mine. I could not recall it and, gasping with laughter, told him so, at which he ceased his inspection and regarded me with raised eyebrows. I am to spend this night lashed to the flying jib, which Captain Murder says might refresh my memory.

23rd August. Strode the deck with Captain Murder. Offered him a coconut, which he knocked to the deck with the others. Told him I run a tight ship, at which he roared with laughter and said he admired a man with a sense of humour, and that he intended to take my ship and kill myself and the crew. Became indignant at my flushed hilarity. Murder's mate came slamming up through the hatch snarl-ing "Calenture, Captain—sunstroke—savage foamin' at the gob" and offered his opinion that "the ship's cursed sir—all barkin' mad as the Ides o' March—coconuts everywhere." At that another dog of fortune burst out of the aft hatch bellowing "Crocodile eatin' soup at the Captain's table." Captain swore that he would find a decent meal aboard if it killed him. Hacked his way into saloon and was eaten by three lions. I climb rigging and watch pirates pursued overboard by lions and vessel uncoupling in alarm, moving off with man-eaters roaring on deck. I eat coconuts and watch their retreat, laughing.

24th August. Crew refuse to come above, hollering that all manner of misery occurs on deck. Leggahorn and myself attempted to negotiate but reasoning marred by sudden appearance on deck of Forfang, who fired musket into darkness—their response was one of screams and abuse. With uncommon bravery, Leggahorn prods Forfang's arm and leaps overboard. Cook has locked himself in galley shouting about "persecution" and smashing his equipment. Darly looked at me today, with his big eye.

25th August. Land sighted—crew erupt above punching each other senseless and straining at the rail. All voiced aloud their notions—"Cadiz! Tobago! Benidorm! The Cape! Purgatory!"—as town and port became visible. Mr Byron lashed himself to wheel and bade the world farewell. John Tunny became frantic and wondered aloud if we should hoist a flag. Nobody could remember. Drifted near to harbour and set off hollering in landing boats. At wall crew pushed past me as I stood on steps speaking of courtesy and caution, and dashed bellowing into town. Foreigner asked me if I was English—embraced me—asked me into tavern. Told me I was in Havana, at which I took up a brace of pistols and threatened every man present. Backed out blasting away with both hands and bumped into old friend, Burdett, who greeted me with delight and invited me into tavern. Occupants shrieked and ran as I re-entered, and Burdett poured wine and told me of recent events—treaty with Spain, no more killing of Spaniards for us and so on. Told him of damage to ship, eating of charts, arrival of Darly, Death, Old Shaky and my mother, and of many other events which had occurred during the voyage, at which he was aghast. I said that stranger things happen at sea, to which he replied with uncommon emphasis that this was not the case. Forfang entered with Darly on chain and I shouted goodbye to Burdett as he left. Forfang has left me Darly to care for and I am to attempt slumber at an inn this night.

26th August. Took Darly for skitter through town this morning—looked for crew. Saw many citizens who turned and ran. Saw Harker at harbour wall, peeing over rail. Passing ladies disturbed at view. I went and spoke with him, suggesting he attend to his toilet elsewhere. "I would," he laughed, "if I 'ad one!" Continued to pee over rail, and soon seemed unaware of my presence. Entered rowdy tavern. Chained Darly to banister. Met woman who threw herself onto my lap from other side of the room. On the way upstairs thought I saw Berringer's arm in crowd, but as I drew near it punched me senseless. This night I am indisposed in house filled with draperies.

27th August. Scarlet Bella and myself walk Darly through town—look for crew. Bella remarks on man peeing over rail. Laughter. Surprised to see Captain Murder's mate with arm in sling—became enraged when I asked what had happened. Scarlet Bella punched him in the nose and we moved on. Taught Darly to stagger short distance on hind legs—how we roared!

28th August. Spent the day in bed, writing, carving dogs from driftwood and singing dirges. Received a visit from Murder's mate, who made a remark and forced a scrap of paper into my hand, leaving with a slam. Unwrapped it but none the wiser—message obscured by great spot of spilt ink. Folded paper into tiny boat which sank in basin.

29th August. Walked out with Scarlet Bella—witnessed Harker being placed under arrest. Interceded on his behalf and was taken to fort in chains. Cuban officer circled me and became bellicose—criticised my ears, asked me my name. Explained to him that I could not recall this information. Slammed his fist on desk and prodded rampantly at statement, demanding a signature. Told him to find a man called Burdett who would probably know my name. Officer said he had no time to waste and told me to sign with a cross. This I did, scribbling above it a rudimentary order promoting him to bosun. As he took it wall exploded with French cannonball and buried him in rubble. I search dungeon, shooting guards and flicking spiders from my apparel. Find Harker and rest of crew, who tell me they have been arrested for witchcraft. Escape to woodland, where by light of campfire Death entertains us with impression of gasping mackerel.

30th August. Hazlitt says we should go to the harbour dressed as dogs. Rest of crew disagree, claiming that beagles would be more appropriate. Death asks "What are beagles" and after startled thought, crew decline to reply. Berringer goes out to kill a bear but returns with some weeds which John Tunny adds to a stew. After eating, everyone blacks out and are finally awoken only by heavy thunderstorm. Mr Byron holds wet finger to wind and nods with a smile. John Conk begins shrieking.

31st August. We wander aboardship at four in morning. Berringer grips me by the arm and claims through clenched teeth that he is "exhausted." John Conk has gone bananas and believes the world is run by a bear playing the trumpet. Sea stormy. At noon three ships appear in pursuit, bringing down our crossjack with cannon fire. I tell Berringer to change his shirt. He comes at me with axe but Leggahorn intercedes, punching my face. Fire amidships. I rush to consult with cook but he is chopping onions. We take another hit and ship water. New bosun—Glasby. Forfang attempts to wrap me in burning canvas. I tell Harker that all is well. Crew celebrate in final moments and fire Glasby from cannon, taking out mainsail of leading ship. Leggahorn remarks amid renewed jubilation that *The Iguana* has no cannons aboard, and that we must be aboard someone else's ship. Crew cease cheering. Forfang makes a remark and fires cannon, sinking *Iguana* with all hands. Crew begin fighting on deck, vaulting over fallen masts and choking each other against the rails. Big seas aboard. I announce my plans to marry. Mr Byron leans back on wheel and chuckles at the progress of his career. John Conk staggers out of the spray holding a fern. We founder on reef and leap into the tempest. Bad omen.

1st September. Spent morning on beach chatting with crew who sit sobbing among rockpools. Announced that it seemed voyage was at an end, that they had performed admirably and I would welcome the chance to sail with them again. Berringer took his hands from his face and, after a pause, lunged at me with animal yell. A flushed Forfang interceded brandishing oar and I awoke on empty beach. Spent a few hours wandering beach looking for driftwood and colourful shells. Found urchin with black eyes. Wear it on my head in rain and start back to England, where I am to present my report.

PIRATES OF THE SUARA SEA

by David Freer & Eric Flint

The ship was on fire.

I ran down to the aft-deck, where, surprise, surprise, a bunch of the Altekar crew were toasting spiky mauve crustaceans on long forks, over a fire made of ripped up deck-planks. On top of other deck-planks.

If you think that sounds unbelievably daft, then you don't know Altekar. Sometimes I wished that I didn't.

"What the hell do you think you're doing!" I shouted, flinging a bucket of water which they had standing next to them at the fire.

"Cooking Perga, Skipper," said Skeer, the bosun, cheerfully. "The cook doesn't like the smell in his galley."

I could tell why.

It stank. Like my being here, in the middle of the Suara Sea on an old scow, a hundred light years—and twenty years too late—from where I wanted to be. "You could have burned the whole ship, you idiots."

"Aw, Skip," said Skeer, waving a taloned flipper at me, "There are lots more deck-planks. Maybe even… five."

Altekar don't count beyond four. Maybe they could if they wanted to, but they don't. And, being amphibians they were less worried about burning the ship under them than I was. They're good in a fight, good for getting drunk with, and good for collecting Marquat pods from the seaweed clumps. Like me, they're not much good for anything else—which is rather why we were all here. Unlike me they never had had much need for numbers. An Altekar has an inbuilt sense of direction and location. I needed a GPS, and that meant numbers. Other than that, I tried to ignore figures too.

Then we heard a yell from the masthead lookout. "Fast boat, Cap'n. Fast boat comin' fast."

Ten out of ten for accuracy and minus three hundred for information… but I didn't need a lot. Out in the endless seaweed drifts of the Suara there were only two kinds of vessels: sailboats working Marquat and those that preyed on the sailboats. Back on Earth when I was a kid playing on a sixteen-foot Hobie off Sydney, and FTL was hot news, there had been the assumption that once the galaxy was our oyster, it would be an oyster like a very large Earth: technologically advanced, and well-ordered.

About the only thing I liked about the galaxy was that it was neither. It was big—far too big for narrow imagining—it was chaotic, and it was technologically speaking as varied as bouillabaisse. And interstellar transport was not cheap. Hence, when harvesting the Marquat pods, for which there was an insatiable demand back on the core-worlds, from the hundreds of thousands of square miles of Altekar's shallow seas, you could use locally made boats or go broke.

Unless, of course, you harvested Marquat pod boats instead of Marquat pods. Then importing a jet-drive, and the fuel for it, could pay for itself. Also the pirates cut out the middleman—the Reyno Corporation buyers in Port Carson. ReynoCo got rich, and the pirates kept the Marquat supply available during our attempts at collective action for a better deal. Piracy had been getting worse over the last few years. Neither Reyno nor the Planetary Authority seemed interested in doing much about it. So it was every ship's crew for itself, and devil take the hindmost. "Prepare for action!" I yelled. There was no need to do so. The Altekar crew were scattering to their stations and tasks. Bales were being strung and jettisoned, and our feeble armory run out: two locally made bronze cannon. I sprinted up to the wheelhouse and threw the wheel hard over, setting the sails belling with the cracking and creaking of booms, as we turned to run directly with the wind.

I looked at the GPS unit. Memorised the figures. Tossed it down to Skeer... Who hooked it up to the last bale of jetsam on the rope, and tossed it overboard.

On the fore-deck, boarding axes and the particularly nasty snake-edged blades the Altekar fancied were readied. Fat lot of good those would be against the pirates' beam-cannon, fléchette rifles and pistols. Hand-to-hand combat the pirates would avoid. They would lie off, demast the ship, rake the decks, and gas grenade the holds, until the Altekar were dead or jumped overboard.

Sure enough, the two sleek jetboats came yowling up on the starboard side, firing at their maximum range. The water boiled ahead of our bow, and, damn them, they punched a hole through the mainsail.

Our cannon boomed on the down-roll. Darko, mister mate and chief gunner both, was good. The ball missed the lead vessel by less than ten yards, showering the jetboat and its crew in warm Suara-water and seaweed, wreathing our deck in maroon Lenka smoke. Lenka, the propellant, was a kind of pollen that would even burn underwater—but it just was lousy at tossing cannonballs. It burned too hot to use twice in a row. There was no point in reloading, since the stuff would melt steel, let alone local bronze.

As the jetboats fired again, I swung the wheel hard the other way, luffing the sail. Beam-cannon ripped into the bottom edge of the mainsail, the uproll effectively protecting the crew. The pirates would not fire through the wooden hull. The last thing they wanted was for the ship to be sunk or the cargo to be damaged.

Darko tossed his linstock over the port side, and he followed it along with the rest of my loyal lads. I huddled down in the titanium-fullerene wheelhouse. That and the GPS were the only two pieces of Earth-made kit we had on board. The wheelhouse came as flat-pak and didn't cost much.

The ship rolled back to reveal our empty decks to their gunners. The one vessel lay off and seared the ocean a bit, looking for the Altekar who were in the water. They boiled some seaweed and a shoal of opal-fish with the beam-cannon. They couldn't do much harm, except to the fish. The crew would be on the bottom fifteen fathoms down by now.

The other jetboat raced in to board us. They were a hard-bitten looking bunch. Mostly New Earthers by the look of them. Tough kids from the slums that technology, progress and welfare had been unable to entirely get rid of. Out here to get rich, or just recruited for the joy of trouble and killing. They packed pistols and a small array of heavier weaponry.

They checked the hold. Cautiously peering over the edge. Altekar sailors had been known to wait in ambush down in the hold. One of the pirates held a gas grenade at the ready...

But the hold was empty, except for one small bale in the far corner. Not big enough to hide three Altekar, let alone a ship's crew. "It's empty! Dammit! There is no friggin' cargo," yelled one.

I listened happily to the cussing and swearing for a while. When one of them got to the inevitable "Let's sink the tub." I called out.

One of the gung-ho live-bait took a shot at the wheelhouse. The others dived for cover.

"Come out!" yelled one of them, trying to get all of himself behind the mainmast. I was almost tempted to take the .03 Lemmer flat out of my boot-heel and trim his belly with a fléchette. But instead I yelled. "No way. You'll kill me."

"We're gonna kill you anyway, asshole," shouted one, running for cover behind the dive-ropes. Like that would have helped.

"Then I won't be able to tell you where we jettisoned the cargo," I yelled back, over a fusillade of remarkable inaccuracy. If these little snots had been my boots, back in MACSA... They'd have been dead. That was the trouble with recruiting inner-city drug-gang kids.

The words finally penetrated the head of whatever passed for an officer in the pirate-crew. "Stop shooting," he yelled.

Eventually they listened to him. Or ran out of ammunition, one of the two. "Come out, " he yelled again. "We won't shoot you."

"If you do shoot me, you'll all be a lot poorer." I hoped that would get through to this bunch of crack-heads. One never quite knew if anything in their brains still functioned.

That was obviously worrying to their commander too. "Reiki. Manson. Keep him covered. The rest of you. Holster them."

With a bit of grumbling, and a fair amount of argument, it happened. "Right." He stood up from behind the strapped-down water-barrels. "Now come out of there. Let's talk. What's a Terran doing here?"

"I got dumped by my ship," I said. "It was this or starve. Look, I don't want to die. I'll make you a deal. "I'll give you the cargo's GPS location, in exchange for my life and my ship."

"Sure," he said, too easily. "Come out of there, with your hands up, mind."

"You're not gonna shoot me?" I whined, staying put. "Anyway, you can't lift the cargo with those little things," I pointed vaguely at the other vessel hanging off on the starboard bow, with its beam-cannon trained on the ship. "You'll have to let me take the *Queen*," I pointed at my ship, "back there. And without my crew and with the wind in this quarter it's going to take us a while. You'll have to man the sails."

"*Queen!*" the commander rolled his eyes heavenward. "Terrence," he said to one of his crew of little scabs. "Call the ship."

He turned back to me. "We've got a winch on that. And dive gear." He started walking towards the wheelhouse.

"You just stop right there," I snapped, forgetting myself. Once a Master Sergeant, always a Master Sergeant... He paused, halted by my tone. It gave me enough time to gather myself again. "I need some guarantees."

"My word on it," he said, far too easily again.

"You'll never find it without me. And there are forty-three bales of prime Marquat pod down there," I said.

He whistled. "Better than the last haul."

"Better than the last three," said one of the men who was supposedly covering the wheelhouse.

I stepped out of my titanium-fullerine weave shelter, holding the button in my hand. It was a box, a tiny battery, a green button and a red LED. That was it. Manufacturing didn't rise to much more out here. But what you don't tell, they don't know.

"Frigging hell. It's a woman," said one of the pirates, licking his lips.

I resisted the temptation to say, "Now, if only you were a man, sonny."

His friends came running up, grinning like sharks.

"Get the GPS unit," said their commander, grabbing me where few live men had before, without invitation. He grinned cruelly. "Stupid bitch. Your back-track is on that."

"How much do you want to bet?" I said. "And I wouldn't do that."

"We can, and we're going to do anything we damn well like to you. Officers first..." He saw my hand and its contents. He let me go. He gestured at the second boat, slowly and carefully. "We're under the other skiff's beam-cannon. Put that down."

"Lieutenant Koscov. It's not in here!" shouted the member of his crew who had followed his orders to the wheelhouse.

I looked at the button I was holding down. Looked at Koscov. "I have nothing to lose. You've got everything to lose. If I stop pressing this button, you'll find that out. So: you need to cut me a deal to change that. And I don't have a lot of reasons to trust you, mister."

"What is that thing?" he asked, eyeing the object in my hand. His crew were slithering away, like the slimeballs they were.

"Insurance," I said. "And you just stay put. All of you. When your ship gets here she can tow the *Queen* along to the site. You boys can just stay on board until the cargo's up. Then we'll work out something that lets me get out of here alive."

"You could join us," said Koscov looking at the two-dollar red LED light. "We're always recruiting. The money is good."

"I'll consider it," I said evenly. I was quite proud of the way I said that. I mean, I never had any formal training, like standing for office or anything.

It took a good half an hour for their ship to arrive. Space-to-water job, very nice. Innocuous looking, no external armaments—well, it was quite hard to look innocent with those. Civ, thank goodness. Old military crates come onto the market every now and again, but they're heavy with armour, not thin steel-plate, and cost a lot to fly. And they don't have much hold space. So the Marquat pirates tend to use Civ boats, which they mostly keep on or under the water, using their radar to pick up targets for the skiffs, coming in to load up when it was all over, and then buying a few moments satellite blindness to launch off-world. This place was officially a Terran dependancy, but there is always someone on the take.

A bit more talky-talk and they hooked us up on the long cable from our chain locker. If the *Queen Anne's Revenge* had been a floating bomb they'd have been quite safe. My hostages were a little less happy about it.

"Look… Captain Van Vyss might just decide to blow you… and us, away when he has the GPS reference," said Koscov uneasily.

I shrugged. "You better point out that I might have lied to him. He won't know for sure until his divers have the stuff hooked up."

"Uh. Did you lie…?"

"That's for me to know. Tell him that I want to know if his word is any better than yours," I grinned nastily at him. "Oh, and tell him we dropped in two strings. I'll start with the first one."

"Uh. Look, Van Vyss could just decide we're expendable once he gets that cargo of yours," said the lieutenant

I raised an eyebrow. "I thought you were always recruiting? I guess I can see why. I reckon that skiff of yours is my best bet. You might consider coming with me, sweetie. Because the man is not likely to be too pleased with you."

Lieutenant Koscov was just a little startled by the idea. And seriously weighing it. There is one born every minute. Maybe I am one too. "Look," he said, wheedlingly. "I can cut you a deal. You want off-world…"

"Can't. That's why I'm stuck here, sunshine. My heart won't take the G-stresses. That's why I got dumped." It was a good story. Better than "I fought on the losing side, and the systems eventually picked up on my fake ID, and I barely had time to skip out of Port Carson on a Marquat boat which then had the misfortune to get taken by pirates." Sometimes being a "war criminal" is a matter of perspective. The Corporates won. The Free World Alliance lost.

The ship lowered its stern loading door to allow a diver to drop into the water. "One diver?" I said scathingly. "Even Altekar go down in threes. There are a lot of murkies down here."

"Murkies? You mean the water?" asked the lieutenant.

I rolled my eyes. "The Suara Sea does look more like thin soup than seawater, Lieutenant Koscov. But that's seaweed, and plankton. I mean Mercosaurus something-or-other. Just big teeth on a long neck and no brains. Fast and nasty. They'll even eat Altekar. You boys are new to this, aren't you?"

"We've been here for two months. Never had any incidents," said Koscov, telling me what I wanted to know. They'd have a nearly full hold, and a lot of Altekar blood on their hands.

"Yeah? And how much time have you spent in the water?" I asked, scathingly. "Better tell that captain of yours."

So he did. And a few minutes later the remains of a diver drifted up. I looked at it dispassionately. "I guess someone should have listened."

It took a bit of time for the next lot to go over the side. In a bunch. They were armed with knives and a couple of makeshift harpoons. Heh.

A few minutes later the rope they'd taken down with them was tugged. Someone hooked it up to a winch. A couple of minutes later they hauled up the first of the bales from the *Queen.*

Koscov chose that moment to get clever. Tried to grab the button. I poked him in the solar plexus and, as he folded, I pushed him into one of his dumb friends and tossed the button at another one, dropping down next to the wheelhouse before the explosions began.

Altekar didn't need GPS readings to find out where we'd dropped the cargo. And the cargo wasn't all Marquat pods either. Some of the load was Lenka limpet mines. And although there were some bales of Marquat—we dived for the pods in between catching our prey—those bales of Marquat were not what the New Earther pirates had hauled aboard. They got the bales we kept for our prey: bales of shrapnel, Lenka and a pressure switch.

They say the way to a pirate's heart is through his chest. And judging by Lieutenant Koscov's earlier behaviour he didn't love me much. So I took the .03 out of my boot-heel and let an exploding fléchette open the way through his chest for me. He was sweet in dumb-bunny boot sense. I kept shooting. It kept them busy and distracted while Skeer and his boys—who had swum back and been waiting—used their boarding axes and talons to get back on board the *Queen Anne's Revenge.*

I got three of the others too, before Skeer and his crew caught up with the rest.

I knew that Darko and his boys would be busy on their ship. A few seconds after the pirates had had their cargo bay—and its loot-eager pirate crew—shredded by shrapnel, Darko and his bullies would have been swarming out of the water, into their ship, butchering the survivors in the cargo bay. I knew my Altekar lads wouldn't have many New Earthers trying to stop them boarding. The explosions almost always made the cargo doors inoperable, but we never gave the pirates a chance to try to close them. Anyway, the pirates' ship wasn't going anywhere, with the hull burned through with the Lenka limpets.

The pirates on the ship were less helpless than a bunch of stupid inner-city boys diving had been, but their ship was sinking. The skiffs and their beam-cannons were matchwood. We really would get the limpet charges right one of these days. That was a lot of good loot wasted.

They liked to use speed and long-range weapons to kill us and keep them safe. We wanted to get in close—and get their mothership too. Get them to fight on our terms and in our environment. It took a little deception. Otherwise we couldn't catch the mothership. This way we did.

"Nice shooting, Skipper!" yelled Skeer, cheerfully. "Better than the first time, eh."

"That was because you jumped left when you should have jumped right," I said. The first time I'd been a desperate passenger, and the pirates had taken the ship unawares. Skeer and Darko were just Marquat divers back then, and it had been an ugly fight with very few survivors. That time I hadn't been expecting it. Times changed. "Let's go. Darko breaks too much if we leave him to himself." One of the lads passed me the rebreather that used to be one of the pirate-diver's possessions before they had to try knife fighting at fifteen fathoms.

Me and the boys dived over the side and headed for their ship. I can't swim as fast as an Altekar, but they helped me along.

We swam in through the hull-breach that we'd melted through with the limpet mines. It was always a bit tricky, that, because there were sharp bits of metal and the water was sucking, but we got in fine. Well, no major loss of blood. The water was doing a good job of flushing the rats out, but having us come up behind them suddenly added a new dimension to the fight. The city-boys had guns and emergency lighting. We had vision tailored for sight in soupy water, knives, axes, and some .3 fléchettes and surprise. Not everything in life is fair. I think they found taking on sail ships with jetboats and beam-cannon was more fun. They preferred it being unfair that way around, it seemed, listening to their screaming.

The emergency lights dimmed. I gritted my teeth. Engineering and the bridge were always our first target. Okay. External aerials went first, outside, but the inside of a twenty-second century ship was an unfamiliar place to the Altekar. Things went wrong. There is always something that you don't expect in a fight. That's reality, as the first bunch of overconfident pirates found out, when they'd targeted an Altekar Marquat boat with a stowaway Marine Master Sergeant.

The ship lurched. Yeah. I was right. Someone had tried to initiate launch—despite the ship being half-full of water, with compromised hull-integrity and probably with open cargo-bay doors. Oh, and three hundred tons of *Queen Anne's Revenge* hooked up to the spaceship by a good solid braided palkar-cable. And a fair amount of the ship's electrical and electronic systems suffering from Suara seawater. Sure death. Still… she was starting to boost, and that would be sure death for all of us too.

The ship was already making a lot of seriously unhappy mechanical noises. Well, I was no Altekar and I knew where engineering and the bridge were on a space-craft. The former was closer, and, as the pirate swayed and sucked to get free of the water, I led Skeer and the lads there. We blew the door, and I took out the crewman huddled behind the generator.

Generators were valuable loot, but I had no hesitation in dropping a Lenka charge into it, before we ran like hell.

The Lenka blast and death of her lift-generators smacked us down in the corridor, but at least it wasn't free-fall. As well as killing us all, free-fall would have wrecked my ship, and I would have been a really upset ghost. We couldn't have been more than twenty feet clear of the water by the impact. Of course the lights were completely down now. There was just the emergency wall-glow trace, reflecting off even more water swirling in.

Still. The dark is better for knife-work than shooting.

We blew a few airtight doors, and the ship continued to settle. The Suara is only about twenty fathoms at its deepest, and around here fifteen fa'am was the norm. So that left a piece of their ship sticking out above water-level. We had to put a Lenka charge to blow a hole in it to haul the last of them out of there. In the meanwhile Skeer had the lads get some ropes down to their cargo hold. There was a good supply of other people's Marquat pods there.

We started loading while Darko wrinkled the last of the hide-aways out of their holes. There was still a lot of fine looting of twenty-second century goods on the ship. Those were worth more than Marquat, here on Altekar. It'd take us a week to strip her.

I was supervising the loading when they brought Captain Van Vyss to the *Queen Anne's Revenge*. They'd found him in a lifepod, which, lucky for us, he'd failed to launch. Sometimes luck breaks your way.

I looked the sorry piece of work over. "I thought there couldn't be too many Van Vysses out there," I said, remembering him all too well. Mowing down people who couldn't get to you to fight back was something he'd done well for the Corporates. He hadn't changed much in peace-time.

"Look," he began, "I'm worth more to you alive than I am dead. You can get a good ransom for me." Then he recognised me. "Bonney!"

He'd kept his cool until then. Now beads of cold sweat stood out on his forehead. "I call myself Teach these days," I said conversationally. "More appropriate, I think. A nice pun, and better ship-name. Now, who would be prepared to pay a ransom for you, ex-Commodore Van Vyss?"

He was too scared to play his cards properly. It was amazing what a bad reputation could do for you. The Corporates had done well at lying off in space and pounding colonies until they surrendered. Might have gone on working too if the Free Worlders hadn't found out what happened to the colonists who had surrendered. So: when they pounded Macquarie's settlement to pieces, Master Sergeant Anne Bonney had been waiting for them when they landed, with a lot of people who hadn't been in the settlement. I hadn't changed that much either. Well, Macquarie was lifeless slag, and I was a war criminal as a result. I'd let Van Vyss get away that time. And he'd testified against me.

He still seemed to think that he could be lucky twice. But fear made him stupid this time. He named names. Gave details about certain well-placed administrators and the officials in the Reyno Corporation. Now he offered me very large sums, instead of trading on my honor and the status of prisoners of war. Of course Marquat-pod harvesters don't make much money, but some people get very rich out of the trade. Isn't that always the truth?

"Well, Van Vyss," I said when he'd finally finished, when he thought he was going to jump the trap. "I'll have to go through your cabin and log details to confirm it, but it could be even more profitable than the last few of our prizes have been."

"Oh yes. Look, Bonney. We could use you," he said, desperately eager.

"Yeah. You could. Of course it would cost you."

He sang a little more about his contacts.

So I turned to Darko. "Got the plank ready? Or did you use it for cooking Perga?"

"Got another one," said Darko, cheerfully.

I knew the next part. "Got lots, maybe even five," I said, grinning wryly. You had to learn to fit in with the Altekar.

Van Vyss didn't speak Altekar, and only understood "five." I guess it meant as much to him as the number did to the Altekar, because he didn't even try to fight or run.

Altekar can't count, but you can count on them. Someone had chummed the opal-fish in close. We were lying maybe three hundred yards from Van Vyss's sunken ship. The water shimmered with hungry little fish. "One of the problems with modern pirates," I said, as he was prodded with sharp snaky-blades onto the plank out over the bright water. "Is that they don't learn enough history. With a name like mine, I took an interest. If you'd recruited anyone other than dropout illiterates, they'd never have taken on a ship called *Queen Anne's Revenge*."

What was happening finally sank in to Van Vyss. "But all the money, Bonney!" he squalled.

"Wasn't worth your life," I said, prodding him forward. I'd been terribly disappointed to find out that walking the plank was one of the pirate myths, and had rarely happened. Well. We had changed that. "I don't think there is enough money in the universe, Van Vyss. And anyway, you and your friends might have talked to their other friends. And then *my* friends would have paid for it. I've been there before, in case you forget, and I learned my lesson. No, you pirates will just have to keep getting lost with all hands. It'll get harder to recruit as less of your gutter-sweepings come back from the Suara, and the price of Marquat will rise without the pirate supply undercutting it. But we'll give your friends a call."

So we pulled up a few spare deck-planks and toasted some Perga on long forks on the aft-deck, and drank Nash Rum (you really don't want to know) while the opal-fish and the meer-crabs pulled Van Vyss's corpse apart. Tomorrow we'd give a call to his backers to come and fetch the rich cargo he had stolen, before his ship's hull was damaged.

Okay, so the ship was on fire. But we had at least another five deck-planks.

A COLD DAY IN HELL

By Paul Batteiger

The sky was dark with the first taste of snow as two ships cut their way across the frozen sea. Their sails pulled taut in the wind as they tacked southward, ropes tight and cracking in the cold, and from their triple runners sprayed tails of ice that caught the dying daylight and shimmered in the air. They were the *Ranger* and the *Jane*, two fore-and-aft rigged sloops hastily fitted for battle, and battle they sought. They were nine days out of Boston, tacking southerly against the changeable winds of late winter, searching like hounds in cry for the spoor of their quarry.

In command of the expedition, aboard the *Ranger*, Leftenant Drake stood on the cramped bow lookout post and scanned the ice ahead for what he sought. He was twenty-seven, broad-chested and powerful, with dark eyes that could be mirthful or mad. Now he was wrapped tight against the killing wind as his ship raced at better than fifty knots, a speed his father—that old sailor of the watery seas—would never have credited.

He looked again through his spyglass, a ring of leather protecting his eye from freezing to the brass. The ice was clear, only slight waves betraying that this had once been a sea of waves and spray, not twenty years ago. A patch of darkness caught his eye and he paused. There—a blot of smoke low on the horizon, boiling up until the wind took it. He smiled under the high-laced leather collar that guarded his face—he would not be one of the old ice-dogs who ended life lipless, nostrils flayed to the bone by cold. He marked the spot on the horizon, then turned and made his way back to the stern.

At the helm, shielded by canvas from the full wind, stood his right hand Dunstan Roark, Chief Warrant Officer. Any ordinary day he would not be steering the ship himself, but this was no ordinary mission, and Roark was a fine steersman for this kind of work. That and he was one of only a few of Drake's men who had seen battle, and a blooded man was not to be wasted. Roark would not flinch when it came to it.

"Smoke two points to port!" Drake had to shout to be heard over the screaming wind. "One more turn and then back!"

"Aye!" Roark was a big man, with the massive arms needed to steer a ship. Even behind the windbreak he was swaddled like a Bedouin. He waved to the signalman and the flags waved to tell their companion ship of the turn. Drake watched as the *Jane* turned to match their tack, keeping fifty yards between them. She was a touch shorter than the *Ranger*, with shallower pitch to her runners for easier maneuvers at close quarters. But she stuttered a bit on the turn and Drake grimaced—there was that cut-skate working loose again. The *Jane*'s steering runner had never been properly finished, and they'd been forced to lash her down with rawhide before they set out. Drake just had to hope it would hold.

Roark laid their course skillfully, coming in towards the source of the black smoke at a steep angle to the wind, sails luffing and snapping as they cut almost straight across. One last turn and they arced sharply into the wind, ice shooting high in the afternoon air as they ground to a stop. The twenty-five men of the crew came instantly out from belowdecks, swarming to take in the sails and swinging over the side to set the anchors for and aft. The *Jane* drew up twenty yards astern and put out her own anchors, sails dropping. Drake nodded, saw that his ships were secured, and then he turned to the sight at hand off the starboard bow.

It was a ship, or had been. Now it was a blackened hulk burned to the ribs, one remaining mast jutting up like the arm of a corpse. He could see two men dead on the ice on the near side, and from the way they lay he could tell they had been thrown from the deck and died when they hit. Blood was frozen around the bodies in starburst pools. The ice was chipped and gouged by cannon-shot, and so he knew this was not a simple accident. He motioned to Roark, and they dropped ropes and went over the side, swung down the dozen feet to the hard, white ice. It was always difficult, standing on the surface, for him to believe it had ever been water, or that there was water yet far, far below him, though he remembered it from when he was a small boy. Boston harbor in summer, the sun shining off the waves. And then the long, long winter of 1697—the winter that never ended. The winter that closed up the seas from Savannah to the pole itself in an armor of ice.

"They were running fast," Roark said. "Sixty, seventy knots. Then they flipped."

Drake pointed. "Five-skater. Must've had one shot away."

"And then it was all over," Roark said.

They came closer to the hulk and Drake put his hand up to the blackened wood, ran his gloved fingers over it. Nails were embedded into the charred remains in clusters. "Double-shot and nails," he said. "They crippled her and then came broadside and blasted her right to the ice."

"Stripped the ship and then torched her. It was him," said Roark.

"Frost." Drake said it without emotion. The dreaded Captain Frost. Not his real name, surely not, but what he called himself. The story said he was caught in the first great freeze at sea, trapped in the ice with his ship for months. Sailors whispered that he went mad, that he butchered and ate his crew to survive, and when he finally escaped, his hair and beard were white as the ice itself. What was true was that he was a pirate, in command of a monstrous seventy-five-foot ship-of-war and a few smaller vessels besides. And Drake had been chosen to bring him in, selected by his captain back on the *Redoubt* to show that even now, the Royal Navy could not be held lightly.

The commander of the *Jane* came from the other side of the ship—Midshipman Crowe. Drake wasn't entirely sure of Crowe, he was a bit too reckless for this work. But he was brave, there was no doubt of that. "Leftenant," Crowe beckoned. "You'd best see this over here."

Roark looked up at the sky. "We can't waste time, it's getting dark."

They walked around the end of the wreck to the landward side. Drake saw a group of Crowe's men gathered around a spot on the ice with their guns held ready, matches burning in the air. He grunted in annoyance. "Get those matches doused! There's nothing out here to shoot. Spread out, find me their track. Snap to it!" The men dispersed and he stopped, heard Roark mutter an oath.

There were three more dead men on this side of the ship. Their wrists were tied with rawhide, the thongs staked through to the ice with anchor spikes. Each of them was ripped open down the center, blood splashed on the ice in terrible gouts. One man was simply gone from the waist down, shards of bone thrusting redly from the place where he ended. All of them bore contorted expressions of agony on their faces, now frozen forever.

"They must have set hooks in them, made them fast to hawsers so when they pulled away—" Crowe turned away, out of the wind.

"Enough, Mr. Crowe. You should have known to keep your men from seeing this, we don't need them more spooked than they already are."

"Sir—"

"Take your men and get them back to the *Jane*, the damage is done now. No help for it. Learn from your mistake."

"Sir!" One of the men was waving from a distance, his voice barely audible over the wind. "Leftenant Drake, sir!"

They made their way to him through the stiffening evening wind. It was the track of the departing pirate ship. They had cut south to gain speed and then tacked back across, heading landward. Roark knelt and put his fingers in the cut made by the runners. "Five-skater, running heavy. Rear starboard skate is a bit off true, see the jagged sides?"

"Too small to be the *Queen's Revenge*," Drake said, looking to the horizon. "Could be the *Lanner*—the one he stole last winter—she was a five-skater."

"Heavy loaded like that," Roark said. "With a bad skate…" He looked up, and Drake could see his pale blue eyes narrow as he grinned under his mask. "She won't be running full-out."

"After all," Drake smiled. "What need to hurry?" He held out a hand and pulled Roark to his feet. He turned to Crowe. "Get your men aboard and make sail, we've a pirate to catch." He turned with Roark and they jogged back to the *Ranger*. "If we make all speed we may catch them before nightfall. We'll give the devil a bellyful of fire for his last meal."

The sun was westering behind golden clouds ahead when their quarry came in sight. The lookout called and Drake went to see, squinting against the light. White sails and the hull washed pale as bone made her hard to see, but her shadow cast behind betrayed her. Drake laughed and clapped the man on the back. "A brace of pistols for you lad! You have eyes for the ice!" He made his way back to the afterdeck, gave orders to the signalman and nodded to Roark.

Flags billowed in the wind, and the *Jane* signaled her acknowledgement and angled straight at the retreating shadow of their prey. Roark steered the *Ranger* slightly downwind, putting on more speed as men raced to adjust the sails in response to his bellowed orders. Drake could feel the deep vibration through his feet as the ship caught more wind and raced at upwards of seventy knots. It took skilled handling to keep a ship steady at this speed, but he trusted Roark's hand at the wheel.

The big Scot turned to him. "You think Crowe can bring him down? He's never run a real falcon before."

"I'd rather have us ready to pursue if he misses than the other way 'round," Drake said. And then they watched, for the moment was close.

To attack at speed was called by icemen "The Falcon," as it was as close to a hunting bird's stoop as man could come. Dive straight at the enemy, full speed, and fire into him as you passed. It took great skill for the gunners to hit a target at that speed, but it was almost impossible for the target's gunners to hit a foe flashing past them at better than sixty knots. They watched as the *Jane* arrowed straight at the pirate sloop even as they turned to cut off retreat downwind.

The gap closed, and now the pirate vessel heeled over, turning to race downwind, trying to gain speed. It turned her more broadside to the attacking *Jane*, and a single cannon-shot echoed across the sea. That was another reason Drake sent her after the enemy. Both his ships carried six guns, but the *Ranger* was rigged three to a side, while the *Jane* held two on a side, one stern chaser, and one at the bow. They saw the impact on the ice where the ball struck and bounced off, but no answering impact struck the pirate ship, and Roark cursed. A bow gun offered a steadier target, and was the best chance for a hit on the approach.

Now it was a true falcon, and the men of the *Ranger* held their breath as the ships passed in a blink. It took a moment for the sound of the guns to reach them, the series of sharp reports, and then both ships were away, the *Jane* arcing away to the north, and then the last shout of a gun as her stern chaser fired a parting shot. The enemy ship showed no sign of distress, she left the billows of smoke behind her and curved south, gaining speed.

"Damn!" Drake pounded his fist on the rail. "Bring us in! I'm going to knock that bird to the ice myself!" Roark spun the wheel, and the *Ranger* stooped for the kill. The other ship was turning towards her, but she was a five-skate ship—not so quick to turn as the *Ranger*, and it seemed to Drake's experienced eye that the captain of his prey was favoring her a bit, going easy on the turn. Perhaps Crowe had damaged her, perhaps it was just the bad skate.

Drake jumped down to the main deck and took a gun himself. They were going to come in almost parallel, and that meant broadsides from both. Pirates almost always fired double-shot at close range, with a fistful of iron nails thrown in to kill and maim crew. Well, he'd see if he could stop her before that. He ordered the crew to pull out the forward braces and with a crash the gun carriage dropped nose-down, the cannon angled down at the ice. Drake sighted down the barrel. "Two points port, Mr. Roark!" he shouted into the wind. He grabbed the burning match as the ship turned, turned. The sails cracked like whips as they caught more wind and the *Ranger* gathered speed. Now they were on what amounted to a collision course with the pirate vessel. A shot boomed from the other ship and Drake saw the blows upon the ice as the ball skipped once, twice, and then was gone behind them.

He sighted down the cannon, judging wind, speed, distance, his eyes unfocused, his lips moving silently. Then he stood aside and touched the match, the gunners set hold fast of the ropes and then the cannon spoke, leaping back against its bonds and filling the air with smoke. Drake flung himself to the rail and counted the ice-shard splashes that skipped across to the enemy. One, two, and the third that burst upon their for'ard port skate. The crew of the *Ranger* leaped from their posts and shouted as the pirate ship shuddered and slewed violently to starboard, ice fountaining mast-high as her runners skipped free of their paths and skidded across the ice. Then she went over in a tangle of sails and flying splinters, the terrific crack of her unmaking whipping out to them a moment later. The gunners shouted and shook their fists in the air. "Drake! Drake! Bloody hell did you see that shot!"

Drake climbed back to the quarterdeck. "Bring us back around to her, Mr. Roark. Let's see what manner of bird we've landed."

It was the sloop *Lanner*, stolen out of Charlestown the winter before. Five skates, copper-plated hull, and a shelled prow for ramming. A fine ship, now she was a wreck. She'd heeled over onto the ice at better than fifty knots and the gouged trail was littered with shattered wood and shattered men. Drake drew the *Ranger* in alongside, guns ready and men waiting below the gunwales with muskets and swords. The *Jane* was already on station to windward.

As soon as they came in close men emerged from the wreck, arms held up and waving torn sails in surrender. Most of them were injured. When a ship crashed like that, survivors rarely tried to fight, they were too shaken up. Drake sent Roark over with a dozen armed men and waited out of the wind. The men were confident now, swaggering like duelists. His one shot had put iron to their courage.

Roark came back aboard, shook his head. "It's not Frost. These are his men though. They were heading back to anchorage."

Drake felt a thrill of excitement inside, like a trickle of fire in his belly. "Did they give the position?"

Roark nodded. "They say Frost has anchored the *Queen's Revenge* in a bay on the lee side of Ocracoke Island. They're emptying her right now and laying in for the spring snows. This was another supply run, to keep them fed through the snow season. They say Frost is there, and the *Revenge* isn't ready to sail. It's a tight slip and they had to tow her in there. He has another sloop, named *Venture* in there, they're using it to ferry supplies across to their base camp."

"Can we slip in ourselves?" Drake asked.

"They say Frost has set rocks across the bay mouth so no one can sail in without giving warning. And they didn't say for certain, but I'm willing to wager as there will be guards looking out."

Drake smiled. "Helpful fellows, aren't they?"

Roark grinned behind his mask. "Well, it's all in how you ask them, sir."

Which was why he'd sent Roark. What he did not see he did not have to know about. "How many prisoners?"

"Eight, three too badly hurt to travel."

Drake nodded. "Well then, see to it."

Roark nodded. "Yes, sir."

This was not the old days, when ships were huge and there was always room for captives. Drake's ships were small, with no space or food for any but the crews already stuffed into them. These men were pirates who had borne arms against the King's Navy. Yet still Drake turned away when the shots rang out, and perhaps inside he cursed the cold, grim age in which his life was spent, and wished for his youth when the world seemed a kinder place.

It was dark and cramped inside Drake's cabin, lit only by a single lamp on one corner of his small table. Spread out on the aged wood was the best map they had of the Outer Banks. Roark and Crowe were wedged in beside him. Outside it was full dark, both ships anchored solidly against the hell-bent northers that blew after nightfall.

Drake tapped the map. "The best anchorage on the island is supposed to be here, on the south end. Frost is supposed to have strung rocks across the mouth, so we can't slip in."

"Even if they see us, we can still trap them in there," Crowe pointed out.

"That's no good," Drake said. "Even at anchor the *Queen's Revenge* still mounts more guns than we have between us. If they can man them in time it won't matter if the ship is lashed down, they'll still blow us to pieces."

"So what then?" Roark asked.

Drake paused, pursing his lips in thought. "We can't know if the *Venture* will be in there or not, or where she'll be. So we will do this. Mister Crowe, you take the *Jane* around the lee side and block off the bay, so they can't get out. Mister Roark, you and myself will take the men from the *Ranger* and cross the island on foot to reach the anchorage. When we find the *Revenge* we will attack her by surprise, board her, and use her guns upon the *Venture* if she is present. If she is not we will lay in wait for her to arrive and then ambush her. Mister Crowe, if you hear cannons firing get men on the ice, clear the channel, and get in the bay to assist us. If you hear nothing, then wait until you do. We will catch them in a vise between us. Mister Roark, get the men ready, and see that they dress as warmly as possible." He paused as a deeper gust shook the *Ranger*, moaning through her spars. "It's a cold night, but we shall soon heat it up a bit, won't we? Very well, be about it."

It was cold, and the sky was low with clouds promising the spring snows that would make the ice too dangerous for weeks at a time. This was the time of year when all icemen went to ground, lashing down their ships and laying in supplies for the season of snows. This was the worst time of it, when the bite of winter was in the air still. Drake checked over each of his twenty men before they left, making sure they were well-wrapped against the chill. Every man had a musket with powder and shot for thirty volleys, extra matches, sword and long knife. Roark and he both carried loaded pistols, expensive flintlocks already loaded. Six men carried live coals in iron pots slung from their belts for lighting the matches when it came time. He asked the men if they were ready, they nodded, and they went.

The island was low, just a sandbar with rolling dunes and saltmarsh long since frozen solid. They carried no lanterns, making their way by the scant starlight and moonlight that caught through the tattered clouds. What light there was reflected from the ice and lit the world with the soft night glow. So they could see well enough to keep their heading, but many men fell, stumbling over rocks or slipping on ice-sheathed hills. Dead marsh grasses lay in windrows like stiff pelt-fur, and they felt they were creeping up the back of some beast. Drake leaned on his musket like the others, driving the butt into the frozen earth for purchase. Inside his mask breath wet the leather and froze, sticking to his lips.

Roark spotted the lights first, stopping him and pointing across the barren landscape of the island. Peering into the wind Drake could see two faint firepoints of yellow and knew them for the fore and aft lanterns of a ship at anchor. Quietly word was passed down the line to the other men and they readied themselves. Now they moved more carefully, and men who fell did not cry out, only cursed softly and struggled back up helped by their fellows. They drew closer, and Drake guessed it was shy of midnight when they crouched among dead brush and looked up at the shadowed hulk of the *Queen's Revenge*, quiet and still as a derelict, no sign on her but those two lanterns.

"Shall we light now, sir?" asked one man, fondling his gun.

Drake shook his head. "No, we'll try and take her without shooting. Leave the guns here. You two stay and guard them, keep the coal-pots as well. Everyone else stand ready with sword and dirk. We'll come on the shore side and climb aboard. You two take the ropes and lead the way. Now listen men," his tone drew them closer to hear. "There will be no prisoners here. There are likely not many men on this ship, just guards, and I'll wager they're malingering out of the cold belowdecks. But they have lanterns lit, which means the other ship may be returning soon, even in darkness—could be returning even now. So we take this ship, and then we wait for her sister to return and we ambush her. We daren't give them a chance to signal danger. So we kill who we find, no matter if they beg for mercy. You hear me?"

The men looked troubled. "Sir—"

"No! Remember those fellows we found at the other ship? No doubt they begged for mercy, did they get it?" The men turned to one another, there were nods. Good.

"Right then, let's be about it. Quick!"

They went then, climbing down to the shore, over the slippery rocks and the rough ice at the edge, and then down onto the smooth floor of the bay. They came up on the dark side of the *Queen's Revenge* silent as thieves. Two men in front hung ropes over their shoulders. One man made a stirrup with his hands and boosted the other one high enough to set a hook over the ship's rail. Then he climbed the last few feet over and set another hook, dropping a knotted rope from each. Drake caught one and went right up, trying not to thump against the side as he climbed. Then he caught the gunwale and the other man was helping him over onto the deck between two canvas-wrapped cannon.

It was quiet as a graveyard. Drake scanned the deck and saw nothing moving, only the bow lantern swinging in the wind to his right, the stern guttering to his left. He moved away from the rail as more men came aboard. Hangers and knives glittered like flat ice in the starlight. He motioned men fore and aft. Roark came up and Drake drew him close. "Check below, quietly." Roark nodded.

Drake crossed to midships to look out over the bay and suddenly there was a human shape before him, eyes wide over the face-mask. He seemed to have risen from the very shadows of the deck. He and Drake stared at each other for an instant that seemed longer, and then the pirate clapped his hand to a pistol in his belt. Drake rushed at him, grabbing for the pistol-arm, pushing the man down between the guns and against the rail. He reached for his hanger but it was too far around his belt—he couldn't reach it. The man still had hold of the pistol and fumbled with it, Drake caught his sleeve and shook, trying to make him drop it.

His sword out of reach, Drake groped instead for his long knife, yanking it from his belt in a poor, overhand grip. The pirate cursed and Drake became frantic that he would shout and give warning. He plunged the blade in from the side and felt it bite, heard the ripping of fabric and the pirate gasped. Drake tried to pull it out for a better blow but he couldn't grip it well through his gloves and it slipped. He thrust the man down against the rail and pounded on the knife-hilt like a hammer upon a wayward nail. The pirate gasped and twisted, and then let out a long, thin sigh that wheezed through his throat. His struggles weakened.

And then there were hands pulling Drake up, helping him back, and another sailor stabbed his sword into the wounded pirate to finish him. The men were patting at him. "You all right, sir? Are you wounded?"

"No, no I'm not hurt," Drake said, shaking them off. He reached down and took hold of his knife-hilt, worked at it until he could pull it free. Blood was soaking through the heavy winter coat the pirate wore and staining the snow-dusted deck. Drake looked at his knife and saw it was red and steaming in the cold.

Roark loomed close to him. "Got one I see, sir."

"Yes," Drake said absently, rubbing at the blood already freezing on the knife-blade, his hand ached from pounding on the handle. "Yes. I wonder what he was doing up here."

"Watering the ice, most likely, sir."

Drake almost laughed, then he seemed to recover himself. "What below?"

"Two," Roark said. "They won't be troubling us." He gestured. "Some dried meats in the hold and other sundries, in nets for offloading. I'd say they're coming back soon enough for the rest of their stores. Only one bit of bad luck." He held up his straight broadsword and began rubbing frozen blood from its edge. "They already unloaded the powder and shot. We can't use the guns against 'em."

Drake swore, watched how Roark chipped the frozen blood off steel with his thumb and began to do the same. "Well, we shall bring up the muskets and lay low until they return, and we shall make things hot for them all the same. We'll wait until they draw alongside and we'll board her. We won't give them time to use their cannon."

Roark mock-saluted with his blade. "Here's to a bloody mornin' then."

They waited. Drake sent the men below to get some sleep once the muskets were passed aboard. Only three of the coal pots had gone out, so they refilled with coals from the crew stoves below and settled in to wait. Men stood two-hour watches, keeping the lanterns lit and watching out for the *Venture*, Drake wasn't willing to gamble that she wouldn't be back before dawn. He worried a little about Crowe out there alone with the *Jane*. Crowe could be impatient, and he had a need to prove himself. Drake hoped he wouldn't do anything foolish. He saw to his men and then bedded down in a hammock to get some sleep himself. There was nothing to do until the enemy showed his face. It was still dark when Roark came and woke him.

Drake rolled out of the hammock, shivering in the chill. It was just before dawn. Roark had his mask pulled down, here out of the wind. He opened the stove front and warmed his hands while he spoke, firelight painting gold on his small beard. "There's a ship coming, be here in a bit. Lanterns are lit."

"Did they signal?"

Roark shrugged. "The lookout didn't see. I'd have told him not to try answerin'. If we got it wrong, they'd know something was up. If we don't answer they just figure the lookout's hiding below. Nothing lost."

Drake nodded. "Good. All right," he raised his voice a little to bring the men in close. "They're coming. Everyone make sure your gun is loaded proper, check that you have spare matches, and everyone light before we go up. Keep low! We don't want them to see us before it's too late. If they see matchglow they'll stand off and rake us with shot until we're all over the decks. So keep your bloody guns down at least. This ship is taller, so they won't see us even when they're right on us. Once they're alongside I'll fire and that's the signal. Stay together at the rail and work across—we don't want to shoot each other. Well? Good. Go."

It was done quickly. All the men gathered their weapons and went up. Drake could smell the acrid sting of burning match and it was a good smell. He came up on deck, keeping low and then moved to the fore lantern. He kept it behind him so the shadows would hide his face. He didn't bring a musket, just the brace of flintlock pistols in his belt that would give no telltale glow. The sky was still dim grey, but the world was beginning to lighten. The ice shone in the predawn, cold as every winter. The air was so still and frigid it bit at him, and he hastily drew up his face-mask. The men gathered along the port side just below the gunwale, huddled low. All he could really see was a trail of sparks where their matches burned.

The other ship came in slow, taking her time, turning her sails to make most use of the light wind. She was low-built and long, bigger than either of his ships and trimly made. Her three skates cut the ice deftly, and Drake knew a good hand was at her tiller. It was too dark to count cannon, but she couldn't mount more than three to a side, maybe four, she was too small. Roark came and crouched nearby, pistol in one hand and his sword in the other, held low to the deck. He was hunkered down to keep out of sight, but his whole body quivered with readiness.

The bow lantern of the approaching ship swung twice deliberately, then again. Then a long halloo floated over the ice. Drake tensed. This was the moment of decision, when they would see just how sharp a nose for danger Captain Frost really had. Beyond the pirate ship, at the mouth of the bay, something dark cut across the ice, and Drake peered to see what it was. It was a little lighter now, and suddenly he could see the dark shape of the *Jane* coming up behind the pirate sloop.

"Ohhhh damn him to Hell," Drake muttered.

Roark looked up. "What is it?"

"See for yourself."

Roark peered over the wale and cursed. Crowe had decided not to wait. They stared as the *Jane* crept upon the pirate vessel like a stalking cat, and even angry Drake had to admire how well Crowe was handling his ship, but then the loose cut skate betrayed them and the *Jane* turned false, her sails snapping with a crack like splitting wood that echoed over the bay.

Shouts rose from the pirate ship and she turned with remarkable speed. Crowe, knowing he was discovered, fired his bow gun and Drake heard it scream through the air, the shot passing astern of the pirate sloop as she turned.

"Damn it all!" Drake swore. "Take the ropes, get on the ice and attack! She'll never come close enough now. To the ice!"

The men seized ropes and threw them over, then swung over and dropped to the ice with guns ready. They were no more than thirty yards from the pirate ship, and in the growing light Drake could see it was indeed the *Venture*. They had to get close; boarding a ship from the ice was only possible if it was moving slow and you could get men in under the guns before they could be brought to bear. He prayed the pirates had no grape shot loaded. He took a rope and prepared to jump, looked up in time to see the *Jane* pass broadside to the *Venture*, and smoke exploded in the air as the guns fired.

The reports lashed and echoed off the frozen bay, and Drake heard screams. Then he was over and down on the ice, in among his men as they raced for the pirate ship. Men slipped and fell, struggled up again. Some of them were shouting, screaming man's ageless, wordless battle-cries. Drake ran, slipping and stumbling but not falling. Cannons pounded, close enough to smell the powder, and the smoke filled the air around him. He heard the shot scream overhead and shouted his own cry. Through the smoke he saw wood and knew they were there.

There was a rope, and around him other men were throwing hooks, pulling ropes, some firing straight up into the smoke and darkness. He caught the knotted line and climbed hand over hand until the rail was before him and he pulled himself up even as a cannon ran out just beside him. He saw a shape coming closer to him and groped for the pistol, couldn't reach it and then another of his men was there, sword in hand and blood splashed his face.

Drake clawed over the rail into a world of dark and boiling smoke and raging blood. He drew a pistol and cocked it, fired at a shadow and flung the gun away. Then he drew his hanger and rushed into the smoke. All around him men were suddenly locked in battle, hacking with sword and knife, battering with their guns, rolling on the deck and fighting like animals with their hands alone. A man staggered back into him and Drake shoved him away, saw he was a pirate and slashed him across the chest. He raised his sword for another blow but the man sat down on the deck and clutched himself, making no move to fight.

A shape closed on his left and Drake whirled, sword ready, and saw it was one of his own men. Drake clapped him on the shoulder and smiled, the man nodded in return and was suddenly struck down by a blow that almost tore him off his feet. Drake stumbled back as the man fell, blood darkening the deck, and then he saw the awful apparition coming for him out of the smoke.

It was Captain Frost, for it could be no other. He was tall as a mountain in the haze and terror of the moment, broad as a tree. His great white beard seemed to trail off and become part of the smoke, his eyes like two points of blue fire above it. His hair streamed like the mane of God himself in all his vengeance, tied in locks with lit matches that burned and smoldered, wreathing his terrible white face with smoke. His black coat billowed like a sail, his sword flashed down and Drake parried, feeling the blow shiver in his arm-bones. He sprang back from the snow-giant, ducked another stroke and then leaped in, aiming a cut of his own that Frost shrugged aside with his own heavy blade.

Drake gave ground before the giant, his arm ringing and numb with the blows he caught on his sword. Frost bellowed, breathing out clouds of steam as though he were a devil who ate smoke and fire. His eyes were alight, truly alight, and it was like nothing Drake had ever seen before. Frost struck at him and Drake evaded the cut, lunged in suddenly with a sharp thrust that struck home at Frost's belt, catching his cartridge box. The stout hanger bent like a bow with the force of the thrust before Frost lashed down his own sword and Drake's blade snapped in three pieces clean as ice.

Drake staggered and Frost caught him low with a stroke that sent him reeling. He felt pain burn his side just above his hip, then the warmth of blood. He leaped back and snatched the other pistol from his belt, cocked it and fired point-blank into that giant body. The pan flash and smoke blinded him for a moment, but then he saw Frost stagger, and a groan came from his white lips. But still he came, red sword uplifted for a killing blow.

Then Roark was there, his own red sword striking, and Frost staggered sideways, free hand grasping at his throat where blood and steam ran out between his fingers. He fell against the mast, eyes wild and blue. He looked at Roark and held out his bloody hand. "Well done, lad," the giant said in a voice that was all scrape and gutter.

"I'll do it better," said Roark, and he struck again, hewing through that great neck and laying the white-bearded head flat on its own shoulder. Blood streamed from the neck, rilling across the deck and adding its steam to the smoke of the battle. The giant body sagged in place, as if even that wound could not stop it, but then it sank down and lay still, pouring its life out upon the cold wood.

Roark leaned on his red dripping sword and pulled down his mask, wiping at the ice gathered in his beard. He looked at Drake and smiled tiredly. The noise of battle was dying away, the smoke was lifting, and the light of day gathered to show the carnage wrought. Like the slow dawn itself it came to Drake that they had won.

"You well, sir?" Roark asked.

"I shall live, I think. You?"

"Oh I'm right as Christmas mornin', sir." He looked around. "Well, this will make a story, what?"

They had eight wounded, two dead out of twenty. The *Jane* was hard-hit. Sixteen men dead, including Crowe and his steersman, killed in that first terrible broadside. Well enough, since the ship was no fit shape to travel. They took what they could use off her and the pirate ships, then loaded the dead into them and burned them to the ice. Men were sent back to the *Ranger* to bring her in and the survivors were loaded aboard. Roark hung Frost's head on a rope and slung it under the bowsprit. Drake watched him do it as they prepared to make for home. His own wound was shallow, though it pained him, and would scar.

"Barbaric, don't you think, Mr. Roark?"

"No less than he would have done to you, sir. Shall I take it down?"

Drake thought for a moment. "No, no leave it. We shall sail into Boston harbor with the awful Captain Frost's head swinging from the prow. And everyone who sees it will tell the story for twenty years."

"Like as not the ones who don't see it will tell the story anyway."

Drake smiled behind his mask. "I daresay they will. It is a good story too, though not so daring as the one you have to tell."

Roark shrugged. "If men buy me drinks for it, then it's a good story." He looked up. "Snow coming, best be on our way."

Drake nodded and gave the orders, felt the wind catch as they turned to sail out of that bay of death, ships burning behind them. The sky was dark, and dust of snow came down all around as they set their course for home.

THE ADVENTURES OF CAPTAIN BLACK HEART WENTWORTH: A NAUTICAL TAIL

by Rachel Swirsky

I. Burial at Sea

With a splash, the body of Cracked Mack the Lack went overboard. Captain Black Heart Wentworth, Rat Pirate of the Gully by the Oak, stared after Mack into the turgid brown waters. Wentworth's first mate, Whiskers Sullivan of the beady eyes and greedy paws, slunk deckside, muttering madly about the pitter patter of fleas rushing along his spine so loud he couldn't sleep or shit or make water—and when a rat can't shit or make water, tis a dark day indeed.

Cracked Mack the Lack had been the last of their dastardly crew. Sully'd found him that morning, gone tail over snout in the stern. Arsenic done him in. Mack had a taste for it, reminded him of that crack in the wall called home when papa took the boys out of a morning to learn their way in the world: how to tweak a cat's whiskers and pry cheese from between spring-loaded jaws. Now Mack was gone, wrapped in a spider web shroud to decay in his watery grave.

"We two rat jacks is all that's left," Wentworth said to Sully. "A ship with but two pirates is hardly a pirate ship at all."

Sully swiveled one ear toward his captain's voice. He scratched his head with his back foot.

"Tis time for a new mission," said Wentworth. "This old girl's been plundering these shores since you and I were press-ganged pups. We coarsened our hair on this route. Its bounty allowed our balls to grow low and pendulous.

"But now, I say, enough! Enough of hustling gulls, robbing their garbage as if twas treasure. Enough of gobbling eggs and spooking minnows. Like our venerable ancestors who carried the plague across Europe on their backs, we must spread our scourge throughout the seven seas! You hark?"

Sully scrabbled in circles, claws scratching on leaf-planks. His naked tail whipped;

his beady eyes sparkled; his snout raised to sniff the invigorating maritime breeze. Whether he danced for joy or to exorcise the demon fleas what haunted him was anyone's guess.

II. Launch

Wentworth oversaw the repairs which would see them off to parts unknown. Finest acorns restocked the canon. Deadfall to replank the deck was collected from the base of the Great Oak on the riverbank, the tree with bark too slick for any cat to climb, where ancestral rats had taken refuge through dark winters. Fresh twigs, roots, and tubers replaced the rotting hull, bound together with whiskers plucked from captured hounds. The old anchor was replaced with a ripe plum, plucked from a pie still cooling on the windowsill belonging to the tabby Sharp Tooth. Under Wentworth's supervision, Sully secured the fruit to a catgut line and dropped it to the riverbottom.

As for the ragged pelts hanging from the fishspine mast, Wentworth ordered them taken down.

"Tis the banner of death what sees us off," said Wentworth. "Our flag should be the same."

Wentworth ordered that a black squirrel should be caught and skinned, one with fur fine as the down on a mother rat's breast and dark as Wentworth's withered heart. Muttering and grumbling, Sully hunted squirrels through the windswept grass. He cornered his quarry near the briar patch, ignoring the squirrel's prayers and promises. He dispatched the creature merciful quick: with but an exhalation of Sully's fetid breath, the squirrel perished.

They hung the pelt—skull and femurs attached—and prepared to launch.

In the stern, Sully stood watch, grumbling to his fleas. Standing at the snail-shell wheel, Wentworth opened the rusty trunk that had belonged to the captain before him, and the captain before him. He pulled out an ancient map. Looking to the overhanging stars, he guided the ship toward a place marked in the shaking script of a rat close to death: The Open Seas.

The ship plunged through dark waters, ghastly sail billowing in the wind, black-furred tail trailing behind them like the hem of death's own garment. Above hung the moon, green as finest rotting cheese.

III. Battle

Dawn rose over the water, shards of reflected orange and rose mingling with foam. The ship bobbed through the estuary leading into the sea. Frogs and toads leapt, squelching, through the mud. Sully drew his scimitar to teach the tadpoles a thing or two about pirates, but Wentworth stayed his hand. "Wait til they have legs. Tis fair play," he advised.

Midmorning waters deepened to cobalt. Sully filled his tin cup and used the water to salt his dried meat ration. The treeline thinned to a distant green fringe.

"At last, the sea," said Wentworth. "I feel its goodness deep in my piratical bones."

Sully appeared to agree, or at least the mad twinkle brightened in his eye.

In the afternoon, they caught sight of a duck followed by a line of puffy yellow ducklings.

"Stand down!" shouted Wentworth, brandishing his sword. "We demand treasure! Give us your eggs and nest lining! Lay algae and water bugs at our feet."

The duck turned a matte eye on him and gave an uncomprehending honk.

"A rebel, eh?" Wentworth turned to Sully. "To the canons, rat!"

The first shot fired across mama's feathered bow. She flapped her wings, but surrendered no treasure.

"Down the fleet!" ordered Wentworth.

The canon boomed. One, two, three fluffy chicks disappeared into a puff of yellow feathers. Mama honked her outrage. She flew at the ship, pecking the prow. The ship careened beneath ardent avian assault. The whittled ears of the rat maiden figurehead snapped free. Wentworth ducked as they crashed around his head. Sully slammed against the hull and slumped.

"Retreat!" shouted Wentworth. He scrambled over Sullivan's unconscious form and wrenched the wheel to the left. The ship veered. The duck flapped after them, feet dragging in the waves, then skidded back to her remaining youngsters.

IV. Uncharted Waters

Sully plucked splinters from his fur. "No lasting damage, eh?" said Wentworth.

They sailed til the water turned the steely grey of their swords. Overhead, web-winged creatures wheeled through the sky. "Wok, wok," they called, "Jabberwock."

Sully tested the depths by dropping anchor. The catgut line unspooled til it broke.

Wentworth went to fill his flask and found the supply of good brisk drink had pitched overboard. Ah, and the water barrels were gone, too.

He found Sully perched on the side of the boat, fishing with the broken catgut line. "We're to die out here," said Wentworth. "There's no booze left and no water neither."

Something tugged at Sully's line. He staggered back to ho-heave-ho.

Up on deck came a-sprawling a strange creature with a fish's bright green tail and the furry, cherubic face of a rat maid not long weaned.

"My whiskers," said Wentworth, "a merrat!"

She was slender for a ratly creature, but huge for a fish. Where her fur merged into scales, it flushed deep emerald like a branch giving way to leaves. Six pink shells covered the delights of her nipples.

Fancies of seduction raced through Wentworth's brain. Sully had other ideas. Drawing his saber, he slashed her tender throat. Her dying squeak rose high above her thumping death throes.

That evening they dined on roast fish while Sully wove himself a coat from the merrat's fur. Twas too close to cannibalism for Wentworth's gut, but a mad rat like Sullivan would slay his mother for her pelt.

"You're a cruel rat, Sully," said Wentworth.

Sully looked up, whiskers twitching. Wentworth could almost see the fleas rushing through his fur.

"Maybe your fleas'll move from your pelt to hers," suggested Wentworth.

Laughter danced in the inky wells of Sully's eyes. Baring the yellowed squares of his teeth, he ripped off a chunk of the merrat's pelt and threaded the needle he'd carved of her bone.

On the horizon, Wentworth glimpsed a white tentacle glowing in the pale dusk. "A monster! Rat, your station! It's like to be guarding a hoard."

V. Here There Be Krakens

Wentworth ordered Sullivan to quiet their running. They cut silently through darkening waters, hushed as a coward's footsteps.

They sailed round the tentacle like a peninsula, for twas almost as massive. Suckers big as pampered housecats pulsed, tasting the briny air.

"We'll sail to its center," Wentworth told Sullivan. "I'd lay ingots the beast's treasure lies near its heart."

The monster's head rose from the ocean like the great white dome of a cathedral. It was garbed in seaweed and encrusted with barnacles. A vast obsidian eye stared with diffuse gaze at the horizon.

Wentworth fetched his best harpoon, point honed to the soul of sharpness, and aimed at the creature. He threw strong, but false. His harpoon sank into the waves.

The wind of its passing woke the monster. Its great, murky eye flashed alert. The massive head reared, barnacles snapping off and falling into the sea. A tentacle crashed across the ship, knocking the wheel askew. A second wrapped Wentworth in its sinuous grip.

Undaunted, Wentworth drew his dagger and hacked away. Green blood burned Wentworth's fur and sprayed across the ocean surface like oil. The tentacle pulsed with pain, squeezing tighter. At last, Wentworth hacked the tentacle through and thumped onto the deck.

Behind him, Sully led another tentacle in circles. It wrapped around the fishspine mast like a maypole.

Wentworth dashed to Sully's side. "Faster! Faster!" he called.

They whirled in a merry, desperate dance. The tentacle spiraled tighter and tighter til white flesh strained.

"Keep running her round," shouted Wentworth. He ran to the merrat's corpse where Sully's half-sewn coat lay, wet and bedraggled. He heaved the coat toward the mast.

Feeling coarse, soaked rat fur, the monster grasped and pulled. The mast came loose in its formidable grip. It dragged both pelt and mast toward gaping maw, stabbing its throat with splintered fishspine. Green blood spurted. It began to sink.

Doused in burning blood, Wentworth and Sullivan danced a celebratory jig. Over the noise of massive tentacles sliding into the water, the pirates heard a female's distressed wail.

"Help! Help!"

VI. Rescue

A pea-green skipper floated beside the nearest tentacle, in danger of being submerged in its wake. Wentworth directed Sullivan to the wheel. "Swiftly, rat," he ordered, buttoning his waistcoat.

They veered toward the small vessel, its deck obscured by churning waters. Wentworth knotted the catgut line and threw it down.

What vision of loveliness awaited them? Wentworth wondered. A sleek sable tail-swinger with cherry-red eyes? A midnight-furred scrambler with whiskers fine as dandelion fluff?

He felt a hitch in the catgut line as the fair maiden trusted her weight to him. "Thank you, kind sir," said she, coming into view: a green-eyed, ginger-coated, ravishing damsel of a… cat.

VII. Dinner at the Captain's Table

They gathered round a knotted pine table stolen from a child's dollhouse. Oil lamps fueled by finest seal fat cast orange light across their repast of roast fish and "recycled" water.

"Avoid the drink," Wentworth advised their guest. "Tis less than potable."

The cat pulled a flask from her lacy garter. "I come supplied for all occasions." Feline she might be, but she still seemed a lady, bonnet and petticoat pristine. "Gin. Would you like a snifter?"

Wentworth grunted. Was it his imagination or had Sullivan polished the bones on his necklace? Did his flea-ridden fur seem fluffier from, perhaps, a mid-ocean bath?

"I'm Pussy La Chat," said the ginger jezebel. "My story is terrible sad. A fortnight ago, I set off with my bridegroom hoping to be married by the turkey on the hill. Alas, now, my love is gone, and I'm alone." She smiled demurely. Lamplight could not help but glisten on her fangs. "How lucky I am to have found two strong sailors."

She set her paw on the table. Wentworth noted the fetching white sock on her foreleg.

Now Wentworth came to think of it, her tail had a rather shapely curve, and her green eyes—well, was not green the color of leaves and grass and cool spring meadows?

"Lucky and lovely," he agreed.

Sullivan glared jealously at his captain.

"I wonder," said Pussy, voice honeyed with purr, "if I might join your crew. Weak though I am, perhaps I could be of some small assistance."

"That could be arranged."

"Purrfect."

Wentworth loosened his ascot. "Would you care to join me for a moonlight stroll?"

"Would that I could, Captain, but I find myself accounted for this evening." Pussy perked her ears. "Your first mate has offered to show me the constellations. Perhaps another time?"

Sullivan offered his arm to the feline intruder. She *mrrowwed*, fur ruffling prettily along her back. Oh, Wentworth had seen the signs of love before. How fast women fell. How illogical and intractable their affections.

He drained his goblet. Blast. He shouldn't have let Sully slay the merrat.

VIII. A Better Battle

Pussy spotted the galleon. "A nautical masterpiece," said Wentworth, admiring the five masts and graceful lateen sail. Plump, well-dressed hamsters bustled along deck.

"To the canons!" called Wentworth.

Sully paused, shoulders hunched.

"To the canons!" Wentworth repeated. "Are you a rat or a mouse?"

Hesitantly, Pussy licked her paw. "Your first mate has regaled me with your adventures," she began. "Your aggressive strategy, while admirable, may not be wise."

"Is that what Sully said?"

Under his captain's betrayed gaze, Sullivan slunk away.

"Innovation is a sailor's way!" Pussy continued. "Else we'd all sail battered skiffs, like me and my poor bridegroom." She sniffed, dabbing her eye.

Wentworth tugged down his waistcoat. "What's your suggestion?"

"Deception!" Pussy licked her chops. "Good nautical men are always eager to assist their fellow voyagers."

"As we assisted you?"

"Our mast is gone. Our figurehead broken. I must say, we're quite a sight."

Grudgingly, Wentworth assented. He and Sullivan secreted themselves beneath the fallen sail, awaiting Pussy's signal.

"We must not allow Pussy to come between us," whispered Wentworth. "We're pirates. We kill without remorse. We do not romance. You hark?"

Sully pricked his ears.

"Good."

Dimly, they heard the galleon nearing. Pussy called, "Oh, sirs! Alack and alas, my ship has been caught in a storm, and all hands lost save me! Help, help!"

In low squeaks, the hamsters considered their options. "What's she worth in salvage?" "We'll get but a pittance for the leaves." "But a gross for the wheel!" Planks creaked as they boarded.

"Now!" shouted Pussy.

Wentworth and Sullivan dashed out, sabers flashing. The merchant's captain drew a fancy fencing foil. "I'll save you, milady!" he shouted. Pussy devoured him in a gulp.

A pretentious poof of a hamster flung a knife at Pussy's tail. Fast as a hopping mad flea, Sully chopped off the fellow's whiskers, tail-nub, and head.

Wentworth made short work of the other quivering wretches. Those who surrendered were marched off the plank with a satisfying splash.

Wentworth surveyed the tatters of his once-sturdy vessel. He turned to the galleon. "The time's come to jump ship."

IX. Treasure at Last

"Pearls!" said Pussy. "Rubies!"

"Sapphires, gold, tea and tin." Wentworth rushed between overflowing trunks. "We're rich, rich, rich!"

He tossed a handful of gems, dancing in their glittering fall. "Ow."

Pussy turned. "What's wrong?"

Sully returned from exploring the ship's bowels, brandishing a master-crafted, jewel-encrusted sword—yet twas the object in Sully's other paw that caught Wentworth's eye.

Wentworth relieved Sullivan of the vintage wine. "Nothing," he said. "Nothing at all."

They drank into the night. Sully and Pussy curled up on a silk rug. Abandoned, the wine bottle emptied its dregs onto fine silk. Amid so much bounty, no one paid heed.

"This is so nice," said Pussy. A pearl necklace looped thrice around her neck. Her claws shone with diamonds.

Wentworth wore the hamster captain's tri-corner hat and tiny velvet waistcoat, unbuttoned. "We should sell our bounty and find a tropical island. We'll have servants and order everyone about. If anyone defies us, our blades will drink their blood!"

"That sounds lovely." Pussy rolled across the rug, paws in the air. "Captain Wentworth, will you marry Sullivan and me?"

The evening's joy bled away like the wine. Wentworth paced to the hull, gazing down at the roiling black sea. "What happened to your last bridegroom?"

Pussy burped. A white feather flew from her mouth. "Nevermind that." She joined Wentworth at the hull. "Here, I want you to have this."

She drew from her petticoats a metal object. It glinted in starlight.

"Tis my runcible spoon. My bridegroom and I ate our last meal from it. It's very precious to me."

Wentworth admired the runcible spoon. "No one's ever given me a gift before. Not without a threat."

Pussy purred. "Will you marry us?"

Wentworth glanced at Sully. He stood, paws folded at his waist, whiskers clean and tidy. For the first time in years, he wasn't twitching.

"Very well."

Wentworth married them there, beneath the green crescent moon. Seeing the two of them, rapturous and silhouetted by starlight, a tear came to Wentworth's crusty pirate's eye.

X. A Brewing Storm

Wentworth woke with a headache. He grabbed the wine and took a swig.

Above, the rosy tint of dawn illuminated the dark underbellies of storm clouds. Distant lightning flashed across the horizon. Thunder followed.

"Storm!" cried Wentworth. He rushed to the captain's cabin where Pussy and Sullivan had made their honeymoon suite. He burst through the door. "No time to lose! A dickens of a squall is on the way!"

He fell silent. Pussy stood over the bed, mouth stretched to reveal shining, dagger-sharp teeth. Sully lay helpless on the sheets, still snoring.

"Stop, you wretch!" Drawing his dagger, Wentworth ran at the cat. She mewled and leapt away.

"You've the wrong idea," began Pussy.

"Cat!" shouted Wentworth. "Feline! Kitten! Domesticated animal!"

Sullivan woke. He jumped to his feet, drawing his sword. He looked between his wife and his friend, unsure which to attack.

Wentworth jabbed at Pussy. "This *Felis domesticus* was about to make you a snack!"

"Do nothing hasty, my beloved," said Pussy. "We can work this out."

Mad eyes bright, Sully charged his friend. Wentworth was too stunned to move. The blade's tip drew close to his fur.

With a burst of lightning like a thousand firecrackers, the ship tilted. Sully's blade clattered to the floor. Wentworth was thrown to the ground after it. Pussy clamored over him, escaping to the deck.

"After her," said Wentworth.

XI. Lightning Strikes

He found the false feline standing by the mast, long white gown wetted to her body.

"I didn't mean to hurt him!" she called into the wind. "Tis just—that flashing tail, that delectable fur, that delicious, rapid heartbeat! Oh, the trials of a cat in love."

"Is that what happened to your former bridegroom?"

"Tis true, I've succumbed to temptation in the past, but not this time! I would have remembered my vows!"

Sully crawled after Wentworth. His eyes were black as the tumbling waves. He twitched beneath a seething mass of fleas.

"My fate is in your paws," Pussy called to him.

Another lightning bolt crashed into the ship. It lit the mast from tip to deck where Pussy stood. Her dress turned ashen. The odor of burned fur filled the air.

Sully rushed to her side. "Don't comfort the harlot," called Wentworth. "There's no time."

Thunder rumbled. The mast creaked. As it fell, Wentworth pushed Sullivan aside. It crashed across the deck. The ship heaved and tilted. Gems and silks slid into the water. The bow tipped into the waves, prow pointing straight up toward the hidden sun.

Wentworth scrabbled for purchase. He pulled the runcible spoon from his sleeve and stuck it into a groove between planks. He gripped it, hind paws dangling over the water.

Pussy fell past him. Her claws slipped, stuck. Sully shivered on her back, twitches so bad they'd become convulsions. Fleas flashed around his body.

Pussy began to slip. "Hold tight," she yelled.

Her claws pulled free. She scrambled, regained her grip. She couldn't support them both.

Sully's eyes blazed past the black of waves and nighttime. They were black as madness now, black as the rotten cheese at the back of the moon.

He let go.

"No!" shouted Pussy and Wentworth, simultaneously.

Sully slid into the water, naked tail cresting the waves before disappearing.

XII. Rat Overboard

The storm cleared to bright, azure sky. Pussy knelt, weeping. Wentworth inventoried the ship to see what treasure remained.

"The jewels are gone. And the rugs and gold and tea and tin and wine. But it looks like some silver survived. Enough to buy a new boat, maybe. A small one."

"Tis my fault," sobbed Pussy. "If I hadn't been tempted, if you hadn't found me, the three of us might have sheltered together."

Long ago as a press-ganged pup, Wentworth had made a vow of solidarity with those who found themselves prematurely estranged from their loved ones. He would not kill orphans or widows. But oh, he was tempted.

"No, we wouldn't," he said. "You'd have eaten him."

Pussy's bitter tears mingled with the drying ocean water on deck. "O, my dark one, my fleet one, my mad dancing one, with eyes black as a moonless night, and fur soft as the master's blanket."

"Should we drink the wine or save it to sell?" asked Wentworth.

"O, that you should die like this, at the hour of my ignominy, sacrificing your noble life for mine!"

"Drink it, I think," said Wentworth.

"Oh, my love! I can't go on without you!"

With a clatter of her claws on the leaf-planks, Pussy mounted the side of the ship. She stood like a figurehead, gown rustling in the wind, tail billowing behind her. Then the leap, and with a splash of spray, she was gone.

Wentworth gazed after her. This journey had been one of death. Cracked Mack had died. Sullivan had died. Even Pussy, poor pirate though she'd been, had taken a watery grave. Wentworth pulled the runcible spoon from his pocket and heaved it overboard. Without the damn thing, he'd be dead too, and maybe it would have been for the best.

XIII. Adrift

Weakened by the storm, exhausted timbers broke apart. The captain's quarters capsized, taking the silver with them. The deck cracked into sections. Wentworth clung to the planks beneath him as they split off like a raft.

Long hours passed. A circling gull woke Wentworth's hope he might be approaching land til the bird pitched dead into the sea. Wentworth fished out its corpse and dined upon it.

Wet and miserable, Wentworth lay down and waited to die. He considered his many sins. As a ratling, he'd oft squabbled with his siblings, nipping their whiskers to make off with their breadcrumbs. He'd swindled apples from pups and woven lies odiferous as rotten cheese. He'd nipped the teats that fed him.

For all that, he didn't think he'd been a bad rat. A bit nasty. A bit merciless. A bit bloodthirsty. No rodent is without flaws.

When he heard the rush of water pushed aside by a well-made prow, he thought perhaps he was gone to heaven. Sharp steel jabbing his ribs set him straight.

"Slavers, eh?" he asked.

"Silence, rat," replied the sword-wielding ferret, cruel nose twitching. He turned tail and two fat guineas marched Wentworth aboard their rickety vessel.

Palm trees swayed on the horizon, black against the sunset. Wentworth stared slack-jawed, aghast that he'd come so close to freedom.

A guinea caught him looking. "That thar's Sweet Summer Isle. They grow sugar thar. You'll spend the rest of yer life workin' the plantations."

He gave a dry and brutal laugh, cuffed Wentworth round the ear for good measure, and led him below decks whence he chained the poor rat to a dank cell wall for the remainder of the journey.

XIV. Deserted Island

But what kind of pirate would Captain Black Heart Wentworth, Oppressor of Puppies and Terror of Things That Go Squeak, be if he couldn't slip free of rusty handcuffs? He knocked out the guinea guard with his own sword and with thundering footsteps marched deckside to conquer his craven captors.

At port, Wentworth sold the slavers for good gold coin and bought a plantation. When no other rat would purchase the cowards, Wentworth reacquired them at a price much reduced and forced them to labor sunup to sundown.

One afternoon, as summer sun shimmered on the sand, Wentworth was surprised to see two familiar figures staggering from the sea. Pussy, fur patched and ears a-tatter, clung to a skinnier flealess Sullivan. Over a feast of tropical fruit, Pussy explained how they'd come to these sunny shores.

Pussy had leapt into the water contrite and ready to die, until accosted by hungry cannibals who dragged her to their camp. Nearby, Sully, having been found inedible, was imprisoned in a cage. When the cannibals dunked Pussy in their wicked cauldron, Sully drew on nameless reserves of strength to wrench apart the cage bars. Quickly, he slew the cannibals and fled with his bride to their captor's ship which they converted to their own piratical ends. Ah, but theft and murder felt wrong without Wentworth to oversee it. The wedded couple spent their gold-strewn hours listless and mournful til they heard rumors of a wealthy white rat with a scurvy temper who ran a tropical sugar plantation. With haste, Pussy and Sully set off, til not two days from the island, their ship was lost to a freak whirlpool. Pussy and Sully swam for shore. Sharks circled and tropical undertows threatened to drag them under, but lo, they arrived at last on this very beach.

Past slights forgiven, Wentworth embraced his long-lost friends. In the sugar cane fields, even the ferret and his crew of guineas, now tanned and sore from their months of punishing labor, wept sentimental tears til Wentworth ordered them back to work.

XV. Piratical Epilogue

So it came to be that the world was not menaced by rat pirates. Port cities flourished unafraid, reaping rich cargos of coffee and tea, sugar and salt, wood and silk and spices and precious stones. Unaccosted gold flowed through marine arteries, sustaining the vast fatherly arms of empires. By turbulent sea, churning river, or trickling tributary, trade reached even the most insignificant peoples stranded in the remotest, uncivilized reaches of the globe.

Sully held Pussy as they sat together on the white sand, admiring the sunset over the water. Wentworth threatened a cowardly guinea with his sword if he did not immediately dash to fetch a goblet of rum and mango juice. The creature scurried off. A smile stirred beneath Wentworth's whitening whiskers. Ah, sun and sand and sea air. Ah, the goodness of reclining on a beach with friends.

ARAMINTA, OR, THE WRECK OF THE AMPHIDRAKE

by Naomi Novik

Lady Araminta was seen off from the docks at Chenstowe-on-Sea with great ceremony if not much affection by her assembled family. She departed in the company of not one but two maids, a hired eunuch swordsman, and an experienced professional chaperone with the Eye of Horus branded upon her forehead, to keep watch at night while the other two were closed.

Sad to say these precautions were not entirely unnecessary. Lady Araminta—the possessor of several other, more notable names besides, here omitted for discretion—had been caught twice trying to climb out her window, and once in her father's library, reading a spellbook. On this last occasion she had fortunately been discovered by the butler, a reliable servant of fifteen years, so the matter was hushed up; but it had decided her fate.

Her father's senior wife informed her husband she refused to pay for the formal presentation to the Court necessary for Araminta to make her debut. "I have five girls to see established besides her," Lady D— said, "and I cannot have them ruined by the antics which are certain to follow."

(Lest this be imagined the fruits of an unfair preference, it will be as well to note here that Araminta was in fact the natural daughter of her Ladyship, and the others in question her daughters-in-marriage, rather than the reverse.)

"It has been too long," Lady D— continued, severely, "and she is spoilt beyond redemption."

Lord D— hung his head: he felt all the guilt of the situation, and deserved to. As a youth, he had vowed never to offer prayers to foreign deities such as Juno; and out of obstinacy he had refused to recant, so it had taken three wives and fourteen years to acquire the necessary son. Even then the boy had proven rather a disappointment: sickly and slight, and as he grew older preferring of all things literature to the manly arts of fencing or shooting, or even sorcery, which would at least have been respectable.

"But it is rather messy," young Avery said, apologetic but unmoving, even at the age of seven: he *had* inherited the family trait of obstinacy, in full measure. It is never wise to offend foreign deities, no matter how many good old-fashioned British fairies one might have invited to the wedding.

185

Meanwhile Araminta, the eldest, had long shown more aptitude for riding and shooting than for the cooler arts, and a distressing tendency to gamble. Where her mother would have seen these inappropriate tendencies nipped in the bud, Lord D—, himself a notable sportsman, had selfishly indulged the girl: he liked to have company hunting when he was required at home to do his duty to his wives—and with three, he was required more often than not.

"It is not too much to ask that at least one of my offspring not embarrass me on the field," had been one of his favorite remarks, when chastised; so while her peers were entering into society as polished young ladies, beginning their study of banking or medicine, Lady Araminta was confirmed only as a sportswoman of excessive skill, with all the unfortunate results heretofore described.

Something of course had to be done, so a match was hastily arranged with the colonial branch of a similarly exalted line. The rumors she had already excited precluded an acceptable marriage at home, but young men of good birth, having gone oversea to seek a better fortune than a second son's portion, often had some difficulty acquiring suitable wives.

In those days, the journey took nearly six months, and was fraught with considerable dangers: storms and pirates both patrolled the shipping lanes; leviathans regularly pulled down ships, mistaking them for whales; and strange fevers and lunacies thrived amid the undersea forests of the Shallow Sea, where ships might find themselves becalmed for months above the overgrown ruins of the Drowned Lands.

Naturally Lady Araminta was sent off with every consideration for her safety. The *Bluegill* was a sleek, modern vessel, named for the long brightly painted iron spikes studded in a ridge down her keel to fend off the leviathans, and armed with no fewer than ten cannon. The cabin had three locks upon the door, the eunuch lay upon the threshold outside, the maids slept to either side of Araminta in the large bed, the chaperone had a cot at the foot; and as the last refuge of virtue she had been provided at hideous expense with a Tiresian amulet.

She was given no instruction for the last, save to keep it in its box, and put it on only if the worst should happen—the worst having been described to her rather hazily by Lady D—, who felt suspiciously that Araminta already knew a good deal too much of such things.

There were not many tears in evidence at the leave-taking, except from Lady Ginevra, the next-oldest, who felt it was her sisterly duty to weep, though privately delighted at the chance of advancing her own debut a year. Araminta herself shed none; only said, "Well, good-bye," and went aboard unrepentant, having unbeknownst to all concealed a sword, a very fine pair of dueling pistols and a most inappropriate grimoire in her dower chest during the upheaval of the packing. She was not very sorry to be leaving home: she was tired of being always lectured, and the colonies seemed to her a hopeful destination: a young man who had gone out to make his fortune, she thought, could not be quite so much a stuffed-shirt.

After all the preparations and warnings, the journey seemed to her so uneventful as to be tiresome: one day after another altered only by the degree of the blowing wind, until they came to the Drowned Lands and the wind died overhead. She enjoyed looking over the railing for the first few days, at the pale white gleam of marble and masonry which could yet be glimpsed in places, when the sailors gave her a bit of spell-light to cast down below.

"There's nowt to see, though, miss," the master said in fatherly tones, while she peered hopefully. Only the occasional shark, or sometimes one of the enormous sea-spiders, clambering over the ruined towers with their long spindly red legs, but that was all—no gleam of lost treasure, no sparks of ancient magic. "There's no treasure to be had here, not without a first-rate sorcerer to raise it up for you."

She sighed, and insisted instead on being taught how to climb the rigging, much to the disgust of the sailors. "Not like having a *proper* woman on board," more than one might be heard quietly muttering.

Araminta was not perturbed, save by the increasing difficulty in coaxing interesting lessons from them. She resorted after a while to the privacy of her cabin, where through snatched moments she learned enough magic to hide the grimoire behind an illusion of *The Wealth of Nations*, so she might read it publicly and no-one the wiser. The amulet she saved for last, and tried quietly in the middle of the night, while the chaperone Mrs. Penulki snored. The maids, at first rather startled, were persuaded with only a little difficulty to keep the secret. (It must be admitted they were somewhat young and flighty creatures, and already overawed by their noble charge.)

Two slow months they spent crossing the dead shallow water, all their sails spread hopefully, and occasionally putting men over the side in boats to row them into one faint bit of current or another. All the crew cheered the night the first storm broke, a great roaring tumult that washed the windows of her high stern cabin with foam and left both of the maids moaning weakly in the water-closet. Mrs. Penulki firmly refused to entertain the possibility that Araminta might go outside for a breath of fresh air, even when the storm had at last died down, so she spent a stuffy, restless night and woke with the changing of the watch.

She lay on her back listening to the footsteps slapping against the wood, the creak of rope and sail. And then she was listening only to an unfamiliar silence, loud in its way as the thunder; no cheerful cursing, not a snatch of morning song or clatter of breakfast.

She pushed her maids until they awoke and let her climb out to hurry into her clothes. Outside, the sailors on deck were standing silent and unmoving at their ropes and tackle, as if preserved in wax, all of them watching Captain Rellowe. He was in the bows, with his long-glass to his eye aimed out to port. The dark tangled mass of storm-clouds yet receded away from them, a thin gray curtain dropped across half the stage of the horizon. The smooth curve of the ocean bowed away to either side, unbroken.

He put down the glass. "Mr. Willis, all hands to make sail, north-northwest. And go to quarters," he added, even as the master cupped his hands around his mouth to bellow orders.

The hands burst into frantic activity, running past her; below she could hear their curses as they ran the ship's guns up into their places, to the complaint of the creaking wheels. "Milady, you will go inside," Captain Rellowe said, crossing before her to the quarterdeck, none of his usual awkward smiles and scraping; he did not even lift his hat.

"Oh, what is it," Liesl, one of the maids said, gasping.

"Pirates, I expect," Araminta said, tugging her enormously heavy dower chest out from under the bed. "Oh, what good will wailing do? *Help* me."

The other ship emerged from the rain-curtain shortly, and became plainly visible out the windows of Araminta's stern cabin. It was a considerable heavier vessel, with a sharp-nosed aggressive bow that plowed the waves into a neat furrow, and no hull-spikes at all: instead her hull was painted a vile greenly color, with white markings like teeth also painted around.

Liesl and Helia both moaned and clutched at one another. "I will die before you are taken," Molloy, the eunuch, informed Araminta.

"Precious little difference it will be to me, if I am taken straightaway after," she said practically, and did not look up from her rummaging. "Go speak to one of those fellows outside: we must all have breeches, and shirts."

The chaperone made some stifled noises of protest, which Araminta ignored, and which were silenced by the emergence of the pistols and the sword.

The jewels and the trinkets were buried amid the linen and silk gowns, well-bundled in cloth against temptation for straying eyes, so they were nearly impossible to work out. The amulet in particular, nothing more than a tiny nondescript silver drachma on a thin chain, would have been nearly impossible to find if Araminta had not previously tucked it with care into the very back corner. It was just as well, she reflected, glancing up to see how the pirate vessel came on, that boredom had driven her to experimentation.

From the quarterdeck, Captain Rellowe too watched the ship coming up on their heels; his glass was good enough to show him the pirates' faces, lean and hungry and grinning. He was a good merchant captain; he had wriggled out of more than one net, but this one drew taut as a clean line drawn from his stern to her bows. The once-longed-for steady wind blew into his sails with no sign of dying, feeding the chase still better.

Amphidrake was her name, blazoned in yellow, and she was a fast ship, if rigged a little slapdash and dirty. Her hull at least was clean, he noted bitterly, mentally counting the knots he was losing to his own hull-spikes. Not one ship in a thousand met a leviathan, in season, and cannon saw them safe as often as not; but spikes the owners would have, and after the crossing of the Shallow Sea, they would surely by now be tangled with great streamers of kelp, to say nothing of barnacles and algae.

(The storm, of course, would have washed away any kelp; but the spikes made as satisfying a target to blame as any, and preferable to considering that perhaps it had not been wise to hold so very close to the regular sea-lanes, even though it was late in the season.)

In any event, the pirate would catch the *Bluegill* well before the hour of twilight, which might otherwise have given them a chance to slip away; and every man aboard knew it. Rellowe did not like to hear the mortal hush that had settled over his ship, nor to feel the eyes pinned upon his back. They could not expect miracles of him, he would have liked to tell them roundly; but of course he could say nothing so disheartening.

The *Amphidrake* gained rapidly. The bo'sun's mates began taking around the grog, and the bo'sun himself the cat, to encourage the men. The hand-axes and cutlasses and pistols were lain down along the rail, waiting.

"Mr. Gilpin," Captain Rellowe said, with a beckon to his first mate, and in undertone said to him, "Will you be so good as to ask the ladies if for their protection they would object to putting on male dress?"

"Already asked for, sir, themselves," Gilpin said, in a strange, stifled tone, his eyes darting meaningfully to the side, and Rellowe turning found himself facing a young man, with Lady Araminta's long black curls pulled back into a queue.

Rellowe stared, and then looked away, and then looked at her head—his head—and then glanced downward again, and then involuntarily a little lower—and then away again—He did not know how to look. It was no trick of dress; the shirt was open too loose for that, the very line of the jaw was different, and the waist.

Of course one heard of such devices, but generally only under intimate circumstances, or as the subject of rude jokes. Rellowe (if he had ever thought of such things at all) had vaguely imagined some sort of more caricaturish alteration; he had not gone very far in studies of sorcery himself. In reality, the line between lady and lord was distressingly thin. Araminta transformed had a sword, and two pistols, and a voice only a little high to be a tenor, in which she informed him, "I should like to be of use, sir, if you please."

He meant of course to refuse, vocally, and have her removed to the medical orlop if necessary by force; and so he should have done, if only the *Amphidrake* had not in that very moment fired her bow-chasers, an early warning-shot, and painfully lucky had taken off an alarming section of the quarterdeck rail.

All went into confusion, and he had no thought for anything but keeping the men from panic. Three men only had been hit even by so much as a splinter, but a drop of blood spilled was enough to spark the built-up store of terror. The mates had been too free with the grog, and now the lash had less effect: a good many of the men had to be thrust bodily back into their places, or pricked with sword-point, and if Araminta joined in the effort, Rellowe managed not to see.

She was perfectly happy, herself; it had not yet occurred to her they might lose. The ship had been very expensive, and the cannon seemed in excellent repair to her eye: bright brass and ebony polished, with fresh paint. Of course there was a personal danger, while she was on-deck, but high spirits made light of that, and she had never balked at a fence yet.

"You cannot mean to be a coward in front of all these other stout fellows," she sternly told one sailor, a scrawny underfed gaol-rat attempting to creep away down the forward ladderway, and helped him back to the rail with a boot at his back end.

The crash of cannon-fire was glorious, one blast after another, and then one whistling by overhead plowed into the mizzenmast. Splinters went flaying skin in all directions, blood in bright arterial spray hot and startling. Araminta reached up and touched her cheek, surprised, and looked down at the bo'sun, staring glassy-eyed back at her, dead at her feet. Her shirt was striped collar to waist with a long sash of red blood.

She did not take it very badly; she had done a great deal of hunting, and stern lecturing from her father had cured her of any tendency to be missish, even when in at the kill. Elves, of course, were much smaller, and with their claws and pointed teeth inhuman, but near enough she was not tempted in the present moment either to swoon or to be inconveniently ill, unlike one small midshipman noisily vomiting upon the deck nearby.

Above her head, the splintered mizzen creaked, moaned, and toppled: the sails making hollow thumping noises like drum skins as it came down, entangling the mainmast. Araminta was buried beneath a choking weight of canvas, stinking with slush. The ship's way was checked so abruptly she could feel the griping through the boards while she struggled to force her way out through the thick smothering folds. All was muffled beneath the sailcloth, screams, pistol-shots all distant, and then for a moment Captain Rellowe's voice rose bellowing over the fray, "Fire!"

But their own cannon spoke only with stuttering, choked voices. Before they had even quite finished, a second tremendous broadside roar thundered out in answer, one ball after another pounding into them so the *Bluegill* shook like a withered old rattle-plant. Splinters rained against the canvas, a shushing noise, and at last with a tremendous heave she managed to buy enough room to draw her sword, and cut a long tear to escape through.

Pirates were leaping across the boards: grappling hooks clawed onto whatever was left of the rail, and wide planks thrust out to make narrow bridges. The deck was awash in blood and wreckage, of the ship and of men, torn limbs and corpses underfoot.

"Parley," Captain Rellowe was calling out, a shrill and unbecoming note in his voice, without much hope: and across the boards on the deck of the other ship, the pirate captain only laughed.

"Late for that now, Captain," he called back. "No, it's to the Drowned Lands for all of you," cheerful and clear as a bell over the water. He was a splendidly looking fellow, six feet tall in an expansive coat of wool dyed priest's-crimson, with lace cuffs and gold braid. It was indeed the notorious Weedle, who had once taken fourteen prizes in a single season, and made hostage Lord Tan Cader's eldest son.

Inexperience was not, in Araminta's case, a synonym for romanticism; defeat was now writ too plainly across the deck for her to mistake it. Molloy, staggering over to her, grasped her arm: he had a gash torn across the forehead and his own sword was wet with blood. She shook him off and shot one pirate leaping towards them. "Come with me, quickly," she ordered, and turning dashed into the cabin again. The maids terrified were clinging to one another huddled by the window, with Mrs. Penulki pale and clutching a dagger in front of them.

"Your Ladyship, you may not go out again," the chaperone said, her voice trembling.

"All of you hide in the water-closet, and do not make a sound if anyone should come in," Araminta said, digging into the dower chest again. She pulled out the great long strand of pearls, her mother's parting gift, and wrapped it around her waist, hidden beneath her sash. She took out also the gold watch, meant to be presented at the betrothal ceremony, and shut and locked the chest. "Bring that, Molloy," she said, and dashing back outside pointed at Weedle, and taking a deep breath whispered, "Parley, or I will throw it overboard. *Dacet.*"

The charm leapt from her lips, and she saw him start and look about suspiciously, as the words curled into his ears. She waved her handkerchief until his eyes fixed on her, and pointed to the chest which Molloy held at the ship's rail.

Pirate captains as a class are generally alive to their best advantage. The value of a ship bound for the colonies, laden with boughten goods, might be ten thousand sovereigns, of which not more than a quarter might be realized; a dower chest might hold such a sum alone, or twice that, in jewels and silks more easily exchanged for gold. Weedle was not unwilling to be put to the little difficulty of negotiation to secure it, when they might finish putting the sword to the survivors afterwards.

"I should tell you at once, it is cursed," Araminta said, "so if anyone but me should open it, everything inside will turn to dust." It was not, of course. Such curses were extremely expensive, and dangerous besides, as an unwitting maid might accidentally ruin all the contents. Fortunately, the bluff would be rather risky to disprove. "There is a Fidelity charm inside, intended for my bride," she added, by way of explaining such a measure.

Weedle scowled a little, and a good deal more when she resolutely refused to open it, even with a dagger at her throat. "No," she said. "I will go with you, and you may take me to Kingsport, and when you have let me off at the docks, I will open it for you there. And I dare say my family will send a ransom too, if you let Captain Rellowe go and inform them," she added, raising her voice for the benefit of the listening pirates, "so you will all be better off than if you had taken the ship."

The better to emphasize her point, she had handed around the gold watch, and the pirates were all murmuring over it, imagining the chest full to the brim of such jewels. Weedle liked a little more blood, in an engagement—the fewer men to share the rewards with after—but for consolation, there was not only the contents of the chest, but what they augured for the value of the ransom.

"What do you say, lads? Shall we give the young gentleman his passage?" he called, and tossed the watch out over their heads, to be snatched for and scrambled after, as they chorused agreement.

"Lord Aramin, I must protest," Captain Rellowe said, resentfully. With the swords sheathed, his mind already began to anticipate the whispers of censure to come, what indignant retribution her family might take. But he had scarcely any alternative; exposing her to rape and murder would certainly be no better, and, after all, he could only be censured if he were alive for it, which was some improvement. So he stood by, burdened with an ashamed sense of relief, as she crossed with unpardonable calm to the pirate ship and the chest trundled over carefully behind her.

The *Amphidrake* sailed away to the south; the *Bluegill* limped on the rest of her way to New Jericho, there to be received with many exclamations of horror and dismay. The family of Lady Araminta's fiancé (whose name let discretion also elide) sent an agent to Kingsport at once; followed by others from her own family.

They waited one month and then two, but the *Amphidrake* never put in. Word eventually came that the ship had been seen instead at port in Redhook Island. It was assumed, for everyone's comfort, that the pirates had yielded to temptation and tried the chest early, and then disposed of a still-disguised Lady Araminta for tricking them.

Now that there was no danger of her rescue, she was much lionized; but for a little while only. She had been most heroic, but it would have been much more decorous to die, ideally on her own dagger. Also, both the maids had been discovered, shortly after their arrival in port, to be increasing.

Her fiancé made the appropriate offerings and, after a decent period of mourning, married a young lady of far less exalted birth, with a reputation for shrewd investing, and a particularly fine hand in the ledger-book. Lord D— gave prayers at the River Waye; his wives lit a candle in Quensington Tower and put her death-date in the family book. A quiet discreet settlement was made upon the maids, and the short affair of her life was laid to rest.

The report, however, was quite wrong; the *Amphidrake* had not put in at Redhook Island, or at Kingsport either, for the simple reason that she had struck on shoals, three weeks before, and sunk to the bottom of the ocean.

As the *Bluegill* sailed away, stripped of all but a little food and water, Captain Weedle escorted Lady Araminta and the dower chest to his own cabin. She accepted the courtesy quite unconsciously, but he did not leave it to her, and instead seated himself at the elegant dining table with every appearance of intending to stay. She stared a little, and recollected her disguise, and suddenly realized that she was about to be ruined.

This understanding might be called a little late in coming, but Araminta had generally considered the laws of etiquette as the rules of the chase, and divided them into categories: those which everyone broke, all the time; those which one could not break without being frowned at; and those which caused one to be quietly and permanently left out of every future invitation to the field. Caught browsing a spellbook was in the very limits of the second category; a bit of quiet fun with a lady friend in the first; but a night alone in the company of an unmarried gentleman was very firmly in the last.

"You aren't married, are you?" she inquired, not with much hope; she was fairly certain that in any case, a hypothetical Mrs. Weedle a thousand sea-miles distant was not the sort of protection Lady D— would ever consider acceptable for a daughter's reputation, magic amulet or no.

Weedle's face assumed a cast of melancholy, and he said, "I am not."

He was the by-blow of an officer of the Navy and a dockside lady of the West Indies sufficiently shrewd to have secured a vow on the hearth before yielding; accordingly he had been given a place aboard his father's ship at a young age. He had gifts, and might well have made a respectable career, but he had been taken too much into society by his father, and while of an impressionable age had fallen in love with a lady of birth considerably beyond his own.

He had presence enough to appeal to the maiden, but her family forbade him the house as soon as they realized his presumption. She in turn laughed with astonishment at his suggestion of an elopement, adding to this injury the insult of drawing him a brutal chart of their expected circumstances and income, five years out, without her dowry.

In a fit of pride and oppression, he had vowed that in five years' time he would be richer than her father or dead; and belatedly realized he had put himself into a very nasty situation, if any god had happened to be listening. One could never be sure. He was at the time only eighteen, several years from his own ship and the chance of substantial prize-money, if he should ever get either; and the lady's father was exceptionally rich.

Pirate ships were rather more open to the advancement of a clever lad, and there was no Navy taking the lion's share of any prize, or inconveniently ordering one into convoy duty. He deserted, changed his name, and in six months' time was third mate on the *Amphidrake* under the vicious Captain Egg, when that gentleman met his end untimely from too much expensive brandy and heatstroke.

A little scuffling had ensued, among the officers, and Weedle had regretfully been forced to kill the first and second mates, when they had tried to assert their claims on grounds of seniority; he was particularly sorry for the second mate, who had been an excellent navigator, and a drinking-companion.

With nothing to lose, Weedle had gone on cheerful and reckless, and now six years later he was alive, exceptionally rich himself, and not very sorry for the turn his life had taken, though he still liked to see himself a tragic figure. "I am not married," he repeated, and sighed, deeply.

He would not have minded in the least to be asked for the whole tale, but Araminta was too much concerned with her own circumstances, to care at all about his. She did not care at all about being ruined for its own sake, and so had forgotten to consider it, in the crisis. But she cared very much to be caught at it, and locked up in a temple the rest of her days, never allowed to do anything but make aspirin or do up accounts for widowers—*that* was not to be borne. She sighed in her own turn, and sat down upon the lid of the chest.

Weedle misunderstood the sigh, and poured her a glass of wine. "Come, sir, there is no need to be afraid, I assure you," he said, with worldly sympathy. "You will come to no harm under my protection, and soon you will be reunited with your friends."

"Oh, yes," she said, unenthusiastically. She was very sorry she had ever mentioned a ransom. "Thank you," she said, politely, and took the wine.

For consolation, it was excellent wine, and an excellent dinner: Weedle was pleased for an excuse to show away his ability to entertain in grand style, and Araminta discovered she was uncommonly hungry. She put away a truly astonishing amount of beef and soused hog's face and mince pie, none of which she had ever been allowed, of course; and she found she could drink three glasses of wine instead of the two which were ordinarily her limit.

By the time the servants cleared away the pudding, she was in too much charity with the world to be anxious. She had worked out several schemes for slipping away, if the pirates should indeed deliver her to her family; and the pearls around her waist, concealed, were a great comfort. She had meant them to pay her passage home, if she were not ransomed; now they would give her the start of an independence. And, best of all, if she were ruined, she need never worry about it again: she might jettison the whole tedious set of restrictions, which she felt was worth nearly every other pain.

And Weedle did not seem to be such a bad fellow, after all; her father's highest requirements for a man had always been, he should be a good host, and show to advantage upon a horse, and play a decent hand at the card-table. She thoughtfully eyed Weedle's leg, encased snugly in his silk knee-breeches and white stockings. It certainly did not need the aid of padding, and if his long curling black hair was a little extravagant, his height and his shoulders rescued that and the red coat from vulgarity. Fine eyes, and fine teeth; nothing not to like, at all.

So it was with renewed complacency of spirit she offered Weedle a toast, and gratified his vanity by saying sincerely, "That was the best dinner I ever ate. Shall we have a round of aughts and sixes?"

He was a little surprised to find his miserable young prisoner already so cheerful: ordinarily, it required a greater investment of patience and liquor, a show of cool, lordly kindness, to settle a delicate young nobleman's nerves, and impress upon him his host's generosity and masterful nature. But Weedle was not at all unwilling to congratulate himself on an early success, and began at once to calculate just how much sooner he might encompass his designs upon Lord Aramin's virtue. Ordinarily he allowed a week; perhaps, he thought judiciously, three days would do, in the present case.

Meanwhile, Araminta, who had spent the last several months housed in a cabin over the sailors' berth, and was already familiar with the means of consolation men found at sea, added, "Winner has first go, after?" and tilted her head towards the bed.

Taken aback, Weedle stared, acquiesced doubtfully, and picked up his cards with a faintly injured sense that the world was failing to arrange itself according to expectations. The sentiment was not soon overcome; Araminta was very good at aughts and sixes.

Araminta liked to be on *Amphidrake* very well. The pirates, most of them deserters from the Navy or the merchant marine, were not very different from the sailors on the *Bluegill*. But they did not know she was a woman, so no-one batted an eye if she wished to learn how to reef and make sail, and navigate by the stars. Instead they pronounced her a good sport and full of pluck, and began to pull their forelocks when she walked past, to show they did not hold it against her for being a nobleman.

Weedle was excellent company in most respects, if occasionally inclined to what Araminta considered inappropriate extremes of sensibility. Whistling while a man was being flogged at the grating could only be called insensitive; and on the other hand, finding one of the ship's kittens curled up dead in the corner of the cabin was not an occasion for mourning, but for throwing it out the window, and having the ship's boys swab the floor.

She enjoyed her food a great deal, and was adding muscle and inches of height at what anyone might have considered a remarkable rate at her age. She began to be concerned, a little, what would happen if she were to take off the amulet, particularly when she began to sprout a beard; but as she was certainly not going to do any such thing amidst a pack of pirates, she put it out of her mind and learned to shave.

The future loomed alarmingly for other reasons entirely. If only they had gone directly to Kingsport, Araminta had hoped they should arrive before the ransom, and she might slip away somehow while the men went on carouse with their winnings. But Weedle meant to try and break his personal record of fourteen prizes, and so he was staying out as long as possible.

"I am sure," she tried, "that they are already there. If you do not go directly, they will not wait forever: surely they will decide that I am dead, and that is why you do not come." She did not consider this a possibility at all: she envisioned nightly a horde of chaperones waiting at the docks, all of them with Horus-eyes glaring at her, and holding a heap of chains.

"I must endure the risk," Weedle said, "of your extended company," with a dangerously sentimental look in his eye: worse and worse. Araminta decidedly did not mean to spend the rest of her days as a pirate captain's paramour, no matter how splendidly muscled his thighs were. Although she depressed herself by considering that it might yet be preferable to a life with the Holy Sisters of The Sangreal.

She was perhaps inappropriately relieved, then, when a shriek of "Leviathan" went up, the next morning; and she dashed out to the deck on Weedle's heels. Now surely he should have to turn about and put in to port, she thought, not realizing they were already caught, until she tripped over the translucent tendril lying over the deck.

She pulled herself up and looked over the side. The leviathan's vast, pulsating, domelike mass was directly beneath the ship and enveloping her hull, glowing phosphorescent blue around the edges and wobbling softly like an aspic jelly. A few half-digested bones floated naked inside that transparent body, leftovers of a whale's ribcage. A faint whitish froth was already forming around the ship, at the waterline, as the leviathan's acid ate into the wood.

The men were firing pistols at it, and hacking at the tough, rubbery tendrils;

without much effect. The leviathan leisurely threw over a few more, and a tip struck one of the pirates; he arched his back and dropped his hand-axe, mouth opening in a silent, frozen scream. The tendril looped half a dozen times around him, quick as lightning, and lifted him up and over the side, drawing him down and into the mass of the leviathan's body. His eyes stared up through the green murk, full of horror and quite alive: Araminta saw them slowly blink even as he was swallowed up into the jelly.

She snatched for a sword herself, and began to help chop away, ducking involuntarily as more of the thin limbs came up, balletic and graceful, to lace over the deck. Thankfully they did nothing once they were there other than to cling on, if one did not touch the glistening pink tips.

"Leave off, you damned lubbers," Weedle was shouting. "Make sail! All hands to make sail—"

He was standing at the wheel. Araminta joined the rush for the rope lines, and shortly they were making nine knots in the direction of the wind, back towards the Drowned Lands. It was a sorry speed, by the *Amphidrake*'s usual standards; the leviathan dragging from below worse than ten thousand barnacles. It did not seem particularly incommoded by their movement, and kept throwing over more arms; an acrid smell, like woodsmoke and poison, rose from the sides. The men had nearly all gone to huddle down below, out of reach of the tendrils. Weedle held the wheel with one arm, and an oar with the other, which he used to beat off any that came at him.

Araminta seized his long-glass, and climbed up to the crow's-nest to go looking out: she could see clearly where the water changed color, and the gorgeous blue-green began; the shipping lanes visible as broad bands of darker blue running through the Shallow Sea. The wind was moderately high, and everywhere she looked there seemed to be a little froth of cresting waves, useless; until at last she glimpsed in the distance a steady bank of white: a reef, or some land near enough the surface to make a breakwater; and she thought even a little green behind it: an island, maybe.

A fist of tendrils had wrapped around the mast since she had gone up, poisonous tips waving hopefully: there would be no climbing down now. She used the whisper-charm to tell Weedle the way: south by southeast, and then she grimly clung on to the swinging nest as he drove them towards the shoals.

What was left of the leviathan, a vile gelatinous mess stinking all the way to the shore, bobbed gently up and down with the waves breaking on the shoals, pinned atop the rocks along with what was left of the *Amphidrake*. This was not very much but a section of the quarterdeck, the roof of the cabin, and, unluckily, the top twelve feet of her mainmast, with the black skull flag gaily flying, planted neatly in a noxious mound of jelly.

The wreckage had so far survived three rainstorms. The survivors gazed at it dismally from the shore, and concocted increasingly desperate and unlikely schemes for tearing away, burning, or explaining the flag, on the arrival of a Navy patrol—these being regular enough, along the nearby shipping lanes, to make a rescue eventual, rather than unlikely.

"And then they put out the yard-arm, and string us all up one by one," the bo'sun Mr. Ribb said, morbidly.

"If so," Araminta snapped, losing patience with all of them, "at least it is better than being et up by the leviathan, and we may as well not sit here on the shore and moan." This was directed pointedly at Weedle, bitter and slumped under a palm tree. He had not been in the least inclined to go down with his ship, although he secretly felt he ought to have done, and it was hard to find that his unromantic escape had only bought him a few weeks of life and an ignominious death.

Araminta did not herself need to worry about hanging, but she was not much less unhappy, being perfectly certain the Navy would take her directly back to her family, under such guard as would make escape impossible. Nevertheless, she was not inclined to only eat coconuts and throw stones at monkeys and complain all day.

The island was an old, old mountaintop, furred with thick green vegetation, and nearly all cliffs rising directly from the ocean. Where the shoals had blocked the full force of the waves, a small natural harbor had developed, and the narrow strip of white sand which had given them shelter. Climbing up to the cliff walls to either side, Araminta could look down into the glass-clear water and see the mountainside dropping down and away, far away, and in a few places even the bleached gray spears of drowned trees below.

They had found the ruins of an old walkway, back in the jungle, while hunting: smooth, uneven bricks of creamy white stone which led up and into the island's interior; but none of the men wanted to follow it. "That's the Drowned Ones' work," they said, with shudders of dismay, and made various superstitious gestures, and refused even to let her go alone.

But after three days and a rainstorm had gone by, leaving the black flag as securely planted as ever, hanging loomed ever larger; and when Araminta again tried to persuade them, a few agreed to go along.

The walkway wound narrowly up the mountainside, pausing occasionally at small niches carved into the rock face, mossy remnants of statues squatting inside. The road was steep, and in places they had to climb on hands and feet with nothing more than narrow ledges for footholds. Araminta did not like to think how difficult a pilgrimage it might have been, three thousand years ago, before the Drowning, when the trail would have begun at the mountain's base and not near its summit. The men flinched at every niche; but nothing happened as they climbed, except that they got dust in their noses, and sneezed a great deal, and Jem Gorey was stung by a wasp.

The trail ended at a shrine, perched precarious and delicate atop the very summit; two massive sculpted lion-women sprawled at the gate, the fine detail of their heavy breasts and beards still perfectly preserved, so many years gone. The roof of the shrine stood some twenty feet in the air, on delicate columns not as thick as Araminta's wrist, each one the elongated graceful figure of a woman, and filmy drapery hung from the rafters still, billowing in great sheets of clean white. An altar of white stone stood in the center, and upon it a wide platter of shining silver.

"Wind goddess," Mr. Ribb said, gloomily. "Wind goddess for sure; we'll get no use here. Don't you be an ass, Porlock," he added, cutting that sailor a hard look. "As much as a man's life is worth, go poking into there."

"I'll just nip in," Porlock said, his eyes on the silver platter, and set his foot on the first stair of the gate.

The lion-women stirred, and cracked ebony-black eyes, and turned to look at him. He recoiled, or tried to: his foot would not come off the stair. "Help, fellows!" he cried, desperately. "Take my arm, heave—"

No-one went anywhere near him. With a grinding noise like millstones, the lion-women rose up onto their massive paws and came leisurely towards him. Taking either one an arm, they tore him in two quite effortlessly; and then tore the parts in two again.

The other men fled, scattering back down the mountainside, as the lion-women turned their heads to look them over. Araminta alone did not flee, but waited until the others had run away. The living statues settled themselves back into their places, but they kept their eyes open and fixed on her, watchfully.

She debated with herself a while; she had read enough stories to know the dangers. She did not care to become a permanent resident, forced to tend the shrine forever; and it might not be only men who were punished for the temerity to enter. In favor of the attempt, however, the shrine plainly did not need much tending: whatever magic had made it, sustained it, with no guardian necessary but the deadly statues. And those stones along the trail had been worn smooth by more than weather: many feet had come this way, once upon a time.

"All right," she said at last, aloud, and reaching up to her neck took off the amulet.

She was braced to find herself abruptly back in her own former body, a good deal smaller; but the alteration was as mild as before. She looked down at her arms, and her legs: the same new length, and still heavy with muscle; she had lost none of the weight she had gained, or the height. Breasts swelled out beneath her shirt, her hips and waist had negotiated the exchange of an inch or two between themselves, and her face when she touched it felt a little different—the beard was gone, she noted gratefully—but that was all.

The guardians peered at her doubtfully when she came up the stairs. They did get up, as she came inside, and paced after her all the way to the altar, occasionally leaning forward for a suspicious sniff. She unwound the strand of pearls from around her waist and poured the whole length of it rattling into the offering-dish, a heap of opalescence and silver.

The lion-women went back to their places, satisfied. The hangings rose and shuddered in a sudden gust of wind, and the goddess spoke: a fine gift, and a long time since anyone had come to worship; what did Araminta want?

It was not like Midwinter Feast, where the medium was taken over and told fortunes; or like church services at Lammas tide. The goddess of the Drowned

Ones spoke rather matter-of-factly, and there was no real sound at all, only the wind rising and falling over the thrumming hangings. But Araminta understood perfectly, and understood also that her prepared answers were all wrong. The goddess was not offering a little favor, a charm to hide her or a key to unlock chains, or even a way off the island; the goddess was asking a question, and the question had to be answered truly.

Easier to say what Araminta did not want: to go home and be put in a convent, to go on to the colonies and be married. Not to be a prisoner, or a fine lady, or a captain's lover, or a man in disguise forever; not, she added, that it was not entertaining enough for a time; but what she really wanted, she told the goddess, was to be a captain herself, of her own life; and free.

A fine wish, the goddess said, for a fine gift. Take one of those pearls, and go down and throw it in the ocean.

Araminta took a pearl out of the dish: it came easily off the strand. She went down the narrow walkway, down to the shore, and past all the men staring at her and crossing themselves in alarm, and she threw the pearl into the clear blue waters of the natural harbor.

For a moment, nothing happened; then a sudden foaming overtook the surface of the water, white as milk. With a roar of parting waves and a shudder, the *Amphidrake* came rising from the deep in all her shattered pieces, seaweed and ocean spilling away. Her ribs and keel showed through the gaps in her half-eaten hull for a moment, and then the foam was climbing up her sides, and leaving gleaming unbroken pearl behind. The decks were rebuilt in smooth white wood; tall slim masts, carved in the shapes of women, climbed up one after another, and vast white sails unfurled in a wind that teased them gently full.

The foam subsided to the water, and solidified into a narrow dock of pearl, running to shore to meet her. Araminta turned to look a rather dazed Weedle in the face.

"This is my ship," she said, "and you and all your men are welcome, if you would rather take service with me than wait for the Navy."

She pulled her hair back from her head, and tied it with a thread from her shirt; and she stepped out onto the dock. She was nearly at the ship when Weedle came out onto the dock at last, and called, "Aramin!" after her.

She turned and smiled at him, a flashing smile. "Araminta," she said, and went aboard.

THE WHALE BELOW

By Jayme Lynn Blaschke

Avispa Feroz dropped below the scattered cloud deck, a lethal silver dart aimed at the whaling squadron. Her long sailing masts were folded tightly along the length of her bow. A black wasp riding jagged lightning bolts cut through the red striping emblazoned upon her nose. Driven by four powerful nacelle props boxing the stern just behind the rearward pilot house, *Avispa Feroz* swept down on her prey. Measuring 445 feet bow-to-stern, she dwarfed even the largest airship of the whaling squadron by a nearly four-to-one margin.

"I count me some five whalers, Capitan. All 'em are chasers, anchored fast to a kelper whale. Big one, too, from the looks of things." Magda Pinzón, the first mate, held the elevator wheel in her left hand with an underhanded grip, her other hand holding a spyglass to her eye. Upon her right forearm the Cydone prayer for the dead was tattooed in landric lettering. Her shoulders were almost as square as her jaw, and her curly red hair was chopped short. She lowered her spyglass and frowned. "I don't see a skybarge."

"Fortunate for us, Magda. That's six less bodies shooting at us, give or take." Capitan Baldomero Valdez sat on the edge of his seat in *Avispa Feroz*'s pilot house, rubbing his thumb and forefinger together with nervous energy. His eyes, almost as dark as his beard, flicked from Magda to the young, wide-eyed pilot Cristobal Tavares, then to the one-armed, bushy-browed bos'n Uriel Zarzamora. "Señor Tavares, inform grapple station one to hold themselves in reserve. Just in case one of those whalers tries a breakaway." His voice was soft as nails.

"Aye, Capitan," Tavares answered from the rudder wheel, relaying the orders through the speaking-tubes.

"Opinion, Magda?" Capitan Valdez asked.

"I'm not seeing any of the fishchasers, Capitan," Magda answered. "None working the whale, no action on the ships."

"Best guess, then."

"Best guess is twenty men total, if they crew four men per whaler like any sane sons-a-bitches do. I'll be damned if they have more than six long-barrel rifles, though," she answered. "They'd be crazy to fight, a squadron this small. Most likely we needs to worry 'bout them scattering like marlowhips."

"Add another six men to that count," said Zarzamora from his station by the gas boards. He looked out the starboard portal to the looming orange-and-gold crescent of Cibola, the motherworld, slicing through half the sky. "Cibola's a crafty bitch. It'd be like her to steal away the skybarge but double up the crew on those five chasers."

"Six either way, it makes no difference—they'll all be shark food by the end of the day," Capitan Valdez said, grinning. His two front teeth flashed gold. "Señor Zarzamora, sound for standard boarding—and by Cibola, they'd better leave one of those fishchasers alive this time if they know what's good for them. How's anyone going to know to fear us if we never leave living witnesses to spread the tales?"

"Aye, Capitan," Zarzamora said, then piped the signal through the speaking-tubes.

"What say we run old *Avispa Feroz* up their arses hard and fast, Magda? The damn fishchasers won't know what hit 'em."

"Aye. That they won't, Capitan." Magda spun her wheel, and *Avispa Feroz* nosed sharply down.

"Trim her up, Señor Tavares. We want to split their lines down the middle, not run 'em under."

Tavares corrected to port. Magda spun her wheel the opposite direction, leveling *Avispa Feroz* out forty feet above the waves. The whaling fleet surged closer.

"There," Capitan Valdez said, pointing. "Second chaser to starboard, flying the Comodoro's pennant. See it, Señor Zarzamora?"

"Aye. That one belongs to Javier's boarding crew." Zarzamora started up the ladder into *Avispa Feroz*'s hull. "I'll make sure they don't ruin anything of value."

"I want the log book!" Capitan Valdez called after him, and Zarzamora acknowledged with a backhanded wave.

"Nothing working up on those whalers," said Magda, discarding her spyglass. Disbelief crept into her voice. "You don't suppose them fishchasers ain't seen us yet, do you?"

"Well, they'll get a damn sight more than an eyeful soon enough, Magda. Get ready to signal Pedemaestro Galindo for full reverse."

Magda grabbed the lever controlling the ship's bell system. The whalers loomed closer.

"Steady… steady…" said Capitan Valdez. "*Now!*"

Magda pumped the lever, sending three bursts of ringing through the ship. Almost instantly, a harsh grinding and groaning sounded from above them as Pedemaestro Galindo shifted gears in the prophouse deep in the gut of *Avispa Feroz*. The propellers spun down, then whipped back to life in reverse. *Avispa Feroz* shuddered but she did slow, like a great shark nosing in amongst a school of frightened minnows.

Five grapples lashed out from the buitre airship in rapid-fire cadence. The great barbed prongs speared the whalers—pierced the outer envelopes and found solid purchase. The grappling teams winched their prey to *Avispa Feroz*. Timbers groaned as the whalers bellied up against *Avispa Feroz*'s hull. Flintlocks cocked and cutlasses drawn, the boarding parties—three men each—slid across, tethered by pisshooks to the cables.

"I'm not hearing any killing. Why am I not hearing any killing?" demanded Capitan Valdez. "Fishchasers always have one or two heroes in their midst—I know this. Those bastards complicate what should otherwise be a simple—"

"Mateo's signaling from the pilot house of his whaler," Magda said, leaning forward against the glass windscreen for a better view. She frowned. "He's shouting something." She unlatched the screen and pushed it open.

"—deserted," Mateo called out. "The whole damn ship's empty."

Magda's frown deepened. She quickly made the Cydone sign of preservation over her heart.

"The crew's got to be somewhere. They can't have just disappeared," grumbled Capitan Valdez. "They're holed up atop their gas cells. Or all together on one of the other chaser ships. I don't care where they are, I want them found before they pull some damn fool stunt that damages *Avispa Feroz!*"

The whaler crew wasn't holed up atop the gas cells. There wasn't a soul—living or dead—aboard the whaler. One by one reports came back from the other captured airships, each one of those deserted as well.

"So what happened to them all? Fishchasers don't leave five perfectly good ships—not to mention a kelper this size—derelict without good reason." Capitan Valdez chewed at the topmost whiskers of his beard, worrying the mystery.

"Zarzamora's party found blood in the pilot house of the second whaler to starboard," Magda reported. "*Something* happened here. Something what made them cut loose the skybarge and take their chances on the winds. Ain't nobody in their right mind cut loose on a skybarge this far from land."

Capitan Valdez pointed a stubby finger at Magda. "When Zarzamora finds the Comodoro's log book have him bring it straight to me… Madre dios!"

Outside, the foremost of the whalers sagged below *Avispa Feroz*'s bow, straining at the grapple line. The rent where the grapple pierced the fabric hull flapped wildly. Below, the kelper whale's massive, flat head was already slipping beneath the waves.

"Damn! They speared it too high," Magda said. "Who's on that team?"

"That's Chago Bonilla's group," said Tavares. "Those two brothers we just signed on—Rubén and Eduardo Campos."

"Figures. You heard me tell them snot-nosed shits, 'Aim low into the underbelly timbers. You shoot high, all you're gonna hit is gas bag.' But did they listen?"

Capitan Valdez gave her a resigned look. "You know what to do."

Magda sighed. "Aye, Capitan. Ol' Magda *always* knows what to do."

She clambered up the pilot house ladder to the keel catwalk, then puffed her way up to the bow double-quick. Just past the copper ballast tanks, Magda unfastened a wood-and-canvas portal and climbed into the tight pigeon well between the first and second gas cells. Startled, a trio of fat green-and-black arañas del seda did an eight-legged scurry away across the cells. She crawled up the rope ladder to the grapple station. It was little more than a wooden cage anchored to one of *Avispa*

Feroz's ribs, but it was solid enough to support a massive ballista and a windlass. Holding onto the railing for balance, Magda ducked under the rolled-up canvas portal cover and assessed the situation.

The grapple line reached down sharply, straining hard against the folded mast and furled sail just below the opening. From this vantage, the gash in the whaler's hull looked much worse, and Magda could hear the escaping helio gas. The whaler's hull already looked flaccid in places. It was going down, and quickly.

"Ah, dios mío." She made the Cydone ward sign for luck, then reached over and released the windlass' brake. Immediately, it began to whirl, feeding out cable. Freed of the dead weight, *Avispa Feroz* nosed upward, sharply enough to force Magda to steady herself against the cage. The whaler dipped down, kissing the green waters. No longer buoyed, the kelper's head slumped fully beneath the surface.

Curses poured out of the whaler, followed by Chago, Rubén and Eduardo swimming away from the airship before the hull completely collapsed over them.

"You listen to Magda next time, right?" she shouted down at them. "You listen, so Magda doesn't have to clean up any more of your shit, understand?"

She waved off their cries for help.

"You idiots free up the grapple first, then we take you back aboard. Maybe. That whaler was a prize worth more than the lot of you combined, so you best thank Cibola I don't kill you all now. Come to think of it, that big ship grapple cost more'n you're worth as well. You best hope it don't take to rusting or I might be reconsidering the killing part."

Chago shouted just what he thought Magda should do with a rusty ship grapple. Magda turned her back to them and made her way back to the pilot house.

"Looks like the wreck'll float well enough. I've reassigned that grapple crew to salvage," she announced, coming down the ladder. "And I'm about to have to kill that Chago, Capitan. Cut him up into little pieces and feed him to the crabs."

Capitan Valdez didn't turn from the open windscreen. He leaned out, looking over the kelper whale carcass below. "Not sure if I can spare the body, Magda. Is it necessary?"

"That sonofabitch been thinking impure thoughts 'bout me for a long time, and now he's giving me lip. I let a man get away with that once before. Ain't making the same mistake twice."

Capitan Valdez nodded thoughtfully. "Well, use your best judgment. But try not to spook the rest of the crew."

"Never been a crew what sailed couldn't stand a good spooking."

Capitan Valdez motioned her over to him. "Look down there. The cutting stage's still tethered to the whale. Why'd they cut the skybarge loose and leave the cutting stage?"

Magda sniffed in disgust. "You think too much, Capitan. Who gives a shit why fishchasers do the crazy things they do? These ships is derelict. We tow them in for auction and won't even have to forge their papers, hardly. That dead fish bound to be taking on water—see how low it's riding? I say cut it loose before it drags the four good whalers we got down with it."

Magda peered down at the kelper, the first time she'd really looked *at* it since their descent. Up close, the enormity of the creature sank in. Massive beyond all reason, its head loomed just below the surface of the water, the crumpled wreckage of the whaler floating atop its snout. Dozens of long spikes clamped the kelper's mouth shut to keep it from taking on water. Its dull, sightless eyes stared up at them. Farther back, a copper drum had been fitted over the blowhole, now submerged. On either flank of the whale, along the parallel dorsal ridges, taut cables ran from deeply embedded harpoons up to the captured whalers on either side of *Avispa Feroz*. Rope ladders ran back down from the whalers to the cutting stage, directly below *Avispa Feroz*.

A raft a hundred or so feet long and maybe a third as wide, the cutting stage floated above the thick forest of inquilinic seaweed that grew from the kelper's back and hid much of the carcass from view. Barrels crowded the rope railing to port and four fat copper try pots sat at the corners of the raft. Salt-gray hoses sprawled along the deck, connected to float-mounted air pumps. Blanket strips of blubber lay rotting on the deck, along with scattered flensing blades. A handful of disheveled black croates worried at the blubber, flapping and squawking. Anchored on either side of the cutting stage, long booms extended out over the water. A system of ropes and pulleys on one held up a hooked strip of blubber still attached to the carcass. At the far end of the cutting stage, the other two whalers were anchored to the whale with ladders running down as well. From the cutting stage on back to where the remaining two whalers were tethered to the tail, the anchoring harpoons hidden beneath the tangled forest of seaweed.

Capitan Valdez shook his head. "Magda, Magda, Magda. Where's your sense of adventure? Your sense of romance?"

Magda narrowed her eyes. "You watch your mouth. Capitan or not, I can cut you up for crab-bait just as easy as Chago."

"*Curiosity*, Magda. I mean curiosity."

"Yeah, only I don't got none of that. It's too much trouble. Say, I have an idea: Let's take what we got and not be here anymore."

"I'm dropping a ladder to the cutting stage," Capitan Valdez said abruptly. "Señor Tavares, is Andrés still on topside lookout? Good. Tell him to stay there and keep alert. Then relay to Pedemaestro Galindo that he's to secure his gigapedes and meet me and Magda down on the cutting stage. The same goes for the boarding parties, once they've secured their whalers. *Avispa Feroz* is in your hands."

He unbolted the side hatchway and pushed the spooled ladder out, then climbed down.

Magda followed. The deck of the cutting stage shifted and swayed with the gentle motion of the waves. It was different from the sway of an airship's deck, she noted. More regular. Continuous. Magda blinked twice, wrinkling her nose. "I ain't smelled nothing this bad since that whorehouse Paōlo took us to on Jaysos," she said. "Though I got to admit, that Carita I had sure knew her business."

"I wouldn'ta thought there'd be enough whores on all of Jaysos to give Magda the business to her liking," said Chago, pulling his dripping self up onto the cutting stage. The two Campos boys swam up behind him, grabbing onto the deck.

Magda pulled her flintlock from her belt in one fluid motion, holding it cocked and aimed at Chago's head. Chago blanched. Rubén and Eduardo ducked back into the water.

"Not now, Magda," said Capitan Valdez, kneeling beside the empty barrels. "Come here—tell me what you see."

Reluctantly, Magda lowered her pistol and Chago breathed a sigh of relief. She examined the barrels, running her finger through a number of rough, splintered holes. Thick, golden whale oil oozed from one.

"Well?"

"They ain't going to be much for holding anything, that's for certain."

"Exactly. And look here in the deck—there're slugs buried here, and here... What's this—shards of glass? No, it's just a piece of seashell." Capitan Valdez looked up at Magda, eyes lively. He held up the finger-long splinter of ivory shell, then tossed it overboard. "Lots of shooting. Blood in some of the whalers. But if it was a mutiny... dios, it still makes no sense."

"Capitan, I think you wanted this," came Zarzamora's voice from above. They looked up at Zarzamora spider-climbing down one of the whaler ladders. His black ponytail flapped eagerly in the breeze, and held between the stub of his left arm and his chest was a leather-bound book. He jumped down the last few feet, flipping the book to Capitan Valdez with practiced ease. "Comodoro's log book, as requested."

As Capitan Valdez submerged himself in the log, Magda turned to Chago, Rubén and Eduardo. "All right, you soggy sons-a-bitches, time to quit loafing and earn your keep! All this rotting blubber, I want it *gone*. Same goes for the nasty shit fermenting in those pots. I'm sick of this rank air. Move it!"

The whaling crew had flensed most of the dorsal blubber from the carcass, exposing dark, discolored meat below. Long fronds of blubber-rooted seaweed waved and tangled along the edges of the harvested area, with dozens of sleek green crabs the size of frying pans clambering through the tangle. The circular drum—a thick, copper-and-brass affair—appeared solidly anchored six yards beyond the flensing and almost as deep under water. The heavy, hinged lid appeared to be latched securely, but a ring of clamps around the edge hadn't been fastened.

When Magda turned back, Pedemaestro Galindo had joined Capitan Valdez. Galindo was round and bald, skin as weathered as the cutting stage's deck. He was also missing his nose, and wore a black patch tied over it. It made him look unbearably ridiculous, but Magda'd seen him without it. She much preferred the patch.

"So, do we know what this drum is, or not?" she asked to no one in particular.

"Indeed we do," answered Capitan Valdez. "It's a blow hatch, to keep the whale watertight and allow access to its inner cavities."

"Why the hell would anyone want to get inside that stinking pile of rot?"

Capitan Valdez grinned. "Pedemaestro Galindo knows, don't you, Segio?"

"Gullet pearls," Galindo said. "Like as not they'd just started in harvesting before whatever it was interrupted 'em.See how that blow hatch ain't bolted, only latched down? That says they cut out in a panic. Any Comodoro worth his salt'd skin 'em alive for that normally."

"Señor Galindo served on a whaler during his misspent youth," Capitan Valdez explained.

"Three weeks, only. Then I jumped ship," Galindo said.

"That's more experience than any of the rest of us have. He's organizing our harvesting efforts. Magda, make what he needs to happen, happen."

Magda stared at him, blinking. "Sounds like work," she grumbled. "Strikes me that if I wanted *honest* work, I wouldn't have signed on with a buitre."

"Magda, you have to have faith," Capitan Valdez said, gripping her shoulder. "You and me, we've pissed away more gold in a single night than most people see in a lifetime. But Magda, I'm telling you—*this* haul will dwarf them all. And the log says all the hard work's already done."

"'Course, the log says they ran this whale down close to five days back. Bound to be mighty ripe inside by now," said Galindo, scratching his head. "And I can't fathom how a squadron this small could harvest a kelper this size. Five chasers? I'm not an expert, mind you, but I'd say this kelper's a eight chaser, minimum."

Magda closed her eyes, pinching the bridge of her nose with her thumb and forefinger. "What needs to be done first?"

"Well," said Galindo, hitching up his pants, "we're going to need more crew on this than just you and me."

"If it's nasty work, I've got the perfect crew in mind," Magda said, eyeing Chago, Rubén and Eduardo as they heaved a four-yard-long strip of blubber overboard. "What else?"

Galindo *tched* through his teeth. "Can't do shit with that sumbitch sunk like it is. Before you go and do nothing else, you best figure out how to get that kelper head up out of the water."

Magda glanced over to the drifting wreckage of the ruined whaler, then up at *Avispa Feroz*. "Way ahead of you."

It took three hours to splice the grapple cable onto the whaler's harpoon line, even after enlisting Zarzamora's help. Then, because Galindo thought the harpoon'd loosened enough that it might tear free, Magda ordered two more harpoons set into the kelper. Lines were run from *Avispa Feroz* to the harpoons. When they'd finally finished, late in the day, the carcass was as secure as anyone could hope.

"We're clear!" Magda gave a thumbs-up as the last man—Eduardo—pulled himself up onto the cutting stage after the final harpoon check.

Galindo nodded, then shouted up to the pilot house, "Ease her up now, nice and gentle."

A deluge rained down upon them as the bow ballast tanks opened. The cables tightened. The timbers far above in the nose of *Avispa Feroz* groaned ominously. The blubber around the harpoons puckered, but held. Slowly, the kelper's head began to rise.

"That's enough!" shouted Galindo, motioning wildly. "Enough!"

The ballast rain shut off, reduced to a spastic trickle. The kelper continued to rise, buoyant momentum lifting the snout above the waves. The head broached the surface, then the blowhole. The bulk swelled up beneath the cutting stage, heaving up the forward edge. The kelper hung there for a moment, threatening to continue up into the sky, but with a ghostly groan retreated. It rose once more before finding equilibrium, then settled as waves agitated around it. Rivulets streamed down the gray-green wrinkled hide.

It stank worse than all the rotten fish in the world gathered together to celebrate the joys of rankness. Rubén vomited on the deck.

"Clean that puke up, before I make you lick it up," Magda barked. "We're all breathing the same air here—you don't see no one else pissing and moaning about it." She turned to Galindo. "You're the expert. What next?"

Galindo shrugged. "Set up the air pumps and open the hatch."

"Fine, let's get it over with."

Magda, Galindo and Zarzamora climbed off the cutting stage onto the kelper. The knotty skin was firm, not as slick as it appeared. The blow hatch glistened brightly, intact and sealed.

"See there? They're made to latch automatically whenever they close, so big waves or somesuch don't swamp the whale and drag her down with a belly full of seawater," Galindo said. He grabbed the latch handle and gave it a pull. It refused to budge. "Bastard's got some nasty internal pressure built up. Must be from the sun's heating."

"Rot gas, I'll bet," Zarzamora said. "It's been dead the better part of a week. A cow'd have bloated up split apart by now. I'm surprised this thing isn't worse off than it is."

"Huh," grunted Galindo, bracing himself against the drum and tugging on the handle again. "The seawater's cold. That keeps the carcass from putrefying fast, see? But it don't stop it completely. Stand clear. With that much pressure, when I do get this open, it's going to—"

The lid burst open with a sudden *foomp*, jerking the handle away and clanging hard against the side of the drum. A geyser of fog billowed out like whalespout. A sticky, curdled stench settled in over them.

"Thanks for the warning," said Magda, peering into the hatch. The septum had been sliced away, the twin blowholes now joined as a single, man-sized tunnel. A rope ladder secured to the inside of the drum disappeared into the darkness. "There is no way," she said, backing away, "that anyone can work in that air."

"That's what those pumps are for. Once they're going, they'll have the air inside breathable in half an hour. Give or take."

Magda wrinkled her nose. "Define 'breathable.'"

"I've got an idea," said Galindo, heading back to the cutting stage. "I'm running up to *Avispa Feroz* for a bit. Don't go down without me."

"Don't worry, amigo. We wouldn't dream of leaving you behind," answered Zarzamora.

"He's the one what ain't got a nose—he should be the first one down." Magda shook her head. "Señor Zarzamora, I don't know what it takes to make those louts up there into pearlmen… but whatever it is, we'd best get to it."

They set Chago's crew to work on the pumps, casting them afloat on either side of the kelper where the gentle, steady wave action would work the bellows. Rubén and Eduardo ran the salt-gray hoses across the seaweed-matted carcass, dropping them down the darkness of the blowhole. More airmen came down from the whalers and gathered along the edge of the cutting stage, watching with idle interest. By the time Galindo returned, Magda and Zarzamora had scavenged enough whale oil lamps, gaffs and blubber spades from the cutting stage to outfit the party.

"Listen up, people, this is the plan, and I'm only gonna say it once," Magda said. "This is just a look-see—once we know the status down below, we come back up and plan our course of action for tomorrow morning. Galindo goes first on account of he ain't got any nose and he's the only one who halfway knows what he's doing. Bonilla, Campos and Campos are next. Zarzamora, you're on pump duty because… well, damn, man—you're down to just the one arm."

Zarzamora shrugged. "No arguments from me."

"Here you go. Take this and tie it over yer noses," Galindo said, handing out dirty red strips of cloth. "Go on! Don't just stand there lookin' like a strangled hollager, unless you want to choke on that whale's stink. I put a dollop of Essence of Numbskull on each what I got from the surgeon's stores. Since we ain't had a ship's surgeon going on two years, I figure nobody'd mind. Take a few breaths of that and your nose'll be dead to the world, mark my words."

"If anyone should know, it's you," Magda said, tying the cloth on. She took a breath and felt as if her eyes would pop out of her skull. The cutting, astringent vapors seared her sinuses. As suddenly as it'd started, the sensation subsided. The stench of the carcass faded as well.

Galindo took a lantern, cocked his leg over the drum and disappeared down the hatch. One-by-one they followed, Magda taking the final lantern as Zarzamora waved a mock farewell.

The walls of the tunnel were close and viscous, raw and wounded and the ugly color of bruises. The thick air stank of rotten fish, blood and salt. Several times Magda had to stop her climb and cling to the ladder as it jerked roughly. Indignant curses rose up from below, muffled and blunt.

Abruptly, the airway curved away but the ladder continued downward through a ragged opening edged with splintered bone. A vast space opened up beneath that, and Magda lowered herself into the eerie yellow glow.

The lanterns cast strange, conflicting shadows against the dark, ribbed roof of the mouth. The massive blue tongue filled the cavity like a mountain laid flat, disappearing into the brushy forest of baleen that ringed the mouth. Dark water pooled beneath the baleen, seepage from the imperfect seals upon the mouth. Black, booted footprints smeared the knotty blue surface, congealed blood thick and gummy in the humid cavern. The entire crew of *Avispa Feroz* could come down here, Magda realized, and the place would still feel empty.

"There's your gullet pearls, Magda," Galindo said, breaking her distraction. He gestured with his pole. "The question is, how do we get at 'em?"

The cavernous mouth constricted rapidly, and the throat itself was barely wide enough for two men to stand abreast, arms spread. Hundreds of broken pieces of shell littered the floor, discolored with the undrying blood. Around the throat, hundreds more mollusks with thick, streamlined shells that tapered, clawlike, down the throat clustered above and below like oysters on a reef. Most were tiny, no bigger than a little finger, but there were raw patches on the flesh of the throat where something large had been cut away. The mottled black-and-tan shells glistened in the lamplight, their sharply pointed tips presenting daunting obstacles for any creature attempting to escape the kelper's belly. There were larger mollusks as well—judging by their thickness, longer than a forearm, but these were all partially buried beneath a massive black... *something*.

"What in Cibola's name is *that?*" demanded Magda. Driftwood and seaweed, along with big chunks of broken shell and bone, were cemented together in a black, irregular mass that blocked the entirety of the throat, overrunning most of the anchored shellfish.

"Damned if I know. The mussel bed should extend another fifteen, twenty feet back. Whatever this is, it's blocking us from most of the pearls," Galindo answered. "Looks like the fishchasers already got everything easy to get at. If anyone else has an idea, now's the time to speak up."

The crew murmured to each other, but nobody spoke up.

"Right. Then we might as well see if these beauties have any pearls to worry about." Galindo jabbed his blubber spade blade into a cluster of palm-sized mussels untouched by the black cement, and with a twist, popped one free. He picked it up and produced a knife in his free hand, opening the shell like a skilled oyster man. "Ah! Look at this, then," he said, holding up a gray-green ball the size of a pea. "We're in a great deal of luck, boys—and Magda. Unless I'm wrong, these here are dewclaw mussels. Tigereyes are the only ones what bring a better price."

"Fat lot of good it'll do us," Chago grumbled, poking at the mass with his blade. The blade came away black. "All the pearls are behind this stuff."

"I'll get you a spoon, Chago, and you can dig through it," said Magda. "Nasty work, sure, but it'll keep you out of trouble."

Chago bristled, but said nothing.

"Look here, this darker part's newer. See? You can follow the seam," Galindo said, running his finger along an irregular arch. Her finger came away inky black. "It looks like the fishchasers tried to cut their way through right here. I don't think... hello, is that a *gouger* stuck in there?"

The business end of the semicircular blade jutted out from the mass, its handle buried deep within.

"Looks to me that whatever hole they cut done closed back up," Magda said.

"You don't... you don't think the fishchasers are all trapped behind that black stuff, do you?" Rubén Campos said softly to his brother.

"Can't be," Galindo said. "Besides, they'd all be dead by now. The air's bad."

"I've seen enough. Everyone back topside," Magda said. "We'll let Capitan Valdez decide what to do next. Myself, I am seven different kinds of sick of whale innards."

The climb back up was slow going, and by the time Magda climbed through the blow hatch, the sun had set and the indigo sky was tinged rose on the horizon. The cutting stage blazed with light from dozens of lanterns, and a rolling chantey danced in the air. "Frost in the Air" it was, with *Avispa Feroz*'s regular trio performing it on fiddle, concertina and zambomba. A dozen airmen or more jostled happily together, passing around long brown bottles from a wooden crate.

Dinner, it seemed, was being served on the raft as well—a thick stew with tough, half-dried beef and rye bread liberated, no doubt, from the whalers' stores. Magda grabbed some for herself and set out to find Capitan Valdez. It wasn't easy in all the coming and going, but she eventually spotted him, seated atop one of the empty barrels and watching the crew's antics with amusement.

"The coral wine, I take it?" she asked. "Not like you to be so generous with the plunder."

"Can't stand the stuff, myself. My taste's always been for metheglin. As is yours," he answered, taking a swallow of yellow-green liquid from his own bottle before handing it to her. "Most of these men never tasted such expensive drink as coral wine. Most never will again. This is shaping up to be our richest haul yet—once we sell off those four whalers. I figure I can afford to be generous for a change."

Magda grunted noncommittally, sucking on the bottle. Out of the corner of her eye, she spotted Chago climbing down the ladder from *Avispa Feroz*, holding a small firkin cask awkwardly under one arm. A contraband stash of brandy? Or maybe cachaça? She bristled, and took a step to intercept him, but stopped herself.

"Dios," she said, turning away and taking another swallow of metheglin. "Let them have their fun."

"Now who's going soft?" Capitan Valdez grinned. From somewhere he'd produced another bottle for himself. "That pearl Galindo has is a real beauty. Small, but quality. I sent him up to my cabin with it. I'm thinking a man could retire on a few dozen of those and live a respectable life."

Magda raised her eyebrows.

"Of course, you and me have never been respectable in any sense of the word," he said, breaking out in a wide grin.

"Paralytic drunk's more like it."

"Aye. But this haul is special, and deserves special celebration. I've always heard the whores in Sevoñia far surpass any others in talent, beauty and artistry. Alas, I've never had the means to verify such grandiose claims…"

"Until now." Magda took another swallow from the bottle of metheglin. "It's a thought," she said simply.

The song wound down, and one of the airmen called out for "Shoals of Cibola." A victory song. Magda smiled. It was bad luck to play that song before starting the homeward leg of a voyage, but the metheglin was so good she found herself humming along. She wondered if she had enough liquor in her personal locker for a proper paralytic bender.

Capitan Valdez sighed. "It is nice to dream."

His words broke her from her reverie. "Capitan?"

"You were down there with Galindo. Do you think it's as bad as he fears?"

Magda frowned, choosing her words with care. "Something ain't right down there. That much I can tell. But if Galindo knows more, didn't say nothing to me."

Capitan Valdez nodded. "Galindo tells me there are some kinds of armored mollusks in these seas that mass together in breeding balls this time of year. They secrete an inky mucus that protects the adults and their eggs."

"He thinks this whale swallowed…?"

"The whale had to be distressed for a squadron this small to take it, or so Galindo says." Capitan Valdez twisted his chin whiskers thoughtfully. "Supposedly, disturbing a breeding ball is much the same as poking a hornet's nest with a stick. Which may well explain why the fishchasers fled the way they did."

Magda's skin prickled, remembering how Chago had prodded the black mass with his flensing blade. "So… what're the capitan's orders?"

Capitan Valdez smiled. "I'll admit I'm not *entirely* immune to greed. I'm seriously considering sending Galindo back down with a few men to harvest what they can—even a few dewclaw pearls would fetch quite a heavy bucket of gold—but I haven't decided yet. I'm inclined to lock down the blow hatch until I decide one way or—"

A distant, muffled *hwump* came up to Magda through her feet. The kelper shuddered, bubbles burping up from various spots along its mouth. The crew stopped cavorting—they'd felt it, too.

Magda and Capitan Valdez looked at each other, worry etched on their faces. "Madre dios!" he said. "What was that?"

"Why don't you ask *him*," Magda said, pointing at Chago's sprawled body before the blow hatch. Thick, gray smoke billowed up through the opening, and as she watched, Rubén Campos heaved out, coughing and hysterical.

"Eduardo's still in there!" Rubén shouted. "Somebody help!"

Capitan Valdez went over the railing a split second before Magda, the rest of the crew close behind.

"What happened?" Capitan Valdez demanded.

"The fuse—it wasn't long enough," managed Rubén between coughing fits. "Chago said we'd have time to get out, but the powder blew too soon."

"Why the hell were you idiots into the powder stores?" bellowed Magda.

"To blow out that shit blocking the gullet," Chago shot back. "What? We wanted to get to all the mussels, right? The pearls, that's why we're here."

"Who cares about pearls? Eduardo is still down there!" Rubén cried.

"Magda! Galindo! We've got to get that hatch locked down!" shouted Capitan Valdez.

"No! You'll kill him!" Rubén lunged at the hatch, bending over it. "Eduardo! Can you hear me? Are you—*gaaak!*"

In the blink of an eye, Rubén disappeared head-first down the hatch.

The gathered airmen exchanged baffled, wary looks.

Magda's skin prickled. She slid one hand to her flintlock, the other to her cutlass.

"Pedemaestro Galindo…"

"Already on it, Capitan." Galindo edged cautiously up to the hatch, his cutlass held between him and the opening. Carefully, he reached out to grasp the lid.

A sucker-lined tentacle, sinuous and purple-red, whipped out of the hatch and around Galindo's neck. The pedemaestro's eyes bulged as his body went limp.

More tentacles followed. Then a snapping beak. Then a pair of shining, black eyes round as the bottom of a bottle of coral wine. The tentacles heaved, and the creature flopped to the ground with a solid thunk before lifting itself up. Its body was nearly as long as a man's, fully encased in a thick, twisting shell of flecked ivory. Another set of tentacles flailed at the hatch.

"¡Kraken swarm!" Capitan Valdez shouted, firing his flintlock at the closest kraken. Splintered shell flew through the air. The creature whipped around to face him.

Magda fired her flintlock into the eye, and the kraken slumped down, tentacles thrashing. "The shell's too thick—aim for the eyes."

"I daresay Galindo's theories have been proven out," Capitan Valdez said, drawing his cutlass as a second and third kraken came through the hatch. "That hatch really, *really* has to be closed."

"I'm glad you're here to tell me these things, Capitan!" Magda slashed with her cutlass as a kraken lunged at her, driving her back.

The crew'd scattered in panic as the first kraken emerged, but now some returned, armed with gaffs and blubber pikes, flintlocks spitting fire at the three kraken. Zarzamora slipped between them and hooked the hatch lid with the tip of his gaff, slamming it onto a newly emerging tentacle. He slashed at it with the barb until it pulled back, then locked the hatch in place with his good arm. The drum clanged as the kraken flailed away inside it.

"The clamps, too!" shouted Magda.

The three kraken twitched listlessly, bloodied and impaled against the kelper's hide. One airman lay screaming in a pool of blood, his left leg sheared off at the knee by a kraken's beak.

"Hell of a time to lose Galindo, but we've made do without a pedemaestro before," Capitan Valdez said grimly. "We're damned lucky as it is."

"*Lucky?* You think…" Magda felt wetness about her feet and looked down. Water lapped at her boots. "Madre dios! Chago's stunt ruptured the mouth spikes. This whale's sinking."

"That's not all," Zarzamora said, pointing with his gaff. "Look."

The sea around the whale's mouth frothed, the spray sparkling like diamonds in the reflected light of the lanterns. Tentacles and ivory shells churned the water.

"The swarm's free," Capitan Valdez said, a simple statement of fact. "We're going to lose a lot of good men."

"To the ships! Move your sorry arses 'less you wanna be kraken food!" Magda bellowed, charging to the cutting stage through rising water already above her ankles. The crew scrambled to get onto the raft, a chaotic scrum of curses and elbows.

The swarm came out of the sea from every side. Kraken lunged out of the water as if flung from a sling. They splashed and clambered along the carcass, grabbing hold of airmen's legs. Men screamed, flailing and stabbing with blubber spades and pikes as they were dragged back into the dark waters.

"Capitan! Up the ladder! Up to *Avispa Feroz!*" Magda stood on the deck, cutlass drawn, slashing at any kraken that came near the edge. Already several airmen were scampering up ladders to the nearest whaling ships, double-quick. At the far end of the stage, several kraken wrapped their tentacles around the rope rungs and followed.

"They can climb," said Capitan Valdez, stopping with one foot on a rung to gawk. "Madre dios, who knew?"

"Just thank Cibola they don't fly as well," Magda said, slapping his leg with the flat of her blade. "Now get your arse up to the damned ship already!"

To starboard, a shot rang out. One of the airmen on a whaler was firing at a kraken making its way up the ladder. Suddenly, a whipping noise sounded from the farthest whaler to port. The cut tether lashed hard against the cutting stage deck, smashing two kraken into stacked barrels. The ladder pulled free of the cutting stage. The whaler groaned and rolled, then abruptly wrenched itself free from *Avispa Feroz*'s grapple, disappearing up into the night sky. They'd cut themselves loose.

"Bastards! Cowards!" Magda shouted. "Stand your ground or I'll kill you myself!"

Freed of the whaler's buoyancy, the carcass abruptly sank half a fathom. The cutting stage lurched as seawater rushed beneath it. Barrels toppled over. The lid flew off one as it fell, spilling whale oil into the sea. Magda snatched a lantern from its hook and flung it down. The oil blazed up, exposed kraken writhing wildly as the flames scorched their shells and cooked their flesh.

Another ladder crashed to the deck as the second whaler to port, taking its cue from the first, cut itself free from the carcass. Water swirled over the uselessly sealed blow hatch.

Magda looked wildly about her through the smoke and flame. Blood streaked the deck. Men screamed and shouted. Random shots rang out. She couldn't tell how many men were dead, how many were still fighting. The kraken kept coming, and the kelper carcass was sinking. There was nothing more she could do.

Magda leapt to the ladder, pulling herself up with her cutlass ready in hand. She was halfway up before she heard the cry for help behind her.

Half a dozen rungs below, a kraken'd caught Chago's leg as he followed her. *Chago.*

"Help me, Magda! Don't let it take me!"

Gritting her teeth, Magda slid down the ladder one-handed, the rope burning her rough palm. She hooked a knee through the rung above Chago's shoulder and threw herself backwards, swinging around and down to drive her cutlass straight through the kraken's eye. It released its grip and dropped away.

"I knew you'd come. I knew you wouldn't leave me," Chago said, helping her pull back upright.

"I saved you 'cause we're short crew. I'd just as soon feed you to the kraken."

"Sure you would," Chago said, winking.

"That damn stunt you pulled is the reason we're in this mess!"

"I did it for you!" Chago took her wounded hand. "I wanted get the pearls on my own, to show I was worthy of you."

Magda stared into his eyes. "You're serious."

Chago nodded.

"I knew it," she snarled, then slashed the ladder in two with her cutlass, dropping Chago into the midst of the blood-maddened kraken.

The dangling ladder lurched wildly as the remaining whalers cut loose. Magda struggled to hold on, climbing hand over fist to *Avispa Feroz*'s pilot house. Capitan Valdez grabbed her shoulders and hauled her in.

"Is there anyone else with you?" Capitan Valdez asked.

Magda shook her head. "Chago was, but I had to kill the stupid sonofabitch."

Capitan Valdez looked ill.

"He had it coming, Capitan," Magda said defensively.

"We need more bodies, Magda. The carcass is dragging us down! We've blown all the ballast tanks, but it hasn't helped."

Magda glanced out the hatch. The sea was disturbingly close, and the kelper wasn't even visible as an outline. The three cables anchoring *Avispa Feroz* to the whale slipped into the smoldering dark water as the bow of the airship sank closer to the waves.

"So who do we have?" asked Magda.

"You, me and Tavares here," Capitan Valdez said. "Andrés doesn't answer his post."

"I'm gonna have to do me a lot of killing once this mess is through," Magda muttered. "Capitan's orders?"

"Orders? Dios, Magda, I've got no crew!"

Magda raised her arms in exasperation. "Can't you do *anything* on your own? There are three of us, and there are three anchor lines. If you want to save *Avispa Feroz*, they need to be cut, pronto."

Capitan Valdez stared at her a moment, then grabbed a lantern and scrambled up the ladder to the keel catwalk. Tavares followed, then Magda. They stumbled down the walk as the floor tilted more and more steeply. Abruptly, water swirled in through the hull seams before them.

"Back!" shouted Magda. "We're too late. To the stern!"

"No! We can still reach them!"

"Only if you've grown gills, Capitan."

The catwalk steepened, moving to nearly vertical. The three abandoned the floor and moved to the walls and ceiling, climbing the braces and supports as ladders.

From below came a *whumpf!* and a sudden wind of helio billowed around them as gas cell number 1 ruptured.

Avispa Feroz dropped thirty feet with a lurch. Capitan Valdez dropped the lantern. Tavares lost his grip and fell, crying in panic until the sharp knocks of flesh on wood silenced him. A swarm of arañas del seda skittered over and past them. Below, the hull flickered as the flames outside chewed away at the ship's skin.

"Arse in gear, Capitan. Keep up or get left behind."

Another gas cell ruptured as they climbed, and another. Each time helio wind rushed past them, followed by a gut-churning drop. The airship sank rapidly now, the dead weight of the whale overwhelming. They climbed past the pilot house access before Magda stopped them. The panicked gigapedes were thrashing against their harnesses.

"Climb out to the nacelle, then jump," Magda said. "We can't reach the stern—going down too fast. Get as far away from the ship as you can, and pray the swarm's following the whale all the way down to the bottom."

They climbed the ladder out to the nacelle as the ship shuddered around them. Below—still a disturbingly long distance away—anemic flames chewed listlessly at the hull. Above the horizon, the fat white crescent of Ansuly gleamed against the starry backdrop, with the smaller, blue half-disk of Cyodne higher still. Despite their light, Magda could see neither cutting stage nor whaling ships.

She closed her eyes and touched her hand to the tattooed Cydone prayer for the dead on her arm. Then she jumped.

The water hit Magda with such force to knock her breath away. Her momentum carried her deep, and she struggled to fight her way back to the surface before burning lungs forced her to suck in water. She broke the surface, gulping in air. Then she swam away from the sinking airship, forcing herself on until her abused body rebelled, and her arms refused to move.

So this is how it ends, she thought, drifting. The waters rose up and covered her face. *Cocked up shit. I wanted to go in a bar fight somewhere. Take plenty of sons-a-bitches with me.*

Something grabbed her hair and pulled. Hands slapped her hard across the face, and Magda coughed, then breathed.

"Don't you dare think I'm letting my first mate off that easily," Capitan Valdez said. Bedraggled hair dripped down his face, one arm draped over a floating barrel. "I'm going to need you at my side, Magda, if I'm to rebuild my fortunes after this debacle."

He pulled her to the barrel, where she grabbed hold. With tears in his eyes, he felt for Magda's hand, and held it tightly. They floated there together, watching as the tail of *Avispa Feroz* disappeared beneath the waves.

"Capitan."

"Aye, Magda?"

"Remember what happened to Chago?"

"Aye." And he let go.

BEYOND THE SEA GATE OF THE SCHOLAR-PIRATES OF SARSKÖE

By Garth Nix

"**R**emind me why the pirates won't sink us with cannon fire at long range," said Sir Hereward as he lazed back against the bow of the skiff, his scarlet-sleeved arms trailing far enough over the side to get his twice folded-back cuffs and hands completely drenched, with occasional splashes going down his neck and back as well. He enjoyed the sensation, for the water in these eastern seas was warm, the swell gentle, and the boat was making a good four or five knots, reaching on a twelve knot breeze.

"For the first part, this skiff formerly belonged to Annim Tel, the pirate's agent in Kerebad," said Mister Fitz. Despite being only three feet, six and a half inches tall and currently lacking even the extra height afforded by his favourite hat, the puppet was easily handling both tiller and main sheet of their small craft. "For the second part, we are both clad in red, the colour favoured by the pirates of this archipelagic trail, so they will account us as brethren until proven otherwise. For the third part, any decent perspective glass will bring close to their view the chest that lies lashed on the thwart there, and they will want to examine it, rather than blow it to smithereens."

"Unless they're drunk, which is highly probable," said Hereward cheerfully. He lifted his arms out of the water and shook his hands, being careful not to wet the tarred canvas bag at his feet that held his small armoury. Given the mission at hand, he had not brought any of his usual, highly identifiable weapons. Instead the bag held a mere four snaphance pistols of quite ordinary though serviceable make, an oiled leather bag of powder, a box of shot, and a blued steel main gauche in a sharkskin scabbard. A sheathed mortuary sword lay across the top of the bag, its half-basket hilt at Hereward's feet.

He had left his armour behind at the inn where they had met the messenger from the Council of the Treaty for the Safety of the World, and though he was currently enjoying the light air upon his skin, and was optimistic by nature, Hereward couldn't help reflect that a scarlet shirt, leather breeches and sea boots were not going to be much protection if the drunken pirates aboard the xebec they were sailing towards chose to conduct some musketry exercise.

Not that any amount of leather and proof steel would help if they happened to hit the chest. Even Mister Fitz's sorcery could not help them in that circumstance, though he might be able to employ some sorcery to deflect bullets or small shot from both boat and chest.

Mister Fitz looked like, and was currently dressed in the puffy-trousered raiment of, one of the self-willed puppets that were made long ago in a gentler age to play merry tunes, declaim epic poetry and generally entertain. This belied his true nature and most people or other beings who encountered the puppet other than casually did not find him entertaining at all. While his full sewing desk was back at the inn with Hereward's gear, the puppet still had several esoteric needles concealed under the red bandanna that was tightly strapped on his pumpkin-sized papier-mâché head, and he was possibly one of the greatest practitioners of his chosen art still to walk—or sail—the known world.

"We're in range of the bow-chasers," noted Hereward. Casually, he rolled over to lie on his stomach, so only his head was visible over the bow. "Keep her head on."

"I have enumerated three excellent reasons why they will not fire upon us," said Mister Fitz, but he pulled the tiller a little and let out the main sheet, the skiff's sails billowing as it ran with the wind, so that it would bear down directly on the bow of the anchored xebec, allowing the pirates no opportunity for a full broadside. "In any case, the bow-chasers are not even manned."

Hereward squinted. Without his artillery glass he couldn't clearly see what was occurring on deck, but he trusted Fitz's superior vision.

"Oh well, maybe they won't shoot us out of hand," he said. "At least not at first. Remind me of my supposed name and title?"

"Martin Suresword, Terror of the Syndical Sea."

"Ludicrous," said Hereward. "I doubt I can say it, let alone carry on the pretense of being such a fellow."

"There is a pirate of that name, though I believe he was rarely addressed by his preferred title," said Mister Fitz. "Or perhaps I should say there was such a pirate, up until some months ago. He was large and blond, as you are, and the Syndical Sea is extremely distant, so it is a suitable cognomen for you to assume."

"And you? Farnolio, wasn't it?"

"Farolio," corrected Fitz. "An entertainer fallen on hard times."

"How can a puppet fall on hard times?" asked Hereward. He did not look back, as some movement on the bow of the xebec fixed his attention. He hoped it was not a gun crew making ready.

"It is not uncommon for a puppet to lose their singing voice," said Fitz. "If their throat was made with a reed, rather than a silver pipe, the sorcery will only hold for five or six hundred years."

"Your throat, I suppose, is silver?"

"An admixture of several metals," said Fitz. "Silver being the most ordinary. I stand corrected on one of my earlier predictions, by the way."

"What?"

"They *are* going to fire," said Fitz, and he pushed the tiller away, the skiff's mainsail flapping as it heeled to starboard. A few seconds later, a small cannon ball splashed down forty or fifty yards to port.

"Keep her steady!" ordered Hereward. "We're as like to steer into a ball as not."

"I think there will only be the one shot," said the puppet. "The fellow who fired it is now being beaten with a musket stock."

Hereward shielded his eyes with his hand to get a better look. The sun was hot in these parts, and glaring off the water. But they were close enough now that he could clearly see a small red-clad crowd gathered near the bow, and in the middle of it, a surprisingly slight pirate was beating the living daylights out of someone who was now crouched—or who had fallen—on the deck.

"Can you make out a name anywhere on the vessel?" Hereward asked.

"I cannot," answered Fitz. "But her gun ports are black, there is a remnant of yellow striping on the rails of her quarterdeck and though the figurehead has been partially shot off, it is clearly a rampant sea-cat. This accords with Annim Tel's description, and is the vessel we seek. She is the *Sea-Cat*, captained by one Romola Fury. I suspect it is she who has clubbed the firer of the bow-chaser to the deck."

"A women pirate," mused Hereward. "Did Annim Tel mention whether she is comely?"

"I can see for myself that you would think her passing fair," said Fitz, his tone suddenly severe. "Which has no bearing on the task that lies ahead."

"Save that it may make the company of these pirates more pleasant," said Hereward. "Would you say we are now close enough to hail?"

"Indeed," said Fitz.

Hereward stood up, pressed his knees against the top strakes of the bow to keep his balance, and cupped his hands around his mouth.

"Ahoy *Sea-Cat!*" he shouted. "Permission for two brethren to come aboard?"

There was a brief commotion near the bow, most of the crowd moving purposefully to the main deck. Only two pirates remained on the bow: the slight figure, who now they were closer they could see was female and so was almost certainly Captain Fury, and a tub-chested giant of a man who stood behind her. A crumpled body lay at their feet.

The huge pirate bent to listen to some quiet words from Fury, then filling his lungs to an extent that threatened to burst the buttons of his scarlet waistcoat, answered the hail with a shout that carried much farther than Hereward's.

"Come aboard then, cullies! Port-side if you please."

Mister Fitz leaned on the tiller and hauled in the main sheet, the skiff turning wide, the intention being to circle in off the port-side of the xebec and then turn bow-first into the wind and drop the sail. If properly executed, the skiff would lose way and bump gently up against the pirate ship. If not, they would run into the vessel, damage the skiff and be a laughing stock.

This was the reason Mister Fitz had the helm. Somewhere in his long past, the puppet had served at sea for several decades, and his wooden limbs were well-salted, his experience clearly remembered and his instincts true.

Hereward, for his part, had served as a gunner aboard a frigate of the Kahlian Mercantile Alliance for a year when he was fifteen and though that lay some ten years behind him, he had since had some shorter-lived nautical adventures and was thus well able to pass himself off as a seaman aboard a fair-sized ship. But he was not a great sailor of small boats and he hastened to follow Mister Fitz's quiet commands to lower sail and prepare to fend off with an oar as they coasted to a stop next to the anchored *Sea-Cat*.

In the event, no fending off was required, but Hereward took a thrown line from the xebec to make the skiff fast alongside, while Fitz secured the head- and main-sail. With the swell so slight, the ship at anchor, and being a xebec low in the waist, it was then an easy matter to climb aboard, using the gun ports and chain-plates as foot- and hand-holds, Hereward only slightly hampered by his sword. He left the pistols in the skiff.

Pirates sauntered and swaggered across the deck to form two rough lines as Hereward and Fitz found their feet. Though they did not have weapons drawn, it was very much a gauntlet, the men and women of the *Sea-Cat* eyeing their visitors with suspicion. Though he did not wonder at the time, presuming it the norm among pirates, Hereward noted that the men in particular were ill-favoured, disfigured, or both. Fitz saw this too, and marked it as a matter for further investigation.

Romola Fury stepped down the short ladder from the forecastle deck to the waist and stood at the open end of the double line of pirates. The red waistcoated bully stood behind, but Hereward hardly noticed him. Though she was sadly lacking in the facial scars necessary for him to consider her a true beauty, Fury was indeed comely, and there was a hint of a powder burn on one high cheek-bone that accentuated her natural charms. She wore a fine blue silk coat embroidered with leaping sea-cats, without a shirt. As her coat was only loosely buttoned, Hereward found his attention very much focussed upon her. Belatedly, he remembered his instructions, and gave a flamboyant but unstructured wave of his open hand, a gesture meant to be a salute.

"Well met, Captain! Martin Suresword and the dread puppet Farolio, formerly of the *Anodyne Pain*, brothers in good standing of the chapter of the Syndical Sea."

Fury raised one eyebrow and tilted her head a little to the side, the long reddish hair on the unshaved half of her head momentarily catching the breeze. Hereward kept his eyes on her, and tried to look relaxed, though he was ready to dive aside, headbutt a path through the gauntlet of pirates, circle behind the mizzen, draw his sword and hold off the attack long enough for Fitz to wreak his havoc...

"You're a long way from the Syndical Sea, Captain Suresword," Fury finally replied. Her voice was strangely pitched and throaty, and Fitz thought it might be the effects of an acid or alkaline burn to the tissues of the throat. "What brings you to these waters, and to the *Sea-Cat*? In Annim Tel's craft, no less, with a tasty-looking chest across the thwarts?"

She made no sign, but something in her tone or perhaps in the words themselves made the two lines of pirates relax and the atmosphere of incipient violence ease.

"A proposition," replied Hereward. "For the mutual benefit of all."

Fury smiled and strolled down the deck, her large enforcer at her heels. She paused in front of Hereward, looked up at him, and smiled a crooked smile, provoking in him the memory of a cat that always looked just so before it sat on his lap and trod its claws into his groin.

"Is it riches we're talking about, Martin Sure... sword? Gold treasure and the like? Not slaves, I trust? We don't hold with slaving on the *Sea-Cat*, no matter what our brothers of the Syndical Sea may care for."

"Not slaves, Captain," said Hereward. "But treasure of all kinds. More gold and silver than you've ever seen. More than anyone has ever seen."

Fury's smile broadened for a moment. She slid a foot forward like a dancer, moved to Hereward's side and linked her arm through his, neatly pinning his sword-arm.

"Do tell, Martin," she said. "Is it to be an assault on the Ingmal Convoy? A cutting-out venture in Hryken Bay?"

Her crew laughed as she spoke, and Hereward felt the mood change again. Fury was mocking him, for it would take a vast fleet of pirates to carry an assault on the fabulous biennial convoy from the Ingmal saffron fields, and Hryken Bay was dominated by the guns of the justly famous Diamond Fort and its red-hot shot.

"I do not bring you dreams and fancies, Captain Fury," said Hereward quietly. "What I offer is a prize greater than even a galleon of the Ingmal."

"What then?" asked Fury. She gestured at the sky, where a small turquoise disc was still visible near the horizon, though it was faded by the sun. "You'll bring the blue moon down for us to plunder?"

"I offer a way through the Secret Channels and the Sea Gate of the Scholar-Pirates of Sarsköe," said Hereward, speaking louder with each word, as the pirates began to shout, most in angry disbelief, but some in excited greed.

Fury's hand tightened on Hereward's arm, but she did not speak immediately. Slowly, as her silence was noted, her crew grew quiet, such was her power over them. Hereward knew very few others who had such presence, and he had known many kings and princes, queens and high priestesses. Not for the first time, he felt a stab of doubt about their plan, or more accurately Fitz's plan. Fury was no cat's-paw, to be lightly used by others.

"What is this way?" asked Fury, when her crew was silent, the only sound the lap of the waves against the hull, the creak of the rigging, and to Hereward at least, the pounding of his own heart.

"I have a dark rutter for the channels," he said. "Farolio here, is a gifted navigator. He will take the star sights."

"So the Secret Channels may be traveled," said Fury. "If the rutter is true."

"It is true, madam," piped up Fitz, pitching his voice higher than usual. He sounded childlike, and harmless. "We have journeyed to the foot of the Sea Gate and returned, this past month."

Fury glanced down at the puppet, who met her look with his unblinking, blue-painted eyes, the sheen of the sorcerous varnish upon them bright. She held the puppet's gaze for several seconds, her eyes narrowing once more, in a fashion reminiscent of a cat that sees something it is not sure whether to flee or fight. Then she slowly looked back at Hereward.

"And the Sea Gate? It matters not to pass the channels if the gate is shut against us."

"The Sea Gate is not what it once was," said Hereward. "If pressure is brought against the correct place, then it will fall."

"Pressure?" asked Fury, and the veriest tip of her tongue thrust out between her lips.

"I am a Master Gunner," said Hereward. "In the chest aboard our skiff is a mortar shell of particular construction—and I believe that not a week past you captured a Harker-built bomb vessel, and have yet to dispose of it."

He did not mention that this ship had been purchased specifically for his command, and its capture had seriously complicated their initial plan.

"You are well-informed," said Fury. "I do have such a craft, hidden in a cove beyond the strand. I have my crew, none better in all this sea. You have a rutter, a navigator, a bomb, and the art to bring the Sea Gate down. Shall we say two-thirds to we Sea-Cats and one-third to you and your puppet?"

"Done," said Hereward.

"Yes," said Fitz.

Fury unlinked her arm from Hereward's, held up her open hand and licked her palm most daintily, before offering it to him. Hereward paused, then spat mostly air on his own palm, and they shook upon the bargain.

Fitz held up his hand, as flexible as any human's, though it was dark brown and grained like wood, and licked his palm with a long blue-stippled tongue that was pierced with a silver stud. Fury slapped more than shook Fitz's hand, and she did not look at the puppet.

"Jabez!" instructed Fury, and her great hulking right-hand man was next to shake on the bargain, his grip surprisingly light and deft, and his eyes warm with humour, a small smile on his battered face. Whether it was for the prospect of treasure or some secret amusement, Hereward could not tell, and Jabez did not smile for Fitz. After Jabez came the rest of the crew, spitting and shaking till the bargain was sealed with all aboard. Like every ship of the brotherhood, the Sea-Cats were in theory a free company, and decisions made by all.

The corpse on the forecastle was an indication that this was merely a theory and that in practice, Captain Fury ruled as she wished. The spitting and handshaking were merely song and dance and moonshadow, but it played well with the pirates, who enjoyed pumping Hereward's hand till his shoulder hurt. They did not take such liberties with Fitz, but this was no sign they had discerned his true nature, but merely the usual wariness of humans towards esoteric life.

When all the hand-clasping was done, Fury took Hereward's arm again and led him towards the great cabin in the xebec's stern. As they strolled along the deck, she called over her shoulder, "Make ready to sail, Jabez. Captain Suresword and I have some matters to discuss."

Fitz followed at Hereward's heels. Jabez's shouts passed over his head, and he had to weave his way past pirates rushing to climb the ratlines or man the capstan that would raise the anchor.

Fury's great cabin was divided by a thick curtain that separated her sleeping quarters from a larger space that was not quite broad enough to comfortably house both the teak-topped table and the two twelve-pounder guns. Fury had to let go of Hereward to slip through the space between the breech of one gun and the table corner, and he found himself strangely relieved by the cessation of physical proximity. He was no stranger to women, and had dallied with courtesans, soldiers, farm girls, priestesses and even a widowed empress, but there was something about Fury that unsettled him more than any of these past lovers.

Consequently he was even more relieved when she did not lead him through the curtain to her sleeping quarters, but sat at the head of the table and gestured for him to sit on one side. He did so, and Fitz hopped up on to the table.

"Drink!" shouted Fury. She was answered by a grunt from behind a half-door in the fore bulkhead that Hereward had taken for a locker. The door opened a fraction and a scrawny, tattooed, handless arm was thrust out, the stump through the leather loop of a wineskin which was unceremoniously thrown upon the table.

"Go get the meat on the forecastle," added Fury. She raised the wineskin and daintily directed a jet of a dark, resinous wine into her mouth, licking her lips most carefully when she finished. She passed the skin to Hereward, who took the merest swig. He was watching the horribly mutilated little man who was crawling across the deck. The pirate's skin was so heavily and completely tattooed that it took a moment to realize he was an albino. He had only his left hand, his right arm ending at the wrist. Both of his legs were gone from the knee, and he scuttled on his stumps like a tricorn beetle.

"M' steward," said Fury, as the fellow left. She took another long drink. "Excellent cook."

Hereward nodded grimly. He had recognized some of the tattoos on the man, which identified him as a member of one of the cannibal societies that infested the decaying city of Coradon, far to the south.

"I'd invite you to take nuncheon with me," said Fury, with a sly look. "But most folk don't share my tastes."

Hereward nodded. He had in fact eaten human flesh, when driven to extremity in the long retreat from Jeminero. It was not something he wished to partake of again, should there be any alternative sustenance.

"We are all but meat and water, in the end," said Fury. "Saving your presence, puppet."

"It is a philosophic position that I find unsurprising in one of your past life," said Fitz. "I, for one, do not think it strange for you to eat dead folk, particularly when there is always a shortage of fresh meat at sea."

"What do you know of my 'past life'?" asked Fury, and she smiled just a little, so her sharp eye teeth protruded over her lower lip.

"Only what I observe," remarked Fitz. "Though the mark is faded, I perceive a Lurquist slave brand in that quarter of the skin above your left breast and below your shoulder. You also have the characteristic scar of a Nagolon manacle on your right wrist. These things indicate you have been a slave at least twice, and so must have freed yourself or been freed, also twice. The Nagolon cook the flesh of their dead rowers to provide for the living, hence your taste—"

"I think that will do," interrupted Fury. She looked at Hereward. "We all need our little secrets, do we not? But there are others we must share. It is enough for the crew to know no more than the song about the Scholar-Pirates of Sarsköe and the dangers of the waters near their isle. But I would know the whole of it. Tell me more about these Scholar-Pirates and their fabled fortress. Do they still lurk behind the Sea Gate?"

"The Sea Gate has been shut fast these last two hundred years or more," Hereward said carefully. He had to answer before Fitz did, as the puppet could not always be trusted to sufficiently skirt the truth, even when engaged on a task that required subterfuge and misdirection. "The Scholar-Pirates have not been seen since that time and most likely the fortress is now no more than a dark and silent tomb."

"If it is not now, we shall make it so," said Fury. She hesitated for a second, then added, "For the Scholar-Pirates," and tapped the table thrice with the bare iron ring she wore on the thumb of her left hand. This was an ancient gesture, and told Fitz even more about the captain.

"The song says they were indeed as much scholars as pirates," said Fury. "I have no desire to seize a mound of dusty parchment or rows of books. Do you know of anything more than legend that confirms their treasure?"

"I have seen inside their fortress," said Fitz. "Some four hundred years past, before the Sea Gate was… permanently raised. There very few true scholars among them even then, and most had long since made learning secondary to the procurement of riches… and riches there were, in plenty."

"How old are you, puppet?"

Fitz shrugged his little shoulders and did not answer, a forbearance that Hereward was pleased to see. Fury was no common pirate, and anyone who knew Fitz's age and a little history could put the two together in a way that might require adjustment, and jeopardize Hereward's current task.

"There will be gold enough for all," Hereward said hastily. "There are four or five accounts extant from ransomed captives of the Scholar-Pirates, and all mention great stores of treasure. Treasure for the taking."

"Aye, after some small journey through famously impassable waters and a legendary gate," said Fury. "As I said, tell me the whole."

"We will," said Hereward. "Farolio?"

"If I may spill a little wine, I will sketch out a chart," said Fitz.

Fury nodded. Hereward poured a puddle of wine on the corner of the table for the puppet, who crouched and dipped his longest finger in it, which was the one next to his thumb, then quickly sketched a rough map of many islands. Though he performed no obvious sorcery, the wet lines were quite sharp and did not dry out as quickly as one might expect.

"The fortress itself is built wholly within a natural vastness inside this isle, in the very heart of the archipelago. The pirates called both island and fortress Cror Holt, though its proper name is Sarsköe, which is also the name of the entire island group."

Fitz made another quick sketch, an enlarged view of the same island, a roughly circular land that was split from its eastern shore to its centre by a jagged, switchbacked line of five turns.

"The sole entry to the Cror Holt cavern is from the sea, through this gorge which cuts a zigzag way for almost nine miles through the limestone. The gorge terminates at a smooth cliff, but here the pirates bored a tunnel through to their cavern. The entrance to the tunnel is barred by the famed Sea Gate, which measures one hundred and seven feet wide and one hundred and ninety-seven feet high. The sea abuts it at near forty feet at low water and sixty-three at the top of the tide.

The gorge is narrow, only broad enough for three ships to pass abreast, so it is not possible to directly fire upon the Sea-Gate with cannon. However, we have devised a scheme to fire a bomb from the prior stretch of the gorge, over the intervening rock wall and into the top of the gate.

Once past the gate, there is a harbour pool capacious enough to host a dozen vessels of a similar size to your *Sea-Cat*, with three timber wharves built out from a paved quay. The treasure- and store-houses of the Scholar-Pirates are built on an inclined crescent above the quay, along with residences and other buildings of no great note."

"You are an unusual puppet," said Fury. She took the wineskin and poured another long stream down her throat. "Go on."

Fitz nodded, and returned to his first sketch, his finger tracing a winding path between the islands.

"To get to the Cror Holt entry in the first place, we must pick our way through the so-called Secret Channels. There are close to two hundred islands and reefs arrayed around the central isle, and the only passage through is twisty indeed. Adding complication to difficulty, we must pass these channels at night, a night with a clear sky, for we have only the dark rutter to guide us through the channels, and the path contained therein is detailed by star sights and soundings.

"We will also have to contend with most difficult tides. This is particularly so in the final approach to the Sea Gate, where the shape of the reefs and islands—and I suspect some sorcerous tinkering—funnel two opposing tidewashes into each other. The resultant *eagre*, or bore as some call it, enters the mouth of the gorge an hour before high water and the backwash returns some fifteen minutes later. The initial wave is taller than your top-masts and very swift, and will destroy any craft caught in the gorge.

"Furthermore, we must also be in the Cror Holt gorge just before the turn of the tide, in order to secure the bomb vessel ready for firing during the slack water. With only one shot, He... Martin, that is, will need the most stable platform possible. I have observed the slack water as lasting twenty-three minutes and we must have the bomb vessel ready to fire.

"Accordingly we must enter after the *eagre* has gone in and come out, anchor and spring the bomb vessel at the top of the tide, fire on the slack and then we will have some eight or nine hours at most to loot and be gone before the *eagre* returns, and without the Sea Gate to block it, floods the fortress completely and drowns all within."

Fury looked from the puppet to Hereward, her face impassive. She did not speak for at least a minute. Hereward and Fitz waited silently, listening to the sounds of the crew in deck and rigging above them, the creak of the vessel's timbers and above all that, the thump of someone chopping something up in the captain's galley that lay somewhat above them and nearer the waist.

"It is a madcap venture, and my crew would mutiny if they knew what lies ahead," said Fury finally. "Nor do I trust either of you to have told me the half of it. But… I grow tired of the easy pickings on this coast. Perhaps it is time to test my luck again. We will join with the bomb vessel, which is called *Strongarm*, by nightfall and sail on in convoy. You will both stay aboard the *Sea-Cat*. How long to gain the outer archipelago, master navigator puppet?"

"Three days with a fair wind," said Fitz. "If the night then is clear, we shall have two of three moons sufficiently advanced to light our way, but not so much they will mar my star sights. Then it depends upon the wind. If it is even passing fair, we should reach the entrance to the Cror Holt gorge two hours after midnight, as the tide nears its flood."

"Madness," said Fury again, but she laughed and slapped Fitz's sketch, a spray of wine peppering Hereward's face. "You may leave me now. Jabez will find you quarters."

Hereward stood and almost bowed, before remembering he was a pirate. He turned the bow into a flamboyant wipe of his wine-stained face and turned away, to follow Fitz, who had jumped down from the table without any attempt at courtesy.

As they left, Fury spoke quietly, but her words carried great force.

"Remember this, Captain Suresword. I eat my enemies—and those that betray my trust I eat alive."

That parting comment was still echoing in Hereward's mind four days later, as the *Sea-Cat* sailed cautiously between two lines of white breakers no more than a mile apart. The surf was barely visible in the moonlight, but all aboard could easily envision the keel-tearing reefs that lay below.

Strongarm wallowed close behind, its ragged wake testament to its inferior sailing properties, much of this due to the fact that it had a huge mortar sitting where it would normally have a foremast. But though it would win no races, *Strongarm* was a beautiful vessel in Hereward's eyes, with her massively reinforced decks and beams, chain rigging and, of course, the great iron mortar itself.

Though Fury had not let him stay overlong away from the *Sea-Cat*, and Fitz had been required to stay on the xebec, Hereward had spent nearly all his daylight hours on the bomb vessel, familiarizing himself with the mortar and training the crew he had been given to serve it. Though he would only have one shot with the special bomb prepared by Mister Fitz, and he would load and aim that himself, Hereward had kept his gunners busy drilling. With a modicum of luck, the special shot would bring the Sea Gate down, but he thought there could well be an eventuality where even commonplace bombs might need to be rained down upon the entrance to Cror Holt.

A touch at Hereward's arm brought his attention back to Fitz. Both stood on the quarterdeck, next to the helmsman, who was peering nervously ahead. Fury was in her cabin, possibly to show her confidence in her chosen navigator—and in all probability, dining once more on the leftovers of the unfortunate pirate who had taken it on himself to fire the bow-chaser.

"We are making good progress," said Fitz. He held a peculiar device at his side that combined a small telescope and a tiny, ten-line abacus of screw-thread beads. Hereward had never seen any other navigator use such an instrument, but by taking sights on the moons and the stars and with the mysterious aid of the silver chronometric egg he kept in his waistcoat, Fitz could and did fix their position most accurately. This could then be checked against the directions contained with the salt-stained leather bindings of the dark rutter.

"Come to the taffrail," whispered Fitz. More loudly, he said, "Keep her steady, helm. I shall give you a new course presently."

Man and puppet moved to the rail at the stern, to stand near the great lantern that was the essential beacon for the following ship. Hereward leaned on the rail and looked back at the *Strongarm* again. In the light of the two moons the bomb vessel was a pallid, ghostly ship, the great mortar giving it an odd silhouette.

Fitz, careless of the roll and pitch of the ship, leaped to the rail. Gripping Hereward's arm, he leaned over and looked intently at the stern below.

"Stern windows shut—we shall not be overheard," whispered Fitz.

"What is it you wish to say?" asked Hereward.

"Elements of our plan may need re-appraisal," said Fitz. "Fury is no easy dupe and once the Sea Gate falls, its nature will be evident. Though she must spare me to navigate our return to open water, I fear she may well attempt to slay you in a fit of pique. I will then be forced into action, which would be unfortunate as we may well need the pirates to carry the day."

"I trust you would be 'forced into action' before she killed me... or started eating me alive," said Hereward.

Fitz did not deign to answer this sally. They both knew Hereward's safety was of *almost* paramount concern to the puppet.

"Perchance we should give the captain a morsel of knowledge," said Fitz. "What do you counsel?"

Hereward looked down at the deck and thought of Fury at her board below, carving off a more literal morsel.

"She is a most uncommon woman, even for a pirate," he said slowly.

"She is that," said Fitz. "On many counts. You recall the iron ring, the three-times tap she did on our first meeting below? That is a grounding action against some minor forms of esoteric attack. She used it as a ward against ill-saying, which is the practice of a number of sects. I would think she was a priestess once, or at least a novice, in her youth."

"Of what god?" asked Hereward. "A listed entity? That might serve us very ill."

"Most probably some benign and harmless godlet," said Fitz. "Else she could not have been wrested from its service to the rowing benches of the Nagolon. But there is something about her that goes against this supposition… it would be prudent to confirm which entity she served."

"If you wish to ask, I have no objection…" Hereward began. Then he stopped and looked at the puppet, favouring his long-time comrade with a scowl.

"I have to take many more star sights," said Fitz. He jumped down from the rail and turned to face the bow. "Not to mention instruct the helmsman on numerous small points of sail. I think it would be in our interest to grant Captain Fury some further knowledge of our destination, and also endeavour to discover which godlet held the indenture of her youth. We have some three or four hours before we will reach the entrance to the gorge."

"I am not sure—" said Hereward.

"Surely that is time enough for such a conversation," interrupted Fitz. "Truly, I have never known you so reluctant to seek private discourse with a woman of distinction."

"A woman who feasts upon human flesh," protested Hereward as he followed Fitz.

"She merely does not waste foodstuffs," said Fitz. "I think it commendable. You have yourself partaken of—"

"Yes, yes, I remember!" said Hereward. "Take your star sight! I will go below and speak to Fury."

The helmsman looked back as Hereward spoke, and he realized he was no longer whispering.

"Captain Fury, I mean. I will speak with you anon, Mister… Farolio!"

Captain Fury was seated at her table when Hereward entered, following a cautious knock. But she was not eating and there were no recognizable human portions upon the platter in front of her. It held only a dark glass bottle and a small silver cup, the kind used in birthing rites or baptismal ceremonies. Fury drank from it, flicking her wrist to send the entire contents down her throat in one gulp. Even from a few paces distant, Hereward could smell the sharp odour of strong spirits.

"Arrack," said Fury. "I have a taste for it at times, though it does not serve me as well as once it did. You wish to speak to me? Then sit."

Hereward sat cautiously, as far away as he dared without giving offence, and angled his chair so as to allow a clean draw of the main gauche from his right hip. Fury appeared less than sober, if not exactly drunk, and Hereward was very wary of the trouble that might come from the admixture of a pirate with cannibalistic tendencies and a powerfully spirituous drink.

"I am not drunk," said Fury. "It would take three bottles of this stuff to send me away, and a better glass to sup it with. I am merely wetting down my powder before we storm the fortress."

"Why?" asked Hereward. He did not move any closer.

"I am cursed," said Fury. She poured herself another tot. "Did you suppose 'Fury' is my birth name?"

Hereward shook his head slowly.

"Perhaps I am blessed," continued the woman. She smiled her small, toothy smile again, and drank. "You will see when the fighting starts. Your puppet knows, doesn't it? Those blue eyes… it will be safe enough, but you'd best keep your distance. It's the tall men and the well-favoured that she must either bed or slay, and it's all I can do to point her towards the foe…"

"Who is she?" asked Hereward. It took some effort to keep his voice calm and level. At the same time he let his hand slowly fall to his side, fingers trailing across the hilt of his parrying dagger.

"What I become," said Fury. "A fury indeed, when battle is begun."

She made a sign with her hand, her fingers making a claw. Her nails had grown, Hereward saw, but not to full talons. Not yet. More discoloured patches—spots— had also appeared on her face, making it obvious the permanent one near her eye was not a powder-burn at all.

"You were a sister of Chelkios, the Leoparde," stated Hereward. He did not have Fitz's exhaustive knowledge of cross-dimensional entities, but Chelkios was one of the more prominent deities of the old Kvarnish Empire. Most importantly from his point of view, at least in the longer term, it was not proscribed.

"I was taken from Her by slavers when I was but a novice, a silly little thing who disobeyed the rules and left the temple," said Fury. She took another drink. "A true sister controls the temper of the beast. I must manage with rum, for the most part, and the occasional…"

She set her cup down, stood up and held her hand out to Hereward and said, "Distraction."

Hereward also stood, but did not immediately take her hand. Two powerful instincts warred against each other, a sensuous thrill that coursed through his whole body versus a panicked sense of self-preservation that emanated from a more rational reckoning of threat and chance.

"Bed or slay, she has no middle course," said Fury. Her hand trembled and the nails on her fingers grew longer and began to curve.

"There are matters pertaining to our task that you must hear," said Hereward, but as he spoke all his caution fell away and he took her hand to draw her close. "You should know that the Sea Gate is now in fact a wall…"

He paused as cool hands found their way under his shirt, muscles tensing in anticipation of those sharp nails upon his skin. But Fury's fingers were soft pads now, and quick, and Hereward's own hands were launched upon a similar voyage of discovery.

"A wall," gulped Hereward. "Built two hundred years ago by the surviving Scholar-Pirates... to... to keep in something they had originally summoned to aid them... the treasure is there... but it is guarded..."

"Later," crooned Fury, close to his ear, as she drew him back through the curtain to her private lair. "Tell me later..."

Many hours later, Fury stood on the quarterdeck and looked down at Hereward as he took his place aboard the boat that was to transfer him to the *Strongarm*. She gave no sign that she viewed him with any particular affection or fondness, or indeed recalled their intimate relations at all. However, Hereward was relieved to see that though the lanterns in the rigging cast shadows on her face, there was only the one leoparde patch there and her nails were of a human dimension.

Fitz stood at her side, his papier-mâché head held at a slight angle so that he might see both sky and boat. Hereward had managed only a brief moment of discourse with him, enough to impart Fury's nature and to tell him that she had seemed to take the disclosure of their potential enemy with equanimity. Or possibly had not heard him properly, or recalled it, having been concerned with more immediate activities.

Both *Sea-Cat* and *Strongarm* were six miles up the gorge, its sheer, grey-white limestone walls towering several hundred feet above them. Only the silver moon was high enough to light their way, the blue moon left behind on the horizon of the open sea. Even so, the silver was a bright three-quarter moon, and the sky clear and full of stars, so on one score at least the night was ideal for the expedition.

But the wind had been dropping by the minute, and now the air was still, and what little sail the *Sea-Cat* had set was limp and useless. *Strongarm*'s poles were bare, as she was already moored in the position Fitz had chosen on their preliminary exploration a month before, with three anchors down and a spring on each line. Hereward would adjust the vessel's lie when he got aboard, thus training the mortar exactly on the Sea Gate, which lay out of sight on the other side of the northern wall, in the next turn of the gorge.

In consequence of the calm, recourse had to be made to oars, so a longboat, two gigs and Annim Tel's skiff were in line ahead of the *Sea-Cat*, ready to tow her the last mile around the bend in the gorge. Hereward would have preferred to undertake the assault entirely in the small craft, but they could not deliver sufficient force. There were more than a hundred and ninety pirates aboard the xebec, and he suspected they might need all of them and more.

"High water," called out someone from near the bow of the *Sea-Cat*. "The flow has ceased."

"Give way!" ordered Hereward, and his boat surged forward, six pirates bending their strength upon the oars. With the gorge so narrow it would only take a few minutes to reach the *Strongarm*, but with the tide at its peak and slack water begun, Hereward had less than a quarter-hour to train, elevate and fire the mortar.

Behind him, he heard Jabez roar, quickly followed by the splash of many oars in the water as the boats began the tow. It would be a slow passage for the *Sea-Cat*, and Hereward's gig would easily catch them up.

The return journey out of the gorge would be just as slow, Hereward thought, and entailed much greater risk. If they lost too many rowers in battle, and if the wind failed to come up, they might well not make it out before the *eagre* came racing up the gorge once more.

He tried to dismiss images of the great wave roaring down the gorge as he climbed up the side of the bomb vessel and quickly ran to the mortar. His crew had everything ready. The chest was open to show the special bomb, the charge bags were laid on oil-cloth next to it and his gunner's quadrant and fuses were laid out likewise on the opposite side.

Hereward looked up at the sky and at the marks Fitz had sorcerously carved into the cliff the month before, small things that caught the moonlight and might be mistaken for a natural pocket of quartz. Using these marks, he ordered a minor adjustment of the springs to warp the bomb vessel around a fraction, a task that took precious minutes as the crew heaved on the lines.

While they heaved, Hereward laid the carefully calculated number and weight of charge bags in the mortar. Then he checked and cut the fuse, measuring it three times and checking it again, before pushing it into the bomb. This was a necessary piece of misdirection for the benefit of the pirates, for in fact Fitz had put a sorcerous trigger in the bomb so that it would explode exactly as required.

"Load!" called Hereward. The six pirates who served the mortar leaped into action, two carefully placing the wadding on the charge bags while the other four gingerly lifted the bomb and let it slide back into the mortar.

"Prepare for adjustment," came the next command. Hereward laid his gunner's quadrant in the barrel and the crew took a grip on the two butterfly-shaped handles that turned the cogs that would raise the mortar's inclination. "Up six turns!"

"Up six turns!" chorused the hands as they turned the handles, bronze cogs ticking as the teeth interlocked with the thread of the inclination screws. The barrel of the mortar slowly rose, till it was pointing up at the clear sky and was only ten degrees from the vertical.

"Down one quarter turn!"

"Down one quarter turn!"

The barrel came down. Hereward checked the angle once more. All would depend upon this one shot.

"Prime her and ready matches!"

The leading hand primed the touch-hole with fine powder from a flask, while his second walked back along the deck to retrieve two linstocks, long poles that held burning lengths of match cord.

"Stand ready!"

Hereward took one linstock and the leading gunner the other. The rest of the gun crew walked aft, away from the mortar, increasing their chances of survival should there be some flaw in weapon or bomb that resulted in early detonation.

"One for the sea, two for the shore, three for the match," Hereward chanted. On three he lit the bomb's fuse and strode quickly away, still chanting, "four for the gunner and five for the bore!"

On "bore" the gunner lit the touch-hole.

Hereward already had his eyes screwed shut and was crouched on the deck fifteen feet from the mortar, with his back to it and a good handhold. Even so, the flash went through his eyelids and the concussion and thunderous report that followed sent him sprawling across the deck. The *Strongarm* pitched and rolled too, so that he was in some danger of going over the side, till he found another handhold.

Hauling himself upright, Hereward looked up to make sure the bomb had cleared the rim of the gorge, though he knew that if it hadn't there would already be broken rock falling all around. Blinking against the spots and luminous blurring that were the after-effects of the flash, he stared up at the sky and a few seconds later, was rewarded by the sight of another, even brighter flash and, hard on its heels, a deep, thunderous rumble.

"A hit, a palpable hit!" cried the leading gunner, who was an educated man who doubtless had some strange story of how he had become a pirate. "Well done, sir!"

"It hit something, sure enough," said Hereward, as the other gunners cheered. "But has it brought the Sea Gate down? We shall see. Gunners, swab out the mortar and stand ready. Crew, to the boat. We must make haste."

As expected, Hereward's gig easily caught the *Sea-Cat* and its towing boats, which were making slow progress, particularly as a small wave had come down from farther up the gorge, setting them momentarily aback, but heartening Hereward as it indicated a major displacement of the water in front of the Sea Gate.

This early portent of success was confirmed some short time later as his craft came in sight of the gorge's terminus. Dust and smoke still hung in the air, and there was a huge dark hole in the middle of what had once been a great wall of pale green bricks.

"Lanterns!" called Hereward as they rowed forward, and his bowman held a lantern high in each hand, the two beams catching spirals of dust and blue-grey gunsmoke which were still twisting their way up towards the silver moon.

The breach in the wall was sixty feet wide, Hereward reckoned, and though bricks were still tumbling on either side, there were none left to fall from above. The *Sea-Cat* could be safely towed inside, to disgorge the pirates upon the wharves or, if they had rotted and fallen away, to the quay itself.

Hereward looked aft. The xebec was some hundred yards behind, its lower yardarms hung with lanterns so that it looked like some strange, blazing-eyed monster slowly wading up the gorge, the small towing craft ahead of it low dark shapes, lesser servants lit by duller lights.

"Rest your oars," said Hereward, louder than he intended. His ears were still damped from the mortar blast. "Ready your weapons and watch that breach."

Most of the pirates hurried to prime pistols or ease dirks and cutlasses in scabbards, but one woman, a broad-faced bravo with a slit nose, laid her elbows on her oars and watched Hereward as he reached into his boot and removed the brassard he had placed there. A simple armband, he had slid it up his arm before he noticed her particular attention, which only sharpened as she saw that the characters embroidered on the brassard shone with their own internal light, far brighter than could be obtained by any natural means.

"What's yon light?" she asked. Others in the crew also turned to look.

"So you can find me," answered Hereward easily. "It is painted with the guts of light-bugs. Now I must pray a moment. If any of you have gods to speak to, now is the time."

He watched for a moment, cautious of treachery or some reaction to the brassard, but the pirates had other concerns. Many of them did bend their heads, or close one eye, or touch their knees with the backs of their hands, or adopt one of the thousands of positions of prayer approved by the godlets they had been raised to worship.

Hereward did none of these things, but spoke under his breath, so that none might hear him.

"In the name of the Council of the Treaty for the Safety of the World, acting under the authority granted by the Three Empires, the Seven Kingdoms, the Palatine Regency, the Jessar Republic and the Forty Lesser Realms, I declare myself an agent of the Council. I identify the godlet manifested in this fortress of Cror Holt as Forjill-Um-Uthrux, a listed entity under the Treaty. Consequently the said godlet and all those who assist it are deemed to be enemies of the World, and the Council authorizes me to pursue any and all actions necessary to banish, repel or exterminate the said godlet."

"Captain Suresword! Advance and clear the channel!"

It was Fury calling, no longer relying on the vasty bellow of Jabez. The xebec was closing more rapidly, the towing craft rowing faster, the prospect of gold reviving tired pirates. Hereward could see Fury in the bow of the *Sea-Cat*, and Fitz beside her, his thin arm a-glow from his own brassard.

Hereward touched the butts of the two pistols in his belt and then the hilt of his mortuary sword. The entity that lay in the darkness within could not be harmed by shot or steel, but it was likely served by those who could die as readily as any other mortal. Hereward's task was to protect Fitz from such servants, while the puppet's sorcery dealt with the god.

"Out oars!" he shouted, loud as he could this time. "Onwards to fortune! Give way!"

Oars dipped, the boat surged forward and they passed the ruins of the Sea Gate into the black interior of Cror Holt.

Out of the moonlight the darkness was immediate and disturbing, though the tunnel was so broad and high and their lantern-light of such small consequence that they had no sense of being within a confined space. Indeed, though Hereward knew the tunnel itself was short, he could only tell when they left it and entered the greater cavern by the difference in the sound of their oar-splashes, immediate echoes being replaced by more distant ones.

"Keep her steady," he instructed, his voice also echoing back across the black water. "Watch for the wharves or submerged piles. It can't be far."

"There, Captain!"

It was not a wharf, but the spreading rings of some disturbance upon the surface of the still water. Something big had popped up and sank again, off the starboard quarter of the boat.

"Pull harder!" instructed Hereward. He drew a pistol and cocked the lock. The *Sea-Cat* was following, and from its many lanterns he could see the lower outline of the tunnel around it.

"I see the wharf!" cried the bowman, his words immediately followed by a sudden thump under the hull, the crack of broken timber and a general falling about in the boat, one of the lanterns going over the side into immediate extinguishment.

"We've struck!" shouted a pirate. He stood as if to leap over the side, but paused and looked down.

Hereward looked too. They had definitely hit something hard and the boat should be sinking beneath them. But it was dry. He looked over the side and saw that the boat was at rest on stony ground. There was no water beneath them at all. Another second of examination, and a backward look confirmed that rather than the boat striking a reef, the ground below them had risen up. There was a wharf some ten yards away but its deck was well above them, and the harbour wall a barrier behind it, that they would now need to climb to come to the treasure houses.

"What's that?" asked the gold-toothed pirate uncertainly.

Hereward looked and fired in the same moment, at a seven-foot-tall yellow starfish that was shuffling forward on two points. The bullet took it in the mid-section, blasting out a hole the size of a man's fist, but the starfish did not falter.

"Shoot it!" he shouted. There were starfish lurching upright all around and he knew there would be even more beyond the lantern-light. "*Sea-Cat*, ware shallows and enemy!"

The closer starfish fell a second later, its lower points shot to pulp. Pirates swore as they reloaded, all of them clustering closer to Hereward as if he might ward them from this sudden, sorcerous enemy.

Louder gunfire echoed in from the tunnel. Hereward saw flashes amid the steady light of the xebec's lanterns. The *Sea-Cat*'s bow-chasers and swivel guns were being fired, so they too must be under attack. He also noted that the ship was moving no closer and in fact, might even be receding.

"Cap'n, the ship! She's backing!" yelled a panicked pirate. He snatched up the remaining lantern and ran from the defensive ring about the boat, intent on the distant lights of the *Sea-Cat*. A few seconds later the others saw pirate and lantern go under a swarm of at least a dozen starfish, and then it was dark once more, save for the glow of the symbols on Hereward's arm.

"Bowman, get a line over the wharf!" shouted Hereward. The mortuary sword was in his hand now, though he could not recall drawing it, and he hacked at a starfish whose points were reaching for him. The things were getting quicker, as if, like battlemounts, they needed to warm their blood . "We must climb up! Hold them back!"

The six of them retreated to the piles of the wharf, the huge, ambulatory starfish pressing their attack. With no time to reload, Hereward and the pirates had to hack and cut at them with sword, cutlasses and a boarding axe, and kick away the pieces that still writhed and sought to fasten themselves on their enemies. Within a minute, all of them had minor wounds to their lower legs, where the rough suckers of the starfish's foul bodies had rasped away clothing and skin.

"Line's fast!" yelled the bowman, and he launched himself up it, faster than any topman had ever climbed a ratline. Two of the other pirates clashed as they tried to climb together, one kicking the other in the face as he wriggled above. The lower pirate fell and was immediately smothered by a starfish that threw itself over him. Muffled screams came from beneath the writhing, yellow five-armed monster, and the pirate's feet drummed violently on the ground for several seconds before they stilled.

"Go!" shouted Hereward to the remaining pirate, who needed no urging. She was halfway up the rope as Hereward knelt down, held his sword with both hands and whirled on his heel in a complete circle, the fine edge of his blade slicing through the lower points of half a dozen advancing starfish. As they fell over, Hereward threw his sword up to the wharf, jumped on the back of the starfish that was hunched over the fallen pirate, leaped to the rope and swarmed up it as starfish points tugged at his heels, rasping off the soles of his boots.

The woman pirate handed Hereward his sword as he reached the deck of the wharf. Once again the surviving quartet huddled close to him, eager to stay within the small circle of light provided by his brassard.

"Watch the end of the wharf!" instructed Hereward. He looked over the side. The huge starfish were everywhere below, but they were either unable or unwilling to climb up, so unless a new enemy presented itself there was a chance of some respite.

"She's gone," whispered one of his crew.

The *Sea-Cat* was indeed no longer visible in the tunnel, though there was still a great noise of gunfire, albeit more distant than before.

"The ground rising up has set her aback," said Hereward. "But Captain Fury will land a reinforcement, I'm sure."

"There are so many of them evil stars," whispered the same man.

"They can be shot and cut to pieces," said Hereward sternly. "We will prevail, have no fear."

He spoke confidently, but was not so certain himself. Particularly as he could see the pieces of all the cut-up starfish wriggling together into a pile below, joining together to make an even bigger starfish, one that could reach up to the wharf.

"We'll move back to the quay," he announced, as two of the five points of the assembling giant starfish below began to flex. "Slow and steady, keep your wits about you."

The five of them moved back along the wharf in a compact huddle, with weapons facing out, like a hedgehog slowly retreating before a predator. Once on the quay, Hereward ordered them to reload, but they had all dropped their pistols, and Hereward had lost one of his pair. He gave his remaining gun to the gold-toothed pirate.

"There are stone houses above," he said, gesturing into the dark. "If we must retreat, we shall find a defensible position there."

"Why wait? Let's get behind some walls now."

"We wait for Captain Fury and the others," said Hereward. "They'll be here any—"

The crack of a small gun drowned out his voice. It was followed a second later by a brilliant flash that lit up the whole cavern and then hard on the heels of the flash came a blinding horizontal bolt of forked lightning that spread across the whole harbour floor, branching into hundreds of lesser jolts that connected with the starfish in a crazed pattern of blue-white sparks.

A strong, nauseatingly powerful stench of salt and rotted meat washed across the pirates on the quay as the darkness returned. Hereward blinked several times and swallowed to try and clear his ears, but neither effort really worked. He knew from experience that both sight and sound would return in a few minutes, and he also knew that the explosion and lightning could only be the work of Mister Fitz. Nevertheless he had an anxious few minutes till he could see enough to make out the fuzzy globes that must be lanterns held by approaching friendly forces, and hear his fellows well enough to know that he would also hear any enemy on the wharf or quay.

"It's the Captain!" cried a pirate. "She's done those stars in."

The starfish had certainly been dealt a savage blow. Fury and Fitz and a column of lantern-bearing pirates were making their way through a charnel field of thousands of pieces of starfish meat, few of them bigger than a man's fist.

But as the pirates advanced, the starfish fragments began to move, pallid horrors wriggling across the stony ground, melding with other pieces to form more mobile gobbets of invertebrate flesh, all of them moving to a central rendezvous somewhere beyond the illumination of the lanterns.

Hereward did not pause to wonder exactly what these disgusting starfish remnants were going to do in the darker reaches of the harbour. He ran along the wharf and took Fitz's hand, helping the puppet to climb the boarding nets that Fury's crew were throwing up. Before Fitz was on his feet, pirates raced past them both, talking excitedly of treasure, the starfish foe forgotten. Hereward's own boat crew, who might have more reason than most to be more thoughtful, had already been absorbed into this flood of looters.

"The starfish are growing back," said Hereward urgently, as he palmed off a too-eager pirate who nearly trod on Fitz.

"Not exactly," corrected Fitz. "Forjill-Um-Uthrux is manifesting itself more completely here. It will use its starfish minions to craft a physical shape. And more importantly—"

"Captain Suresword!" cried Fury, clapping him on the back. Her eyes were bright, there were several dark spots on her face and her ears were long and furred, but she evidently had managed to halt or slow the full transformation. "On to the treasure!"

She laughed and ran past him, with many pirates behind her. Up ahead, the sound of ancient doors being knocked down was already being replaced by gleeful and astonished cries as many hundredweight of loose gold and silver coinage poured out around the looter's thighs.

"More importantly perhaps, Um-Uthrux is doing something to manipulate the sea," continued Fitz. "It has tilted the harbour floor significantly and I can perceive energistic tendrils extending well beyond this island. I fear it is raising the tide ahead of time and with it—"

"The *eagre*," said Hereward. "Do we have time to get out?"

"No," said Fitz. "It will be at the mouth of the gorge within minutes. We must swiftly deal with Um-Uthrux and then take refuge in one of the upper buildings, the strongest possible, where I will spin us a bubble of air."

"How big a bubble?" asked Hereward, as he took a rapid glance around. There were lanterns bobbing all about the slope above the quay, and it looked like all two hundred odd of Fury's crew were in amongst the Scholar-Pirates' buildings.

"A single room, sufficient for a dozen mortals," said Fitz. "Ah, Um-Uthrux has made its host. Please gather as many pirates as you can to fire on it, Hereward. I will require some full minutes of preparation."

The puppet began to take off his bandanna and Hereward shielded his face with his hand. A terrible, harsh light filled the cavern as Fitz removed an esoteric needle that had been glued to his head, the light fading as he closed his hand around it. Any mortal that dared to hold such a needle unprotected would no longer have hand or arm, but Fitz had been specifically made to deal with such things.

In the brief flash of light, Hereward saw a truly giant starfish beginning to stand on its lower points. It was sixty feet wide and at least that tall, and was not pale yellow like its lesser predecessors, but a virulent colour like infected pus, and its broad surface was covered not in a rasping, lumpy structure of tiny suckers but in hundreds of foot-wide puckered mouths that were lined with sharp teeth.

"Fury!" roared Hereward as he sprinted back along the wharf, ignoring the splinters in his now bare feet, his ruined boots flapping about his ankles. "Fury! Sea-Cats! To arms, to arms!"

He kept shouting, but he could not see Fury, and the pirates in sight were gold-drunk, bathing uproariously in piles of coin and articles of virtu that had spilled out of the broken treasure houses and into the cobbled streets between the buildings.

"To arms! The enemy!" Hereward shouted again. He ran to the nearest knot of pirates and dragged one away from a huge gold-chased silver cup that was near as big as he was. "Form line on the quay!"

The pirate shrugged him off and clutched his cup.

"It's mine!" he yelled. "You'll not have it!"

"I don't want it!" roared Hereward. He pointed back at the harbour. "The enemy! Look you fools!"

The nearer pirates stared at him blankly. Hereward turned and saw... nothing but darkness.

"Fitz! Light the cursed monster up!"

He was answered by a blinding surge of violet light that shot from the wharf and washed across the giant starfish, which was now completely upright and lifting one point to march forwards.

There was silence for several seconds, the silence of the shocked. Then a calm, carrying voice snatched order from the closing jaws of panic.

"Sea-cats! First division form line on the quay, right of the wharf! Second to load behind them! Move you knaves! The loot will wait!"

Fury emerged from behind a building, a necklace of gold and yellow diamonds around her neck. She marched to Hereward and placed her arm through his, and together they walked to the quay as if they had not a care in the world, while pirates ran past them.

"You have not become a leoparde," said Hereward. He spoke calmly but he couldn't help but look up at the manifested godlet. Like the smaller starfish, it was becoming quicker with every movement, and Fitz stood alone before it on the end of the wharf. There was a nimbus of sorcerous light around the puppet, indicating that he was working busily with one or more energistic needles, either stitching something otherworldly together or unpicking some aspect of what was commonly considered to be reality.

"Cold things from the sea, no matter their size, do not arouse my ire," replied Fury. "Or perhaps it is the absence of red blood… Stand ready!"

The last words were for the hundred pirates who stood in line along the quay, sporting a wide array of muskets, musketoons, blunderbusses, pistols and even some crossbows. Behind them, the second division knelt with their own firearms ready to pass on, and the necessaries for reloading laid out at their feet.

"Fire!" shouted Fury. A ragged volley rang out and a cloud of smoke rolled back across Hereward and drifted up towards the treasure houses. Many shots struck home, but their effect was much less than on the smaller starfish, with no visible holes being torn in the strange stuff of Um-Uthrux.

"Firsts, fire as you will!" called Fury. "Seconds, reload!"

Though the shots appeared to have no affect, the frantic movement of the pirates shooting and reloading did attract Um-Uthrux's attention. It swiveled and took a step towards the quay, one huge point crashing down on the middle wharf to the left of Mister Fitz. Rather than pulling the point out of the wreckage it just pushed it forward, timber flying as it bulled its way to the quay. Then with one sweep of a middle point, it swept up a dozen pirates and, rolling the point to form a tight circle, held them while its many mouths went to work.

"Fire and fall back!" shouted Fury. "Fire and fall back!"

She fired a long-barrelled pistol herself, but it too had no effect. Um-Uthrux seized several more pirates as they tried to flee, wrapping around them, bones and bloody fragments falling upon shocked companions who were snatched up themselves by another point seconds later.

Hereward and Fury ran back to the corner of one of the treasure houses. Hereward tripped over a golden salt-boat and a pile of coins and would have fallen, had not Fury dragged him on even as the tip of a starfish point crashed down where he had been, flattening the masterwork of some long-forgotten goldsmith.

"Your sorcerer-puppet had best do something," said Fury.

"He will," panted Hereward. But he could not see Fitz, and Um-Uthrux was now bending over the quay with its central torso as well as its points, so its reach would be greater. The quay was crumbling under its assault, and the stones were awash with the blood of many pirates. "We must go higher up!"

"Back Sea-Cats!" shouted Fury. "Higher up!"

The treasure house that had sheltered them was pounded into dust and fragments as they struggled up the steep, cobbled street. Panicked pirates streamed past them, most without their useless weapons. There was no screaming now, just the groans and panting of the tired and wounded, and the sobbing of those whose nerve was entirely gone.

Hereward pointed to a door at the very top of the street. It had already been broken in by some pirate, but the building's front appeared to be a mere façade built over a chamber dug into the island itself, and so would be stronger than any other.

"In there!" he shouted, but the pirates were running down the side alleys as one of Um-Uthrux's points slammed down directly behind, sending bricks, masonry and treasure in all directions. Hereward pushed Fury towards the door, and turned back to see if he could see Fitz.

But there was only the vast starfish in view. It had slid its lower body up on to the quay and was reaching forth with three of its points, each as large as an angled artillery bastion. First it brought them down to smash the buildings, then it used the fine ends to pluck out any pirates, like an anteater digging out its lunch.

"Fitz!" shouted Hereward. "Fitz!"

One of Um-Uthrux's points rose up, high above Hereward. He stepped back, then stopped as the godlet suddenly halted, its upper points writhing in the air and lower points staggering. A tiny, glowing hole appeared in its middle, and grew larger. The godlet lurched back still farther and reached down with its points, clawing at itself as the glowing void in its guts yawned wider still. Then, with a crack that rocked the cavern and knocked Hereward over again, the giant starfish's points were sucked through the hole, it turned inside out and the hole closed taking with it all evidence of Um-Uthrux's existence upon the earth and with it most of the light.

"Your puppet has done well," said Fury. "Though I perceive it is called Fitz and not Farolio."

"Yes," said Hereward. He did not look at her, but waved his arm, the brassard leaving a luminous trail in the air. "Fitz! To me!"

"It has become a bloody affair after all," said Fury. Her voice was a growl and now Hereward did look. Fury still stood on two legs, but she had grown taller and her proportions had changed. Her skin had become spotted fur, and her skull transformed, her jaw thrust out to contain savage teeth, including two incisors as long as Hereward's thumbs. Long curved nails sprouted from her rounded hands, her eyes had become bright with a predatory gleam, and a tail whisked the ground behind.

"Fury," said Hereward. He looked straight at her and did not back away. "We have won. The fight is done."

"I told you that I ate my enemies," said Fury huskily. Her tail twitched and she bobbed her head in a manner no human neck could mimic. Hereward could barely understand her, human speech almost lost in growls and snarls.

"You did not tell me your name, or your true purpose."

"My name is Hereward," said Hereward, and he raised his open hands. If she attacked, his only chance would be to grip her neck and break it before those teeth and nails did mortal damage. "I am not your enemy."

Fury growled, speech entirely gone, and began to crouch.

"Fury! I am not your—"

The leoparde sprang. He caught her on his forearms and felt the nails rake his skin. Fending her off with his left hand, he seized hold of the necklace of yellow diamonds with his right and twisted it hard to cut off her air. But before he could apply much pressure, the beast gave a sudden, human gasp, strange and sad from that bestial jaw. The leoparde's bright eyes dulled as if by sea-mist, and Hereward felt the full weight of the animal in his hands.

The necklace broke, scattering diamonds, as the beast slid down Hereward's chest. Fitz rode on the creature's shoulders all the way down, before he withdrew the stiletto that he had thrust with inhuman strength up through the nape of her neck into her brain.

Hereward closed his hand on the last diamond. He held it just for a second, before he let that too slip through his fingers.

"Inside!" called Fitz, and the puppet was at his companion's knees, pushing Hereward through the door. The knight fell over the threshold as Fitz turned and gestured with an esoteric needle, threads of blinding white whipping about faster than any weaver's shuttle.

His work was barely done before the wave hit. The ground shook and the sorcerous bubble of air bounced to the ceiling and back several times, tumbling Hereward and Fitz over in a mad crush. Then as rapidly as it had come, the wave receded.

Fitz undid the bubble with a deft twitch of his needle and cupped it in his hand. Hereward lay back on the sodden floor and groaned. Blood trickled down his shredded sleeves, bruises he had not even suspected till now made themselves felt, and his feet were unbelievably sore.

Fitz crouched over him and inspected his arms.

"Scratches," he proclaimed. He carefully put the esoteric needle away inside his jerkin and took off his bandanna, ripping it in half to bind the wounds. "Bandages will suffice."

When the puppet was finished, Hereward sat up. He cupped his face in his hands for a second, but his rope-burned palms made him wince and drop them again.

"We have perhaps six hours to gather materials, construct a raft and make our way out the gorge," said Fitz. "Presuming the *eagre* comes again at the usual time, in the absence of Um-Uthrux. We'd best hurry."

Hereward nodded and lurched upright, holding the splintered doorframe for support. He could see nothing beyond Fitz, who stood a few paces away, but he could easily envision the many corpses that would be floating in the refilled harbour pool, or drifting out to the gorge beyond.

"She was right," he said.

Fitz cocked his head in question.

"Meat and water," replied Hereward. "I suppose that *is* all we are, in the end."

Fitz did not answer, but still looked on, his pose unchanged.

"Present company excepted," added Hereward.

AUTHOR NOTES

Steve Aylett is the author of *Lint, Slaughtermatic, Toxicology, Shamanspace, Fain the Sorcerer*, and many others.

Kage Baker has worked as a graphic artist, mural painter, and instructor of Elizabethan English for the stage. She has been nominated for a Hugo Award and is the author of the wildly successful Company novels.

Kelly Barnhill currently writes and teaches writing. Her work is forthcoming from *Weird Tales* and *Postscripts*. Additionally, she is the author of *Animals with No Eyes* and *Monsters of the Deep* and other funny nonfiction books for children.

Paul Batteiger lives with a wife, three cats, and unnumbered serpents. He wrote this story as a reaction to all the tropic-set pirate tales he was sure would come flooding in, and wanted to otherwise keep it as realistic as possible. The ice-sailing is as accurate as extrapolation could make it.

Elizabeth Bear was born on the same day as Frodo and Bilbo Baggins, but in a different year. Her novels include the Jenny Casey trilogy for which she won the 2006 Locus Award for Best First Novel.

Jayme Lynn Blaschke is best-known for writing fiction with an unhealthy fixation on dirigibles, some of which has appeared in *Interzone*. His interview collection, *Voices of Vision: Creators of Science Fiction and Fantasy Speak,* is notable for its complete lack of buccaneer content.

Brendan Connell has had fiction published in *McSweeney's, Adbusters, Nemonymous, Leviathan 3, Album Zutique*, and *Strange Tales*. His first novel, *The Translation of Father Torturo*, was published in 2005.

Eric Flint has collaborated with David Drake on the six-volume Belisarius series, as well as a novel entitled *The Tyrant*. His alternate history novel *1632* was published in 2000, and has led to a long-running series with several novels and anthologies in print.

David Freer grew up as a fisherman's brat, spending his time in trouble on the boat and in the harbor or diving for spiny lobster with other reprobates. He went on to become an Ichthyologist, ending up as the Chief Scientist for the Commercial Shark Fishery in Western Cape, South Africa. Since then he's written nine novels, some with Eric Flint or Eric and Mercedes Lackey, with the tenth, *Slow Train to Arcturus*, coming out in October.

Justin Howe has published fiction in *Strange Horizons, The Internet Review of Science Fiction*, and *Abyss & Apex*. He works for a New York-based architectural preservation company and belongs to the Homelessmoon.com.

Rhys Hughes plans to write exactly one thousand "items" of linked fiction. He hopes the resultant story cycle will be as improbable and startling as a Spanish galleon overgrown with orchids found in a jungle. His books to date include *Worming the Harpy* and *A New Universal History of Infamy*.

Sarah Monette has published four novels in her Doctrine of Labyrinths series, as well as a collaboration with Elizabeth Bear from Tor Books.

Michael Moorcock has won almost every major literary award both in and out of genre. *The Guardian* recently listed him as one of the top fifty most influential British writers since World War II.

Garth Nix is an internationally bestselling author best known for his Old Kingdom trilogy and *The Keys to the Kingdom* series. A previous Sir Hereward & Mr. Fitz novella appeared in *Jim Baen's Universe*.

Naomi Novik has won the John W. Campbell Award for Best New Writer, the Compton Crook Award for Best First Novel, and the Locus Award for Best First Novel. The fourth volume of her Temeraire series, *Empire of Ivory*, published in September 2007, was a *New York Times* bestseller.

Katherine Sparrow has sold stories to *Escape Pod, Aeon, Cleis Press*, and several others. She recently moved from Seattle to Santa Cruz where her apartment faces the sea, there is rum in the cupboard, and all the radio stations seem to constantly play sea shanties.

Rachel Swirsky was inspired to write this story—which she thinks of as being somewhat like Beatrix Potter on a drug trip—by her pet rats, Wentworth and Sullivan. Sullivan died before the release of this anthology, when his teeth grew in at a fatal angle. He has been replaced with a small, white female rat named Alba who at the time of this writing is completely dominant over the pompous Wentworth, despite his being thrice her weight.

Ann and Jeff VanderMeer have edited several books this year, including *The New Weird, Steampunk*, and *Best American Fantasy 2*. A former World Fantasy Award-winner, Jeff has just published *Predator: South China Seas*, which includes pirates. Ann serves as fiction editor for *Weird Tales*, which is celebrating its eighty-fifth birthday. Find out more at: http://www.jeffvandermeer.com.

Carrie Vaughn was raised by landlubbers, but learned to sail when her father was stationed at the US Naval Academy. She now lives in landlocked Colorado. She's the author of a series of novels about a werewolf named Kitty, the most recent of which is *Kitty and the Silver Bullet*.

Howard Waldrop is the author of numerous collections and novels. An American master of short fiction, he has won the Nebula Award and World Fantasy Award.

Conrad Williams received, as a gift from his father on his second birthday, a hardback copy of a Czechoslovakian edition of *Treasure Island*, which contains horribly beautiful illustrations by Josef Hochman. Some of those pictures have haunted him ever since and might have something to do with why he writes novels such as *Head Injuries, London Revenant*, and *The Unblemished*, which won an International Horror Guild Award.

Night Shade Books Is an Independent Publisher of Quality SF, Fantasy and Horror

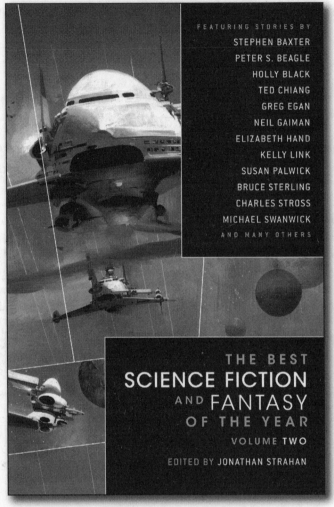

FEATURING STORIES BY
STEPHEN BAXTER
PETER S. BEAGLE
HOLLY BLACK
TED CHIANG
GREG EGAN
NEIL GAIMAN
ELIZABETH HAND
KELLY LINK
SUSAN PALWICK
BRUCE STERLING
CHARLES STROSS
MICHAEL SWANWICK
AND MANY OTHERS

THE BEST
SCIENCE FICTION
AND FANTASY
OF THE YEAR
VOLUME TWO
EDITED BY JONATHAN STRAHAN

ISBN 978-1-59780-124-9 , Trade Paperback; $19.95

The depth and breadth of what science fiction and fantasy fiction is changes with every passing year. The roughly two dozen stories chosen each year for this series, by award-winning anthologist Jonathan Strahan carefully maps this evolution, giving readers a captivating and always-entertaining look at the very best the genre has to offer.

Jonathan Strahan has edited more than twenty anthologies and collections, including The Locus Awards, The New Space Opera, The Jack Vance Treasury, and a number of year's best annuals. He has won the Ditmar, William J. Atheling Jr. and Peter McNamara Awards for his work as an anthologist, and is the reviews editor for Locus.

Don't miss each new volumes in this series, available every year in March.

Night Shade Books Is an Independent Publisher of Quality SF, Fantasy and Horror

ISBN 978-1-59780-105-8, Trade Paperback; $15.95

Famine, Death, War, and Pestilence: The Four Horsemen of the Apocalypse, the harbingers of Armageddon - these are our guides through the Wastelands.

Gathering together the best post-apocalyptic literature of the last two decades from many of today's most renowned authors of speculative fiction, including George R.R. Martin, Gene Wolfe, Orson Scott Card, Carol Emshwiller, Jonathan Lethem, Octavia E. Butler, and Stephen King, Wastelands explores the scientific, psychological, and philosophical questions of what it means to remain human in the wake of Armageddon. Whether the end of the world comes through nuclear war, ecological disaster, or cosmological cataclysm, these are tales of survivors, in some cases struggling to rebuild the society that was, in others, merely surviving, scrounging for food in depopulated ruins and defending themselves against monsters, mutants, and marauders.

Night Shade Books Is an Independent Publisher of Quality SF, Fantasy and Horror

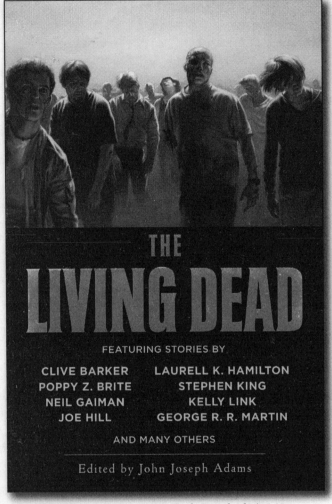

THE LIVING DEAD

FEATURING STORIES BY

CLIVE BARKER	LAURELL K. HAMILTON
POPPY Z. BRITE	STEPHEN KING
NEIL GAIMAN	KELLY LINK
JOE HILL	GEORGE R. R. MARTIN

AND MANY OTHERS

Edited by John Joseph Adams

ISBN 978-1-59780-143-0 , Trade Paperback; $15.95

"When there's no more room in hell, the dead will walk the earth."

From *White Zombie* to *Dawn of the Dead*; from *Resident Evil* to *World War Z*, zombies have invaded popular culture, becoming the monsters that best express the fears and anxieties of the modern west. The ultimate consumers, zombies rise from the dead and feed upon the living, their teeming masses ever hungry, ever seeking to devour or convert, like mindless, faceless eating machines. Zombies have been depicted as mind-controlled minions, the shambling infected, the disintegrating dead, the ultimate lumpenproletariat, but in all cases, they reflect us, mere mortals afraid of death in a society on the verge of collapse.   *The Living Dead* collects together in one book the best Zombie fiction from the last 30 years.